Marian Wood Kolisch

About the Author

URSULA K. LE GUIN is the author of more than one hundred short stories, two collections of essays, four volumes of poetry, and eighteen novels. Her best-known fantasy works, the Earthsea books, have sold millions of copies in America and England, and have been translated into sixteen languages. Her first major work of science fiction, *The Left Hand of Darkness,* is considered epoch-making in the field because of its radical investigation of gender roles and its moral and literary complexity.

Three of Le Guin's books have been finalists for the American Book Award and the Pulitzer Prize, and among the many honors her writing has received are the National Book Award, five Hugo Awards, five Nebula Awards, the Kafka Award, a Pushcart Prize, and the Howard Vursell Award of the American Academy of Arts and Letters. She lives in Portland, Oregon.

NOVELS AND STORY COLLECTIONS BY URSULA K. LE GUIN

NOVELS

Always Coming Home

The Beginning Place

City of Illusion

The Dispossessed

The Eye of the Heron

The Farthest Shore

The Lathe of Heaven

The Left Hand of Darkness

Malafrena

The Other Wind

Planet of Exile

Rocannon's World

Tehanu

The Telling

The Tombs of Atuan

Very Far Away from Anywhere Else

A Wizard of Earthsea

The Word for World is Forest

STORY COLLECTIONS

Buffalo Gals

The Compass Rose

A Fisherman of the Inland Sea

Four Ways to Forgiveness

Orsinian Tales

Searoad

Tales from Earthsea

Unlocking the Air

The Wind's Twelve Quarters

PRAISE FOR URSULA LE GUIN AND

THE BIRTHDAY OF THE WORLD

"Like John le Carré's spy novels, or Larry McMurtry's Westerns, [Le Guin's] work transcends the usual limitations of the genre, and this collection is no exception." —*The New Yorker*

"She is a splendid short-story writer. . . . Fiction, like Borges's, that finds its life in the interstices between the borders of speculative fiction and realism." —*San Francisco Chronicle Book Review*

"The strength of this superior collection, characteristic of Le Guin's work, is that she ignores melodrama for the real drama of the mundane. Which is to say that Le Guin writes about how the future actually will be." —*Sunday Oregonian*

"Le Guin is a writer of enormous intelligence and wit, a master storyteller with the humor and the force of a Twain." —*Boston Globe*

"Pure starlight." —*Kirkus Reviews*

"Once again, Le Guin's powerful work illustrates that fantasy need not be escapist, that gender studies need not be dry or strident, and that entertainment need not be mindless." —*The Onion*

"Le Guin's prose is so very luminous and simple, and she always tells the truth, and when I'm with her people, I'm with living people, on worlds as solid and real as my own. Le Guin has a gift, which is to transform words into worlds. That gift has never been more in evidence than in *The Birthday of the World*." —Molly Gloss, author of *The Jump-off Creek* and *Wild Life*

"A beautiful, profound, irresistible collection—eight wise and wonderful stories by one of the great masters of science fiction." —Robert Silverberg, author of *The King of Dreams* and *The Longest Way Home*

"*The Birthday of the World* is full of wisdom and knowledge, ethnology, and all kinds of sex. Ursula Le Guin's writing touches something ancient in all of us—something atavistic, of folktales and sagas, that comes from deep inside."
—Carol Emshwiller, author of
Ledoyt and *Leaping Man Hill*

"'Beauty' is the word for what Ursula K. Le Guin has wrought here. She explores ways in which we can be foreign and alien to each other, yet still love. Sometimes I don't even know why the tears had sprung to my eyes; I just knew that I was deeply moved." —Nalo Hopkinson, author of
Brown Girl in the Ring and *Skin Folk*

"*The Birthday of the World* is a truly fine book. I don't know anyone else who can do what Le Guin does. Her work is simple and brilliantly clear, like a Buddha's laugh: joyfully serious, delighted with the joke that is life. Le Guin writes about love, pure and simple—love and all the ways in which it refuses to be bound— and she does so beautifully." —Nicola Griffith, author of
Ammonite and *Stay*

"Ursula K. Le Guin's science fiction is an anthropology of the imagination. With telescope and stethoscope, she examines the most public of politics and the most intimate of emotions, constantly challenging her readers to reconsider what it means to be human and humane." —Mary Doria Russell, author of
The Sparrow and *A Thread of Grace*

"*The Birthday of the World* is probably Ursula K. Le Guin's most important book since *Always Coming Home* (1985) and her most satisfactory collection since her first, the brilliant *The Wind's Twelve Quarters* (1975)." —*Locus*

THE BIRTHDAY
OF THE WORLD

AND OTHER STORIES

URSULA K. LE GUIN

Perennial

An Imprint of HarperCollinsPublishers

"Coming of Age in Karhide," copyright © 1995 by Ursula K. Le Guin; first appeared in *New Legends*, edited by Greg Bear with Martin Greenberg (Legend Books, an imprint of Random House UK Limited).

"The Matter of Seggri," copyright © 1994 by Ursula K. Le Guin; first appeared in *Crank!* (Spring 1994; Issue no. 3).

"Unchosen Love," copyright © 1994 by Ursula K. Le Guin; first appeared in *Amazing Stories* (Fall 1994; vol. 69, no. 2).

"Mountain Ways," copyright © 1996 by Ursula K. Le Guin; first appeared in *Asimov's Science Fiction* (August 1996; vol. 20, no. 8).

"Solitude," copyright © 1994 by Ursula K. Le Guin; first appeared in *The Magazine of Fantasy and Science Fiction* (December 1994; vol. 87, no. 6).

"Old Music and the Slave Women," copyright © 1999 by Ursula K. Le Guin; first appeared in *Far Horizons*, edited by Robert Silverberg (Avon Eos).

"The Birthday of the World," copyright © 2000 by Ursula K. Le Guin; first appeared in *The Magazine of Fantasy and Science Fiction* (June 2000; vol. 98, no. 6).

The foreword to this volume and "Paradises Lost" appear for the first time in this work.

A hardcover edition of this book was published in 2002 by HarperCollins Publishers.

THE BIRTHDAY OF THE WORLD. Copyright © 2002 by Ursula K. Le Guin. All rights reserved. Printed in the United States of America. No part of this book may be used or reproduced in any manner whatsoever without written permission except in the case of brief quotations embodied in critical articles and reviews. For information address HarperCollins Publishers Inc., 10 East 53rd Street, New York, NY 10022.

HarperCollins books may be purchased for educational, business, or sales promotional use. For information please write: Special Markets Department, HarperCollins Publishers Inc., 10 East 53rd Street, New York, NY 10022.

First Perennial edition published 2003.

Designed by Jackie McKee

The Library of Congress has catalogued the hardcover edition as follows:

Le Guin, Ursula K.
    The birthday of the world and other stories / Ursula K. Le Guin. — 1st ed.
        p. cm.
    Contents: Coming of age in Karhide — The matter of Seggri — Unchosen love — Mountain ways — Solitude — Old music and the slave women — The birthday of the world — Paradises lost.
    ISBN 0-06-621253-7
    1. Science fiction, American. I. Title.

PS3562.E42 B44 2002
813'.54—dc21   20011039508

ISBN 0-06-050906-6 (pbk.)

03 04 05 06 07 ❖\RRD 10 9 8 7 6 5 4 3 2 1

Contents

FOREWORD

Inventing a universe is tough work. Jehovah took a sabbatical. Vishnu takes naps. Science-fiction universes are only tiny bits of word-worlds, but even so they take some thinking; and rather than think out a new universe for every story, a writer may keep coming back and using the same universe, sometimes till it gets a bit worn at the seams, softens up, feels natural, like an old shirt.

Though I've put a good deal of work into my fictional universe, I don't exactly feel that I invented it. I blundered into it, and have been blundering around in it unsystematically ever since — dropping a millennium here, forgetting a planet there. Honest and earnest people, calling it the Hainish Universe, have tried to plot its history onto Time Lines. I call it the Ekumen, and I say it's hopeless. Its Time Line is like something the kitten pulled out of the knitting basket, and its history consists largely of gaps.

There are reasons for this incoherence, other than authorial carelessness, forgetfulness, and impatience. Space, after all, is essentially gap. Inhabited worlds are a long, long way apart. Einstein said people couldn't travel faster than light, so I generally let my people travel only nearly as fast as light. This means that whenever they cross space, they scarcely age, thanks to Einsteinian time dilation, but they do end up decades or centuries after they set out, and can only find out what happened meanwhile back on the farm by using my handy device, the ansible. (It's interesting to think that the ansible is older than the Internet, and faster — I do let information travel instantaneously.) So in my universe, as in this one, now here is then there, and vice versa, which is a good way to keep history from being either clear or useful.

Of course you can ask the Hainish, who have been around for a long time, and whose historians not only know a lot of what happened, but also know that it keeps happening and will happen again. . . . They're somewhat like Ecclesiastes, seeing no new thing under the, or any, sun; but they're much more cheerful about it than he was.

The people on all the other worlds, who all descended from the Hainish, naturally don't want to believe what the old folks say, so they start making history; and so it all happens again.

I did not plan these worlds and people. I found them, gradually, piecemeal, while writing stories. I'm still finding them.

In my first three science-fiction novels there is a League of Worlds, vaguely embracing known planets in our local bit of the local galaxy, including Earth. This rather suddenly morphs into the Ekumen, a non-directive, information-gathering consortium of worlds, which occasionally disobeys its own directive to be non-directive. I had met the Greek word meaning household, *oikumene*, as in ecumenical, in one of my father's anthropology books, and remembered it when I needed a word that might imply a still wider humanity spread out from one original hearth. I spelled it "Ekumen." If you write science fiction you can spell things the way you like, sometimes.

The first six of these eight stories take place on worlds of the Ekumen, in my pseudo-coherent universe with holes in the elbows.

In my 1969 novel *The Left Hand of Darkness* the first voice is that of a Mobile of the Ekumen, a traveller, making a report back to the

Stabiles, who stay put on Hain. This vocabulary came to me along with the narrator. He said his name was Genly Ai. He began telling the story, and I wrote it.

Gradually, and not easily, he and I found out where we were. He had not been on Gethen before, but I had, in a short story, "Winter's King." That first visit was so hurried I hadn't even noticed there was something a bit weird about Gethenian gender. Just like a tourist. Androgynes? Were there androgynes?

During the writing of *Left Hand*, pieces of myth and legend came to me as needed, when I didn't understand where the story was going; and a second voice, a Gethenian one, took over the story from time to time. But Estraven was a deeply reserved person. And the plot led both my narrators so quickly into so much trouble that many questions didn't get answered or even asked.

Writing the first story in this book, "Coming of Age in Karhide," I came back to Gethen after twenty-five or thirty years. This time I didn't have an honest but bewildered male Terran alongside to confuse my perceptions. I could listen to an open-hearted Gethenian who, unlike Estraven, had nothing to hide. This time I didn't have a damned plot. I could ask questions. I could see how the sex works. I could finally get into a kemmerhouse. I could really have fun.

"The Matter of Seggri" is a compendium of reports on the society of a world called Seggri written by various observers over a period of many years. These documents are from the archives of the Historians of Hain, who are to reports as squirrels are to nuts.

The germ of the story was in an article I read about the gender imbalance that persistent abortion and infanticide of female fetuses and babies are causing in parts of the world — our world, Earth — where only males are considered worth the bother. Out of irrational and insatiable curiosity, in a thought experiment that became the story, I reversed and increased the imbalance and made it permanent. Though I liked the people I met on Seggri, and very much enjoyed channeling their various voices, the experiment was not a happy one.

(I do not really mean channeling. The word is just shorthand for my relation with characters in my fiction. *Fiction* — right? Please do not write me any letters about other lives. I have quite as many as I can handle.)

In the title story of the collection *A Fisherman of the Inland Sea*, I invented some social rules for the people of the world called O, which is quite near Hain, as worlds go. The world, as usual, seemed to be something I just found myself on and had to explore; but I did spend genuine thought, respectable, *systematic* thought, on the marriage and kinship customs of the people of O. I drew charts, with male and female symbols, and lines with arrows, very scientific. I needed those charts. I kept getting confused. The blessed editor of the magazine in which the story first appeared saved me from a horrible blunder, worse than incest. I had gotten my moieties mixed up. She caught it, we fixed it.

Since it took a while to work out these complexities, it may be mere conservation of energy that has brought me back twice to O; but I think it's because I like it. I like thinking about being married to three other people only two of whom you can have sex with (one of each gender but both of the other moiety). I like thinking about complex social relationships which produce and frustrate highly charged emotional relationships.

In this sense, you could say that "Unchosen Love" and "Mountain Ways" are comedies of manners, odd as that may sound to those who think science fiction is written ray-gun in hand. The society of O is different than ours here now, but not very much more different than that of Jane Austen's England; perhaps less different than that of *The Tale of Genji*.

•   •   •

In "Solitude" I went out on the fringes of the Ekumen, to a place somewhat like the Earth we used to write about in the sixties and seventies when we believed in Atomic Holocaust and the End of the World as We Know It and mutants in the glowing ruins of Peoria. I still believe in Atomic Holocaust, you betcha, but the time for writing stories about it is not now; and the world as I knew it has already ended several times.

Whatever caused the population crash in "Solitude" — probably the population itself — it was long ago, and is not the concern of the story, which is about survival, loyalty, and introversion. Hardly anybody ever writes anything nice about introverts. Extraverts rule. This is really rather odd when you realise that about nineteen writers out of twenty are introverts.

We have been taught to be ashamed of not being "outgoing." But a writer's job is ingoing.

The people, the survivors, in this story, like most people in these stories, have some peculiar arrangements of gender and sexuality; but they have no arrangements at all for marriage. Marriage is too extraverted for real introverts. They just see each other sometimes. For a while. Then they go off and be alone again and be happy.

"Old Music and the Slave Women" is a fifth wheel.

My book *Four Ways to Forgiveness* consists of four connected stories. Once more I plead for a name, and thus recognition, for this fictional form (which goes back as least as far as Elizabeth Gaskell's *Cranford* and has become increasingly frequent and interesting): a book of stories linked by place, characters, theme, and movement, so as to form not a novel but a whole. There's a sneering British term "fix-up" for books by authors who, told that collections "don't sell," patch unconnected stories together with verbal duct tape. But the real thing is not a random collection, any more than a Bach cello suite is. It does things a novel doesn't do. It is a real form, and deserves a real name.

Maybe we could call it a story suite? I think I will.

So the story suite *Four Ways* gives a view of the recent history of two worlds, Werel and Yeowe. (This Werel is not the Werel of the early novel *Planet of Exile*. It's a different one. I told you already, I forget whole planets.) The slave-based society and economy of these worlds is in process of revolutionary change. One critic scoffed at me for treating slavery as an issue worth writing about. I wonder what planet he lives on?

"Old Music" is the translated name of a Hainishman, Esdardon Aya, who turns up in three of the stories in the suite. Chronologically, this new story follows the suite, a fifth movement, telling an incident of the civil war on Werel. But it's also its own piece. Its origin was a visit to one of the great slave plantations upriver from Charleston, South Carolina. Readers who have seen that beautiful, terrible place may recognise the garden, the house, the haunted ground.

The title story, "The Birthday of the World," may or may not take place on a world of the Ekumen. I honestly don't know. Does it matter? It's not Earth; its people are physically a little different from us; but the model I used for their society is in some respects clearly that of the Inca. As in the great ancient societies of Egypt or India or Peru, king and god are one, and the sacred is as close and common as bread or breath. And as easy to lose.

These seven stories share a pattern: they exhibit in one way or another, from inside or through an observer (who is liable to go native), people whose society differs from ours, even whose physiology may differ from ours, but who feel the way we do. First to create difference — to establish strangeness — then to let the fiery arc of human emotion leap and close the gap: this acrobatics of the imagination fascinates and satisfies me as almost no other.

The last, long story, "Paradises Lost," is not of this pattern, and is definitely not an Ekumen story. It takes place in another universe, also a well-used one: the generic, shared, science-fiction "future." In this version of it, Earth sends forth ships to the stars at speeds that are, according to our present knowledge, more or less realistic, at least potentially attainable. Such a ship takes decades, centuries, to get where it's going. No Warp Nine, no time-dilation — just real time.

In other words, this is a generation-ship story. Two remarkable books, Martinson's *Aniara* and Gloss's *The Dazzle of Day*, and many short stories have used the theme. Most of the short stories put the crew/colonists into some kind of deepfreeze so that the people who left Earth wake up at the destination. I always wanted to write about people who truly lived out the journey, the middle generations knowing neither departure nor arrival. I tried several times. I never could get the story, until a religious theme began to entwine itself with the idea of the sealed ship in the dead vacuum of space, like a cocoon, full of transformation, transmutation, invisible life: the pupa body, the winged soul.

Ursula K. Le Guin
2001

THE BIRTHDAY OF THE WORLD

Coming of Age in Karhide

By Sov Thade Tage em Ereb, of Rer, in Karhide, on Gethen.

I live in the oldest city in the world. Long before there were kings in Karhide, Rer was a city, the marketplace and meeting ground for all the Northeast, the Plains, and Kerm Land. The Fastness of Rer was a center of learning, a refuge, a judgment seat fifteen thousand years ago. Karhide became a nation here, under the Geger kings, who ruled for a thousand years. In the thousandth year Sedern Geger, the Unking, cast the crown into the River Arre from the palace towers, proclaiming an end to dominion. The time they call the Flowering of Rer, the Summer Century, began then. It ended when the Hearth of Harge took power and moved their capital across the mountains to Erhenrang. The Old Palace has been empty for centuries. But it stands. Nothing in Rer falls down. The Arre floods through the street-tunnels every year in the Thaw, winter blizzards may bring thirty feet of snow, but the city stands. Nobody knows how old the houses are, because they have been rebuilt forever. Each one sits in its gardens without respect to the position of any of the others, as vast and random and ancient as hills. The roofed streets and canals angle about among them. Rer is all corners. We say that the Harges left because they were afraid of what might be around the corner.

Time is different here. I learned in school how the Orgota, the Ekumen, and most other people count years. They call the year of some portentous event Year One and number forward from it. Here it's always Year One. On Getheny Thern, New Year's Day, the Year One becomes one-ago, one-to-come becomes One, and so on. It's like Rer, everything always changing but the city never changing.

When I was fourteen (in the Year One, or fifty-ago) I came of age. I have been thinking about that a good deal recently.

It was a different world. Most of us had never seen an Alien, as we called them then. We might have heard the Mobile talk on the radio, and at school we saw pictures of Aliens — the ones with hair around their mouths were the most pleasingly savage and repulsive. Most of the pictures were disappointing. They looked too much like us. You couldn't even tell that they were always in kemmer. The female Aliens were supposed to have enormous breasts, but my mothersib Dory had bigger breasts than the ones in the pictures.

When the Defenders of the Faith kicked them out of Orgoreyn, when King Emran got into the Border War and lost Erhenrang, even when their Mobiles were outlawed and forced into hiding at Estre in Kerm, the Ekumen did nothing much but wait. They had waited for two hundred years, as patient as Handdara. They did one thing: they took our young king offworld to foil a plot, and then brought the same king back sixty years later to end her wombchild's disastrous reign. Argaven XVII is the only king who ever ruled four years before her heir and forty years after.

The year I was born (the Year One, or sixty-four-ago) was the year Argaven's second reign began. By the time I was noticing anything beyond my own toes, the war was over, the West Fall was part of Karhide again, the capital was back in Erhenrang, and most of the damage done to Rer during the Overthrow of Emran had been repaired. The old houses had been rebuilt again. The Old Palace had been patched again. Argaven XVII was miraculously back on the throne again. Everything was the way it used to be, ought to be, back to normal, just like the old days — everybody said so.

Indeed those were quiet years, an interval of recovery before Argaven, the first Gethenian who ever left our planet, brought us at last fully into the Ekumen; before we, not they, became the Aliens; before we came of age. When I was a child we lived the way people had lived in Rer forever. It is that way, that timeless world, that world around the corner, I have been thinking about, and trying to describe for people who never knew it. Yet as I write I see how also nothing changes, that it is truly the Year One always, for each child that comes of age, each lover who falls in love.

There were a couple of thousand people in the Ereb Hearths, and a hundred and forty of them lived in my Hearth, Ereb Tage. My name is Sov Thade Tage em Ereb, after the old way of naming we still use in Rer. The first thing I remember is a huge dark place full of shouting and shadows, and I am falling upward through a golden light into the darkness. In thrilling terror, I scream. I am caught in my fall, held, held close; I weep; a voice so close to me that it seems to speak through my body says softly, "Sov, Sov, Sov." And then I am given something wonderful to eat, something so sweet, so delicate that never again will I eat anything quite so good. . . .

I imagine that some of my wild elder hearthsibs had been throwing me about, and that my mother comforted me with a bit of festival cake. Later on when I was a wild elder sib we used to play catch with babies for balls; they always screamed, with terror or with delight, or both. It's the nearest to flying anyone of my generation knew. We had dozens of different words for the way snow falls, descends, glides, blows, for the way clouds move, the way ice floats, the way boats sail; but not that word. Not yet. And so I don't remember "flying." I remember falling upward through the golden light.

Family houses in Rer are built around a big central hall. Each story has an inner balcony clear round that space, and we call the whole story, rooms and all, a balcony. My family occupied the whole second balcony of Ereb Tage. There were a lot of us. My grandmother had borne four children, and all of them had children, so I had a bunch of cousins as well as a younger and an older wombsib. "The Thades always kemmer as women and always get pregnant," I heard neighbors say, variously envious, disapproving, admiring. "And they never keep kemmer," somebody would add. The former was an exaggeration, but the latter was true. Not one of us kids had a father. I didn't know for years who my getter was, and never gave it a thought. Clannish, the Thades preferred not to bring outsiders, even other members of our own Hearth, into the family. If young people fell in love and started talking about keeping kemmer or making vows, Grandmother and the mothers were ruthless. "Vowing kemmer, what do you think you are, some kind of noble? some kind of fancy person? The kemmerhouse was good enough for me and it's good enough for you," the mothers said to their lovelorn children, and sent them away, clear off to the old Ereb Domain in the country, to hoe braties till they got over being in love.

So as a child I was a member of a flock, a school, a swarm, in and out of our warren of rooms, tearing up and down the staircases, working together and learning together and looking after the babies — in our own fashion — and terrorising quieter hearthmates by our numbers and our noise. As far as I know we did no real harm. Our escapades were well within the rules and limits of the sedate, ancient Hearth, which we felt not as constraints but as protection, the walls that kept us safe. The only time we got punished was when my cousin Sether decided it would be exciting if we tied a long rope we'd found to the second-floor balcony railing, tied a big knot in the rope, held onto the knot, and jumped. "I'll go first," Sether said. Another misguided attempt at flight. The railing and Sether's broken leg were mended, and the rest of us had to clean the privies, all the privies of the Hearth, for a month. I think the rest of the Hearth had decided it was time the young Thades observed some discipline.

Although I really don't know what I was like as a child, I think that if I'd had any choice I might have been less noisy than my playmates, though just as unruly. I used to love to listen to the radio, and while the rest of them were racketing around the balconies or the centerhall in winter, or out in the streets and gardens in summer, I would crouch for hours in my mother's room behind the bed, playing her old serem-wood radio very softly so that my sibs wouldn't know I was there. I listened to anything, lays and plays and hearth-tales, the Palace news, the analyses of grain harvests and the detailed weather-reports; I listened every day all one winter to an ancient saga from the Pering Storm-Border about snowghouls, perfidious traitors, and bloody ax-murders, which haunted me at night so that I couldn't sleep and would crawl into bed with my mother for comfort. Often my younger sib was already there in the warm, soft, breathing dark. We would sleep all entangled and curled up together like a nest of pesthry.

My mother, Guyr Thade Tage em Ereb, was impatient, warmhearted, and impartial, not exerting much control over us three wombchildren, but keeping watch. The Thades were all tradespeople working in Ereb shops and masteries, with little or no cash to spend; but when I was ten Guyr bought me a radio, a new one, and said where my sibs could hear, "You don't have to share it." I treasured it for years and finally shared it with my own wombchild.

So the years went along and I went along in the warmth and density and certainty of a family and a Hearth embedded in tradition, threads on the quick ever-repeating shuttle weaving the timeless web of custom and act and work and relationship, and at this distance I can hardly tell one year from the other or myself from the other children: until I turned fourteen.

The reason most people in my Hearth would remember that year is for the big party known as Dory's Somer-Forever Celebration. My mothersib Dory had stopped going into kemmer that winter. Some people didn't do anything when they stopped going into kemmer; others went to the Fastness for a ritual; some stayed on at the Fastness for months after, or even moved there. Dory, who wasn't spiritually inclined, said, "If I can't have kids and can't have sex any more and have to get old and die, at least I can have a party."

I have already had some trouble trying to tell this story in a language that has no somer pronouns, only gendered pronouns. In their last years of kemmer, as the hormone balance changes, most people mostly go into kemmer as men. Dory's kemmers had been male for over a year, so I'll call Dory "he," although of course the point was that he would never be either he or she again.

In any event, his party was tremendous. He invited everyone in our Hearth and the two neighboring Ereb Hearths, and it went on for three days. It had been a long winter and the spring was late and cold; people were ready for something new, something hot to happen. We cooked for a week, and a whole storeroom was packed full of beerkegs. A lot of people who were in the middle of going out of kemmer, or had already and hadn't done anything about it, came and joined in the ritual. That's what I remember vividly: in the fire-lit three-story centerhall of our Hearth, a circle of thirty or forty people, all middle-aged or old, singing and dancing, stamping the drumbeats. There was a fierce energy in them, their grey hair was loose and wild, they stamped as if their feet would go through the floor, their voices were deep and strong, they were laughing. The younger people watching them seemed pallid and shadowy. I looked at the dancers and wondered, why are they happy? Aren't they old? Why do they act like they'd got free? What's it like, then, kemmer?

No, I hadn't thought much about kemmer before. What would be the use? Until we come of age we have no gender and no sexuality, our hormones don't give us any trouble at all. And in a city Hearth we never see adults in kemmer. They kiss and go. Where's Maba? In the kemmerhouse, love, now eat your porridge. When's

Maba coming back? Soon, love. — And in a couple of days Maba comes back, looking sleepy and shiny and refreshed and exhausted. Is it like having a bath, Maba? Yes, a bit, love, and what have you been up to while I was away?

Of course we played kemmer, when we were seven or eight. This here's the kemmerhouse and I get to be the woman. No, *I* do. No, *I* do, I thought of it! — And we rubbed our bodies together and rolled around laughing, and then maybe we stuffed a ball under our shirt and were pregnant, and then we gave birth, and then we played catch with the ball. Children will play whatever adults do; but the kemmer game wasn't much of a game. It often ended in a tickling match. And most children aren't even very ticklish, till they come of age.

After Dory's party, I was on duty in the Hearth creche all through Tuwa, the last month of spring; come summer I began my first apprenticeship, in a furniture workshop in the Third Ward. I loved getting up early and running across the city on the wayroofs and up on the curbs of the open ways; after the late Thaw some of the ways were still full of water, deep enough for kayaks and pole-boats. The air would be still and cold and clear; the sun would come up behind the old towers of the Unpalace, red as blood, and all the waters and the windows of the city would flash scarlet and gold. In the workshop there was the piercing sweet smell of fresh-cut wood and the company of grown people, hard-working, patient, and demanding, taking me seriously. I wasn't a child any more, I said to myself. I was an adult, a working person.

But why did I want to cry all the time? Why did I want to sleep all the time? Why did I get angry at Sether? Why did Sether keep bumping into me and saying "Oh sorry" in that stupid husky voice? Why was I so clumsy with the big electric lathe that I ruined six chair-legs one after the other? "Get that kid off the lathe," shouted old Marth, and I slunk away in a fury of humiliation. I would never be a carpenter, I would never be adult, who gave a shit for chair-legs anyway?

"I want to work in the gardens," I told my mother and grand-mother. "Finish your training and you can work in the gardens next summer," Grand said, and Mother nodded. This sensible counsel appeared to me as a heartless injustice, a failure of love, a condemnation to despair. I sulked. I raged.

"What's wrong with the furniture shop?" my elders asked after several days of sulk and rage.

"Why does stupid Sether have to be there!" I shouted. Dory, who was Sether's mother, raised an eyebrow and smiled.

"Are you all right?" my mother asked me as I slouched into the balcony after work, and I snarled, "I'm fine," and rushed to the privies and vomited.

I was sick. My back ached all the time. My head ached and got dizzy and heavy. Something I could not locate anywhere, some part of my soul, hurt with a keen, desolate, ceaseless pain. I was afraid of myself: of my tears, my rage, my sickness, my clumsy body. It did not feel like my body, like me. It felt like something else, an ill-fitting garment, a smelly, heavy overcoat that belonged to some old person, some dead person. It wasn't mine, it wasn't me. Tiny needles of agony shot through my nipples, hot as fire. When I winced and held my arms across my chest, I knew that everybody could see what was happening. Anybody could smell me. I smelled sour, strong, like blood, like raw pelts of animals. My clitopenis was swollen hugely and stuck out from between my labia, and then shrank nearly to nothing, so that it hurt to piss. My labia itched and reddened as with loathsome insect-bites. Deep in my belly something moved, some monstrous growth. I was utterly ashamed. I was dying.

"Sov," my mother said, sitting down beside me on my bed, with a curious, tender, complicitous smile, "shall we choose your kem-merday?"

"I'm not in kemmer," I said passionately.

"No," Guyr said. "But next month I think you will be."

"I *won't*!"

My mother stroked my hair and face and arm. *We shape each other to be human*, old people used to say as they stroked babies or children or one another with those long, slow, soft caresses.

After a while my mother said, "Sether's coming in, too. But a month or so later than you, I think. Dory said let's have a double kemmerday, but I think you should have your own day in your own time."

I burst into tears and cried, "I don't want one, I don't want to, I just want, I just want to go away. . . ."

"Sov," my mother said, "if you want to, you can go to the kemmerhouse at Gerodda Ereb, where you won't know anybody. But I think it would be better here, where people do know you. They'd like it. They'll be so glad for you. Oh, your Grand's so proud of you! 'Have you seen that grandchild of mine, Sov, have you seen what a beauty, what a *mahad*!' Everybody's bored to tears hearing about you. . . ."

Mahad is a dialect word, a Rer word; it means a strong, handsome, generous, upright person, a reliable person. My mother's stern mother, who commanded and thanked but never praised, said I was a mahad? A terrifying idea that dried my tears.

"All right," I said desperately. "Here. But not next month! It isn't. I'm not."

"Let me see," my mother said. Fiercely embarrassed yet relieved to obey, I stood up and undid my trousers.

My mother took a very brief and delicate look, hugged me, and said, "Next month, yes, I'm sure. You'll feel much better in a day or two. And next month it'll be different. It really will."

Sure enough, the next day the headache and the hot itching were gone, and though I was still tired and sleepy a lot of the time, I wasn't quite so stupid and clumsy at work. After a few more days I felt pretty much myself, light and easy in my limbs. Only if I thought about it there was still that queer feeling that wasn't quite in any part of my body, and that was sometimes very painful and sometimes only strange, almost something I wanted to feel again.

My cousin Sether and I had been apprenticed together at the furniture shop. We didn't go to work together because Sether was still slightly lame from that rope trick a couple of years earlier, and got a lift to work in a poleboat so long as there was water in the streets. When they closed the Arre Watergate and the ways went dry, Sether had to walk. So we walked together. The first couple of days we didn't talk much. I still felt angry at Sether. Because I couldn't run through the dawn any more but had to walk at a lame-leg pace. And because Sether was always around. Always there. Taller than me, and quicker at the lathe, and with that long, heavy, shining hair. Why did anybody want to wear their hair so long, anyhow? I felt as if Sether's hair was in front of my own eyes.

We were walking home, tired, on a hot evening of Ockre, the first month of summer. I could see that Sether was limping and trying to hide or ignore it, trying to swing right along at my quick pace, very erect, scowling. A great wave of pity and admiration overwhelmed me, and that thing, that growth, that new being, whatever it was in my bowels and in the ground of my soul moved and turned again, turned towards Sether, aching, yearning.

"Are you coming into kemmer?" I said in a hoarse, husky voice I had never heard come out of my mouth.

"In a couple of months," Sether said in a mumble, not looking at me, still very stiff and frowning.

"I guess I have to have this, do this, you know, this stuff, pretty soon."

"I wish I could," Sether said. "Get it over with."

We did not look at each other. Very gradually, unnoticeably, I was slowing my pace till we were going along side by side at an easy walk.

"Sometimes do you feel like your tits are on fire?" I asked without knowing that I was going to say anything.

Sether nodded.

After a while, Sether said, "Listen, does your pisser get. . . ."
I nodded.

"It must be what the Aliens look like," Sether said with revulsion. "This, this thing sticking out, it gets so *big* . . . it gets in the way."

We exchanged and compared symptoms for a mile or so. It was a relief to talk about it, to find company in misery, but it was also frightening to hear our misery confirmed by the other. Sether burst out, "I'll tell you what I hate, what I really *hate* about it — it's dehumanising. To get jerked around like that by your own body, to lose control, I can't stand the idea. Of being just a sex machine. And everybody just turns into something to have sex with. You know that people in kemmer go crazy and *die* if there isn't anybody else in kemmer? That they'll even attack people in somer? Their own mothers?"

"They can't," I said, shocked.

"Yes they can. Tharry told me. This truck driver up in the High Kargav went into kemmer as a male while their caravan was stuck in the snow, and he was big and strong, and he went crazy and he, he did it to his cabmate, and his cabmate was in somer and got hurt, really hurt, trying to fight him off. And then the driver came out of kemmer and committed suicide."

This horrible story brought the sickness back up from the pit of my stomach, and I could say nothing.

Sether went on, "People in kemmer aren't even human any more! And we have to do that — to be that way!"

Now that awful, desolate fear was out in the open. But it was not a relief to speak it. It was even larger and more terrible, spoken.

"It's stupid," Sether said. "It's a primitive device for continuing the species. There's no need for civilised people to undergo it. People who want to get pregnant could do it with injections. It would be genetically sound. You could choose your child's getter. There wouldn't be all this inbreeding, people fucking with their sibs, like animals. Why do we have to be animals?"

Sether's rage stirred me. I shared it. I also felt shocked and excited by the word "fucking," which I had never heard spoken. I looked again at my cousin, the thin, ruddy face, the heavy, long, shining hair. My age, Sether looked older. A half year in pain from a shattered leg had darkened and matured the adventurous, mischievous child, teaching anger, pride, endurance. "Sether," I said, "listen, it doesn't matter, you're human, even if you have to do that stuff, that fucking. You're a mahad."

"Getheny Kus," Grand said: the first day of the month of Kus, midsummer day.

"I won't be ready," I said.

"You'll be ready."

"I want to go into kemmer with Sether."

"Sether's got a month or two yet to go. Soon enough. It looks like you might be on the same moontime, though. Dark-of-the-mooners, eh? That's what I used to be. So, just stay on the same wavelength, you and Sether. . . ." Grand had never grinned at me this way, an inclusive grin, as if I were an equal.

My mother's mother was sixty years old, short, brawny, broad-hipped, with keen clear eyes, a stonemason by trade, an unquestioned autocrat in the Hearth. I, equal to this formidable person? It was my first intimation that I might be becoming more, rather than less, human.

"I'd like it," said Grand, "if you spent this halfmonth at the Fastness. But it's up to you."

"At the Fastness?" I said, taken by surprise. We Thades were all Handdara, but very inert Handdara, keeping only the great festivals, muttering the grace all in one garbled word, practising none of the disciplines. None of my older hearthsibs had been sent off to the Fastness before their kemmerday. Was there something wrong with me?

"You've got a good brain," said Grand. "You and Sether. I'd like to see some of you lot casting some shadows, some day. We Thades sit here in our Hearth and breed like pesthry. Is that enough? It'd be a good thing if some of you got your heads out of the bedding."

"What do they do in the Fastness?" I asked, and Grand answered frankly, "I don't know. Go find out. They teach you. They can teach you how to control kemmer."

"All right," I said promptly. I would tell Sether that the Indwellers could control kemmer. Maybe I could learn how to do it and come home and teach it to Sether.

Grand looked at me with approval. I had taken up the challenge.

Of course I didn't learn how to control kemmer, in a halfmonth in the Fastness. The first couple of days there, I thought I wouldn't even be able to control my homesickness. From our warm, dark warren of rooms full of people talking, sleeping, eating, cooking, washing, playing remma, playing music, kids running around, noise, family, I went across the city to a huge, clean, cold, quiet house of strangers. They were courteous, they treated me with respect. I was terrified. Why should a person of forty, who knew magic disciplines of superhuman strength and fortitude, who could walk barefoot through blizzards, who could Foretell, whose eyes were the wisest and calmest I had ever seen, why should an Adept of the Handdara respect me?

"Because you are so ignorant," Ranharrer the Adept said, smiling, with great tenderness.

Having me only for a halfmonth, they didn't try to influence the nature of my ignorance very much. I practised the Untrance several hours a day, and came to like it: that was quite enough for them, and they praised me. "At fourteen, most people go crazy moving slowly," my teacher said.

During my last six or seven days in the Fastness certain symptoms began to show up again, the headache, the swellings and shooting pains, the irritability. One morning the sheet of my cot in my bare, peaceful little room was bloodstained. I looked at the smear with horror and loathing. I thought I had scratched my itching labia to bleeding in my sleep, but I knew also what the blood was. I began to cry. I had to wash the sheet somehow. I had fouled, defiled this place where everything was clean, austere, and beautiful.

An old Indweller, finding me scrubbing desperately at the sheet in the washrooms, said nothing, but brought me some soap that bleached away the stain. I went back to my room, which I had come to love with the passion of one who had never before known any actual privacy, and crouched on the sheetless bed, miserable, checking every few minutes to be sure I was not bleeding again. I missed my Untrance practice time. The immense house was very quiet. Its peace sank into me. Again I felt that strangeness in my soul, but it was not pain now; it was a desolation like the air at evening, like the peaks of the Kargav seen far in the west in the clarity of winter. It was an immense enlargement.

Ranharrer the Adept knocked and entered at my word, looked at me for a minute, and asked gently, "What is it?"

"Everything is strange," I said.

The Adept smiled radiantly and said, "Yes."

I know now how Ranharrer cherished and honored my ignorance, in the Handdara sense. Then I knew only that somehow or other I had said the right thing and so pleased a person I wanted very much to please.

"We're doing some singing," Ranharrer said, "you might like to hear it."

They were in fact singing the Midsummer Chant, which goes on for the four days before Getheny Kus, night and day. Singers and drummers drop in and out at will, most of them singing on certain syllables in an endless group improvisation guided only by the drums and by melodic cues in the Chantbook, and falling into harmony with the soloist if one is present. At first I heard only a pleasantly thick-textured, droning sound over a quiet and subtle beat. I listened till I got bored and decided I could do it too. So I opened my mouth and sang "Aah" and heard all the other voices singing "Aah" above and with and below mine until I lost mine and heard only all the voices, and then only the music itself, and then suddenly the startling silvery rush of a single voice running across the weaving, against the current, and sinking into it and vanishing, and rising out of it again. . . . Ranharrer touched my arm. It was time for dinner, I had been singing since Third Hour. I went back to the chantry after dinner, and after supper. I spent the next three days there. I would have spent the nights there if they had let me. I wasn't sleepy at all any more. I had sudden, endless energy, and couldn't sleep. In my little room I sang to myself, or read the strange Handdara poetry which was the only book they had given me, and practised the Untrance, trying to ignore the heat and cold, the fire and ice in my body, till dawn came and I could go sing again.

And then it was Ottormenbod, midsummer's eve, and I had to go home to my Hearth and the kemmerhouse.

To my surprise, my mother and grandmother and all the elders came to the Fastness to fetch me, wearing ceremonial hiebs and looking solemn. Ranharrer handed me over to them, saying to me only, "Come back to us." My family paraded me through the streets in the hot summer morning; all the vines were in flower, perfuming the air, all the gardens were blooming, bearing, fruiting. "This is an excellent time," Grand said judiciously, "to come into kemmer."

The Hearth looked very dark to me after the Fastness, and somehow shrunken. I looked around for Sether, but it was a workday, Sether was at the shop. That gave me a sense of holiday, which was not unpleasant. And then up in the hearthroom of our balcony, Grand and the Hearth elders formally presented me with a whole set of new clothes, new everything, from the boots up, topped by a magnificently embroidered hieb. There was a spoken ritual that went with the clothes, not Handdara, I think, but a tradition of our Hearth; the words were all old and strange, the language of a thousand years ago. Grand rattled them out like somebody spitting rocks, and put the hieb on my shoulders. Everybody said, "Haya!"

All the elders, and a lot of younger kids, hung around helping me put on the new clothes as if I was a king or a baby, and some of the elders wanted to give me advice — "last advice," they called it, since you gain shifgrethor when you go into kemmer, and once you have shifgrethor advice is insulting. "Now you just keep away from that old Ebbeche," one of them told me shrilly. My mother took offense, snapping, "Keep your shadow to yourself, Tadsh!" And to me, "Don't listen to the old fish. Flapmouth Tadsh! But now listen, Sov."

I listened. Guyr had drawn me a little away from the others, and spoke gravely, with some embarrassment. "Remember, it will matter who you're with first."

I nodded. "I understand," I said.

"No, you don't," my mother snapped, forgetting to be embarrassed. "Just keep it in mind!"

"What, ah," I said. My mother waited. "If I, if I go into, as a, as female," I said. "Don't I, shouldn't I — ?"

"Ah," Guyr said. "Don't worry. It'll be a year or more before you can conceive. Or get. Don't worry, this time. The other people will see to it, just in case. They all know it's your first kemmer. But do keep it in mind, who you're with first! Around, oh, around Karrid, and Ebbeche, and some of them."

"Come on!" Dory shouted, and we all got into a procession again to go downstairs and across the centerhall, where everybody cheered "Haya Sov! Haya Sov!" and the cooks beat on their saucepans. I wanted to die. But they all seemed so cheerful, so happy about me, wishing me well; I wanted also to live.

We went out the west door and across the sunny gardens and came to the kemmerhouse. Tage Ereb shares a kemmerhouse with two other Ereb Hearths; it's a beautiful building, all carved with deep-figure friezes in the Old Dynasty style, terribly worn by the weather of a couple of thousand years. On the red stone steps my family all kissed me, murmuring, "Praise then Darkness," or "In the act of Creation praise," and my mother gave me a hard push on my shoulders, what they call the sledge-push, for good luck, as I turned away from them and went in the door.

The Doorkeeper was waiting for me; a queer-looking, rather stooped person, with coarse, pale skin.

Now I realised who this "Ebbeche" they'd been talking about was. I'd never met him, but I'd heard about him. He was the Doorkeeper of our kemmerhouse, a halfdead — that is, a person in permanent kemmer, like the Aliens.

There are always a few people born that way here. Some of them can be cured; those who can't or choose not to be usually live in a Fastness and learn the disciplines, or they become Doorkeepers. It's convenient for them, and for normal people too. After all, who else would want to *live* in a kemmerhouse? But there are drawbacks. If you come to the kemmerhouse in thorharmen, ready to gender, and the first person you meet is fully male, his pheromones are likely to gender you female right then, whether that's what you had in mind this month or not. Responsible Doorkeepers, of course, keep well away from anybody who doesn't invite them to come close. But permanent kemmer may not lead to responsibility of character; nor does being called *halfdead* and *pervert* all your life, I imagine. Obviously my family didn't trust Ebbeche to keep his hands and his pheromones off me. But they were unjust. He honored a first kemmer as much as anyone else. He greeted me by name and showed me where to take off my new boots. Then he began to speak the ancient ritual welcome, backing down the hall before me; the first time I ever heard the words I would hear so many times again for so many years.

> You cross earth now.
> You cross water now.
> You cross the Ice now. . . .

And the exulting ending, as we came into the centerhall:

> *Together we have crossed the Ice.*
> *Together we come into the Hearthplace,*
> *Into life, bringing life!*
> *In the act of creation, praise!*

The solemnity of the words moved me and distracted me some-what from my intense self-consciousness. As I had in the Fastness, I felt the familiar reassurance of being part of something immensely older and larger than myself, even if it was strange and new to me. I must entrust myself to it and be what it made me. At the same time I was intensely alert. All my senses were extraordinarily keen, as they had been all morning. I was aware of everything, the beautiful blue color of the walls, the lightness and vigor of my steps as I walked, the texture of the wood under my bare feet, the sound and meaning of the ritual words, the Doorkeeper himself. He fascinated me. Ebbeche was certainly not handsome, and yet I noticed how musical his rather deep voice was; and pale skin was more attractive than I had ever thought it. I felt that he had been maligned, that his life must be a strange one. I wanted to talk to him. But as he finished the welcome, standing aside for me at the doorway of the centerhall, a tall person strode forward eagerly to meet me.

I was glad to see a familiar face: it was the head cook of my Hearth, Karrid Arrage. Like many cooks a rather fierce and temper-amental person, Karrid had often taken notice of me, singling me out in a joking, challenging way, tossing me some delicacy — "Here, youngun! Get some meat on your bones!" As I saw Karrid now I went through the most extraordinary multiplicity of awarenesses: that Karrid was naked and that this nakedness was not like the nakedness of people in the Hearth, but a significant nakedness — that he was not the Karrid I had seen before but transfigured into great beauty — that he was *he* — that my mother had warned me

about him — that I wanted to touch him — that I was afraid of
him.

He picked me right up in his arms and pressed me against him. I
felt his clitopenis like a fist between my legs. "Easy, now," the
Doorkeeper said to him, and some other people came forward from
the room, which I could see only as large, dimly glowing, full of
shadows and mist.

"Don't worry, don't worry," Karrid said to me and them, with his
hard laugh. "I won't hurt my own get, will I? I just want to be the
one that gives her kemmer. As a woman, like a proper Thade. I want
to give you that joy, little Sov." He was undressing me as he spoke,
slipping off my hieb and shirt with big, hot, hasty hands. The
Doorkeeper and the others kept close watch, but did not interfere. I
felt totally defenseless, helpless, humiliated. I struggled to get free,
broke loose, and tried to pick up and put on my shirt. I was shaking
and felt terribly weak, I could hardly stand up. Karrid helped me
clumsily; his big arm supported me. I leaned against him, feeling his
hot, vibrant skin against mine, a wonderful feeling, like sunlight,
like firelight. I leaned more heavily against him, raising my arms so
that our sides slid together. "Hey, now," he said. "Oh, you beauty,
oh, you Sov, here, take her away, this won't do!" And he backed
right away from me, laughing and yet really alarmed, his clitopenis
standing up amazingly. I stood there half-dressed, on my rubbery
legs, bewildered. My eyes were full of mist, I could see nothing
clearly.

"Come on," somebody said, and took my hand, a soft, cool
touch totally different from the fire of Karrid's skin. It was a person
from one of the other Hearths, I didn't know her name. She seemed
to me to shine like gold in the dim, misty place. "Oh, you're going so
fast," she said, laughing and admiring and consoling. "Come on,
come into the pool, take it easy for a while. Karrid shouldn't have
come on to you like that! But you're lucky, first kemmer as a
woman, there's nothing like it. I kemmered as a man three times

before I got to kemmer as a woman, it made me so mad, every time I got into thorharmen all my damn friends would all be women already. Don't worry about me — I'd say Karrid's influence was decisive," and she laughed again. "Oh, you are so pretty!" and she bent her head and licked my nipples before I knew what she was doing.

It was wonderful, it cooled that stinging fire in them that nothing else could cool. She helped me finish undressing, and we stepped together into the warm water of the big, shallow pool that filled the whole center of this room. That was why it was so misty, why the echoes were so strange. The water lapped on my thighs, on my sex, on my belly. I turned to my friend and leaned forward to kiss her. It was a perfectly natural thing to do, it was what she wanted and I wanted, and I wanted her to lick and suck my nipples again, and she did. For a long time we lay in the shallow water playing, and I could have played forever. But then somebody else joined us, taking hold of my friend from behind, and she arched her body in the water like a golden fish leaping, threw her head back, and began to play with him.

I got out of the water and dried myself, feeling sad and shy and forsaken, and yet extremely interested in what had happened to my body. It felt wonderfully alive and electric, so that the roughness of the towel made me shiver with pleasure. Somebody had come closer to me, somebody that had been watching me play with my friend in the water. He sat down by me now.

It was a hearthmate a few years older than I, Arrad Tehemmy. I had worked in the gardens with Arrad all last summer, and liked him. He looked like Sether, I now thought, with heavy black hair and a long, thin face, but in him was that shining, that glory they all had here — all the kemmerers, the *women*, the *men* — such vivid beauty as I had never seen in any human beings. "Sov," he said, "I'd like — Your first — Will you — " His hands were already on me, and mine on him. "Come," he said, and I went with him. He took me into a beautiful little room, in which there was nothing but a fire burning in a fireplace, and a wide bed. There Arrad took me into his arms and I took Arrad into my arms, and then between my legs, and fell upward, upward through the golden light.

Arrad and I were together all that first night, and besides fucking a great deal, we ate a great deal. It had not occurred to me that there would be food at a kemmerhouse; I had thought you weren't allowed to do anything but fuck. There was a lot of food, very good, too, set out so that you could eat whenever you wanted. Drink was more limited; the person in charge, an old woman-halfdead, kept her canny eye on you, and wouldn't give you any more beer if you showed signs of getting wild or stupid. I didn't need any more beer. I didn't need any more fucking. I was complete. I was in love forever for all time all my life to eternity with Arrad. But Arrad (who was a day farther into kemmer than I) fell asleep and wouldn't wake up, and an extraordinary person named Hama sat down by me and began talking and also running his hand up and down my back in the most delicious way, so that before long we got further entangled, and began fucking, and it was entirely different with Hama than it had been with Arrad, so that I realised that I must be in love with Hama, until Gehardar joined us. After that I think I began to understand that I loved them all and they all loved me and that that was the secret of the kemmerhouse.

It's been nearly fifty years, and I have to admit I do not recall everyone from my first kemmer; only Karrid and Arrad, Hama and Gehardar, old Tubanny, the most exquisitely skillful lover as a male that I ever knew — I met him often in later kemmers — and Berre, my golden fish, with whom I ended up in drowsy, peaceful, blissful lovemaking in front of the great hearth till we both fell asleep. And when we woke we were not women. We were not men. We were not in kemmer. We were very tired young adults.

"You're still beautiful," I said to Berre.

"So are you," Berre said. "Where do you work?"

"Furniture shop, Third Ward."

I tried licking Berre's nipple, but it didn't work; Berre flinched a little, and I said "Sorry," and we both laughed.

"I'm in the radio trade," Berre said. "Did you ever think of trying that?"

"Making radios?"

"No. Broadcasting. I do the Fourth Hour news and weather."

"That's you?" I said, awed.

"Come over to the tower some time, I'll show you around," said Berre.

Which is how I found my lifelong trade and a lifelong friend. As I tried to tell Sether when I came back to the Hearth, kemmer isn't exactly what we thought it was; it's much more complicated.

Sether's first kemmer was on Getheny Gor, the first day of the first month of autumn, at the dark of the moon. One of the family brought Sether into kemmer as a woman, and then Sether brought me in. That was the first time I kemmered as a man. And we stayed on the same wavelength, as Grand put it. We never conceived together, being cousins and having some modern scruples, but we made love in every combination, every dark of the moon, for years. And Sether brought my child, Tamor, into first kemmer — as a woman, like a proper Thade.

Later on Sether went into the Handdara, and became an Indweller in the old Fastness, and now is an Adept. I go over there often to join in one of the Chants or practise the Untrance or just to visit, and every few days Sether comes back to the Hearth. And we talk. The old days or the new times, somer or kemmer, love is love.

THE MATTER OF SEGGRI

The first recorded contact with Seggri was in year 242 of Hainish Cycle 93. A Wandership six generations out from Iao (4-Taurus) came down on the planet, and the captain entered this report in his ship's log.

CAPTAIN AOLAO-OLAO'S REPORT

We have spent near forty days on this world they call Se-ri or Ye-ha-ri, well entertained, and leave with as good an estimation of the natives as is consonant with their unregenerate state. They live in fine great buildings they call castles, with large parks all about. Outside the walls of the parks lie well-tilled fields and abundant orchards, reclaimed by diligence from the parched and arid desert of stone that makes up the greatest part of the land. Their women live in villages and towns huddled outside the walls. All the common work of farm and mill is performed by the women, of whom there is a vast superabundance. They are ordinary drudges, living in towns which belong to the lords of the castle. They live amongst the cattle and brute animals of all kinds, who are permitted into the houses, some of which are of fair size. These women go about drably clothed, always in groups and bands. They are never allowed within the walls of the park, leaving the food and necessaries with which they provide the men at the outer gate of the castle. They evinced great fear and distrust of us. A few of my men following some girls on the road, women rushed from the town like a pack of wild beasts, so that the men thought it best to return forthwith to the castle. Our hosts advised us that it were best for us to keep away from their towns, which we did.

The men go freely about their great parks, playing at one sport or another. At night they go to certain houses which they own in the town, where they may have their pick among the women and satisfy their lust upon them as they will. The women pay them, we were told, in their money, which is copper, for a night of pleasure, and pay them yet more if they get a child on them. Their nights thus are spent in carnal satisfaction as often as they desire, and their days in a diversity of sports and games, notably a kind of wrestling, in which they throw each other through the air so that we marveled that they seemed never to take hurt, but rose up and returned to the combat with wonderful dexterity of hand and foot. Also they fence with blunt swords, and combat with long light sticks. Also they play a game with balls on a great field, using the arms to catch or throw the ball and the legs to kick the ball and trip or catch or kick the men of the other team, so that many are bruised and lamed in the passion of the sport, which was very fine to see, the teams in their contrasted garments of bright colors much gauded out with gold and finery seething now this way, now that, up and down the field in a mass, from which the balls were flung up and caught by runners breaking free of the struggling crowd and fleeting towards the one or the other goal with all the rest in hot pursuit. There is a "battle-field" as they call it of this game lying without the walls of the castle park, near to the town, so that the women may come watch and cheer, which they do heartily, calling out the names of favorite players and urging them with many uncouth cries to victory.

Boys are taken from the women at the age of eleven and brought to the castle to be educated as befits a man. We saw such a child brought into the castle with much ceremony and rejoicing. It is said that the women find it difficult to bring a pregnancy of a manchild to term, and that of those born many die in infancy despite the care lavished upon them, so that there are far more women than men. In this we see the curse of GOD laid upon this race as upon all those who acknowledge HIM not, unrepentant heathens whose ears are stopped to true discourse and blind to the light.

These men know little of art, only a kind of leaping dance, and their science is little beyond that of savages. One great man of a castle to whom I talked, who was dressed out in cloth of gold and crimson and whom all called Prince and Grandsire with much respect and deference, yet was so ignorant he believed the stars to be worlds full of people and beasts, asking us from which star we descended. They have only vessels driven by steam along the surface of the land and water, and no notion of flight either in the air or in space, nor any curiosity about such things, saying with disdain, "That is all women's work," and indeed I found that if I asked these great men about matters of common knowledge such as the working of machinery, the weaving of cloth, the transmission of holovision, they would soon chide me for taking interest in womanish things as they called them, desiring me to talk as befit a man.

In the breeding of their fierce cattle within the parks they are very knowledgeable, as in the sewing up of their clothing, which they make from cloth the women weave in their factories. The men vie in the ornamentation and magnificence of their costumes to an extent which we might indeed have thought scarcely manly, were they not withal such proper men, strong and ready for any game or sport, and full of pride and a most delicate and fiery honor.

The log including Captain Aolao-olao's entries was (after a 12-generation journey) returned to the Sacred Archives of the Universe on Iao, which were dispersed during the period called The Tumult, and eventually preserved in fragmentary form on Hain. There is no record of further contact with Seggri until the First

*Observers were sent by the Ekumen in 93/1333: an Alterran man
and a Hainish woman, Kaza Agad and G. Merriment. After a year
in orbit mapping, photographing, recording and studying broad-
casts, and analysing and learning a major regional language, the
Observers landed. Acting upon a strong persuasion of the vulnerability of the planetary culture, they presented themselves as survivors of the wreck of a fishing boat, blown far off course, from a
remote island. They were, as they had anticipated, separated at
once, Kaza Agad being taken to the Castle and Merriment into the
town. Kaza kept his name, which was plausible in the native context; Merriment called herself Yude. We have only her report, from
which three excerpts follow.*

FROM MOBILE GERINDU'UTTAHAYUDETWE'MENRADE MERRIMENT'S
NOTES FOR A REPORT TO THE EKUMEN, 93/1334

34/223. Their network of trade and information, hence their awareness of what goes on elsewhere in their world, is too sophisticated
for me to maintain my Stupid Foreign Castaway act any longer.
Ekhaw called me in today and said, "If we had a sire here who was
worth buying or if our teams were winning their games, I'd think
you were a spy. Who are you, anyhow?"

I said, "Would you let me go to the College at Hagka?"

She said, "Why?"

"There are scientists there, I think? I need to talk with them."

This made sense to her; she made their "Mh" noise of assent.

"Could my friend go there with me?"

"Shask, you mean?"

We were both puzzled for a moment. She didn't expect a woman
to call a man "friend," and I hadn't thought of Shask as a friend.
She's very young, and I haven't taken her very seriously.

"I mean Kaza, the man I came with."

"A man — to the college?" she said, incredulous. She looked at me and said, "Where *do* you come from?"

It was a fair question, not asked in enmity or challenge. I wish I could have answered it, but I am increasingly convinced that we can do great damage to these people; we are facing Resehavanar's Choice here, I fear.

Ekhaw paid for my journey to Hagka, and Shask came along with me. As I thought about it I saw that of course Shask was my friend. It was she who brought me into the motherhouse, persuading Ekhaw and Azman of their duty to be hospitable; it was she who had looked out for me all along. Only she was so conventional in everything she did and said that I hadn't realised how radical her compassion was. When I tried to thank her, as our little jitney-bus purred along the road to Hagka, she said things like she always says — "Oh, we're all family," and "People have to help each other," and "Nobody can live alone."

"Don't women ever live alone?" I asked her, for all the ones I've met belong to a motherhouse or a daughterhouse, whether a couple or a big family like Ekhaw's, which is three generations: five older women, three of their daughters living at home, and four children — the boy they all coddle and spoil so, and three girls.

"Oh yes," Shask said. "If they don't want wives, they can be singlewomen. And old women, when their wives die, sometimes they just live alone till they die. Usually they go live at a daughterhouse. In the colleges, the *vev* always have a place to be alone." Conventional she may be, but Shask always tries to answer a question seriously and completely; she thinks about her answer. She has been an invaluable informant. She has also made life easy for me by not asking questions about where I come from. I took this for the incuriosity of a person securely embedded in an unquestioned way of life, and for the self-centeredness of the young. Now I see it as delicacy.

"A vev is a teacher?"

"Mh."

"And the teachers at the college are very respected?"

"That's what vev means. That's why we call Eckaw's mother Vev Kakaw. She didn't go to college, but she's a thoughtful person, she's learned from life, she has a lot to teach us."

So respect and teaching are the same thing, and the only term of respect I've heard women use for women means teacher. And so in teaching me, young Shask respects herself? And/or earns my respect? This casts a different light on what I've been seeing as a society in which wealth is the important thing. Zadedr, the current mayor of Reha, is certainly admired for her very ostentatious display of possessions; but they don't call her Vev.

I said to Shask, "You have taught me so much, may I call you Vev Shask?"

She was equally embarrassed and pleased, and squirmed and said, "Oh no no no no." Then she said, "If you ever come back to Reha I would like very much to have love with you, Yude."

"I thought you were in love with Sire Zadr!" I blurted out.

"Oh, I am," she said, with that eye-roll and melted look they have when they speak of the sires, "aren't you? Just think of him fucking you, oh! Oh, I get all wet thinking about it!" She smiled and wriggled. I felt embarrassed in my turn and probably showed it. "Don't you like him?" she inquired with a naivety I found hard to bear. She was acting like a silly adolescent, and I know she's not a silly adolescent. "But I'll never be able to afford him," she said, and sighed.

So you want to make do with me, I thought nastily.

"I'm going to save my money," she announced after a minute. "I think I want to have a baby next year. Of course I can't afford Sire Zadr, he's a Great Champion, but if I don't go to the Games at Kadaki this year I can save up enough for a really good sire at our fuckery, maybe Master Rosra. I wish, I know this is silly, I'm going to say it anyway, I've been wishing you could be its lovemother. I know you can't, you have to go to the college. I just wanted to tell you. I love you." She took my hands, drew them to her face, pressed my palms on her eyes for a moment, and then released me. She was smiling, but her tears were on my hands.

"Oh, Shask," I said, floored.

"It's all right!" she said. "I have to cry a minute." And she did. She wept openly, bending over, wringing her hands, and wailing softly. I patted her arm and felt unutterably ashamed of myself. Other passengers looked round and made little sympathetic grunting noises. One old woman said, "That's it, that's right, lovey!" In a few minutes Shask stopped crying, wiped her nose and face on her sleeve, drew a long, deep breath, and said, "All right." She smiled at me. "Driver," she called, "I have to piss, can we stop?"

The driver, a tense-looking woman, growled something, but stopped the bus on the wide, weedy roadside; and Shask and another woman got off and pissed in the weeds. There is an enviable simplicity to many acts in a society which has, in all its daily life, only one gender. And which, perhaps — I don't know this but it occurred to me then, while I was ashamed of myself — has no shame?

34/245. (Dictated) Still nothing from Kaza. I think I was right to give him the ansible. I hope he's in touch with somebody. I wish it was me. I need to know what goes on in the castles.

Anyhow I understand better now what I was seeing at the Games in Reha. There are sixteen adult women for every adult man. One conception in six or so is male, but a lot of nonviable male fetuses and defective male births bring it down to one in sixteen by puberty. My ancestors must have really had fun playing with these people's chromosomes. I feel guilty, even if it was a million years ago. I have to learn to do without shame but had better not forget the one good use of guilt. Anyhow. A fairly small town like Reha shares its castle with other towns. That confusing spectacle I was taken to on my tenth day down was Awaga Castle trying to keep its place in the Maingame against a castle from up north, and losing. Which means Awaga's team can't play in the big game this year in Fadrga, the city south of here, from which the winners go on to compete in the *big* big game at Zask, where people come from all over the continent — hundreds of contestants and thousands of spectators. I saw some holos of last year's Maingame at Zask. There were 1,280 players, the comment said, and forty balls in play. It looked to me like a total mess, my idea of a battle between two unarmed armies, but I gather that great skill and strategy is involved. All the members of the winning team get a special title for the year, and another one for life, and bring glory back to their various castles and the towns that support them.

I can now get some sense of how this works, see the system from outside it, because the college doesn't support a castle. People here aren't obsessed with sports and athletes and sexy sires the way the young women in Reha were, and some of the older ones. It's a kind of obligatory obsession. Cheer your team, support your brave men, adore your local hero. It makes sense. Given their situation, they need strong, healthy men at their fuckery; it's social selection reinforcing natural selection. But I'm glad to get away from the rah-rah and the swooning and the posters of fellows with swelling muscles and huge penises and bedroom eyes.

I have made Resehavanar's Choice. I chose the option: Less than the truth. Shoggrad and Skodr and the other teachers, professors we'd call them, are intelligent, enlightened people, perfectly capable of understanding the concept of space travel, etc., making decisions about technological innovation, etc. I limit my answers to their questions to technology. I let them assume, as most people naturally assume, particularly people from a monoculture, that our society is pretty much like theirs. When they find how it differs, the effect will be revolutionary, and I have no mandate, reason, or wish to cause such a revolution on Seggri.

Their gender imbalance has produced a society in which, as far as I can tell, the men have all the privilege and the women have all the power. It's obviously a stable arrangement. According to their histories, it's lasted at least two millennia, and probably in some form or another much longer than that. But it could be quickly and disastrously destabilised by contact with us, by their experiencing the human norm. I don't know if the men would cling to their privileged status or demand freedom, but surely the women would resist giving up their power, and their sexual system and affectional relationships would break down. Even if they learned to undo the genetic program that was inflicted on them, it would take several generations to restore normal gender distribution. I can't be the whisper that starts that avalanche.

34/266. (Dictated) Skodr got nowhere with the men of Awaga Castle. She had to make her inquiries very cautiously, since it would endanger Kaza if she told them he was an alien or in any way unique. They'd take it as a claim of superiority, which he'd have to defend in trials of strength and skill. I gather that the hierarchies within the castles are a rigid framework, within which a man moves up or down issuing challenges and winning or losing obligatory and optional trials. The sports and games the women watch are only the showpieces of an endless series of competitions going on inside the castles. As an untrained, grown man Kaza would be at a total disadvantage in such trials. The only way he might get out of them, she said, would be by feigning illness or idiocy. She thinks he must have done so, since he is at least alive; but that's all she could find out — "The man who was cast away at Taha-Reha is alive."

Although the women feed, house, clothe, and support the lords of the castle, they evidently take their noncooperation for granted. She seemed glad to get even that scrap of information. As I am.

But we have to get Kaza out of there. The more I hear about it from Skodr the more dangerous it sounds. I keep thinking "spoiled brats!" but actually these men must be more like soldiers in the training camps that militarists have. Only the training never ends. As they win trials they gain all kinds of titles and ranks you could translate as "generals" and the other names militarists have for all their power-grades. Some of the "generals," the Lords and Masters and so on, are the sports idols, the darlings of the fuckeries, like the one poor Shask adored; but as they get older apparently they often trade glory among the women for power among the men, and become tyrants within their castle, bossing the "lesser" men around, until they're overthrown, kicked out. Old sires often live alone, it seems, in little houses away from the main castle, and are considered crazy and dangerous — rogue males.

It sounds like a miserable life. All they're allowed to do after age eleven is compete at games and sports inside the castle, and compete in the fuckeries, after they're fifteen or so, for money and number of fucks and so on. Nothing else. No options. No trades. No skills of making. No travel unless they play in the big games. They aren't allowed into the colleges to gain any kind of freedom of mind. I asked Skodr why an intelligent man couldn't at least come study in the college, and she told me that learning was very bad for men: it weakens a man's sense of honor, makes his muscles flabby, and leaves him impotent. "'What goes to the brain takes from the testicles,'" she said. "Men have to be sheltered from education for their own good."

I tried to "be water," as I was taught, but I was disgusted. Probably she felt it, because after a while she told me about "the secret college." Some women in colleges do smuggle information to men in castles. The poor things meet secretly and teach each other. In the castles, homosexual relationships are encouraged among boys under fifteen, but not officially tolerated among grown men; she says the "secret colleges" often are run by the homosexual men. They have to be secret because if they're caught reading or talking about ideas they may be punished by their Lords and Masters.

There have been some interesting works from the "secret colleges," Skodr said, but she had to think to come up with examples. One was a man who had smuggled out an interesting mathematical theorem, and one was a painter whose landscapes, though primitive in technique, were admired by professionals of the art. She couldn't remember his name.

Arts, sciences, all learning, all professional techniques, are *haggyad*, skilled work. They're all taught at the colleges, and there are no divisions and few specialists. Teachers and students cross and mix fields all the time, and being a famous scholar in one field doesn't keep you from being a student in another. Skodr is a vev of physiology, writes plays, and is currently studying history with one of the history vevs. Her thinking is informed and lively and fearless. My School on Hain could learn from this college. It's a wonderful place, full of free minds. But only minds of one gender. A hedged freedom.

I hope Kaza has found a secret college or something, some way to fit in at the castle. He's strong, but these men have trained for years for the games they play. And a lot of the games are violent. The women say don't worry, we don't let the men kill each other, we protect them, they're our treasures. But I've seen men carried off with concussions, on the holos of their martial-art fights, where they throw each other around spectacularly. "Only inexperienced fighters get hurt." Very reassuring. And they wrestle bulls. And in that melee they call the Maingame they break each other's legs and ankles deliberately. "What's a hero without a limp?" the women say. Maybe that's the safe thing to do, get your leg broken so you don't have to prove you're a hero any more. But what else might Kaza have to prove?

I asked Shask to let me know if she ever heard of him being at the Reha fuckery. But Awaga Castle services (that's their word, the same word they use for their bulls) four towns, so he might get sent to one of the others. But probably not, because men who don't win at things aren't allowed to go to the fuckeries. Only the champions. And boys between fifteen and nineteen, the ones the older women call *dippida*, baby animals — puppy, kitty, lamby. They use the dippida for pleasure. They only pay for a champion when they go to the fuckery to get pregnant. But Kaza's thirty-six, he isn't a puppy or a kitten or a lamb. He's a man, and this is a terrible place to be a man.

> Kaza Agad had been killed; the Lords of Awaga Castle finally disclosed the fact, but not the circumstances. A year later, Merriment radioed her lander and left Seggri for Hain. Her recommendation was to observe and avoid. The Stabiles, however, decided to send another pair of observers; these were both women, Mobiles Alee Iyoo and Zerin Wu. They lived for eight years on Seggri, after the third year as First Mobiles; Iyoo stayed as Ambassador another fifteen years. They made Resehavanar's Choice as "all the truth slowly." A limit of two hundred visitors from offworld was set. During the next several generations the people of Seggri, becoming accustomed to the alien presence, considered their own options as members of the Ekumen. Proposals for a planetwide referendum on genetic alteration were abandoned, since the men's vote would be insignificant unless the women's vote were handicapped. As of the date of this report the Seggri have not undertaken major genetic alteration, though they have learned and applied various repair techniques, which have resulted in a higher proportion of full-term male infants; the gender balance now stands at about 12:1.
>
> The following is a memoir given to Ambassador Eritho te Ves in 93/1569 by a woman in Ush on Seggri.

You asked me, dear friend, to tell you anything I might like people on other worlds to know about my life and my world. That's not easy! Do I want anybody anywhere else to know anything about my life? I know how strange we seem to all the others, the half-and-half races; I know they think us backward, provincial, even perverse. Maybe in a few more decades we'll decide that we should remake ourselves. I won't be alive then; I don't think I'd want to be. I like my people. I like our fierce, proud, beautiful men, I don't want them to become like women. I like our trustful, powerful, generous women, I don't want them to become like men. And yet I see that among you each man has his own being and nature, each woman has hers, and I can hardly say what it is I think we would lose.

When I was a child I had a brother a year and a half younger than me. His name was Ittu. My mother had gone to the city and paid five years' savings for my sire, a Master Champion in the Dancing. Ittu's sire was an old fellow at our village fuckery; they called him "Master Fallback." He'd never been a champion at anything, hadn't sired a child for years, and was only too glad to fuck for free. My mother always laughed about it — she was still suckling me, she didn't even use a preventive, and she tipped him two coppers! When she found herself pregnant she was furious. When they tested and found it was a male fetus she was even more disgusted at having, as they say, to wait for the miscarriage. But when Ittu was born sound and healthy, she gave the old sire two hundred coppers, all the cash she had.

He wasn't delicate like so many boy babies, but how can you keep from protecting and cherishing a boy? I don't remember when I wasn't looking after Ittu, with it all very clear in my head what Little Brother should do and shouldn't do and all the perils I must keep him from. I was proud of my responsibility, and vain, too, because I had a brother to look after. Not one other motherhouse in my village had a son still living at home.

Ittu was a lovely child, a star. He had the fleecy soft hair that's common in my part of Ush, and big eyes; his nature was sweet and cheerful, and he was very bright. The other children loved him and always wanted to play with him, but he and I were happiest playing by ourselves, long elaborate games of make-believe. We had a herd of twelve cattle an old woman of the village had carved from gourd-shell for Ittu — people always gave him presents — and they were the actors in our dearest game. Our cattle lived in a country called Shush, where they had great adventures, climbing mountains, discovering new lands, sailing on rivers, and so on. Like any herd, like our village herd, the old cows were the leaders; the bull lived apart; the other males were gelded; and the heifers were the adventurers. Our bull would make ceremonial visits to service the cows, and then he might have to go fight with men at Shush Castle. We made the castle of clay and the men of sticks, and the bull always won, knocking the stick-men to pieces. Then sometimes he knocked the castle to pieces too. But the best of our stories were told with two of the heifers. Mine was named Op and my brother's was Utti. Once our hero heifers were having a great adventure on the stream that runs past our village, and their boat got away from us. We found it caught against a log far downstream where the stream was deep and quick. My heifer was still in it. We both dived and dived, but we never found Utti. She had drowned. The Cattle of Shush had a great funeral for her, and Ittu cried very bitterly.

He mourned his brave little toy cow so long that I asked Djerdji the cattleherd if we could work for her, because I thought being with the real cattle might cheer Ittu up. She was glad to get two cowhands for free (when Mother found out we were really working, she made Djerdji pay us a quarter-copper a day). We rode two big, goodnatured old cows, on saddles so big Ittu could lie down on his. We took a herd of two-year-old calves out onto the desert every day to forage for the *edta* that grows best when it's grazed. We were supposed to keep them from wandering off and from trampling streambanks, and when they wanted to settle down and chew the cud we were supposed to gather them in a place where their droppings would nourish useful plants. Our old mounts did most of the work. Mother came out and checked on what we were doing and decided it was all right, and being out in the desert all day was certainly keeping us fit and healthy.

We loved our riding cows, but they were serious-minded and responsible, rather like the grown-ups in our motherhouse. The calves were something else; they were all riding breed, not fine animals of course, just villagebred; but living on edta they were fat and had plenty of spirit. Ittu and I rode them bareback with a rope rein. At first we always ended up on our own backs watching a calf's heels and tail flying off. By the end of a year we were good riders, and took to training our mounts to tricks, trading mounts at a full run, and hornvaulting. Ittu was a marvelous hornvaulter. He trained a big three-year-old roan ox with lyre horns, and the two of them danced like the finest vaulters of the great castles that we saw on the holos. We couldn't keep our excellence to ourselves out in the desert; we started showing off to the other children, inviting them to come out to Salt Springs to see our Great Trick Riding Show. And so of course the adults got to hear of it.

My mother was a brave woman, but that was too much for even her, and she said to me in cold fury, "I trusted you to look after Ittu. You let me down."

All the others had been going on and on about endangering the precious life of a boy, the Vial of Hope, the Treasurehouse of Life, and so on, but it was what my mother said that hurt.

"I do look after Ittu, and he looks after me," I said to her, in that passion of justice that children know, the birthright we seldom honor. "We both know what's dangerous and we don't do stupid things and we know our cattle and we do everything together. When he has to go to the castle he'll have to do lots more dangerous things, but at least he'll already know how to do one of them. And there he has to do them alone, but we did everything together. And I didn't let you down."

My mother looked at us. I was nearly twelve, Ittu was ten. She burst into tears, she sat down on the dirt and wept aloud. Ittu and I both went to her and hugged her and cried. Ittu said, "I won't go. I won't go to the damned castle. They can't make me!"

And I believed him. He believed himself. My mother knew better.

Maybe some day it will be possible for a boy to choose his life. Among your peoples a man's body does not shape his fate, does it? Maybe some day that will be so here.

Our Castle, Hidjegga, had of course been keeping their eye on Ittu ever since he was born; once a year Mother would send them the doctor's report on him, and when he was five Mother and her wives took him out there for the ceremony of Confirmation. Ittu had been embarrassed, disgusted, and flattered. He told me in secret, "There were all these old *men* that smelled funny and they made me take off my clothes and they had these measuring things and they measured my peepee! And they said it was very good. They said it was a good one. What happens when you descend?" It wasn't the first question he had ever asked me that I couldn't answer, and as usual I made up the answer. "Descend means you can have babies," I said, which, in a way, wasn't so far off the mark.

Some castles, I am told, prepare boys of nine and ten for the Severance, woo them with visits from older boys, tickets to games, tours of the park and the buildings, so that they may be quite eager to go to the castle when they turn eleven. But we "outyonders," villagers of the edge of the desert, kept to the harsh old-fashioned ways. Aside from Confirmation, a boy had no contact at all with men until his eleventh birthday. On that day everybody he had ever known brought him to the Gate and gave him to the strangers with whom he would live the rest of his life. Men and women alike believed and still believe that this absolute severance makes the man.

Vev Ushiggi, who had borne a son and had a grandson, and had been mayor five or six times, and was held in great esteem even though she'd never had much money, heard Ittu say that he wouldn't go to the damned Castle. She came next day to our motherhouse and asked to talk to him. He told me what she said. She didn't do any wooing or sweetening. She told him that he was born to the service of his people and had one responsibility, to sire children when he got old enough; and one duty, to be a strong, brave man, stronger and braver than other men, so that women would choose him to sire their children. She said he had to live in the Castle because men could not live among women. At this, Ittu asked her, "Why can't they?"

"You did?" I said, awed by his courage, for Vev Ushiggi was a formidable old woman.

"Yes. And she didn't really answer. She took a long time. She looked at me and then she looked off somewhere and then she stared at me for a long time and then finally she said, 'Because we would destroy them.'"

"But that's crazy," I said. "Men are our treasures. What did she say that for?"

Ittu, of course, didn't know. But he thought hard about what she had said, and I think nothing she could have said would have so impressed him.

After discussion, the village elders and my mother and her wives decided that Ittu could go on practicing hornvaulting, because it really would be a useful skill for him in the Castle; but he could not herd cattle any longer, nor go with me when I did, nor join in any of the work children of the village did, nor their games. "You've done everything together with Po," they told him, "but she should be doing things together with the other girls, and you should be doing things by yourself, the way men do."

They were always very kind to Ittu, but they were stern with us girls; if they saw us even talking with Ittu they'd tell us to go on about our work, leave the boy alone. When we disobeyed — when Ittu and I sneaked off and met at Salt Springs to ride together, or just hid out in our old playplace down in the draw by the stream to talk — he got treated with cold silence to shame him, but I got punished. A day locked in the cellar of the old fiber-processing mill, which was what my village used for a jail; next time it was two days;

and the third time they caught us alone together, they locked me in that cellar for ten days. A young woman called Fersk brought me food once a day and made sure I had enough water and wasn't sick, but she didn't speak; that's how they always used to punish people in the villages. I could hear the other children going by up on the street in the evening. It would get dark at last and I could sleep. All day I had nothing to do, no work, nothing to think about except the scorn and contempt they held me in for betraying their trust, and the injustice of my getting punished when Ittu didn't.

When I came out, I felt different. I felt like something had closed up inside me while I was closed up in that cellar.

When we ate at the motherhouse they made sure Ittu and I didn't sit near each other. For a while we didn't even talk to each other. I went back to school and work. I didn't know what Ittu was doing all day. I didn't think about it. It was only fifty days to his birthday.

One night I got into bed and found a note under my clay pillow: *in the draw to-nt.* Ittu never could spell; what writing he knew I had taught him in secret. I was frightened and angry, but I waited an hour till everybody was asleep, and got up and crept outside into the windy, starry night, and ran to the draw. It was late in the dry season and the stream was barely running. Ittu was there, hunched up with his arms round his knees, a little lump of shadow on the pale, cracked clay at the waterside.

The first thing I said was, "You want to get me locked up again? They said next time it would be thirty days!"

"They're going to lock me up for fifty years," Ittu said, not looking at me.

"What am I supposed to do about it? It's the way it has to be! You're a man. You have to do what men do. They won't lock you up, anyway, you get to play games and come to town to do service and all that. You don't even know what being locked up is!"

"I want to go to Seradda," Ittu said, talking very fast, his eyes shining as he looked up at me. "We could take the riding cows to the bus station in Redang, I saved my money, I have twenty-three coppers, we could take the bus to Seradda. The cows would come back home if we turned them loose."

"What do you think you'd do in Seradda?" I asked, disdainful but curious. Nobody from our village had ever been to the capital.

"The Ekkamen people are there," he said.

"The Ekumen," I corrected him. "So what?"

"They could take me away," Ittu said.

I felt very strange when he said that. I was still angry and still disdainful but a sorrow was rising in me like dark water. "Why would they do that? What would they talk to some little boy for? How would you find them? Twenty-three coppers isn't enough anyway. Seradda's way far off. That's a really stupid idea. You can't do that."

"I thought you'd come with me," Ittu said. His voice was softer, but didn't shake.

"I wouldn't do a stupid thing like that," I said furiously.

"All right," he said. "But you won't tell. Will you?"

"No, I won't tell!" I said. "But you can't run away, Ittu. You can't. It would be — it would be dishonorable."

This time when he answered his voice shook. "I don't care," he said. "I don't care about honor. I want to be free!"

We were both in tears. I sat down by him and we leaned together the way we used to, and cried a while; not long; we weren't used to crying.

"You can't do it," I whispered to him. "It won't work, Ittu."

He nodded, accepting my wisdom.

"It won't be so bad at the Castle," I said.

After a minute he drew away from me very slightly.

"We'll see each other," I said.

He said only, "When?"

"At games. I can watch you. I bet you'll be the best rider and hornvaulter there. I bet you win all the prizes and get to be a Champion."

He nodded, dutiful. He knew and I knew that I had betrayed our love and our birthright of justice. He knew he had no hope.

That was the last time we talked together alone, and almost the last time we talked together.

Ittu ran away about ten days after that, taking the riding cow and heading for Redang; they tracked him easily and had him back in the village before nightfall. I don't know if he thought I had told them where he would be going. I was so ashamed of not having gone with him that I could not look at him. I kept away from him; they didn't have to keep me away any more. He made no effort to speak to me.

I was beginning my puberty, and my first blood was the night before Ittu's birthday. Menstruating women are not allowed to come near the Gates at conservative castles like ours, so when Ittu was made a man I stood far back among a few other girls and women, and could not see much of the ceremony. I stood silent while they sang, and looked down at the dirt and my new sandals and my feet in the sandals, and felt the ache and tug of my womb and the secret movement of the blood, and grieved. I knew even then that this grief would be with me all my life.

Ittu went in and the Gates closed.

He became a Young Champion Hornvaulter, and for two years, when he was eighteen and nineteen, came a few times to service in our village, but I never saw him. One of my friends fucked with him and started to tell me about it, how nice he was, thinking I'd like to hear, but I shut her up and walked away in a blind rage which neither of us understood.

He was traded away to a castle on the east coast when he was twenty. When my daughter was born I wrote him, and several times after that, but he never answered my letters.

I don't know what I've told you about my life and my world. I don't know if it's what I want you to know. It is what I had to tell.

The following is a short story written in 93/1586 by a popular writer of the city of Adr, Sem Gridji. The classic literature of Seggri was the narrative poem and the drama. Classical poems and plays were written collaboratively, in the original version and also by re-writers of subsequent generations, usually anonymous. Small value was placed on preserving a "true" text, since the work was seen as an ongoing process. Probably under Ekumenical influence, individual writers in the late sixteenth century began writing short prose narratives, historical and fictional. The genre became popular, particularly in the cities, though it never obtained the immense audience of the great classical epics and plays. Literally everyone knew the plots and many quotations from the epics and plays, from books and holo, and almost every adult woman had seen or participated in a staged performance of several of them. They were one of the principal unifying influences of the Seggrian monoculture. The prose narrative, read in silence, served rather as a device by which the culture might question itself, and a tool for individual moral self-examination. Conservative Seggrian women disapproved of the genre as antagonistic to the intensely cooperative, collaborative structure of their society. Fiction was not included in the curriculum of the literature departments of the colleges, and was often dismissed contemptuously — "fiction is for men."

Sem Gridji published three books of stories. Her bare, blunt style is characteristic of the Seggrian short story.

LOVE OUT OF PLACE

by Sem Gridji

Azak grew up in a motherhouse in the Downriver Quarter, near the textile mills. She was a bright girl, and her family and neighborhood were proud to gather the money to send her to college. She came back to the city as a starting manager at one of the mills. Azak worked well with other people; she prospered. She had a clear idea of what she wanted to do in the next few years: to find two or three partners with whom to found a daughterhouse and a business.

A beautiful woman in the prime of youth, Azak took great pleasure in sex, especially liking intercourse with men. Though she saved money for her plan of founding a business, she also spent a good deal at the fuckery, going there often, sometimes hiring two men at once. She liked to see how they incited each other to prowess beyond what they would have achieved alone, and shamed each other when they failed. She found a flaccid penis very disgusting, and did not hesitate to send away a man who could not penetrate her three or four times an evening.

The castle of her district bought a Young Champion at the Southeast Castles Dance Tournament, and soon sent him to the fuckery. Having seen him dance in the finals on the holovision and been captivated by his flowing, graceful style and his beauty, Azak was eager to have him service her. His price was twice that of any other man there, but she did not hesitate to pay it. She found him handsome and amiable, eager and gentle, skillful and compliant. In their first evening they came to orgasm together five times. When she left she gave him a large tip. Within the week she was back, asking for Toddra. The pleasure he gave her was exquisite, and soon she was quite obsessed with him.

"I wish I had you all to myself," she said to him one night as they lay still conjoined, languorous and fulfilled.

"That is my heart's desire," he said. "I wish I were your servant. None of the other women that come here arouse me. I don't want them. I want only you."

She wondered if he was telling the truth. The next time she came, she inquired casually of the manager if Toddra were as popular as they had hoped. "No," the manager said. "Everybody else reports that he takes a lot of arousing, and is sullen and careless towards them."

"How strange," Azak said.

"Not at all," said the manager. "He's in love with you."

"A man in love with a woman?" Azak said, and laughed.

"It happens all too often," the manager said.

"I thought only women fell in love," said Azak.

"Women fall in love with a man, sometimes, and that's bad too," said the manager. "May I warn you, Azak? Love should be between women. It's out of place here. It can never come to any good end. I hate to lose the money, but I wish you'd fuck with some of the other men and not always ask for Toddra. You're encouraging him, you see, in something that does harm to him."

"But he and you are making lots of money from me!" said Azak, still taking it as a joke.

"He'd make more from other women if he wasn't in love with you," said the manager. To Azak that seemed a weak argument against the pleasure she had in Toddra, and she said, "Well, he can fuck them all when I've done with him, but for now, I want him."

After their intercourse that evening, she said to Toddra, "The manager here says you're in love with me."

"I told you I was," Toddra said. "I told you I wanted to belong to you, to serve you, you alone. I would die for you, Azak."

"That's foolish," she said.

"Don't you like me? Don't I please you?"

"More than any man I ever knew," she said, kissing him. "You are beautiful and utterly satisfying, my sweet Toddra."

"You don't want any of the other men here, do you?" he asked.

"No. They're all ugly fumblers, compared to my beautiful dancer."

"Listen, then," he said, sitting up and speaking very seriously. He was a slender man of twenty-two, with long, smooth-muscled limbs, wide-set eyes, and a thin-lipped, sensitive mouth. Azak lay stroking his thigh, thinking how lovely and lovable he was. "I have a plan," he said. "When I dance, you know, in the story-dances, I play a woman, of course; I've done it since I was twelve. People always say they can't believe I really am a man, I play a woman so well. If I escaped — from here, from the Castle — as a woman — I could come to your house as a servant — "

"What?" cried Azak, astounded.

"I could live there," he said urgently, bending over her. "With you. I would always be there. You could have me every night. It would cost you nothing, except my food. I would serve you, service you, sweep your house, do anything, anything, Azak, please, my beloved, my mistress, let me be yours!" He saw that she was still incredulous, and hurried on, "You could send me away when you got tired of me — "

"If you tried to go back to the Castle after an escapade like that they'd whip you to death, you idiot!"

"I'm valuable," he said. "They'd punish me, but they wouldn't damage me."

"You're wrong. You haven't been dancing, and your value here has slipped because you don't perform well with anybody but me. The manager told me so."

Tears stood in Toddra's eyes. Azak disliked giving him pain, but she was genuinely shocked at his wild plan. "And if you were discovered, my dear," she said more gently, "I would be utterly disgraced. It is a very childish plan, Toddra. Please never dream of such a thing again. But I am truly, truly fond of you, I adore you and want no other man but you. Do you believe that, Toddra?"

He nodded. Restraining his tears, he said, "For now."

"For now and for a long, long, long time! My dear, sweet, beautiful dancer, we have each other as long as we want, years and years! Only do your duty by the other women that come, so that you don't get sold away by your Castle, please! I couldn't bear to lose you, Toddra." And she clasped him passionately in her arms, and arousing him at once, opened to him, and soon both were crying out in the throes of delight.

Though she could not take his love entirely seriously, since what could come of such a misplaced emotion, except such foolish schemes as he had proposed? — still he touched her heart, and she felt a tenderness towards him that greatly enhanced the pleasure of their intercourse. So for more than a year she spent two or three nights a week with him at the fuckery, which was as much as she could afford. The manager, trying still to discourage his love, would not lower Toddra's fee, even though he was unpopular among the other clients of the fuckery; so Azak spent a great deal of money on him, although he would never, after the first night, accept a tip from her.

Then a woman who had not been able to conceive with any of the sires at the fuckery tried Toddra, and at once conceived, and being tested found the fetus to be male. Another woman conceived by him, again a male fetus. At once Toddra was in demand as a sire. Women began coming from all over the city to be serviced by him. This meant, of course, that he must be free during their period of ovulation. There were now many evenings that he could not meet Azak, for the manager was not to be bribed. Toddra disliked his popularity, but Azak soothed and reassured him, telling him how proud she was of him, and how his work would never interfere with their love. In fact, she was not altogether sorry that he was so much in demand, for she had found another person with whom she wanted to spend her evenings.

This was a young woman named Zedr, who worked in the mill as a machine-repair specialist. She was tall and handsome; Azak noticed first how freely and strongly she walked and how proudly she stood. She found a pretext to make her acquaintance. It seemed to Azak that Zedr admired her; but for a long time each behaved to the other as a friend only, making no sexual advances. They were much in each other's company, going to games and dances together, and Azak found that she enjoyed this open and sociable life better than always being in the fuckery alone with Toddra. They talked about how they might set up a machine-repair service in partnership. As time went on, Azak found that Zedr's beautiful body was always in her thoughts. At last, one evening in her singlewoman's flat, she told her friend that she loved her, but did not wish to burden their friendship with an unwelcome desire.

Zedr replied, "I have wanted you ever since I first saw you, but I didn't want to embarrass you with my desire. I thought you preferred men."

"Until now I did, but I want to make love with you," Azak said.

She found herself quite timid at first, but Zedr was expert and subtle, and could prolong Azak's orgasms till she found such consummation as she had not dreamed of. She said to Zedr, "You have made me a woman."

"Then let's make each other wives," said Zedr joyfully.

They married, moved to a house in the west of the city, and left the mill, setting up in business together.

All this time, Azak had said nothing of her new love to Toddra, whom she had seen less and less often. A little ashamed of her cowardice, she reassured herself that he was so busy performing as a sire that he would not really miss her. After all, despite his romantic talk of love, he was a man, and to a man fucking is the most important thing, instead of being merely one element of love and life as it is to a woman.

When she married Zedr, she sent Toddra a letter, saying that their lives had drifted apart, and she was now moving away and would not see him again, but would always remember him fondly.

She received an immediate answer from Toddra, a letter begging her to come and talk with him, full of avowals of unchanging love, badly spelled and almost illegible. The letter touched, embarrassed, and shamed her, and she did not answer it.

He wrote again and again, and tried to reach her on the holonet at her new business. Zedr urged her not to make any response, saying, "It would be cruel to encourage him."

Their new business went well from the start. They were home one evening busy chopping vegetables for dinner when there was a knock at the door. "Come in," Zedr called, thinking it was Chochi, a friend they were considering as a third partner. A stranger entered, a tall, beautiful woman with a scarf over her hair. The stranger went straight to Azak, saying in a strangled voice, "Azak, Azak, please, please let me stay with you." The scarf fell back from his long hair. Azak recognised Toddra.

She was astonished and a little frightened, but she had known Toddra a long time and been very fond of him, and this habit of affection made her put out her hands to him in greeting. She saw fear and despair in his face, and was sorry for him.

But Zedr, guessing who he was, was both alarmed and angry. She kept the chopping knife in her hand. She slipped from the room and called the city police.

When she returned she saw the man pleading with Azak to let him stay hidden in their household as a servant. "I will do anything," he said. "Please, Azak, my only love, please! I can't live without you. I can't service those women, those strangers who only want to be impregnated. I can't dance any more. I think only of you, you are my only hope. I will be a woman, no one will know. I'll cut my hair, no one will know!" So he went on, almost threatening in his passion, but pitiful also. Zedr listened coldly, thinking he was mad. Azak listened with pain and shame. "No, no, it is not possible," she said over and over, but he would not hear.

When the police came to the door and he realised who they were, he bolted to the back of the house seeking escape. The policewomen caught him in the bedroom; he fought them desperately, and they subdued him brutally. Azak shouted at them not to hurt him, but they paid no heed, twisting his arms and hitting him about the head till he stopped resisting. They dragged him out. The chief of the troop stayed to take evidence. Azak tried to plead for Toddra, but Zedr stated the facts and added that she thought he was insane and dangerous.

After some days, Azak inquired at the police office and was told that Toddra had been returned to his Castle with a warning not to send him to the fuckery again for a year or until the Lords of the Castle found him capable of responsible behavior. She was uneasy thinking of how he might be punished. Zedr said, "They won't hurt him, he's too valuable," just as he himself had said. Azak was glad to believe this. She was, in fact, much relieved to know that he was out of the way.

She and Zedr took Chochi first into their business and then into their household. Chochi was a woman from the dockside quarter, tough and humorous, a hard worker and an undemanding, comfortable lovemaker. They were happy with one another, and prospered.

A year went by, and another year. Azak went to her old quarter to arrange a contract for repair work with two women from the mill where she had first worked. She asked them about Toddra. He was back at the fuckery from time to time, they told her. He had been named the year's Champion Sire of his Castle, and was much in demand, bringing an even higher price, because he impregnated so many women and so many of the conceptions were male. He was not in demand for pleasure, they said, as he had a reputation for roughness and even cruelty. Women asked for him only if they wanted to conceive. Thinking of his gentleness with her, Azak found it hard to imagine him behaving brutally. Harsh punishment at the Castle, she thought, must have altered him. But she could not believe that he had truly changed.

Another year passed. The business was doing very well, and Azak and Chochi both began talking seriously about having children. Zedr was not interested in bearing, though happy to be a mother.

Chochi had a favorite man at their local fuckery to whom she went now and then for pleasure; she began going to him at ovulation, for he had a good reputation as a sire.

Azak had not been to a fuckery since she and Zedr married. She honored fidelity highly, and made love with no one but Zedr and Chochi. When she thought of being impregnated, she found that her old interest in fucking with men had quite died out or even turned to distaste. She did not like the idea of self-impregnation from the sperm bank, but the idea of letting a strange man penetrate her was even more repulsive. Thinking what to do, she thought of Toddra, whom she had truly loved and had pleasure with. He was again a Champion Sire, known throughout the city as a reliable impregnator. There was certainly no other man with whom she could take any pleasure. And he had loved her so much he had put his career and even his life in danger, trying to be with her. That irresponsibility was over and done with. He had never written to her again, and the Castle and the managers of the fuckery would never have let him service women if they thought him mad or untrustworthy. After all this time, she thought, she could go back to him and give him the pleasure he had so desired.

She notified the fuckery of the expected period of her next ovulation, requesting Toddra. He was already engaged for that period, and they offered her another sire; but she preferred to wait till the next month.

Chochi had conceived, and was elated. "Hurry up, hurry up!" she said to Azak. "We want twins!"

Azak found herself looking forward to being with Toddra. Regretting the violence of their last encounter and the pain it must have given him, she wrote the following letter to him:

> "*My dear, I hope our long separation and the distress of our last meeting will be forgotten in the joy of being together again, and*

that you still love me as I still love you. I shall be very proud to
bear your child, and let us hope it may be a son! I am impatient to
see you again, my beautiful dancer. Your Azak."

There had not been time for him to answer this letter when her ovulation period began. She dressed in her best clothes. Zedr still distrusted Toddra and had tried to dissuade her from going to him; she bade her "Good luck!" rather sulkily. Chochi hung a mother-charm around her neck, and she went off.

There was a new manager on duty at the fuckery, a coarse-faced young woman who told her, "Call out if he gives you any trouble. He may be a Champion but he's rough, and we don't let him get away with hurting anybody."

"He won't hurt me," Azak said, smiling, and went eagerly into the familiar room where she and Toddra had enjoyed each other so often. He was standing waiting at the window just as he had used to stand. When he turned he looked just as she remembered, long-limbed, his silky hair flowing like water down his back, his wide-set eyes gazing at her.

"Toddra!" she said, coming to him with outstretched hands.

He took her hands and said her name.

"Did you get my letter? Are you happy?"

"Yes," he said, smiling.

"And all that unhappiness, all that foolishness about love, is it over? I am so sorry you were hurt, Toddra, I don't want any more of that. Can we just be ourselves and be happy together as we used to be?"

"Yes, all that is over," he said. "And I am happy to see you." He drew her gently to him. Gently he began to undress her and caress her body, just as he had used to, knowing what gave her pleasure, and she remembering what gave him pleasure. They lay down naked together. She was fondling his erect penis, aroused and yet a little reluctant to be penetrated after so long, when he moved his arm as if uncomfortable. Drawing away from him a little, she saw that he had a knife in his hand, which he must have hidden in the bed. He was holding it concealed behind his back.

Her womb went cold, but she continued to fondle his penis and testicles, not daring to say anything and not able to pull away, for he was holding her close with the other hand.

Suddenly he moved onto her and forced his penis into her vagina with a thrust so painful that for an instant she thought it was the knife. He ejaculated instantly. As his body arched she writhed out from under him, scrambled to the door, and ran from the room crying for help.

He pursued her, striking with the knife, stabbing her in the shoulderblade before the manager and other women and men seized him. The men were very angry and treated him with a violence which the manager's protests did not lessen. Naked, bloody, and half-conscious, he was bound and taken away immediately to the Castle.

Everyone now gathered around Azak, and her wound, which was slight, was cleaned and covered. Shaken and confused, she could ask only, "What will they do to him?"

"What do you think they do to a murdering rapist? Give him a prize?" the manager said. "They'll geld him."

"But it was my fault," Azak said.

The manager stared at her and said, "Are you mad? Go home."

She went back into the room and mechanically put on her clothes. She looked at the bed where they had lain. She stood at the window where Toddra had stood. She remembered how she had seen him dance long ago in the contest where he had first been made champion. She thought, "My life is wrong." But she did not know how to make it right.

Alteration in Seggrian social and cultural institutions did not take the disastrous course Merriment feared. It has been slow and its direction is not clear. In 93/1602 Terhada College invited men from two neighboring castles to apply as students, and three men

*did so. In the next decades, most colleges opened their doors to
men. Once they were graduated, male students had to return to
their castle, unless they left the planet, since native men were not
allowed to live anywhere but as students in a college or in a castle,
until the Open Gate Law was passed in 93/1662.*

*Even after passage of that law, the castles remained closed to
women; and the exodus of men from the castles was much slower
than opponents of the measure feared. Social adjustment to the
Open Gate Law has been slow. In several regions programs to train
men in basic skills such as farming and construction have met with
moderate success; the men work in competitive teams, separate
from and managed by the women's companies. A good many Seggri have come to Hain to study in recent years — more men than
women, despite the great numerical imbalance that still exists.*

*The following autobiographical sketch by one of these men is of
particular interest, since he was involved in the event which
directly precipitated the Open Gate Law.*

AUTOBIOGRAPHICAL SKETCH BY MOBILE ARDAR DEZ

I was born in Ekumenical Cycle 93, Year 1641, in Rakedr on Seggri.
Rakedr was a placid, prosperous, conservative town, and I was
brought up in the old way, the petted boychild of a big motherhouse. Altogether there were seventeen of us, not counting the
kitchen staff — a great-grandmother, two grandmothers, four
mothers, nine daughters, and me. We were well off; all the women
were or had been managers or skilled workers in the Rakedr Pottery,
the principal industry of the town. We kept all the holidays with
pomp and energy, decorating the house from roof to foundation
with banners for Hillalli, making fantastic costumes for the Harvest
Festival, and celebrating somebody's birthday every few weeks with

gifts all round. I was petted, as I said, but not, I think, spoiled. My birthday was no grander than my sisters', and I was allowed to run and play with them just as if I were a girl. Yet I was always aware, as were they, that our mothers' eyes rested on me with a different look, brooding, reserved, and sometimes, as I grew older, desolate.

After my Confirmation, my birthmother or her mother took me to Rakedr Castle every spring on Visiting Day. The gates of the park, which had opened to admit me alone (and terrified) for my Confirmation, remained shut, but rolling stairs were placed against the park walls. Up these I and a few other little boys from the town climbed, to sit on top of the park wall in great state, on cushions, under awnings, and watch demonstration dancing, bull-dancing, wrestling, and other sports on the great gamefield inside the wall. Our mothers waited below, outside, in the bleachers of the public field. Men and youths from the Castle sat with us, explaining the rules of the games and pointing out the fine points of a dancer or wrestler, treating us seriously, making us feel important. I enjoyed that very much, but as soon as I came down off the wall and started home it all fell away like a costume shrugged off, a part played in a play; and I went on with my work and play in the motherhouse with my family, my real life.

When I was ten I went to Boys' Class downtown. The class had been set up forty or fifty years before as a bridge between the motherhouses and the Castle, but the Castle, under increasingly reactionary governance, had recently withdrawn from the project. Lord Fassaw forbade his men to go anywhere outside the walls but directly to the fuckery, in a closed car, returning at first light; and so no men were able to teach the class. The townswomen who tried to tell me what to expect when I went to the Castle did not really know much more than I did. However well-meaning they were, they mostly frightened and confused me. But fear and confusion were an appropriate preparation.

I cannot describe the ceremony of Severance. I really cannot describe it. Men on Seggri, in those days, had this advantage: they knew what death is. They had all died once before their body's death. They had turned and looked back at their whole life, every place and face they had loved, and turned away from it as the gate closed.

At the time of my Severance, our small Castle was internally divided into "collegials" and "traditionals," a liberal faction left from the regime of Lord Ishog and a younger, highly conservative faction. The split was already disastrously wide when I came to the Castle. Lord Fassaw's rule had grown increasingly harsh and irrational. He governed by corruption, brutality, and cruelty. All of us who lived there were of course infected, and would have been destroyed if there had not been a strong, constant, moral resistance, centered around Ragaz and Kohadrat, who had been protégés of Lord Ishog. The two men were open partners; their followers were all the homosexuals in the Castle, and a good number of other men and older boys.

My first days and months in the Scrubs' dormitory were a bewildering alternation: terror, hatred, shame, as the boys who had been there a few months or years longer than I were incited to humiliate and abuse the newcomer, in order to make a man of him — and comfort, gratitude, love, as boys who had come under the influence of the collegials offered me secret friendship and protection. They helped me in the games and competitions and took me into their beds at night, not for sex but to keep me from the sexual bullies. Lord Fassaw detested adult homosexuality and would have reinstituted the death penalty if the Town Council had allowed it. Though he did not dare punish Ragaz and Kohadrat, he punished consenting love between older boys with bizarre and appalling physical mutilations — ears cut into fringes, fingers branded with red-hot iron rings. Yet he encouraged the older boys to rape the eleven- and twelve-year-olds, as a manly practice. None of us escaped. We particularly dreaded four youths, seventeen or eighteen years old when I came there, who called themselves the Lordsmen. Every few nights they raided the Scrubs' dormitory for a victim, whom they raped as a group. The collegials protected us as best they could by ordering us to their beds, where we wept and protested loudly, while they pretended to abuse us, laughing and jeering. Later, in the dark and silence, they comforted us with candy, and sometimes, as we grew older, with a desired love, gentle and exquisite in its secrecy.

There was no privacy at all in the Castle. I have said that to women who asked me to describe life there, and they thought they understood me. "Well, everybody shares everything in a mother-house," they would say, "everybody's in and out of the rooms all the time. You're never really alone unless you have a singlewoman's flat." I could not tell them how different the loose, warm commonality of the motherhouse was from the rigid, deliberate publicity of the forty-bed, brightly-lighted Castle dormitories. Nothing in Rakedr was private: only secret, only silent. We ate our tears.

I grew up; I take some pride in that, along with my profound gratitude to the boys and men who made it possible. I did not kill myself, as several boys did during those years, nor did I kill my mind and soul, as some did so their body could survive. Thanks to the maternal care of the collegials — the resistance, as we came to call ourselves — I grew up.

Why do I say maternal, not paternal? Because there were no fathers in my world. There were only sires. I knew no such word as father or paternal. I thought of Ragaz and Kohadrat as my mothers. I still do.

Fassaw grew quite mad as the years went on, and his hold over the Castle tightened to a deathgrip. The Lordsmen now ruled us all. They were lucky in that we still had a strong Maingame team, the pride of Fassaw's heart, which kept us in the First League, as well as two Champion Sires in steady demand at the town fuckeries. Any protest the resistance tried to bring to the Town Council could be dismissed as typical male whining, or laid to the demoralising influence of the aliens. From the outside Rakedr Castle seemed all right.

Look at our great team! Look at our champion studs! The women looked no further.

How could they abandon us? — the cry every Seggrian boy must make in his heart. How could she leave me here? Doesn't she know what it's like? Why doesn't she know? Doesn't she want to know?

"Of course not," Ragaz said to me when I came to him in a passion of righteous indignation, the Town Council having denied our petition to be heard. "Of course they don't want to know how we live. Why do they never come into the castles? Oh, we keep them out, yes; but do you think we could keep them out if they wanted to enter? My dear, we collude with them and they with us in maintaining the great foundation of ignorance and lies on which our civilisation rests."

"Our own mothers abandon us," I said.

"Abandon us? Who feeds us, clothes us, houses us, pays us? We're utterly dependent on them. If ever we made ourselves independent, perhaps we could rebuild society on a foundation of truth."

Independence was as far as his vision could reach. Yet I think his mind groped further, towards what he could not see, the body's obscure, inalterable dream of mutuality.

Our effort to make our case heard at the Council had no effect except within the Castle. Lord Fassaw saw his power threatened. Within a few days Ragaz was seized by the Lordsmen and their bully boys, accused of repeated homosexual acts and treasonable plots, arraigned, and sentenced by the Lord of the Castle. Everyone was summoned to the Gamefield to witness the punishment. A man of fifty with a heart ailment — he had been a Maingame racer in his twenties and had overtrained — Ragaz was tied naked across a bench and beaten with "Lord Long," a heavy leather tube filled with lead weights. The Lordsman Berhed, who wielded it, struck repeatedly at the head, the kidneys, and the genitals. Ragaz died an hour or two later in the infirmary.

The Rakedr Mutiny took shape that night. Kohadrat, older than

Ragaz and devastated by his loss, could not restrain or guide us. His vision had been of a true resistance, longlasting and nonviolent, through which the Lordsmen would in time destroy themselves. We had been following that vision. Now we let it go. We dropped the truth and grabbed weapons. "How you play is what you win," Kohadrat said, but we had heard all those old saws. We would not play the patience game any more. We would win, now, once for all.

And we did. We won. We had our victory. Lord Fassaw, the Lordsmen and their bullies had been slaughtered by the time the police got to the Gate.

I remember how those tough women strode in among us, staring at the rooms of the Castle which they had never seen, staring at the mutilated bodies, eviscerated, castrated, headless — at Lordsman Berhed, who had been nailed to the floor with "Lord Long" stuffed down his throat — at us, the rebels, the victors, with our bloody hands and defiant faces — at Kohadrat, whom we thrust forward as our leader, our spokesman.

He stood silent. He ate his tears.

The women drew closer to one another, clutching their guns, staring around. They were appalled, they thought us all insane. Their utter incomprehension drove one of us at last to speak — a young man, Tarsk, who wore the iron ring that had been forced onto his finger when it was red-hot. "They killed Ragaz," he said. "They were all mad. Look." He held out his crippled hand.

The chief of the troop, after a pause, said, "No one will leave here till this is looked into," and marched her women out of the Castle, out of the park, locking the gate behind them, leaving us with our victory.

The hearings and judgments on the Rakedr Mutiny were all broadcast, of course, and the event has been studied and discussed ever since. My own part in it was the murder of the Lordsman Tatiddi. Three of us set on him and beat him to death with exercise-clubs in the gymnasium where we had cornered him.

How we played was what we won.

We were not punished. Men were sent from several castles to form a government over Rakedr Castle. They learned enough of Fassaw's behavior to see the cause of our rebellion, but the contempt of even the most liberal of them for us was absolute. They treated us not as men, but as irrational, irresponsible creatures, untamable cattle. If we spoke they did not answer.

I do not know how long we could have endured that cold regime of shame. It was only two months after the Mutiny that the World Council enacted the Open Gate Law. We told one another that that was our victory, we had made that happen. None of us believed it. We told one another we were free. For the first time in history, any man who wanted to leave his castle could walk out the gate. We were free!

What happened to the free man outside the gate? Nobody had given it much thought.

I was one who walked out the gate, on the morning of the day the law came into force. Eleven of us walked into town together.

Several of us, men not from Rakedr, went to one or another of the fuckeries, hoping to be allowed to stay there; they had nowhere else to go. Hotels and inns of course would not accept men. Those of us who had been children in the town went to our motherhouses.

What is it like to return from the dead? Not easy. Not for the one who returns, nor for his people. The place he occupied in their world has closed up, ceased to be, filled with accumulated change, habit, the doings and needs of others. He has been replaced. To return from the dead is to be a ghost: a person for whom there is no room.

Neither I nor my family understood that, at first. I came back to them at twenty-one as trustingly as if I were the eleven-year-old who had left them, and they opened their arms to their child. But he did not exist. Who was I?

For a long time, months, we refugees from the Castle hid in our motherhouses. The men from other towns all made their way home, usually by begging a ride with teams on tour. There were seven or eight of us in Rakedr, but we scarcely ever saw one another. Men had no place on the street; for hundreds of years a man seen alone on the street had been arrested immediately. If we went out, women ran from us, or reported us, or surrounded and threatened us — "Get back into your Castle where you belong! Get back to the fuckery where you belong! Get out of our city!" They called us drones, and in fact we had no work, no function at all in the community. The fuckeries would not accept us for service, because we had no guarantee of health and good behavior from a castle.

This was our freedom: we were all ghosts, useless, frightened, frightening intruders, shadows in the corners of life. We watched life going on around us — work, love, childbearing, childrearing, getting and spending, making and shaping, governing and adventuring — the women's world, the bright, full, real world — and there was no room in it for us. All we had ever learned to do was play games and destroy one another.

My mothers and sisters racked their brains, I know, to find some place and use for me in their lively, industrious household. Two old live-in cooks had run our kitchen since long before I was born, so cooking, the one practical art I had been taught in the Castle, was superfluous. They found household tasks for me, but they were all make-work, and they and I knew it. I was perfectly willing to look after the babies, but one of the grandmothers was very jealous of that privilege, and also some of my sisters' wives were uneasy about a man touching their baby. My sister Pado broached the possibility of an apprenticeship in the clayworks, and I leaped at the chance; but the managers of the Pottery, after long discussion, were unable to agree to accept men as employees. Their hormones would make male workers unreliable, and female workers would be uncomfortable, and so on.

The holonews was full of such proposals and discussions, of

course, and orations about the unforeseen consequences of the Open Gate Law, the proper place of men, male capacities and limitations, gender as destiny. Feeling against the Open Gate policy ran very strong, and it seemed that every time I watched the holo there was a woman talking grimly about the inherent violence and irresponsibility of the male, his biological unfitness to participate in social and political decision-making. Often it was a man saying the same things. Opposition to the new law had the fervent support of all the conservatives in the castles, who pleaded eloquently for the gates to be closed and men to return to their proper station, pursuing the true, masculine glory of the games and the fuckeries.

Glory did not tempt me, after the years at Rakedr Castle; the word itself had come to mean degradation to me. I ranted against the games and competitions, puzzling most of my family, who loved to watch the Maingames and wrestling, and complained only that the level of excellence of most of the teams had declined since the gates were opened. And I ranted against the fuckeries, where, I said, men were used as cattle, stud bulls, not as human beings. I would never go there again.

"But my dear boy," my mother said at last, alone with me one evening, "will you live the rest of your life celibate?"

"I hope not," I said.

"Then . . . ?"

"I want to get married."

Her eyes widened. She brooded a bit, and finally ventured, "To a man."

"No. To a woman. I want a normal, ordinary marriage. I want to have a wife and be a wife."

Shocking as the idea was, she tried to absorb it. She pondered, frowning.

"All it means," I said, for I had had a long time with nothing to do but ponder, "is that we'd live together just like any married pair. We'd set up our own daughterhouse, and be faithful to each other, and if she had a child I'd be its lovemother along with her. There isn't any reason why it wouldn't work!"

"Well, I don't know — I don't know of any," said my mother, gentle and judicious, and never happy at saying no to me. "But you do have to find the woman, you know."

"I know," I said glumly.

"It's such a problem for you to meet people," she said. "Perhaps if you went to the fuckery . . . ? I don't see why your own motherhouse couldn't guarantee you just as well as a castle. We could try — ?"

But I passionately refused. Not being one of Fassaw's sycophants, I had seldom been allowed to go to the fuckery; and my few experiences there had been unfortunate. Young, inexperienced, and without recommendation, I had been selected by older women who wanted a plaything. Their practiced skill at arousing me had left me humiliated and enraged. They patted and tipped me as they left. That elaborate, mechanical excitation and their condescending coldness were vile to me, after the tenderness of my lover-protectors in the Castle. Yet women attracted me physically as men never had; the beautiful bodies of my sisters and their wives, all around me constantly now, clothed and naked, innocent and sensual, the wonderful heaviness and strength and softness of women's bodies, kept me continually aroused. Every night I masturbated, fantasising my sisters in my arms. It was unendurable. Again I was a ghost, a raging, yearning impotence in the midst of untouchable reality.

I began to think I would have to go back to the Castle. I sank into a deep depression, an inertia, a chill darkness of the mind.

My family, anxious, affectionate, busy, had no idea what to do for me or with me. I think most of them thought in their hearts that it would be best if I went back through the gate.

One afternoon my sister Pado, with whom I had been closest as a child, came to my room — they had cleared out a dormer attic for me, so that I had room at least in the literal sense. She found me in my now constant lethargy, lying on the bed doing nothing at all. She breezed in, and with the indifference women often show to moods and signals, plumped down on the foot of the bed and said, "Hey, what do you know about the man who's here from the Ekumen?"

I shrugged and shut my eyes. I had been having rape fantasies lately. I was afraid of her.

She talked on about the offworlder, who was apparently in Rakedr to study the Mutiny. "He wants to talk to the resistance," she said. "Men like you. The men who opened the gates. He says they won't come forward, as if they were ashamed of being heroes."

"Heroes!" I said. The word in my language is gendered female. It refers to the semi-divine, semi-historic protagonists of the Epics.

"It's what you are," Pado said, intensity breaking through her assumed breeziness. "You took responsibility in a great act. Maybe you did it wrong. Sassume did it wrong in the *Founding of Emmo*, didn't she, she let Faradr get killed. But she was still a hero. She took the responsibility. So did you. You ought to go talk to this Alien. Tell him what happened. Nobody really knows what happened at the Castle. You owe us the story."

That was a powerful phrase, among my people. "The untold story mothers the lie," was the saying. The doer of any notable act was held literally *accountable* for it to the community.

"So why should I tell it to an Alien?" I said, defensive of my inertia.

"Because he'll listen," my sister said drily. "We're all too damned busy."

It was profoundly true. Pado had seen a gate for me and opened it; and I went through it, having just enough strength and sanity left to do so.

Mobile Noem was a man in his forties, born some centuries earlier on Terra, trained on Hain, widely travelled; a small, yellow-brown, quick-eyed person, very easy to talk to. He did not seem at all masculine to me, at first; I kept thinking he was a woman, because he acted like one. He got right to business, with none of the maneuvering to assert his authority or jockeying for position that men of my society felt obligatory in any relationship with another man. I was used to men being wary, indirect, and competitive. Noem, like a woman, was direct and receptive. He was also as subtle and powerful as any man or woman I had known, even Ragaz. His authority was in fact immense; but he never stood on it. He sat down on it, comfortably, and invited you to sit down with him.

I was the first of the Rakedr mutineers to come forward and tell our story to him. He recorded it, with my permission, to use in making his report to the Stabiles on the condition of our society, "the matter of Seggri," as he called it. My first description of the Mutiny took less than an hour. I thought I was done. I didn't know, then, the inexhaustible desire to learn, to understand, to hear *all* the story, that characterises the Mobiles of the Ekumen. Noem asked questions, I answered; he speculated and extrapolated, I corrected; he wanted details, I furnished them — telling the story of the Mutiny, of the years before it, of the men of the Castle, of the women of the Town, of my people, of my life — little by little, bit by bit, all in fragments, a muddle. I talked to Noem daily for a month. I learned that the story has no beginning, and no story has an end. That the story is all muddle, all middle. That the story is never true, but that the lie is indeed a child of silence.

By the end of the month I had come to love and trust Noem, and of course to depend on him. Talking to him had become my reason for being. I tried to face the fact that he would not stay in Rakedr much longer. I must learn to do without him. Do what? There were things for men to do, ways for men to live, he proved it by his mere existence; but could I find them?

He was keenly aware of my situation, and would not let me withdraw, as I began to do, into the lethargy of fear again; he would not let me be silent. He asked me impossible questions. "What would you be if you could be anything?" he asked me, a question children ask each other.

I answered at once, passionately — "A wife!"

I know now what the flicker that crossed his face was. His quick, kind eyes watched me, looked away, looked back.

"I want my own family," I said. "Not to live in my mothers' house, where I'm always a child. Work. A wife, wives — children — to be a mother. I want life, not games!"

"You can't bear a child," he said gently.

"No, but I can mother one!"

"We gender the word," he said. "I like it better your way. . . . But tell me, Ardar, what are the chances of your marrying — meeting a woman willing to marry a man? It hasn't happened, here, has it?"

I had to say no, not to my knowledge.

"It will happen, certainly, I think," he said (his certainties were always uncertain). "But the personal cost, at first, is likely to be high. Relationships formed against the negative pressure of a society are under terrible strain; they tend to become defensive, over-intense, unpeaceful. They have no room to grow."

"Room!" I said. And I tried to tell him my feeling of having no room in my world, no air to breathe.

He looked at me, scratching his nose; he laughed. "There's plenty of room in the galaxy, you know," he said.

"Do you mean . . . I could . . . That the Ekumen . . ." I didn't even know what the question I wanted to ask was. Noem did. He began to answer it thoughtfully and in detail. My education so far had been so limited, even as regards the culture of my own people, that I would have to attend a college for at least two or three years, in order to be ready to apply to an offworld institution such as the Ekumenical Schools on Hain. Of course, he went on, where I went and what kind of training I chose would depend on my interests, which I would go to a college to discover, since neither my schooling as a child nor my training at the Castle had really given me any idea of what there was to be interested in. The choices offered me had been unbelievably limited, addressing neither the needs of a nor-mally intelligent person nor the needs of my society. And so the

Open Gate Law instead of giving me freedom had left me "with no air to breathe but airless Space," said Noem, quoting some poet from some planet somewhere. My head was spinning, full of stars. "Hagka College is quite near Rakedr," Noem said, "did you never think of applying? If only to escape from your terrible Castle?"

I shook my head. "Lord Fassaw always destroyed the application forms when they were sent to his office. If any of us had tried to apply. . . ."

"You would have been punished. Tortured, I suppose. Yes. Well, from the little I know of your colleges, I think your life there would be better than it is here, but not altogether pleasant. You will have work to do, a place to be; but you will be made to feel marginal, inferior. Even highly educated, enlightened women have difficulty accepting men as their intellectual equals. Believe me, I have experienced it myself! And because you were trained at the Castle to compete, to want to excel, you may find it hard to be among people who either believe you incapable of excellence, or to whom the concept of competition, of winning and defeating, is valueless. But just there, there is where you will find air to breathe."

Noem recommended me to women he knew on the faculty of Hagka College, and I was enrolled on probation. My family were delighted to pay my tuition. I was the first of us to go to college, and they were genuinely proud of me.

As Noem had predicted, it was not always easy, but there were enough other men there that I found friends and was not caught in the paralysing isolation of the motherhouse. And as I took courage, I made friends among the women students, finding many of them unprejudiced and companionable. In my third year, one of them and I managed, tentatively and warily, to fall in love. It did not work very well or last very long, yet it was a great liberation for both of us, our liberation from the belief that the only communication or commonality possible between us was sexual, that an adult man and woman had nothing to join them but their genitals. Emadr loathed the professionalism of the fuckery as I did, and our lovemaking was always shy and brief. Its true significance was not as a consummation of desire, but as proof that we could trust each other. Where our real passion broke loose was when we lay together talking, telling each other what our lives had been, how we felt about men and women and each other and ourselves, what our nightmares were, what our dreams were. We talked endlessly, in a communion that I will cherish and honor all my life, two young souls finding their wings, flying together, not for long, but high. The first flight is the highest.

Emadr has been dead two hundred years; she stayed on Seggri, married into a motherhouse, bore two children, taught at Hagka, and died in her seventies. I went to Hain, to the Ekumenical Schools, and later to Werel and Yeowe as part of the Mobile's staff; my record is herewith enclosed. I have written this sketch of my life as part of my application to return to Seggri as a Mobile of the Ekumen. I want very much to live among my people, to learn who they are, now that I know with at least an uncertain certainty who I am.

UNCHOSEN LOVE

INTRODUCTION

By Heokad'd Arhe of Inanan Farmhold of Tag Village on the Southwest Watershed of the Budran River on Okets on the Planet O.

S ex, for everybody, on every world, is a complicated business, but nobody seems to have complicated marriage quite as much as my people have. To us, of course, it seems simple, and so natural that it's foolish to describe it, like trying to describe how we walk, how we breathe. Well, you know, you stand on one leg and move the other one forward . . . you let the air come into your lungs and then you let it out . . . you marry a man and woman from the other moiety. . . .

What is a moiety? a Gethenian asked me, and I realised that it's easier for me to imagine not knowing which sex I'll be tomorrow morning, like the Gethenian, than to imagine not knowing whether I was a Morning person or an Evening person. So complete, so universal a division of humanity — how can there be a society without it? How do you know who anyone is? How can you give worship without the one to ask and the other to answer, the one to pour and the other to drink? How can you couple indiscriminately without regard to incest? I have to admit that in the unswept, unenlightened basements of my hindbrain I agree with my great-uncle Gambat, who said, "Those people from off the world, they all try to stand on one leg. Two legs, two sexes, two moieties — it only makes sense!"

A moiety is half a population. We call our two halves the Morning and the Evening. If your mother's a Morning woman, you're a Morning person; and all Morning people are in certain respects your brothers or sisters. You have sex, marry, have children only with Evening people.

When I explained our concept of incest to a fellow student on Hain, she said, shocked, "But that means you can't have sex with half the population!" And I in turn said, shocked, "Do you *want* sex with half the population?"

Moieties are in fact not an uncommon social structure within the Ekumen. I have had comfortable conversations with people from several bipartite societies. One of them, a Nadir Woman of the Umna on Ithsh, nodded and laughed when I told her my great-uncle's opinion. "But you ki'O," she said, "you marry on all fours."

Few people from other worlds are willing to believe that our form of marriage works. They prefer to think that we endure it. They forget that human beings, while whining after the simple life, thrive on complexity.

When I marry — for love, for stability, for children — I marry three people. I am a Morning man: I marry an Evening woman and an Evening man, with both of whom I have a sexual relationship, and a Morning woman, with whom I have no sexual relationship. Her sexual relationships are with the Evening man and the Evening woman. The whole marriage is called a sedoretu. Within it there are four submarriages; the two heterosexual pairs are called Morning and Evening, according to the woman's moiety; the male homosexual pair is called the Night marriage, and the female homosexual pair is called the Day.

Brothers and sisters of the four primary people can join the sedoretu, so that the number of people in the marriage sometimes gets to six or seven. The children are variously related as siblings, germanes, and cousins.

Clearly a sedoretu takes some arranging. We spend a lot of our time arranging them. How much of a marriage is founded on love and in which couples the love is strongest, how much of it is founded on convenience, custom, profit, friendship, will depend on regional tradition, personal character, and so on. The complexities are so evident that I am always surprised when an offworlder sees, in the multiple relationship, only the forbidden, the illicit one. "How can you be married to three people and never have sex with one of them?" they ask.

The question makes me uncomfortable; it seems to assume that sexuality is a force so dominant that it cannot be contained or shaped by any other relationship. Most societies expect a father and daughter, or a brother and sister, to have a nonsexual family relationship, though I gather that in some the incest ban is often violated by people empowered by age and gender to ignore it. Evidently such societies see human beings as divided into two kinds, the fundamental division being power, and they grant one gender superior power. To us, the fundamental division is moiety; gender is a great but secondary difference; and in the search for power no one starts from a position of innate privilege. It certainly leads to our looking at things differently.

The fact is, the people of O admire the simple life as much as anyone else, and we have found our own peculiar way of achieving it. We are conservative, conventional, self-righteous, and dull. We suspect change and resist it blindly. Many houses, farms, and shrines on O have been in the same place and called by the same name for fifty or sixty centuries, some for hundreds of centuries. We have mostly been doing the same things in the same way for longer than that. Evidently, we do things carefully. We honor self-restraint, often to the point of harboring demons, and are fierce in defense of our privacy. We despise the outstanding. The wise among us do not live in solitude on mountain tops; they live in houses on farms, have many relatives, and keep careful accounts. We have no cities, only dispersed villages composed of a group of farmholds and a community center; educational and technological centers are supported by each region. We do without gods and, for a long time now, without wars. The question strangers most often ask us is, "In those marriages of yours, do you all go to bed together?" and the answer we give is, "No."

That is in fact how we tend to answer any question from a stranger. It is amazing that we ever got into the Ekumen. We are near Hain — sidereally near, 4.2 light years — and the Hainish simply kept coming here and talking to us for centuries, until we got used to them and were able to say Yes. The Hainish, of course, are our ancestral race, but the stolid longevity of our customs makes them feel young and rootless and dashing. That is probably why they like us.

UNCHOSEN LOVE

There was a hold down near the mouths of the Saduun, built on a rock island that stands up out of the great tidal plain south of where the river meets the sea. The sea used to come in and swirl around the island, but as the Saduun slowly built up its delta over the centuries, only the great tides reached it, and then only the storm tides, and at last the sea never came so far, but lay shining all along the west.

Meruo was never a farmhold; built on rock in a salt marsh, it was a seahold, and lived by fishing. When the sea withdrew, the people dug a channel from the foot of the rock to the tideline. Over the years, as the sea withdrew farther, the channel grew longer and longer, till it was a broad canal three miles long. Up and down it fishing boats and trading ships went to and from the docks of

Meruo that sprawled over the rocky base of the island. Right beside the docks and the netyards and the drying and freezing plants began the prairies of saltgrass, where vast flocks of yama and flightless baro grazed. Meruo rented out those pastures to farmholds of Sadahun Village in the coastal hills. None of the flocks belonged to Meruo, whose people looked only to the sea, and farmed only the sea, and never walked if they could sail. More than the fishing, it was the prairies that had made them rich, but they spent their wealth on boats and on digging and dredging the great canal. We throw our money in the sea, they said.

They were known as a stiff-necked lot, holding themselves apart from the village. Meruo was a big hold, often with a hundred people living in it, so they seldom made sedoretu with village people, but married one another. They're all germanes at Meruo, the villagers said.

A Morning man from eastern Oket came to stay in Sadahun, studying saltmarsh grazing for his farmhold on the other coast. He chanced to meet a Evening man of Meruo named Suord, in town for a village meeting. The next day, there came Suord again, to see him; and the next day too; and by the fourth night Suord was making love to him, sweeping him off his feet like a storm-wave. The Easterner, whose name was Hadri, was a modest, inexperienced young man to whom the journey and the unfamiliar places and the strangers he met had been a considerable adventure. Now he found one of the strangers wildly in love with him, beseeching him to come out to Meruo and stay there, live there — "We'll make a sedoretu," Suord said. "There's half a dozen Evening girls. Any, any of the Morning women, I'd marry any one of them to keep you. Come out, come out with me, come out onto the Rock!" For so the people of Meruo called their hold.

Hadri thought he owed it to Suord to do what he asked, since Suord loved him so passionately. He got up his courage, packed his bag, and went out across the wide, flat prairies to the place he had seen all along dark against the sky far off, the high roofs of Meruo, hunched up on its rock above its docks and warehouses and boat-basin, its windows looking away from the land, staring always down the long canal to the sea that had forsaken it.

Suord brought him in and introduced him to the household, and Hadri was terrified. They were all like Suord, dark people, handsome, fierce, abrupt, intransigent — so much alike that he could not tell one from the other and mistook daughter for mother, brother for cousin, Evening for Morning. They were barely polite to him. He was an interloper. They were afraid Suord would bring him in among them for good. And so was he.

Suord's passion was so intense that Hadri, a moderate soul, assumed it must burn out soon. "Hot fires don't last," he said to himself, and took comfort in the adage. "He'll get tired of me and I can go," he thought, not in words. But he stayed a tenday at Meruo, and a month, and Suord burned as hot as ever. Hadri saw too that among the sedoretu of the household there were many passionate matings, sexual tensions running among them like a network of ungrounded wires, filling the air with the crackle and spark of electricity; and some of these marriages were many years old.

He was flattered and amazed at Suord's insatiable, yearning, worshipping desire for a person Hadri himself was used to considering as quite ordinary. He felt his response to such passion was never enough. Suord's dark beauty filled his mind, and his mind turned away, looking for emptiness, a space to be alone. Some nights, when Suord lay flung out across the bed in deep sleep after lovemaking, Hadri would get up, naked, silent; he would sit in the windowseat across the room, gazing down the shining of the long canal under the stars. Sometimes he wept silently. He cried because he was in pain, but he did not know what the pain was.

One such night in early winter his feeling of being chafed, rubbed raw, like an animal fretting in a trap, all his nerve-ends exposed, was too much to endure. He dressed, very quietly for fear of waking Suord, and went barefoot out of their room, to get outdoors — anywhere out from under the roofs, he thought. He felt that he could not breathe.

The immense house was bewildering in the dark. The seven sedoretu living there now had each their own wing or floor or suite of rooms, all spacious. He had never even been into the regions of the First and Second Sedoretu, way off in the south wing, and always got confused in the ancient central part of the house, but he thought he knew his way around these floors in the north wing. This corridor, he thought, led to the landward stairs. It led only to narrow stairs going up. He went up them into a great shadowy attic, and found a door out onto the roof itself.

A long railed walk led along the south edge. He followed it, the peaks of the roofs rising up like black mountains to his left, and the prairies, the marshes, and then as he came round to the west side, the canal, all lying vast and dim in starlight below. The air was soft and damp, smelling of rain to come. A low mist was coming up from the marshes. As he watched, his arms on the rail, the mist thickened and whitened, hiding the marshes and the canal. He welcomed that softness, that slowness of the blurring, healing, concealing fog. A little peace and solace came into him. He breathed deep and thought, "Why, why am I so sad? Why don't I love Suord as much as he loves me? Why does he love me?"

He felt somebody was near him, and looked round. A woman had come out onto the roof and stood only a few yards away, her arms on the railing like his, barefoot like him, in a long dressing-gown. When he turned his head, she turned hers, looking at him.

She was one of the women of the Rock, no mistaking the dark skin and straight black hair and a certain fine cut of brow, cheekbone, jaw; but which one he was not sure. At the dining rooms of the north wing he had met a number of Evening women in their twenties, all sisters, cousins, or germanes, all unmarried. He was afraid of them all, because Suord might propose one of them as his wife in sedoretu. Hadri was a little shy sexually and found the gender difference hard to cross; he had found his pleasure and solace mostly with other young men, though some women attracted him very much. These women of Meruo were powerfully attractive, but he could not imagine himself touching one of them. Some of the pain he suffered here was caused by the distrustful coldness of the Evening women, always making it clear to him that he was the outsider. They scorned him and he avoided them. And so he was not perfectly certain which one was Sasni, which one was Lamateo, or Saval, or Esbuai.

He thought this was Esbuai, because she was tall, but he wasn't sure. The darkness might excuse him, for one could barely make out the features of a face. He murmured, "Good evening," and said no name.

There was a long pause, and he thought resignedly that a woman of Meruo would snub him even in the dead of night on a rooftop.

But then she said, "Good evening," softly, with a laugh in her voice, and it was a soft voice, that lay on his mind the way the fog did, mild and cool. "Who is that?" she said.

"Hadri," he said, resigned again. Now she knew him and would snub him.

"Hadri? You aren't from here."

Who was she, then?

He said his farmhold name. "I'm from the east, from the Fadan'n Watershed. Visiting."

"I've been away," she said. "I just came back. Tonight. Isn't it a lovely night? I like these nights best of all, when the fog comes up, like a sea of its own . . ."

Indeed the mists had joined and risen, so that Meruo on its rock seemed to float suspended in darkness over a faintly luminous void.

"I like it too," he said. "I was thinking. . . ." Then he stopped.

"What?" she said after a minute, so gently that he took courage and went on.

"That being unhappy in a room is worse than being unhappy

out of doors," he said, with a self-conscious and unhappy laugh. "I wonder why that is."

"I knew," she said. "By the way you were standing. I'm sorry. What do you . . . what would you need to make you happier?" At first he had thought her older than himself, but now she spoke like a quite young girl, shy and bold at the same time, awkwardly, with sweetness. It was the dark and the fog that made them both bold, released them, so they could speak truly.

"I don't know," he said. "I think I don't know how to be in love."

"Why do you think so?"

"Because I — It's Suord, he brought me here," he told her, trying to go on speaking truly. "I do love him, but not — not the way he deserves — "

"Suord," she said thoughtfully.

"He is strong. Generous. He gives me everything he is, his whole life. But I'm not, I'm not able to . . ."

"Why do you stay?" she asked, not accusingly, but asking for an answer.

"I love him," Hadri said. "I don't want to hurt him. If I run away I'll be a coward. I want to be worth him." They were four separate answers, each spoken separately, painfully.

"Unchosen love," she said with a dry, rough tenderness. "Oh, it's hard."

She did not sound like a girl now, but like a woman who knew what love is. While they talked they had both looked out westward over the sea of mist, because it was easier to talk that way. She turned now to look at him again. He was aware of her quiet gaze in the darkness. A great star shone bright between the line of the roof and her head. When she moved again her round, dark head occulted the star, and then it shone tangled in her hair, as if she was wearing it. It was a lovely thing to see.

"I always thought I'd choose love," he said at last, her words working in his mind. "Choose a sedoretu, settle down, some day, somewhere near my farm. I never imagined anything else. And then I came out here, to the edge of the world. . . . And I don't know what to do. I was chosen, I can't choose. . . ."

There was a little self-mockery in his voice.

"This is a strange place," he said.

"It is," she said. "Once you've seen the great tide. . . ."

He had seen it once. Suord had taken him to a headland that stood above the southern floodplain. Though it was only a few miles southwest of Meruo, they had to go a long way round inland and then back out west again, and Hadri asked, "Why can't we just go down the coast?"

"You'll see why," Suord said. They sat up on the rocky headland eating their picnic, Suord always with an eye on the brown-grey mud flats stretching off to the western horizon, endless and dreary, cut by a few worming, silted channels. "Here it comes," he said, standing up; and Hadri stood up to see the gleam and hear the distant thunder, see the advancing bright line, the incredible rush of the tide across the immense plain for seven miles till it crashed in foam on the rocks below them and flooded on round the headland.

"A good deal faster than you could run," Suord said, his dark face keen and intense. "That's how it used to come in around our Rock. In the old days."

"Are we cut off here?" Hadri had asked, and Suord had answered, "No, but I wish we were."

Thinking of it now, Hadri imagined the broad sea lying under the fog all around Meruo, lapping on the rocks, under the walls. As it had been in the old days.

"I suppose the tides cut Meruo off from the mainland," he said, and she said, "Twice every day."

"Strange," he murmured, and heard her slight intaken breath of laughter.

"Not at all," she said. "Not if you were born here. . . . Do you know that babies are born and the dying die on what they call the lull? The low point of the low tide of morning."

Her voice and words made his heart clench within him, they were so soft and seemed so strange. "I come from inland, from the hills, I never saw the sea before," he said. "I don't know anything about the tides."

"Well," she said, "there's their true love." She was looking behind him. He turned and saw the waning moon just above the sea of mist, only its darkest, scarred crescent showing. He stared at it, unable to say anything more.

"Hadri," she said, "don't be sad. It's only the moon. Come up here again if you are sad, though. I liked talking with you. There's nobody here to talk to. . . . Good night," she whispered. She went away from him along the walk and vanished in the shadows.

He stayed a while watching the mist rise and the moon rise; the mist won the slow race, blotting out moon and all in a cold dimness at last. Shivering, but no longer tense and anguished, he found his way back to Suord's room and slid into the wide, warm bed. As he stretched out to sleep, he thought, I don't know her name.

Suord woke in an unhappy mood. He insisted that Hadri come out in the sailboat with him down the canal, to check the locks on the side-canals, he said; but what he wanted was to get Hadri alone, in a boat, where Hadri was not only useless but slightly uneasy and had no escape at all. They drifted in the mild sunshine on the glassy side-canal. "You want to leave, don't you," Suord said, speaking as if the sentence was a knife that cut his tongue as he spoke it.

"No," Hadri said, not knowing if it was true, but unable to say any other word.

"You don't want to get married here."

"I don't know, Suord."

"What do you mean, you don't know?"

"I don't think any of the Evening women want a marriage with me," he said, and trying to speak true, "I know they don't. They want you to find somebody from around here. I'm a foreigner."

"They don't know you," Suord said with a sudden, pleading gentleness. "People here, they take a long time to get to know people. We've lived too long on our Rock. Seawater in our veins instead of blood. But they'll see — they'll come to know you if you — If you'll stay — " He looked out over the side of the boat and after a while said almost inaudibly, "If you leave, can I come with you?"

"I'm not leaving," Hadri said. He went and stroked Suord's hair and face and kissed him. He knew that Suord could not follow him, couldn't live in Oket, inland; it wouldn't work, it wouldn't do. But that meant he must stay here with Suord. There was a numb coldness in him, under his heart.

"Sasni and Duun are germanes," Suord said presently, sounding like himself again, controlled, intense. "They've been lovers ever since they were thirteen. Sasni would marry me if I asked her, if she can have Duun in the Day marriage. We can make a sedoretu with them, Hadri."

The numbness kept Hadri from reacting to this for some time; he did not know what he was feeling, what he thought. What he finally said was, "Who is Duun?" There was a vague hope in him that it was the woman he had talked with on the roof, last night — in a different world, it seemed, a realm of fog and darkness and truth.

"You know Duun."

"Did she just come back from somewhere else?"

"No," Suord said, too intent to be puzzled by Hadri's stupidity. "Sasni's germane, Lasudu's daughter of the Fourth Sedoretu. She's short, very thin, doesn't talk much."

"I don't know her," Hadri said in despair, "I can't tell them apart, they don't talk to me," and he bit his lip and stalked over to the other end of the boat and stood with his hands in his pockets and his shoulders hunched.

Suord's mood had quite changed; he splashed about happily in the water and mud when they got to the lock, making sure the mechanisms were in order, then sailed them back to the great canal with a fine following wind. Shouting, "Time you got your sea legs!" to Hadri, he took the boat west down the canal and out onto the open sea. The misty sunlight, the breeze full of salt spray, the fear of the depths, the exertion of working the boat under Suord's capable directions, the triumph of steering it back into the canal at sunset, when the light lay red-gold on the water and vast flocks of stilts and marshbirds rose crying and circling around them — it made a great day, after all, for Hadri.

But the glory dropped away as soon as he came under the roofs of Meruo again, into the dark corridors and the low, wide, dark rooms that all looked west. They took meals with the Fourth and Fifth Sedoretu. In Hadri's farmhold there would have been a good deal of teasing when they came in just in time for dinner, having been out all day without notice and done none of the work of it; here nobody ever teased or joked. If there was resentment it stayed hidden. Maybe there was no resentment, maybe they all knew each other so well and were so much of a piece that they trusted one other the way you trust your own hands, without question. Even the children joked and quarrelled less than Hadri was used to. Conversation at the long table was always quiet, many not speaking a word.

As he served himself, Hadri looked around among them for the woman of last night. Had it in fact been Esbuai? He thought not; the height was like, but Esbuai was very thin, and had a particularly arrogant carriage to her head. The woman was not here. Maybe she was First Sedoretu. Which of these women was Duun?

That one, the little one, with Sasni; he recalled her now. She was always with Sasni. He had never spoken to her, because Sasni of them all had snubbed him most hatefully, and Duun was her shadow.

"Come on," said Suord, and went round the table to sit down beside Sasni, gesturing Hadri to sit beside Duun. He did so. I'm Suord's shadow, he thought.

"Hadri says he's never talked to you," Suord said to Duun. The girl hunched up a bit and muttered something meaningless. Hadri saw Sasni's face flash with anger, and yet there was a hint of a challenging smile in it, as she looked straight at Suord. They were very much alike. They were well matched.

Suord and Sasni talked — about the fishing, about the locks — while Hadri ate his dinner. He was ravenous after the day on the water. Duun, having finished her meal, sat and said nothing. These people had a capacity for remaining perfectly motionless and silent, like predatory animals, or fishing birds. The dinner was fish, of course; it was always fish. Meruo had been wealthy once and still had the manners of wealth, but few of the means. Dredging out the great canal took more of their income every year, as the sea relentlessly pulled back from the delta. Their fishing fleet was large, but the boats were old, often rebuilt. Hadri had asked why they did not build new ones, for a big shipyard loomed above the drydocks; Suord explained that the cost of the wood alone was prohibitive. Having only the one crop, fish and shellfish, they had to pay for all other food, for clothing, for wood, even for water. The wells for miles around Meruo were salt. An aqueduct led to the seahold from the village in the hills.

They drank their expensive water from silver cups, however, and ate their eternal fish from bowls of ancient, translucent blue Edia ware, which Hadri was always afraid of breaking when he washed them.

Sasni and Suord went on talking, and Hadri felt stupid and sullen, sitting there saying nothing to the girl who said nothing.

"I was out on the sea for the first time today," he said, feeling the blood flush his face.

She made some kind of noise, mhm, and gazed at her empty bowl.

"Can I get you some soup?" Hadri asked. They ended the meal with broth, here, fish broth of course.

"No," she said, with a scowl.

"In my farmhold," he said, "people often bring dishes to each other; it's a minor kind of courtesy; I am sorry if you find it offensive." He stood up and strode off to the sideboard, where with shaking hands he served himself a bowl of soup. When he got back Suord was looking at him with a speculative eye and a faint smile, which he resented. What did they take him for? Did they think he had no standards, no people, no place of his own? Let them marry each other, he would have no part of it. He gulped his soup, got up without waiting for Suord, and went to the kitchen, where he spent an hour in the washing-up crew to make up for missing his time in the cooking crew. Maybe they had no standards about things, but he did.

Suord was waiting for him in their room — Suord's room — Hadri had no room of his own here. That in itself was insulting, unnatural. In a decent hold, a guest was always given a room.

Whatever Suord said — he could not remember later what it was — was a spark to blasting-powder. "I will not be treated this way!" he cried passionately, and Suord firing up at once demanded what he meant, and they had at it, an explosion of rage and frustration and accusation that left them staring grey-faced at each other, appalled. "Hadri," Suord said, the name a sob; he was shivering, his whole body shaking. They came together, clinging to each other. Suord's small, rough, strong hands held Hadri close. The taste of Suord's skin was salt as the sea. Hadri sank, sank and was drowned.

But in the morning everything was as it had been. He did not dare ask for a room to himself, knowing it would hurt Suord. If they do make this sedoretu, then at least I'll have a room, said a small, unworthy voice in his head. But it was wrong, wrong. . . .

He looked for the woman he had met on the roof, and saw half a dozen who might have been her and none he was certain was her. Would she not look at him, speak to him? Not in daylight, not in front of the others? Well, so much for her, then.

It occurred to him only now that he did not know whether she was a woman of the Morning or the Evening. But what did it matter?

That night the fog came in. Waking suddenly, deep in the night, he saw out the window only a formless grey, glowing very dimly with diffused light from a window somewhere in another wing of the house. Suord slept, as he always did, flat out, lying like a bit of jetsam flung on the beach of the night, utterly absent and abandoned. Hadri watched him with an aching tenderness for a while. Then he got up, pulled on clothes, and found the corridor to the stairs that led up to the roof.

The mist hid even the roof-peaks. Nothing at all was visible over the railing. He had to feel his way along, touching the railing. The wooden walkway was damp and cold to the soles of his feet. Yet a kind of happiness had started in him as he went up the attic stairs, and it grew as he breathed the foggy air, and as he turned the corner to the west side of the house. He stood still a while and then spoke, almost in a whisper. "Are you there?" he said.

There was a pause, as there had been the first time he spoke to her, and then she answered, the laugh just hidden in her voice, "Yes, I'm here. Are you there?"

The next moment they could see each other, though only as shapes bulking in the mist.

"I'm here," he said. His happiness was absurd. He took a step closer to her, so that he could make out her dark hair, the darkness of her eyes in the lighter oval of her face. "I wanted to talk to you again," he said.

"I wanted to talk to you again," she said.

"I couldn't find you. I hoped you'd speak to me."

"Not down there," she said, her voice turning light and cold.

"Are you in the First Sedoretu?"

"Yes," she said. "The Morning wife of the First Sedoretu of Meruo. My name is An'nad. I wanted to know if you're still unhappy."

"Yes," he said, "no — " He tried to see her face more clearly, but there was little light. "Why is it that you talk to me, and I can talk to you, and not to anybody else in this household?" he said. "Why are you the only kind one?"

"Is — Suord unkind?" she asked, with a little hesitation on the name.

"He never means to be. He never is. Only he — he drags me, he pushes me, he . . . He's stronger than I am."

"Maybe not," said An'nad, "maybe only more used to getting his way."

"Or more in love," Hadri said, low-voiced, with shame.

"You're not in love with him?"

"Oh yes!"

She laughed.

"I never knew anyone like him — he's more than — his feelings are so deep, he's — I'm out of my depth," Hadri stammered. "But I love him — immensely — "

"So what's wrong?"

"He wants to marry," Hadri said, and then stopped. He was talking about her household, probably her blood kin; as a wife of the First Sedoretu she was part of all the network of relationships of Meruo. What was he blundering into?

"Who does he want to marry?" she asked. "Don't worry. I won't interfere. Is the trouble that you don't want to marry him?"

"No, no," Hadri said. "It's only — I never meant to stay here, I thought I'd go home. . . . Marrying Suord seems — more than I, than I deserve — But it would be amazing, it would be wonderful! But . . . the marriage itself, the sedoretu, it's not right. He says that Sasni will marry him, and Duun will marry me, so that she and Duun can be married."

"Suord and Sasni," again the faint pause on the name, "don't love each other, then?"

"No," he said, a little hesitant, remembering that challenge between them, like a spark struck.

"And you and Duun?"

"I don't even know her."

"Oh, no, that is dishonest," An'nad said. "One should choose love, but not that way. . . . Whose plan is it? All three of them?"

"I suppose so. Suord and Sasni have talked about it. The girl, Duun, she never says anything."

"Talk to her," said the soft voice. "Talk to her, Hadri." She was looking at him; they stood quite close together, close enough that he felt the warmth of her arm on his arm though they did not touch.

"I'd rather talk to you," he said, turning to face her. She moved back, seeming to grow insubstantial even in that slight movement, the fog was so dense and dark. She put out her hand, but again did not quite touch him. He knew she was smiling.

"Then stay and talk with me," she said, leaning again on the rail. "Tell me . . . oh, tell me anything. What do you do, you and Suord, when you're not making love?"

"We went out sailing," he said, and found himself telling her what it had been like for him out on the open sea for the first time, his terror and delight. "Can you swim?" she asked, and he laughed and said, "In the lake at home, it's not the same," and she laughed and said, "No, I imagine not." They talked a long time, and he asked her what she did — "in daylight. I haven't seen you yet, down there."

"No," she said. "What do I do? Oh, I worry about Meruo, I suppose. I worry about my children. . . . I don't want to think about that now. How did you come to meet Suord?"

Before they were done talking the mist had begun to lighten very faintly with moonrise. It had grown piercingly cold. Hadri was shivering. "Go on," she said. "I'm used to it. Go on to bed."

"There's frost," he said, "look," touching the silvered wooden rail. "You should go down too."

"I will. Good night, Hadri." As he turned she said, or he thought she said, "I'll wait for the tide."

"Good night, An'nad." He spoke her name huskily, tenderly. If only the others were like her. . . .

He stretched himself out close to Suord's inert, delicious warmth, and slept.

The next day Suord had to work in the records office, where Hadri was utterly useless and in the way. Hadri took his chance, and by asking several sullen, snappish women, found where Duun was: in the fish-drying plant. He went down to the docks and found her, by luck, if it was luck, eating her lunch alone in the misty sunshine at the edge of the boat basin.

"I want to talk with you," he said.

"What for?" she said. She would not look at him.

"Is it honest to marry a person you don't even like in order to marry a person you love?"

"No," she said fiercely. She kept looking down. She tried to fold up the bag she had carried her lunch in, but her hands shook too much.

"Why are you willing to do it, then?"

"Why are *you* willing to do it?"

"I'm not," he said. "It's Suord. And Sasni."

She nodded.

"Not you?"

She shook her head violently. Her thin, dark face was a very young face, he realised.

"But you love Sasni," he said a little uncertainly.

"Yes! I love Sasni! I always did, I always will! That doesn't mean I, I, I have to do everything she says, everything she wants, that I have to, that I have to — " She was looking at him now, right at him, her face burning like a coal, her voice quivering and breaking. "I don't *belong* to Sasni!"

"Well," he said, "I don't belong to Suord, either."

"I don't know anything about men," Duun said, still glaring at him. "Or any other women. Or anything. I never was with anybody but Sasni, all my life! She thinks she *owns* me."

"She and Suord are a lot alike," Hadri said cautiously.

There was a silence. Duun, though tears had spouted out of her eyes in the most childlike fashion, did not deign to wipe them away. She sat straight-backed, cloaked in the dignity of the women of Meruo, and managed to get her lunch-bag folded.

"I don't know very much about women," Hadri said. His was perhaps a simpler dignity. "Or men. I know I love Suord. But I . . . I need freedom."

"Freedom!" she said, and he thought at first she was mocking him, but quite the opposite — she burst right into tears, and put her head down on her knees, sobbing aloud. "I do too," she cried, "I do too."

Hadri put out a timid hand and stroked her shoulder. "I didn't mean to make you cry," he said. "Don't cry, Duun. Look. If we, if we feel the same way, we can work something out. We don't have to get married. We can be friends."

She nodded, though she went on sobbing for a while. At last she raised her swollen face and looked at him with wet-lidded, luminous eyes. "I would like to have a friend," she said. "I never had one."

"I only have one other one here," he said, thinking how right she had been in telling him to talk to Duun. "An'nad."

She stared at him. "Who?"

"An'nad. The Morning woman of the First Sedoretu."

"What do you mean?" She was not scornful, merely very surprised. "That's Teheo."

"Then who is An'nad?"

"She was the Morning woman of the First Sedoretu four hundred years ago," the girl said, her eyes still on Hadri's, clear and puzzled.

"Tell me," he said.

"She was drowned — here, at the foot of the Rock. They were all down on the sands, her sedoretu, with the children. That was when the tides had begun not to come in as far as Meruo. They were all out on the sands, planning the canal, and she was up in the house. She saw there was a storm in the west, and the wind might bring one of the great tides. She ran down to warn them. And the tide did come in, all the way round the Rock, the way it used to. They all kept ahead of it, except An'nad. She was drowned. . . ."

With all he had to wonder about then, about An'nad, and about Duun, he did not wonder why Duun answered his question and asked him none.

It was not until much later, half a year later, that he said, "Do you remember when I said I'd met An'nad — that first time we talked — by the boat basin?"

"I remember," she said.

They were in Hadri's room, a beautiful, high room with windows looking east, traditionally occupied by a member of the Eighth Sedoretu. Summer morning sunlight warmed their bed, and a soft, earth-scented land-wind blew in the windows.

"Didn't it seem strange?" he asked. His head was pillowed on her shoulder. When she spoke he felt her warm breath in his hair.

"Everything was so strange then . . . I don't know. And anyhow, if you've heard the tide. . . ."

"The tide?"

"Winter nights. Up high in the house, in the attics. You can hear the tide come in, and crash around the Rock, and run on inland to the hills. At the true high tide. But the sea is miles away. . . ."

Suord knocked, waited for their invitation, and came in, already dressed. "Are you still in bed? Are we going into town or not?" he demanded, splendid in his white summer coat, imperious. "Sasni's already down in the courtyard."

"Yes, yes, we're just getting up," they said, secretly entwining further.

"Now!" he said, and went out.

Hadri sat up, but Duun pulled him back down. "You saw her? You talked with her?"

"Twice. I never went back after you told me who she was. I was afraid. . . . Not of her. Only afraid she wouldn't be there."

"What did she do?" Duun asked softly.

"She saved us from drowning," Hadri said.

Mountain Ways

Note for readers unfamiliar with the planet O:

Ki'O society is divided into two halves or moieties, called (for ancient religious reasons) the Morning and the Evening. You belong to your mother's moiety, and you can't have sex with anybody of your moiety.

Marriage on O is a foursome, the sedoretu — a man and a woman from the Morning moiety and a man and a woman from the Evening moiety. You're expected to have sex with both your spouses of the other moiety, and not to have sex with your spouse of your own moiety. So each sedoretu has two expected heterosexual relationships, two expected homosexual relationships, and two forbidden heterosexual relationships.

The expected relationships within each sedoretu are:
The Morning woman and the Evening man (the "Morning marriage")
The Evening woman and the Morning man (the "Evening marriage")
The Morning woman and the Evening woman (the "Day marriage")
The Morning man and the Evening man (the "Night marriage")

The forbidden relationships are between the Morning woman and the Morning man, and between the Evening woman and the Evening man, and they aren't called anything, except sacrilege.

It's just as complicated as it sounds, but aren't most marriages?

In the stony uplands of the Deka Mountains the farmholds are few and far between. Farmers scrape a living out of that cold earth, planting on sheltered slopes facing south, combing the yama for fleece, carding and spinning and weaving the prime wool, selling pelts to the carpet-factories. The mountain yama, called ariu, are a small wiry breed; they run wild, without shelter, and are not fenced in, since they never cross the invisible, immemorial boundaries of the herd territory. Each farmhold is in fact a herd territory. The animals are the true farmholders. Tolerant and aloof, they allow the farmers to comb out their thick fleeces, to assist them in difficult births, and to skin them when they die. The farmers are dependent on the ariu; the ariu are not dependent on the farmers. The question of ownership is moot. At Danro Farmhold they don't say, "We have nine hundred ariu," they say, "The herd has nine hundred."

Danro is the farthest farm of Oro Village in the High Watershed of the Mane River on Oniasu on O. The people up there in the mountains are civilised but not very civilised. Like most ki'O they pride themselves on doing things the way they've always been done, but in fact they are a wilful, stubborn lot who change the rules to suit themselves and then say the people "down there" don't know the rules, don't honor the old ways, the true ki'O ways, the mountain ways.

Some years ago, the First Sedoretu of Danro was broken by a landslide up on the Farren that killed the Morning woman and her husband. The widowed Evening couple, who had both married in from other farmholds, fell into a habit of mourning and grew old early, letting the daughter of the Morning manage the farm and all its business.

Her name was Shahes. At thirty, she was a straight-backed, strong, short woman with rough red cheeks, a mountaineer's long stride, and a mountaineer's deep lungs. She could walk down the road to the village center in deep snow with a sixty-pound pack of pelts on her back, sell the pelts, pay her taxes and visit a bit at the village hearth, and stride back up the steep zigzags to be home before nightfall, forty kilometers round trip and six hundred meters of altitude each way. If she or anyone else at Danro wanted to see a new face they had to go down the mountain to other farms or to the village center. There was nothing to bring anybody up the hard road to Danro. Shahes seldom hired help, and the family wasn't sociable. Their hospitality, like their road, had grown stony through lack of use.

But a travelling scholar from the lowlands who came up the Mane all the way to Oro was not daunted by another near-vertical stretch of ruts and rubble. Having visited the other farms, the scholar climbed on around the Farren from Ked'din and up to Danro, and there made the honorable and traditional offer: to share worship at the house shrine, to lead conversation about the Discussions, to instruct the children of the farmhold in spiritual matters, for as long as the farmers wished to lodge and keep her.

This scholar was an Evening woman, over forty, tall and long-limbed, with cropped dark-brown hair as fine and curly as a yama's. She was quite fearless, expected nothing in the way of luxury or even comfort, and had no small talk at all. She was not one of the subtle and eloquent expounders of the great Centers. She was a farm woman who had gone to school. She read and talked about the Discussions in a plain way that suited her hearers, sang the Offerings and the praise songs to the oldest tunes, and gave brief, undemanding lessons to Danro's one child, a ten-year-old Morning half-nephew. Otherwise she was as silent as her hosts, and as hard-working. They were up at dawn; she was up before dawn to sit in meditation. She studied her few books and wrote for an hour or two after that. The rest of the day she worked alongside the farm people at whatever job they gave her.

It was fleecing season, midsummer, and the people were all out every day, all over the vast mountain territory of the herd, following the scattered groups, combing the animals when they lay down to chew the cud.

The old ariu knew and liked the combing. They lay with their legs folded under them or stood still for it, leaning into the comb-strokes a little, sometimes making a small, shivering whisper-cough of enjoyment. The yearlings, whose fleece was the finest and brought the best price raw or woven, were ticklish and frisky; they sidled, bit, and bolted. Fleecing yearlings called for a profound and resolute patience. To this the young ariu would at last respond, growing quiet and even drowsing as the long, fine teeth of the comb bit in and stroked through, over and over again, in the rhythm of the comber's soft monotonous tune, "Hunna, hunna, na, na. . . ."

The travelling scholar, whose religious name was Enno, showed such a knack for handling newborn ariu that Shahes took her out to try her hand at fleecing yearlings. Enno proved to be as good with them as with the infants, and soon she and Shahes, the best fine-fleecer of Oro, were working daily side by side. After her meditation and reading, Enno would come out and find Shahes on the great slopes where the yearlings still ran with their dams and the new-borns. Together the two women could fill a forty-pound sack a day with the airy, silky, milk-colored clouds of combings. Often they would pick out a pair of twins, of which there had been an unusual number this mild year. If Shahes led out one twin the other would follow it, as yama twins will do all their lives; and so the women could work side by side in a silent, absorbed companionship. They talked only to the animals. "Move your fool leg," Shahes would say to the yearling she was combing, as it gazed at her with its great, dark, dreaming eyes. Enno would murmur "Hunna, hunna, hunna, na," or hum a fragment of an Offering, to soothe her beast when it shook its disdainful, elegant head and showed its teeth at her for tickling its belly. Then for half an hour nothing but the crisp whis-per of the combs, the flutter of the unceasing wind over stones, the soft bleat of a calf, the faint rhythmical sound of the nearby beasts biting the thin, dry grass. Always one old female stood watch, the alert head poised on the long neck, the large eyes watching up and down the vast, tilted planes of the mountain from the river miles below to the hanging glaciers miles above. Far peaks of stone and snow stood distinct against the dark-blue, sun-filled sky, blurred off into cloud and blowing mists, then shone out again across the gulfs of air.

Enno took up the big clot of milky fleece she had combed, and Shahes held open the long, loose-woven, double-ended sack.

Enno stuffed the fleece down into the sack. Shahes took her hands.

Leaning across the half-filled sack they held each other's hands, and Shahes said, "I want — " and Enno said, "Yes, yes!"

Neither of them had had much love, neither had had much pleasure in sex. Enno, when she was a rough farm girl named Akal, had the misfortune to attract and be attracted by a man whose pleasure was in cruelty. When she finally understood that she did not have to endure what he did to her, she ran away, not knowing how else to escape him. She took refuge at the school in Asta, and there found the work and learning much to her liking, as she did the spiritual discipline, and later the wandering life. She had been an itinerant scholar with no family, no close attachments, for twenty years. Now Shahes's passion opened to her a spirituality of the body, a revelation that transformed the world and made her feel she had never lived in it before.

As for Shahes, she'd given very little thought to love and not much more to sex, except as it entered into the question of marriage. Marriage was an urgent matter of business. She was thirty years old. Danro had no whole sedoretu, no childbearing women, and only one child. Her duty was plain. She had gone courting in a grim, reluctant fashion to a couple of neighboring farms where there were Evening men. She was too late for the man at Beha Farm, who ran off with a lowlander. The widower at Upper Ked'd was receptive, but he also was nearly sixty and smelled like piss. She tried to force herself to accept the advances of Uncle Mika's half-cousin from Okba Farm down the river, but his desire to own a share of Danro was clearly the sole substance of his desire for Shahes, and he was even lazier and more shiftless than Uncle Mika.

Ever since they were girls, Shahes had met now and then with Temly, the Evening daughter of the nearest farmhold, Ked'din, round on the other side of the Farren. Temly and Shahes had a sexual friendship that was a true and reliable pleasure to them both. They both wished it could be permanent. Every now and then they talked, lying in Shahes's bed at Danro or Temly's bed at Ked'din, of getting married, making a sedoretu. There was no use going to the village matchmakers; they knew everybody the matchmakers knew. One by one they would name the men of Oro and the very few men they knew from outside the Oro Valley, and one by one they would dismiss them as either impossible or inaccessible. The only name that always stayed on the list was Otorra, a Morning man who worked at the carding sheds down in the village center. Shahes liked his reputation as a steady worker; Temly liked his looks and conversation. He evidently liked Temly's looks and conversation too, and would certainly have come courting her if there were any chance of a marriage at Ked'din, but it was a poor farmhold, and there was the same problem there as at Danro: there wasn't an eligible Evening man. To make a sedoretu, Shahes and Temly and Otorra would have to marry the shiftless, shameless fellow at Okba or the sour old widower at Ked'd. To Shahes the idea of sharing her farm and her bed with either of them was intolerable.

"If I could only meet a man who was a match for me!" she said with bitter energy.

"I wonder if you'd like him if you did," said Temly.

"I don't know that I would."

"Maybe next autumn at Manebo . . ."

Shahes sighed. Every autumn she trekked down sixty kilometers to Manebo Fair with a train of pack-yama laden with pelts and wool, and looked for a man; but those she looked at twice never looked at her once. Even though Danro offered a steady living, nobody wanted to live way up there, on the roof, as they called it. And Shahes had no prettiness or nice ways to interest a man. Hard work, hard weather, and the habit of command had made her tough; solitude had made her shy. She was like a wild animal among the jovial, easy-talking dealers and buyers. Last autumn once more she had gone to the fair and once more strode back up into her mountains, sore and dour, and said to Temly, "I wouldn't touch a one of 'em."

Enno woke in the ringing silence of the mountain night. She saw the small square of the window ablaze with stars and felt Shahes's warm body beside her shake with sobs.

"What is it? What is it, my dear love?"

"You'll go away. You're going to go away!"

"But not now — not soon — "

"You can't stay here. You have a calling. A resp —" the word broken by a gasp and sob — "responsibility to your school, to your work, and I can't keep you. I can't give you the farm. I haven't anything to give you, anything at all!"

Enno — or Akal, as she had asked Shahes to call her when they were alone, going back to the girl-name she had given up — Akal knew only too well what Shahes meant. It was the farmholder's duty to provide continuity. As Shahes owed life to her ancestors she owed life to her descendants. Akal did not question this; she had grown up on a farmhold. Since then, at school, she had learned about the joys and duties of the soul, and with Shahes she had learned the joys and duties of love. Neither of them in any way invalidated the duty of a farmholder. Shahes need not bear children herself, but she must see to it that Danro had children. If Temly and Otorra made the Evening marriage, Temly would bear the children of Danro. But a sedoretu must have a Morning marriage; Shahes must find an

Evening man. Shahes was not free to keep Akal at Danro, nor was Akal justified in staying there, for she was in the way, an irrelevance, ultimately an obstacle, a spoiler. As long as she stayed on as a lover, she was neglecting her religious obligations while compromising Shahes's obligation to her farmhold. Shahes had said the truth: she had to go.

She got out of bed and went over to the window. Cold as it was she stood there naked in the starlight, gazing at the stars that flared and dazzled from the far grey slopes up to the zenith. She had to go and she could not go. Life was here, life was Shahes's body, her breasts, her mouth, her breath. She had found life and she could not go down to death. She could not go and she had to go.

Shahes said across the dark room, "Marry me."

Akal came back to the bed, her bare feet silent on the bare floor. She slipped under the bedfleece, shivering, feeling Shahes's warmth against her, and turned to her to hold her; but Shahes took her hand in a strong grip and said again, "Marry me."

"Oh if I could!"

"You can."

After a moment Akal sighed and stretched out, her hands behind her head on the pillow. "There's no Evening men here; you've said so yourself. So how can we marry? What can I do? Go fishing for a husband down in the lowlands, I suppose. With the farmhold as bait. What kind of man would that turn up? Nobody I'd let share you with me for a moment. I won't do it."

Shahes was following her own train of thought. "I can't leave Temly in the lurch," she said.

"And that's the other obstacle," Akal said. "It's not fair to Temly. If we do find an Evening man, then she'll get left out."

"No, she won't."

"Two Day marriages and no Morning marriage? Two Evening women in one sedoretu? There's a fine notion!"

"Listen," Shahes said, still not listening. She sat up with the bedfleece round her shoulders and spoke low and quick. "You go away. Back down there. The winter goes by. Late in the spring, people come up the Mane looking for summer work. A man comes to Oro and says, is anybody asking for a good finefleecer? At the sheds they tell him, yes, Shahes from Danro was down here looking for a hand. So he comes on up here, he knocks at the door here. My name is Akal, he says, I hear you need a fleecer. Yes, I say, yes, we do. Come in. Oh come in, come in and stay forever!"

Her hand was like iron on Akal's wrist, and her voice shook with exultation. Akal listened as to a fairytale.

"Who's to know, Akal? Who'd ever know you? You're taller than most men up here — you can grow your hair, and dress like a man — you said you liked men's clothes once. Nobody will know. Who ever comes here anyway?"

"Oh, come on, Shahes! The people here, Magel and Madu — Shest — "

"The old people won't see anything. Mika's a halfwit. The child won't know. Temly can bring old Barres from Ked'din to marry us. He never knew a tit from a toe anyhow. But he can say the marriage ceremony."

"And Temly?" Akal said, laughing but disturbed; the idea was so wild and Shahes was so serious about it.

"Don't worry about Temly. She'd do anything to get out of Ked'din. She wants to come here, she and I have wanted to marry for years. Now we can. All we need is a Morning man for her. She likes Otorra well enough. And he'd like a share of Danro."

"No doubt, but he gets a share of me with it, you know! A woman in a Night marriage?"

"He doesn't have to know."

"You're crazy, of course he'll know!"

"Only after we're married."

Akal stared through the dark at Shahes, speechless. Finally she said, "What you're proposing is that I go away now and come back after half a year dressed as a man. And marry you and Temly and a man I never met. And live here the rest of my life pretending to be a man. And nobody is going to guess who I am or see through it or object to it. Least of all my husband."

"He doesn't matter."

"Yes he does," said Akal. "It's wicked and unfair. It would desecrate the marriage sacrament. And anyway it wouldn't work. I couldn't fool everybody! Certainly not for the rest of my life!"

"What other way have we to marry?"

"Find an Evening husband — somewhere — "

"But I want you! I want you for my husband and my wife. I don't want any man, ever. I want you, only you till the end of life, and nobody between us, and nobody to part us. Akal, think, think about it, maybe it's against religion, but who does it hurt? Why is it unfair? Temly likes men, and she'll have Otorra. He'll have her, and Danro. And Danro will have their children. And I will have you, I'll have you forever and ever, my soul, my life and soul."

"Oh don't, oh don't," Akal said with a great sob.

Shahes held her.

"I never was much good at being a woman," Akal said. "Till I met you. You can't make me into a man now! I'd be even worse at that, no good at all!"

"You won't be a man, you'll be my Akal, my love, and nothing and nobody will ever come between us."

They rocked back and forth together, laughing and crying, with the fleece around them and the stars blazing at them. "We'll do it, we'll do it!" Shahes said, and Akal said, "We're crazy, we're crazy!"

Gossips in Oro had begun to ask if that scholar woman was going to spend the winter up in the high farmholds, where was she now, Danro was it or Ked'din? — when she came walking down the zigzag road. She spent the night and sang the Offerings for the mayor's family, and caught the daily freighter to the suntrain station down at Dermane. The first of the autumn blizzards followed her down from the peaks.

Shahes and Akal sent no message to each other all through the winter. In the early spring Akal telephoned the farm. "When are you coming?" Shahes asked, and the distant voice replied, "In time for the fleecing."

For Shahes the winter passed in a long dream of Akal. Her voice sounded in the empty next room. Her tall body moved beside Shahes through the wind and snow. Shahes's sleep was peaceful, rocked in a certainty of love known and love to come.

For Akal, or Enno as she became again in the lowlands, the winter passed in a long misery of guilt and indecision. Marriage was a sacrament, and surely what they planned was a mockery of that sacrament. Yet as surely it was a marriage of love. And as Shahes had said, it harmed no one — unless to deceive them was to harm them. It could not be right to fool the man, Otorra, into a marriage where his Night partner would turn out to be a woman. But surely no man knowing the scheme beforehand would agree to it; deception was the only means at hand. They must cheat him.

The religion of the ki'O lacks priests and pundits who tell the common folk what to do. The common folk have to make their own moral and spiritual choices, which is why they spend a good deal of time discussing the Discussions. As a scholar of the Discussions, Enno knew more questions than most people, but fewer answers.

She sat all the dark winter mornings wrestling with her soul. When she called Shahes, it was to tell her that she could not come. When she heard Shahes's voice her misery and guilt ceased to exist, were gone, as a dream is gone on waking. She said, "I'll be there in time for the fleecing."

In the spring, while she worked with a crew rebuilding and repainting a wing of her old school at Asta, she let her hair grow. When it was long enough, she clubbed it back, as men often did. In the summer, having saved a little money working for the school, she bought men's clothes. She put them on and looked at herself in the mirror in the shop. She saw Akal. Akal was a tall, thin man with a thin face, a bony nose, and a slow, brilliant smile. She liked him.

Akal got off the High Deka freighter at its last stop, Oro, went to the village center, and asked if anybody was looking for a fleecer.

"Danro." — "The farmer was down from Danro, twice already." — "Wants a finefleecer." — "Coarsefleecer, wasn't it?" — It took a while, but the elders and gossips agreed at last: a finefleecer was wanted at Danro.

"Where's Danro?" asked the tall man.

"Up," said an elder succinctly. "You ever handled ariu yearlings?"

"Yes," said the tall man. "Up west or up east?"

They told him the road to Danro, and he went off up the zigzags, whistling a familiar praise song.

As Akal went on he stopped whistling, and stopped being a man, and wondered how she could pretend not to know anybody in the household, and how she could imagine they wouldn't know her. How could she deceive Shest, the child whom she had taught the water rite and the praise-songs? A pang of fear and dismay and shame shook her when she saw Shest come running to the gate to let the stranger in.

Akal spoke little, keeping her voice down in her chest, not meeting the child's eyes. She was sure he recognised her. But his stare was simply that of a child who saw strangers so seldom that for all he knew they all looked alike. He ran in to fetch the old people, Magel and Madu. They came out to offer Akal the customary hospitality, a religious duty, and Akal accepted, feeling mean and low at deceiving these people, who had always been kind to her in their rusty, stingy way, and at the same time feeling a wild impulse of laughter, of triumph. They did not see Enno in her, they did not know her. That meant that she was Akal, and Akal was free.

She was sitting in the kitchen drinking a thin and sour soup of summer greens when Shahes came in — grim, stocky, weather-beaten, wet. A summer thunderstorm had broken over the Farren soon after Akal reached the farm. "Who's that?" said Shahes, doffing her wet coat.

"Come up from the village." Old Magel lowered his voice to address Shahes confidentially: "He said they said you said you wanted a hand with the yearlings."

"Where've you worked?" Shahes demanded, her back turned, as she ladled herself a bowl of soup.

Akal had no life history, at least not a recent one. She groped a long time. No one took any notice, prompt answers and quick talk being unusual and suspect practices in the mountains. At last she said the name of the farm she had run away from twenty years ago. "Bredde Hold, of Abba Village, on the Oriso."

"And you've finefleeced? Handled yearlings? Ariu yearlings?"

Akal nodded, dumb. Was it possible that Shahes did not recognise her? Her voice was flat and unfriendly, and the one glance she had given Akal was dismissive. She had sat down with her soupbowl and was eating hungrily.

"You can come out with me this afternoon and I'll see how you work," Shahes said. "What's your name, then?"

"Akal."

Shahes grunted and went on eating. She glanced up across the table at Akal again, one flick of the eyes, like a stab of light.

Out on the high hills, in the mud of rain and snowmelt, in the stinging wind and the flashing sunlight, they held each other so tight neither could breathe, they laughed and wept and talked and kissed and coupled in a rock shelter, and came back so dirty and with such a sorry little sack of combings that old Magel told Madu that he couldn't understand why Shahes was going to hire the tall fellow from down there at all, if that's all the work was in him, and Madu said what's more he eats for six.

But after a month or so, when Shahes and Akal weren't hiding the fact that they slept together, and Shahes began to talk about making a sedoretu, the old couple grudgingly approved. They had no other kind of approval to give. Maybe Akal was ignorant, didn't know a hassel-bit from a cold-chisel; but they were all like that down there. Remember that travelling scholar, Enno, stayed here last year, she was just the same, too tall for her own good and ignorant, but willing to learn, same as Akal. Akal was a prime hand with the beasts, or had the makings of it anyhow. Shahes could look farther and do worse. And it meant she and Temly could be the Day marriage of a sedoretu, as they would have been long since if there'd been any kind of men around worth taking into the farmhold, what's wrong with this generation, plenty of good men around in my day.

Shahes had spoken to the village matchmakers down in Oro. They spoke to Otorra, now a foreman at the carding sheds; he accepted a formal invitation to Danro. Such invitations included meals and an overnight stay, necessarily, in such a remote place, but the invitation was to share worship with the farm family at the house shrine, and its significance was known to all.

So they all gathered at the house shrine, which at Danro was a low, cold, inner room walled with stone, with a floor of earth and stones that was the unlevelled ground of the mountainside. A tiny spring, rising at the higher end of the room, trickled in a channel of cut granite. It was the reason why the house stood where it did, and had stood there for six hundred years. They offered water and accepted water, one to another, one from another, the old Evening couple, Uncle Mika, his son Shest, Asbi who had worked as a packtrainer and handyman at Danro for thirty years, Akal the new hand, Shahes the farmholder, and the guests: Otorra from Oro and Temly from Ked'din.

Temly smiled across the spring at Otorra, but he did not meet her eyes, or anyone else's.

Temly was a short, stocky woman, the same type as Shahes, but fairer-skinned and a bit lighter all round, not as solid, not as hard. She had a surprising, clear singing voice that soared up in the praise-songs. Otorra was also rather short and broad-shouldered, with good features, a competent-looking man, but just now extremely ill at ease; he looked as if he had robbed the shrine or murdered the mayor, Akal thought, studying him with interest, as well she might. He looked furtive; he looked guilty.

Akal observed him with curiosity and dispassion. She would share water with Otorra, but not guilt. As soon as she had seen Shahes, touched Shahes, all her scruples and moral anxieties had dropped away, as if they could not breathe up here in the mountains. Akal had been born for Shahes and Shahes for Akal; that was all there was to it. Whatever made it possible for them to be together was right.

Once or twice she did ask herself, what if I'd been born into the Morning instead of the Evening moiety? — a perverse and terrible thought. But perversity and sacrilege were not asked of her. All she had to do was change sex. And that only in appearance, in public. With Shahes she was a woman, and more truly a woman and herself than she had ever been in her life. With everybody else she was Akal, whom they took to be a man. That was no trouble at all. She was Akal; she liked being Akal. It was not like acting a part. She never had been herself with other people, had always felt a falsity in her relationships with them; she had never known who she was at all, except sometimes for a moment in meditation, when her *I am* became *It is*, and she breathed the stars. But with Shahes she was herself utterly, in time and in the body, Akal, a soul consumed in love and blessed by intimacy.

So it was that she had agreed with Shahes that they should say nothing to Otorra, nothing even to Temly. "Let's see what Temly makes of you," Shahes said, and Akal agreed.

Last year Temly had entertained the scholar Enno overnight at her farmhold for instruction and worship, and had met her two or three times at Danro. When she came to share worship today she met Akal for the first time. Did she see Enno? She gave no sign of it.

She greeted Akal with a kind of brusque goodwill, and they talked about breeding ariu. She quite evidently studied the newcomer, judging, sizing up; but that was natural enough in a woman meeting a stranger she might be going to marry. "You don't know much about mountain farming, do you?" she said kindly after they had talked a while. "Different from down there. What did you raise? Those big flatland yama?" And Akal told her about the farm where she grew up, and the three crops a year they got, which made Temly nod in amazement.

As for Otorra, Shahes and Akal colluded to deceive him without ever saying a word more about it to each other. Akal's mind shied away from the subject. They would get to know each other during the engagement period, she thought vaguely. She would have to tell him, eventually, that she did not want to have sex with him, of course, and the only way to do that without insulting and humiliating him was to say that she, that Akal, was averse to having sex with other men, and hoped he would forgive her. But Shahes had made it clear that she mustn't tell him that till they were married. If he knew it beforehand he would refuse to enter the sedoretu. And even worse, he might talk about it, expose Akal as a woman, in revenge. Then they would never be able to marry. When Shahes had spoken about this, Akal had felt distressed and trapped, anxious, guilty again; but Shahes was serenely confident and untroubled, and somehow Akal's guilty feelings would not stick. They dropped off. She simply hadn't thought much about it. She watched Otorra now with sympathy and curiosity, wondering what made him look so hangdog. He was scared of something, she thought.

After the water was poured and the blessing said, Shahes read from the Fourth Discussion; she closed the old boxbook very carefully, put it on its shelf and put its cloth over it, and then, speaking to Magel and Madu as was proper, they being what was left of the First Sedoretu of Danro, she said, "My Othermother and my Otherfather, I propose that a new sedoretu be made in this house."

Madu nudged Magel. He fidgeted and grimaced and muttered inaudibly. Finally Madu said in her weak, resigned voice, "Daughter of the Morning, tell us the marriages."

"If all be well and willing, the marriage of the Morning will be Shahes and Akal, and the marriage of the Evening will be Temly and Otorra, and the marriage of the Day will be Shahes and Temly, and the marriage of the Night will be Akal and Otorra."

There was a long pause. Magel hunched his shoulders. Madu said at last, rather fretfully, "Well, is that all right with everybody?" — which gave the gist, if not the glory, of the formal request for consent, usually couched in antique and ornate language.

"Yes," said Shahes, clearly.

"Yes," said Akal, manfully.

"Yes," said Temly, cheerfully.

A pause.

Everybody looked at Otorra, of course. He had blushed purple and, as they watched, turned greyish.

"I am willing," he said at last in a forced mumble, and cleared his throat. "Only — " He stuck there.

Nobody said anything.

The silence was horribly painful.

Akal finally said, "We don't have to decide now. We can talk. And, and come back to the shrine later, if . . ."

"Yes," Otorra said, glancing at Akal with a look in which so much emotion was compressed that she could not read it at all — terror, hate, gratitude, despair? — "I want to — I need to talk — to Akal."

"I'd like to get to know my brother of the Evening too," said Temly in her clear voice.

"Yes, that's it, yes, that is — " Otorra stuck again, and blushed again. He was in such an agony of discomfort that Akal said, "Let's go on outside for a bit, then," and led Otorra out into the yard, while the others went to the kitchen.

Akal knew Otorra had seen through her pretense. She was dismayed, and dreaded what he might say; but he had not made a scene, he had not humiliated her before the others, and she was grateful to him for that.

"This is what it is," Otorra said in a stiff, forced voice, coming to a stop at the gate. "It's the Night marriage." He came to a stop there, too.

Akal nodded. Reluctantly, she spoke, to help Otorra do what he had to do. "You don't have to — " she began, but he was speaking again:

"The Night marriage. Us. You and me. See, I don't — There's some — See, with men, I — "

The whine of delusion and the buzz of incredulity kept Akal from hearing what the man was trying to tell her. He had to stammer on even more painfully before she began to listen. When his words came clear to her she could not trust them, but she had to. He had stopped trying to talk.

Very hesitantly, she said, "Well, I . . . I was going to tell you. . . . The only man I ever had sex with, it was . . . It wasn't good. He made me — He did things — I don't know what was wrong. But I never have — I have never had any sex with men. Since that. I can't. I can't make myself want to."

"Neither can I," Otorra said.

They stood side by side leaning on the gate, contemplating the miracle, the simple truth.

"I just only ever want women," Otorra said in a shaking voice.

"A lot of people are like that," Akal said.

"They are?"

She was touched and grieved by his humility. Was it men's boastfulness with other men, or the hardness of the mountain people, that had burdened him with this ignorance, this shame?

"Yes," she said. "Everywhere I've been. There's quite a lot of men who only want sex with women. And women who only want sex with men. And the other way round, too. Most people want both, but there's always some who don't. It's like the two ends of," she was about to say "a spectrum," but it wasn't the language of Akal the fleecer or Otorra the carder, and with the adroitness of the old teacher she substituted "a sack. If you pack it right, most of the fleece is in the middle. But there's some at both ends where you tie off, too. That's us. There's not as many of us. But there's nothing wrong with us." As she said this last it did not sound like what a man would say to a man. But it was said; and Otorra did not seem to think it peculiar, though he did not look entirely convinced. He pondered. He had a pleasant face, blunt, unguarded, now that his unhappy secret was out. He was only about thirty, younger than she had expected.

"But in a marriage," he said. "It's different from just . . . A marriage is — Well, if I don't — and you don't — "

"Marriage isn't just sex," Akal said, but said it in Enno's voice, Enno the scholar discussing questions of ethics, and Akal cringed.

"A lot of it is," said Otorra, reasonably.

"All right," Akal said in a consciously deeper, slower voice. "But if I don't want it with you and you don't want it with me why can't we have a good marriage?" It came out so improbable and so banal at the same time that she nearly broke into a fit of laughter. Controlling herself, she thought, rather shocked, that Otorra was laughing at her, until she realised that he was crying.

"I never could tell anybody," he said.

"We don't ever have to," she said. She put her arm around his shoulders without thinking about it at all. He wiped his eyes with his fists like a child, cleared his throat, and stood thinking. Obviously he was thinking about what she had just said.

"Think," she said, also thinking about it, "how lucky we are!"

"Yes. Yes, we are." He hesitated. "But . . . but is it religious . . . to marry each other knowing . . . Without really meaning to. . . ." He stuck again.

After a long time, Akal said, in a voice as soft and nearly as deep as his, "I don't know."

She had withdrawn her comforting, patronising arm from his shoulders. She leaned her hands on the top bar of the gate. She looked at her hands, long and strong, hardened and dirt-engrained from farm work, though the oil of the fleeces kept them supple. A farmer's hands. She had given up the religious life for love's sake and never looked back. But now she was ashamed.

She wanted to tell this honest man the truth, to be worthy of his honesty.

But it would do no good, unless not to make the sedoretu was the only good.

"I don't know," she said again. "I think what matters is if we try to give each other love and honor. However we do that, that's how we do it. That's how we're married. The marriage — the religion is in the love, in the honoring."

"I wish there was somebody to ask," Otorra said, unsatisfied. "Like that travelling scholar that was here last summer. Somebody who knows about religion."

Akal was silent.

"I guess the thing is to do your best," Otorra said after a while. It sounded sententious, but he added, plainly, "I would do that."

"So would I," Akal said.

A mountain farmhouse like Danro is a dark, damp, bare, grim place to live in, sparsely furnished, with no luxuries except the warmth of the big kitchen and the splendid bedfleeces. But it offers privacy, which may be the greatest luxury of all, though the ki'O consider it a necessity. "A three-room sedoretu" is a common expression in Okets, meaning an enterprise doomed to fail.

At Danro, everyone had their own room and bathroom. The two old members of the First Sedoretu, and Uncle Mika and his child, had rooms in the center and west wing; Asbi, when he wasn't sleeping out on the mountain, had a cozy, dirty nest behind the kitchen. The new Second Sedoretu had the whole east side of the house. Temly chose a little attic room, up a half-flight of stairs from the others, with a fine view. Shahes kept her room, and Akal hers, adjoining; and Otorra chose the southeast corner, the sunniest room in the house.

The conduct of a new sedoretu is to some extent, and wisely, prescribed by custom and sanctioned by religion. The first night after the ceremony of marriage belongs to the Morning and Evening couples; the second night to the Day and Night couples. Thereafter the four spouses may join as and when they please, but always and only by invitation given and accepted, and the arrangements are to be known to all four. Four souls and bodies and all the years of their four lives to come are in the balance in each of those decisions and invitations; passion, negative and positive, must find its channels, and trust must be established, lest the whole structure fail to found itself solidly, or destroy itself in selfishness and jealousy and grief.

Akal knew all the customs and sanctions, and she insisted that they be followed to the letter. Her wedding night with Shahes was tender and a little tense. Her wedding night with Otorra was also tender; they sat in his room and talked softly, shy with each other but each very grateful; then Otorra slept in the deep windowseat, insisting that Akal have the bed.

Within a few weeks Akal knew that Shahes was more intent on having her way, on having Akal as her partner, than on maintaining any kind of sexual balance or even a pretense of it. As far as Shahes was concerned, Otorra and Temly could look after each other and that was that. Akal had of course known many sedoretu where one or two of the partnerships dominated the others completely, through passion or the power of an ego. To balance all four relationships perfectly was an ideal seldom realised. But this sedoretu, already built on a deception, a disguise, was more fragile than most. Shahes wanted what she wanted and consequences be damned. Akal had followed her far up the mountain, but would not follow her over a precipice.

It was a clear autumn night, the window full of stars, like that night last year when Shahes had said, "Marry me."

"You have to give Temly tomorrow night," Akal repeated.

"She's got Otorra," Shahes repeated.

"She wants you. Why do you think she married you?"

"She's got what she wants. I hope she gets pregnant soon," Shahes said, stretching luxuriously, and running her hand over Akal's breasts and belly. Akal stopped her hand and held it.

"It isn't fair, Shahes. It isn't right."

"A fine one you are to talk!"

"But Otorra doesn't want me, you know that. And Temly does want you. And we owe it to her."

"Owe her what?"

"Love and honor."

"She's got what she wanted," Shahes said, and freed her hand from Akal's grasp with a harsh twist. "Don't preach at me."

"I'm going back to my room," Akal said, slipping lithely from the bed and stalking naked through the starry dark. "Good night."

She was with Temly in the old dye room, unused for years until Temly, an expert dyer, came to the farm. Weavers down in the Centers would pay well for fleece dyed the true Deka red. Her skill had been Temly's dowry. Akal was her assistant and apprentice now.

"Eighteen minutes. Timer set?"

"Set."

Temly nodded, checked the vents on the great dye-boiler, checked the read-out again, and went outside to catch the morning sun. Akal joined her on the stone bench by the stone doorway. The smell of the vegetable dye, pungent and acid-sweet, clung to them, and their clothes and hands and arms were raddled pink and crimson.

Akal had become attached to Temly very soon, finding her reliably good-tempered and unexpectedly thoughtful — both qualities that had been in rather short supply at Danro. Without knowing it, Akal had formed her expectation of the mountain people on Shahes — powerful, wilful, undeviating, rough. Temly was strong and quite self-contained, but open to impressions as Shahes was not. Relationships within her moiety meant little to Shahes; she called Otorra brother because it was customary, but did not see a brother in him. Temly called Akal brother and meant it, and Akal, who had had no family for so long, welcomed the relationship, returning Temly's warmth. They talked easily together, though Akal had constantly to guard herself from becoming too easy and letting her woman-self speak out. Mostly it was no trouble at all being Akal and she gave little thought to it, but sometimes with Temly it was very hard to keep up the pretense, to prevent herself from saying what a woman would say to her sister. In general she had found that the main drawback in being a man was that conversations were less interesting.

They talked about the next step in the dyeing process, and then Temly said, looking off over the low stone wall of the yard to the huge purple slant of the Farren, "You know Enno, don't you?"

The question seemed innocent and Akal almost answered automatically with some kind of deceit — "The scholar that was here . . . ?"

But there was no reason why Akal the fleecer should know Enno the scholar. And Temly had not asked, do you remember Enno, or did you know Enno, but, "You know Enno, don't you?" She knew the answer.

"Yes."

Temly nodded, smiling a little. She said nothing more.

Akal was amazed by her subtlety, her restraint. There was no difficulty in honoring so honorable a woman.

"I lived alone for a long time," Akal said. "Even on the farm where I grew up I was mostly alone. I never had a sister. I'm glad to have one at last."

"So am I," said Temly.

Their eyes met briefly, a flicker of recognition, a glance planting trust deep and silent as a tree-root.

"She knows who I am, Shahes."

Shahes said nothing, trudging up the steep slope.

"Now I wonder if she knew from the start. From the first water-sharing. . . ."

"Ask her if you like," Shahes said, indifferent.

"I can't. The deceiver has no right to ask for the truth."

"Humbug!" Shahes said, turning on her, halting her in mid-stride. They were up on the Farren looking for an old beast that Asbi had reported missing from the herd. The keen autumn wind had blown Shahes's cheeks red, and as she stood staring up at Akal she squinted her watering eyes so that they glinted like knifeblades. "Quit preaching! Is that who you are? 'The deceiver'? I thought you were my wife!"

"I am, and Otorra's too, and you're Temly's — you can't leave them out, Shahes!"

"Are they complaining?"

"Do you want them to complain?" Akal shouted, losing her temper. "Is that the kind of marriage you want? — Look, there she is," she added in a suddenly quiet voice, pointing up the great rocky mountainside. Farsighted, led by a bird's circling, she had caught the movement of the yama's head near an outcrop of boulders. The quarrel was postponed. They both set off at a cautious trot towards the boulders.

The old yama had broken a leg in a slip from the rocks. She lay neatly collected, though the broken foreleg would not double under her white breast but stuck out forward, and her whole body had a lurch to that side. Her disdainful head was erect on the long neck, and she gazed at the women, watching her death approach, with clear, unfathomable, uninterested eyes.

"Is she in pain?" Akal asked, daunted by that great serenity.

"Of course," Shahes said, sitting down several paces away from the yama to sharpen her knife on its emery-stone. "Wouldn't you be?"

She took a long time getting the knife as sharp as she could get it, patiently retesting and rewhetting the blade. At last she tested it again and then sat completely still. She stood up quietly, walked over to the yama, pressed its head up against her breast and cut its throat in one long fast slash. Blood leaped out in a brilliant arc. Shahes slowly lowered the head with its gazing eyes down to the ground.

Akal found that she was speaking the words of the ceremony for the dead, *Now all that was owed is repaid and all that was owned, returned. Now all that was lost is found and all that was bound, free.* Shahes stood silent, listening till the end.

Then came the work of skinning. They would leave the carcass to be cleaned by the scavengers of the mountain; it was a carrion-bird circling over the yama that had first caught Akal's eye, and there were now three of them riding the wind. Skinning was fussy, dirty work, in the stink of meat and blood. Akal was inexpert, clumsy, cutting the hide more than once. In penance she insisted on carrying the pelt, rolled as best they could and strapped with their belts. She felt like a grave robber, carrying away the white-and-dun fleece, leaving the thin, broken corpse sprawled among the rocks in the indignity of its nakedness. Yet in her mind as she lugged the heavy fleece along was Shahes standing up and taking the yama's beautiful head against her breast and slashing its throat, all one long movement, in which the woman and the animal were utterly one.

It is need that answers need, Akal thought, as it is question that answers question. The pelt reeked of death and dung. Her hands were caked with blood, and ached, gripping the stiff belt, as she followed Shahes down the steep rocky path homeward.

"I'm going down to the village," Otorra said, getting up from the breakfast table.

"When are you going to card those four sacks?" Shahes said.

He ignored her, carrying his dishes to the washer-rack. "Any errands?" he asked of them all.

"Everybody done?" Madu asked, and took the cheese out to the pantry.

"No use going into town till you can take the carded fleece," said Shahes.

Otorra turned to her, stared at her, and said, "I'll card it when I choose and take it when I choose and I don't take orders at my own work, will you understand that?"

Stop, stop now! Akal cried silently, for Shahes, stunned by the uprising of the meek, was listening to him. But he went on, firing grievance with grievance, blazing out in recriminations. "You can't give all the orders, we're your sedoretu, we're your household, not a lot of hired hands, yes it's your farm but it's ours too, you married us, you can't make all the decisions, and you can't have it all your way either," and at this point Shahes unhurriedly walked out of the room.

"Shahes!" Akal called after her, loud and imperative. Though Otorra's outburst was undignified it was completely justified, and his anger was both real and dangerous. He was a man who had been used, and he knew it. As he had let himself be used and had colluded in that misuse, so now his anger threatened destruction. Shahes could not run away from it.

She did not come back. Madu had wisely disappeared. Akal told Shest to run out and see to the pack-beasts' feed and water.

The three remaining in the kitchen sat or stood silent. Temly looked at Otorra. He looked at Akal.

"You're right," Akal said to him.

He gave a kind of satisfied snarl. He looked handsome in his anger, flushed and reckless. "Damn right I'm right. I've let this go on for too long. Just because she owned the farmhold — "

"And managed it since she was fourteen," Akal cut in. "You think she can quit managing just like that? She's always run things here. She had to. She never had anybody to share power with. Everybody has to learn how to be married."

"That's right," Otorra flashed back, "and a marriage isn't two pairs. It's four pairs!"

That brought Akal up short. Instinctively she looked to Temly for help. Temly was sitting, quiet as usual, her elbows on the table, gathering up crumbs with one hand and pushing them into a little pyramid.

"Temly and me, you and Shahes, Evening and Morning, fine," Otorra said. "What about Temly and her? What about you and me?"

Akal was now completely at a loss. "I thought . . . When we talked . . ."

"I said I didn't like sex with men," said Otorra.

She looked up and saw a gleam in his eye. Spite? Triumph? Laughter?

"Yes. You did," Akal said after a long pause. "And I said the same thing."

Another pause.

"It's a religious duty," Otorra said.

Enno suddenly said very loudly in Akal's voice, "Don't come onto me with your religious duty! I studied religious duty for twenty years and where did it get me? Here! With you! In this mess!"

At this, Temly made a strange noise and put her face in her hands. Akal thought she had burst into tears, and then saw she was laughing, the painful, helpless, jolting laugh of a person who hasn't had much practice at it.

"There's nothing to laugh about," Otorra said fiercely, but then had no more to say; his anger had blown up leaving nothing but smoke. He groped for words for a while longer. He looked at Temly, who was indeed in tears now, tears of laughter. He made a despairing gesture. He sat down beside Temly and said, "I suppose it is funny if you look at it. It's just that I feel like a chump." He laughed, ruefully, and then, looking up at Akal, he laughed genuinely. "Who's the biggest chump?" he asked her.

"Not you," she said. "How long. . . ."

"How long do you think?"

It was what Shahes, standing in the passageway, heard: their laughter. The three of them laughing. She listened to it with dismay, fear, shame, and terrible envy. She hated them for laughing. She wanted to be with them, she wanted to laugh with them, she wanted to silence them. Akal, Akal was laughing at her.

She went out to the workshed and stood in the dark behind the door and tried to cry and did not know how. She had not cried when her parents were killed; there had been too much to do. She thought the others were laughing at her for loving Akal, for wanting her, for needing her. She thought Akal was laughing at her for being such a fool, for loving her. She thought Akal would sleep with the man and they would laugh together at her. She drew her knife and tested its edge. She had made it very sharp yesterday on the Farren to kill the yama. She came back to the house, to the kitchen.

They were all still there. Shest had come back and was pestering Otorra to take him into town and Otorra was saying, "Maybe, maybe," in his soft lazy voice.

Temly looked up, and Akal looked round at Shahes — the small head on the graceful neck, the clear eyes gazing.

Nobody spoke.

"I'll walk down with you, then," Shahes said to Otorra, and sheathed her knife. She looked at the women and the child. "We might as well all go," she said sourly. "If you like."

SOLITUDE

*An addition to "POVERTY: The Second Report on Eleven-Soro" by Mobile
Entselenne'temharyonoterregwis Leaf, by her daughter, Serenity.*

My mother, a field ethnologist, took the difficulty of learning
anything about the people of Eleven-Soro as a personal challenge. The fact that she used her children to meet that challenge
might be seen as selfishness or as selflessness. Now that I have read
her report I know that she finally thought she had done wrong.
Knowing what it cost her, I wish she knew my gratitude to her for
allowing me to grow up as a person.

Shortly after a robot probe reported people of the Hainish
Descent on the eleventh planet of the Soro system, she joined the
orbital crew as backup for the three First Observers down on-
planet. She had spent four years in the tree-cities of nearby Huthu.
My brother In Joy Born was eight years old and I was five; she
wanted a year or two of ship duty so we could spend some time in a
Hainish-style school. My brother had enjoyed the rainforests of
Huthu very much, but though he could brachiate he could barely
read, and we were all bright blue with skin fungus. While Borny
learned to read and I learned to wear clothes and we all had anti-

fungus treatments, my mother became as intrigued by Eleven-Soro as the Observers were frustrated by it.

All this is in her report, but I will say it as I learned it from her, which helps me remember and understand. The language had been recorded by the probe and the Observers had spent a year learning it. The many dialectical variations excused their accents and errors, and they reported that language was not a problem. Yet there was a communication problem. The two men found themselves isolated, faced with suspicion or hostility, unable to form any connection with the native men, all of whom lived in solitary houses as hermits, or in pairs. Finding communities of adolescent males, they tried to make contact with them, but when they entered the territory of such a group the boys either fled or rushed desperately at them trying to kill them. The women, who lived in what they called "dispersed villages," drove them away with volleys of stones as soon as they came anywhere near the houses. "I believe," one of them reported, "that the only community activity of the Sorovians is throwing rocks at men."

Neither of them succeeded in having a conversation of more than three exchanges with a man. One of them mated with a woman who came by his camp; he reported that though she made unmistakable and insistent advances, she seemed disturbed by his attempts to converse, refused to answer his questions, and left him, he said, "as soon as she got what she came for."

The woman Observer was allowed to settle in an unused house in a "village" (auntring) of seven houses. She made excellent observations of daily life, insofar as she could see any of it, and had several conversations with adult women and many with children; but she found that she was never asked into another woman's house, nor expected to help or ask for help in any work. Conversation concerning normal activities was unwelcome to the other women; the children, her only informants, called her Aunt Crazy-Jabber. Her aberrant behavior caused increasing distrust and dislike among the women, and they began to keep their children away from her. She left. "There's no way," she told my mother, "for an adult to learn anything. They don't ask questions, they don't answer questions. Whatever they learn, they learn when they're children."

Aha! said my mother to herself, looking at Borny and me. And she requested a family transfer to Eleven-Soro with Observer status. The Stabiles interviewed her extensively by ansible, and talked with Borny and even with me — I don't remember it, but she told me I told the Stabiles all about my new stockings — and agreed to her request. The ship was to stay in close orbit, with the previous Observers in the crew, and she was to keep radio contact with it, daily if possible.

I have a dim memory of the tree-city, and of playing with what must have been a kitten or a ghole-kit on the ship; but my first clear memories are of our house in the auntring. It is half underground, half aboveground, with wattle-and-daub walls. Mother and I are standing outside it in the warm sunshine. Between us is a big mud puddle, into which Borny pours water from a basket; then he runs off to the creek to get more water. I muddle the mud with my hands, deliciously, till it is thick and smooth. I pick up a big double handful and slap it onto the walls where the sticks show through. Mother says, "That's good! That's right!" in our new language, and I realise that this is work, and I am doing it. I am repairing the house. I am making it right, doing it right. I am a competent person.

I have never doubted that, so long as I lived there.

We are inside the house at night, and Borny is talking to the ship on the radio, because he misses talking the old language, and anyway he is supposed to tell them stuff. Mother is making a basket and swearing at the split reeds. I am singing a song to drown out Borny so nobody in the auntring hears him talking funny, and anyway I like singing. I learned this song this afternoon in Hyuru's house. I play every day with Hyuru. "Be aware, listen, listen, be aware," I sing. When Mother stops swearing she listens, and then she turns on the recorder. There is a little fire still left from cooking dinner, which was lovely pigi root, I never get tired of pigi. It is dark and warm and smells of pigi and of burning duhur, which is a strong, sacred smell to drive out magic and bad feelings, and as I sing "Listen, be aware," I get sleepier and sleepier and lean against Mother, who is dark and warm and smells like Mother, strong and sacred, full of good feelings.

Our daily life in the auntring was repetitive. On the ship, later, I learned that people who live in artificially complicated situations call such a life "simple." I never knew anybody, anywhere I have been, who found life simple. I think a life or a time looks simple when you leave out the details, the way a planet looks smooth, from orbit.

Certainly our life in the auntring was easy, in the sense that our needs came easily to hand. There was plenty of food to be gathered or grown and prepared and cooked, plenty of temas to pick and rett and spin and weave for clothes and bedding, plenty of reeds to make baskets and thatch with; we children had other children to play with, mothers to look after us, and a great deal to learn. None of this is simple, though it's all easy enough, when you know how to do it, when you are aware of the details.

It was not easy for my mother. It was hard for her, and complicated. She had to pretend she knew the details while she was learning them, and had to think how to report and explain this way of living to people in another place who didn't understand it. For Borny it was easy until it got hard because he was a boy. For me it was all easy. I learned the work and played with the children and listened to the mothers sing.

The First Observer had been quite right: there was no way for a grown woman to learn how to make her soul. Mother couldn't go listen to another mother sing, it would have been too strange. The aunts all knew she hadn't been brought up well, and some of them taught her a good deal without her realising it. They had decided her mother must have been irresponsible and had gone on scouting instead of settling in an auntring, so that her daughter didn't get educated properly. That's why even the most aloof of the aunts always let me listen with their children, so that I could become an educated person. But of course they couldn't ask another adult into their houses. Borny and I had to tell her all the songs and stories we learned, and then she would tell them to the radio, or we told them to the radio while she listened to us. But she never got it right, not really. How could she, trying to learn it after she'd grown up, and after she'd always lived with magicians?

"Be aware!" She would imitate my solemn and probably irritating imitation of the aunts and the big girls. "Be aware! How many times a day do they say that? Be aware of what? They aren't aware of *what* the ruins are, their own history — they aren't aware of each other! They don't even talk to each other! Be aware, indeed!"

When I told her the stories of the Before Time that Aunt Sadne and Aunt Noyit told their daughters and me, she often heard the wrong things in them. I told her about the People, and she said, "Those are the ancestors of the people here now." When I said, "There aren't any people here now," she didn't understand. "There are persons here now," I said, but she still didn't understand.

Borny liked the story about the Man Who Lived with Women, how he kept some women in a pen, the way some persons keep rats in a pen for eating, and all of them got pregnant, and they each had a hundred babies, and the babies grew up as horrible monsters and ate the man and the mothers and each other. Mother explained to us that that was a parable of the human overpopulation of this planet thousands of years ago. "No, it's not," I said, "it's a moral story." — "Well, yes," Mother said. "The moral is, don't have too many babies." — "No, it's not," I said. "Who could have a hundred babies even if they wanted to? The man was a sorcerer. He did magic. The women did it with him. So their children were monsters."

The key, of course, is the word "tekell," which translates so nicely into the Hainish word "magic," an art or power that violates natural law. It was hard for Mother to understand that some persons truly consider most human relationships unnatural; that marriage, for instance, or government, can be seen as an evil spell woven by sorcerers. It is hard for her people to believe magic.

The ship kept asking if we were all right, and every now and then a Stabile would hook up the ansible to our radio and grill Mother and us. She always convinced them that she wanted to stay, for despite her frustrations, she was doing the work the First Observers had not been able to do, and Borny and I were happy as mudfish, all those first years. I think Mother was happy too, once she got used to the slow pace and the indirect way she had to learn things. She was lonely, missing other grown-ups to talk to, and told us that she would have gone crazy without us. If she missed sex she never showed it. I think, though, that her report is not very complete about sexual matters, perhaps because she was troubled by them. I know that when we first lived in the auntring, two of the aunts, Hedimi and Behyu, used to meet to make love, and Behyu courted my mother; but Mother didn't understand, because Behyu wouldn't talk the way Mother wanted to talk. She couldn't understand having sex with a person whose house you wouldn't enter.

Once when I was nine or so, and had been listening to some of the older girls, I asked her why didn't she go out scouting. "Aunt Sadne would look after us," I said hopefully. I was tired of being the uneducated woman's daughter. I wanted to live in Aunt Sadne's house and be just like the other children.

"Mothers don't scout," she said, scornfully, like an aunt.

"Yes, they do, sometimes," I insisted. "They have to, or how could they have more than one baby?"

"They go to settled men near the auntring. Behyu went back to the Red Knob Hill Man when she wanted a second child. Sadne goes and sees Downriver Lame Man when she wants to have sex. They know the men around here. None of the mothers scout."

I realised that in this case she was right and I was wrong, but I stuck to my point. "Well, why don't you go see Downriver Lame Man? Don't you ever want sex? Migi says she wants it all the time."

"Migi is seventeen," Mother said drily. "Mind your own nose." She sounded exactly like all the other mothers.

Men, during my childhood, were a kind of uninteresting mystery to me. They turned up a lot in the Before Time stories, and the singing-circle girls talked about them; but I seldom saw any of them. Sometimes I'd glimpse one when I was foraging, but they never came near the auntring. In summer the Downriver Lame Man would get lonesome waiting for Aunt Sadne and would come lurking around, not very far from the auntring — not in the bush or down by the river, of course, where he might be mistaken for a rogue and stoned — but out in the open, on the hillsides, where we could all see who he was. Hyuru and Didsu, Aunt Sadne's daughters, said she had had sex with him when she went out scouting the first time, and always had sex with him and never tried any of the other men of the settlement.

She had told them, too, that the first child she bore was a boy, and she drowned it, because she didn't want to bring up a boy and send him away. They felt queer about that and so did I, but it wasn't an uncommon thing. One of the stories we learned was about a drowned boy who grew up underwater, and seized his mother when she came to bathe, and tried to hold her under till she too drowned; but she escaped.

At any rate, after the Downriver Lame Man had sat around for several days on the hillsides, singing long songs and braiding and unbraiding his hair, which was long too, and shone black in the sun, Aunt Sadne always went off for a night or two with him, and came back looking cross and self-conscious.

Aunt Noyit explained to me that Downriver Lame Man's songs

were magic; not the usual bad magic, but what she called the great good spells. Aunt Sadne never could resist his spells. "But he hasn't half the charm of some men I've known," said Aunt Noyit, smiling reminiscently.

Our diet, though excellent, was very low in fat, which Mother thought might explain the rather late onset of puberty; girls seldom menstruated before they were fifteen, and boys often weren't mature till they were considerably older than that. But the women began looking askance at boys as soon as they showed any signs at all of adolescence. First Aunt Hedimi, who was always grim, then Aunt Noyit, then even Aunt Sadne began to turn away from Borny, to leave him out, not answering when he spoke. "What are you doing playing with the children?" old Aunt Dnemi asked him so fiercely that he came home in tears. He was not quite fourteen.

Sadne's younger daughter Hyuru was my soulmate, my best friend, you would say. Her elder sister Didsu, who was in the singing-circle now, came and talked to me one day, looking serious. "Borny is very handsome," she said. I agreed proudly.

"Very big, very strong," she said, "stronger than I am."

I agreed proudly again, and then I began to back away from her.

"I'm not doing magic, Ren," she said.

"Yes you are," I said. "I'll tell your mother!"

Didsu shook her head. "I'm trying to speak truly. If my fear causes your fear, I can't help it. It has to be so. We talked about it in the singing-circle. I don't like it, " she said, and I knew she meant it; she had a soft face, soft eyes, she had always been the gentlest of us children. "I wish he could be a child," she said. "I wish I could. But we can't."

"Go be a stupid old woman, then," I said, and ran away from her. I went to my secret place down by the river and cried. I took the holies out of my soulbag and arranged them. One holy — it doesn't matter if I tell you — was a crystal that Borny had given me, clear at the top, cloudy purple at the base. I held it a long time and then I gave it back. I dug a hole under a boulder, and wrapped the holy in duhur leaves inside a square of cloth I tore out of my kilt, beautiful, fine cloth Hyuru had woven and sewn for me. I tore the square right from the front, where it would show. I gave the crystal back, and then sat a long time there near it. When I went home I said nothing of what Didsu had said. But Borny was very silent, and my mother had a worried look. "What have you done to your kilt, Ren?" she asked. I raised my head a little and did not answer; she started to speak again, and then did not. She had finally learned not to talk to a person who chose to be silent.

Borny didn't have a soulmate, but he had been playing more and more often with the two boys nearest his age, Ednede who was a year or two older, a slight, quiet boy, and Bit who was only eleven, but boisterous and reckless. The three of them went off somewhere all the time. I hadn't paid much attention, partly because I was glad to be rid of Bit. Hyuru and I had been practising being aware, and it was tiresome to always have to be aware of Bit yelling and jumping around. He never could leave anyone quiet, as if their quietness took something from him. His mother, Hedimi, had educated him, but she wasn't a good singer or storyteller like Sadne and Noyit, and Bit was too restless to listen even to them. Whenever he saw me and Hyuru trying to slow-walk or sitting being aware, he hung around making noise till we got mad and told him to go, and then he jeered, "Dumb girls!"

I asked Borny what he and Bit and Ednede did, and he said, "Boy stuff."

"Like what?"

"Practising."

"Being aware?"

After a while he said, "No."

"Practising what, then?"

"Wrestling. Getting strong. For the boygroup." He looked gloomy, but after a while he said, "Look," and showed me a knife he had hidden under his mattress. "Ednede says you have to have a knife, then nobody will challenge you. Isn't it a beauty?" It was metal, old metal from the People, shaped like a reed, pounded out and sharpened down both edges, with a sharp point. A piece of polished flintshrub wood had been bored and fitted on the handle to protect the hand. "I found it in an empty man's-house," he said. "I made the wooden part." He brooded over it lovingly. Yet he did not keep it in his soulbag.

"What do you *do* with it?" I asked, wondering why both edges were sharp, so you'd cut your hand if you used it.

"Keep off attackers," he said.

"Where was the empty man's-house?"

"Way over across Rocky Top."

"Can I go with you if you go back?"

"No," he said, not unkindly, but absolutely.

"What happened to the man? Did he die?"

"There was a skull in the creek. We think he slipped and drowned."

He didn't sound quite like Borny. There was something in his voice like a grown-up; melancholy; reserved. I had gone to him for reassurance, but came away more deeply anxious. I went to Mother and asked her, "What do they do in the boygroups?"

"Perform natural selection," she said, not in my language but in hers, in a strained tone. I didn't always understand Hainish any more and had no idea what she meant, but the tone of her voice upset me; and to my horror I saw she had begun to cry silently. "We have to move, Serenity," she said — she was still talking Hainish without realising it. "There isn't any reason why a family can't move, is there? Women just move in and move out as they please. Nobody cares what anybody does. Nothing is anybody's business. Except hounding the boys out of town!"

I understood most of what she said, but got her to say it in my language; and then I said, "But anywhere we went, Borny would be the same age, and size, and everything."

"Then we'll leave," she said fiercely. "Go back to the ship."

I drew away from her. I had never been afraid of her before: she had never used magic on me. A mother has great power, but there is nothing unnatural in it, unless it is used against the child's soul.

Borny had no fear of her. He had his own magic. When she told him she intended leaving, he persuaded her out of it. He wanted to go join the boygroup, he said; he'd been wanting to for a year now. He didn't belong in the auntring any more, all women and girls and little kids. He wanted to go live with other boys. Bit's older brother Yit was a member of the boygroup in the Four Rivers Territory, and would look after a boy from his auntring. And Ednede was getting ready to go. And Borny and Ednede and Bit had been talking to some men, recently. Men weren't all ignorant and crazy, the way Mother thought. They didn't talk much, but they knew a lot.

"What do they know?" Mother asked grimly.

"They know how to be men," Borny said. "It's what I'm going to be."

"Not that kind of man — not if I can help it! In Joy Born, you must remember the men on the ship, real men — nothing like these poor, filthy hermits. I can't let you grow up thinking that that's what you have to be!"

"They're not like that," Borny said. "You ought to go talk to some of them, Mother."

"Don't be naive," she said with an edgy laugh. "You know perfectly well that women don't go to men to *talk*."

I knew she was wrong; all the women in the auntring knew all the settled men for three days' walk around. They did talk with them, when they were out foraging. They only kept away from the ones they didn't trust; and usually those men disappeared before long. Noyit had told me, "Their magic turns on them." She meant the other men drove them away or killed them. But I didn't say any of this, and Borny said only, "Well, Cave Cliff Man is really nice. And he took us to the place where I found those People things" — some ancient artifacts that Mother had been excited about. "The men know things the women don't," Borny went on. "At least I could go to the boygroup for a while, maybe. I ought to. I could learn a lot! We don't have any solid information on them at all. All we know anything about is this auntring. I'll go and stay long enough to get material for our report. I can't ever come back to either the auntring or the boygroup once I leave them. I'll have to go to the ship, or else try to be a man. So let me have a real go at it, please, Mother?"

"I don't know why you think you have to learn how to be a man," she said after a while. "You know how already."

He really smiled then, and she put her arm around him.

What about me? I thought. I don't even know what the ship is. I want to be here, where my soul is. I want to go on learning to be in the world.

But I was afraid of Mother and Borny, who were both working magic, and so I said nothing and was still, as I had been taught.

Ednede and Borny went off together. Noyit, Ednede's mother, was as glad as Mother was about their keeping company, though she said nothing. The evening before they left, the two boys went to every house in the auntring. It took a long time. The houses were each just within sight or hearing of one or two of the others, with bush and gardens and irrigation ditches and paths in between. In each house the mother and the children were waiting to say good-bye, only they didn't say it; my language has no word for hello or goodbye. They asked the boys in and gave them something to eat, something they could take with them on the way to the Territory. When the boys went to the door everybody in the household came and touched their hand or cheek. I remembered when Yit had gone around the auntring that way. I had cried then, because even though I didn't much like Yit, it seemed so strange for somebody to leave forever, like they were dying. This time I didn't cry; but I kept waking and waking again, until I heard Borny get up before the first light and pick up his things and leave quietly. I know Mother was awake too, but we did as we should do, and lay still while he left, and for a long time after.

I have read her description of what she calls "An Adolescent Male leaves the Auntring: a Vestigial Survival of Ceremony."

She had wanted him to put a radio in his soulbag and get in touch with her at least occasionally. He had been unwilling. "I want to do it right, Mother. There's no use doing it if I don't do it right."

"I simply can't handle not hearing from you at all, Borny," she had said in Hainish.

"But if the radio got broken or taken or something, you'd worry a lot more, maybe with no reason at all."

She finally agreed to wait half a year, till the first rain; then she would go to a landmark, a huge ruin near the river that marked the southern end of the Territory, and he would try and come to her there. "But only wait ten days," he said. "If I can't come, I can't." She agreed. She was like a mother with a little baby, I thought, saying yes to everything. That seemed wrong to me; but I thought Borny was right. Nobody ever came back to their mother from boygroup.

But Borny did.

Summer was long, clear, beautiful. I was learning to starwatch; that is when you lie down outside on the open hills in the dry season at night, and find a certain star in the eastern sky, and watch it cross the sky till it sets. You can look away, of course, to rest your eyes, and doze, but you try to keep looking back at the star and the stars around it, until you feel the earth turning, until you become aware of how the stars and the world and the soul move together. After the certain star sets you sleep until dawn wakes you. Then as always you greet the sunrise with aware silence. I was very happy on the hills those warm great nights, those clear dawns. The first time or two Hyuru and I starwatched together, but after that we went alone, and it was better alone.

I was coming back from such a night, along the narrow valley between Rocky Top and Over Home Hill in the first sunlight, when a man came crashing through the bush down onto the path and stood in front of me. "Don't be afraid," he said. "Listen!" He was heavyset, half-naked; he stank. I stood still as a stick. He had said "Listen!" just as the aunts did, and I listened. "Your brother and his friend are all right. Your mother shouldn't go there. Some of the boys are in a gang. They'd rape her. I and some others are killing the leaders. It takes a while. Your brother is with the other gang. He's all right. Tell her. Tell me what I said."

I repeated it word for word, as I had learned to do when I listened.

"Right. Good," he said, and took off up the steep slope on his short, powerful legs, and was gone.

Mother would have gone to the Territory right then, but I told the man's message to Noyit, too, and she came to the porch of our house to speak to Mother. I listened to her, because she was telling things I didn't know well and Mother didn't know at all. Noyit was a small, mild woman, very like her son Ednede; she liked teaching and singing, so the children were always around her place. She saw Mother was getting ready for a journey. She said, "House on the Skyline Man says the boys are all right." When she saw Mother wasn't listening, she went on; she pretended to be talking to me, because women don't teach women: "He says some of the men are breaking up the gang. They do that, when the boygroups get wicked. Sometimes there are magicians among them, leaders, older boys, even men who want to make a gang. The settled men will kill the magicians and make sure none of the boys gets hurt. When gangs come out of the Territories, nobody is safe. The settled men don't like that. They see to it that the auntring is safe. So your brother will be all right."

My mother went on packing pigi-roots into her net.

"A rape is a very, very bad thing for the settled men," said Noyit to me. "It means the women won't come to them. If the boys raped some woman, probably the men would kill *all* the boys."

My mother was finally listening.

She did not go to the rendezvous with Borny, but all through the rainy season she was utterly miserable. She got sick, and old Dnemi sent Didsu over to dose her with gagberry syrup. She made notes while she was sick, lying on her mattress, about illnesses and medicines and how the older girls had to look after sick women, since grown women did not enter one another's houses. She never stopped working and never stopped worrying about Borny.

Late in the rainy season, when the warm wind had come and the yellow honey-flowers were in bloom on all the hills, the Golden World time, Noyit came by while Mother was working in the garden. "House on the Skyline Man says things are all right in the boy-group," she said, and went on.

Mother began to realise then that although no adult ever entered another's house, and adults seldom spoke to one another, and men and women had only brief, often casual relationships, and men lived all their lives in real solitude, still there was a kind of community, a wide, thin, fine network of delicate and certain intention and restraint: a social order. Her reports to the ship were filled with this new understanding. But she still found Sorovian life impoverished, seeing these persons as mere survivors, poor fragments of the wreck of something great.

"My dear," she said, in Hainish; there is no way to say "my dear" in my language. She was speaking Hainish with me in the house so that I wouldn't forget it entirely. "My dear, the explanation of an uncomprehended technology as magic *is* primitivism. It's not a criticism, merely a description."

"But technology isn't magic," I said.

"Yes, it is, in their minds; look at the story you just recorded. Before-Time sorcerers who could fly in the air and undersea and underground in magic boxes!"

"In *metal* boxes," I corrected.

"In other words, airplanes, tunnels, submarines; a lost technology explained as supernatural."

"The *boxes* weren't magic," I said. "The *people* were. They were sorcerers. They used their power to get power over other persons. To live rightly a person has to keep away from magic."

"That's a cultural imperative, because a few thousand years ago uncontrolled technological expansion led to disaster. Exactly. There's a perfectly rational reason for the irrational taboo."

I did not know what "rational" and "irrational" meant in my language; I could not find words for them. "Taboo" was the same as "poisonous." I listened to my mother because a daughter must learn from her mother, and my mother knew many, many things no other person knew; but my education was very difficult, sometimes. If only there were more stories and songs in her teaching, and not so many words, words that slipped away from me like water through a net!

The Golden Time passed, and the beautiful summer; the Silver Time returned, when the mists lie in the valleys between the hills, before the rains begin; and the rains began, and fell long and slow and warm, day after day after day. We had heard nothing of Borny and Ednede for over a year. Then in the night the soft thrum of rain on the reed roof turned into a scratching at the door and a whisper, "Shh — it's all right — it's all right."

We wakened the fire and crouched at it in the dark to talk. Borny had got tall and very thin, like a skeleton with the skin dried on it. A cut across his upper lip had drawn it up into a kind of snarl that bared his teeth, and he could not say *p, b,* or *m*. His voice was a man's voice. He huddled at the fire trying to get warmth into his bones. His clothes were wet rags. The knife hung on a cord around his neck. "It was all right," he kept saying. "I don't want to go on there, though."

He would not tell us much about the year and a half in the boy-group, insisting that he would record a full description when he got to the ship. He did tell us what he would have to do if he stayed on Soro. He would have to go back to the Territory and hold his own among the older boys, by fear and sorcery, always proving his strength, until he was old enough to walk away — that is, to leave the Territory and wander alone till he found a place where the men would let him settle. Ednede and another boy had paired, and were going to walk away together when the rains stopped. It was easier for a pair, he said, if their bond was sexual; so long as they offered no competition for women, settled men wouldn't challenge them. But a new man in the region anywhere within three days' walk of an auntring had to prove himself against the settled men there. "It would 'e three or four years of the sa'e thing," he said, "challenging, fighting, always watching the others, on guard, showing how strong you are, staying alert all night, all day. To go on living alone your whole life. I can't do it." He looked at me. "I'ne not a 'erson," he said. "I want to go ho'e."

"I'll radio the ship now," Mother said quietly, with infinite relief.

"No," I said.

Borny was watching Mother, and raised his hand when she turned to speak to me.

"I'll go," he said. "She doesn't have to. Why should she?" Like me, he had learned not to use names without some reason to.

Mother looked from him to me and finally gave a kind of laugh. "I can't leave her here, Borny!"

"Why should you go?"

"Because I want to," she said. "I've had enough. More than enough. We've got a tremendous amount of material on the women, over seven years of it, and now you can fill the information gaps on the men's side. That's enough. It's time, past time, that we all got back to our own people. All of us."

"I have no people," I said. "I don't belong to people. I am trying to be a person. Why do you want to take me away from my soul? You want me to do magic! I won't. I won't do magic. I won't speak your language. I won't go with you!"

My mother was still not listening; she started to answer angrily.

Borny put up his hand again, the way a woman does when she is going to sing, and she looked at him.

"We can talk later," he said. "We can decide. I need to slee'."

He hid in our house for two days while we decided what to do and how to do it. That was a miserable time. I stayed home as if I were sick so that I would not lie to the other persons, and Borny and Mother and I talked and talked. Borny asked Mother to stay with me; I asked her to leave me with Sadne or Noyit, either of whom would certainly take me into their household. She refused. She was the mother and I the child and her power was sacred. She radioed the ship and arranged for a lander to pick us up in a barren area two days' walk from the auntring. We left at night, sneaking away. I carried nothing but my soulbag. We walked all next day, slept a little when it stopped raining, walked on and came to the desert. The ground was all lumps and hollows and caves, Before-Time ruins; the soil was tiny bits of glass and hard grains and fragments, the way it is in the deserts. Nothing grew there. We waited there.

The sky broke open and a shining thing fell down and stood before us on the rocks, bigger than any house, though not as big as the ruins of the Before Time. My mother looked at me with a queer, vengeful smile. "Is it magic?" she said. And it was very hard for me not to think that it was. Yet I knew it was only a thing, and there is no magic in things, only in minds. I said nothing. I had not spoken since we left my home.

I had resolved never to speak to anybody until I got home again; but I was still a child, used to listening and obeying. In the ship, that utterly strange new world, I held out only for a few hours, and then began to cry and ask to go home. Please, please, can I go home now.

Everyone on the ship was very kind to me.

Even then I thought about what Borny had been through and what I was going through, comparing our ordeals. The difference seemed total. He had been alone, without food, without shelter, a frightened boy trying to survive among equally frightened rivals against the brutality of older youths intent on having and keeping power, which they saw as manhood. I was cared for, clothed, fed so richly I got sick, kept so warm I felt feverish, guided, reasoned with, praised, befriended by citizens of a very great city, offered a share in their power, which they saw as humanity. He and I had both fallen among sorcerers. Both he and I could see the good in the people we were among, but neither he nor I could live with them.

Borny told me he had spent many desolate nights in the Territory crouched in a fireless shelter, telling over the stories he had learned from the aunts, singing the songs in his head. I did the same thing every night on the ship. But I refused to tell the stories or sing to the people there. I would not speak my language, there. It was the only way I had to be silent.

My mother was enraged, and for a long time unforgiving. "You owe your knowledge to our people," she said. I did not answer, because all I had to say was that they were not my people, that I had no people. I was a person. I had a language that I did not speak. I had my silence. I had nothing else.

I went to school; there were children of different ages on the ship, like an auntring, and many of the adults taught us. I learned Ekumenical history and geography, mostly, and Mother gave me a report to learn about the history of Eleven-Soro, what my language calls the Before Time. I read that the cities of my world had been the greatest cities ever built on any world, covering two of the continents entirely, with small areas set aside for farming; there had been 120 billion people living in the cities, while the animals and the sea and the air and the dirt died, until the people began dying too. It was a hideous story. I was ashamed of it and wished nobody else on the ship or in the Ekumen knew about it. And yet, I thought, if they knew the stories I knew about the Before Time, they would understand how magic turns on itself, and that it must be so.

After less than a year, Mother told us we were going to Hain. The ship's doctor and his clever machines had repaired Borny's lip; he and Mother had put all the information they had into the records; he was old enough to begin training for the Ekumenical Schools, as he wanted to do. I was not flourishing, and the doctor's machines were not able to repair me. I kept losing weight, I slept badly, I had terrible headaches. Almost as soon as we came aboard the ship, I had begun to menstruate; each time the cramps were agonizing. "This is no good, this ship life," Mother said. "You need to be outdoors. On a planet. On a civilised planet."

"If I went to Hain," I said, "when I came back, the persons I know would all be dead hundreds of years ago."

"Serenity," she said, "you must stop thinking in terms of Soro. We have left Soro. You must stop deluding and tormenting yourself, and look forward, not back. Your whole life is ahead of you. Hain is where you will learn to live it."

I summoned up my courage and spoke in my own language: "I am not a child now. You have no power over me. I will not go. Go without me. You have no power over me!"

Those are the words I had been taught to say to a magician, a sorcerer. I don't know if my mother fully understood them, but she did understand that I was deathly afraid of her, and it struck her into silence.

After a long time she said in Hainish, "I agree. I have no power over you. But I have certain rights; the right of loyalty; of love."

"Nothing is right that puts me in your power," I said, still in my language.

She stared at me. "You are like one of them," she said. "You are one of them. You don't know what love is. You're closed into yourself like a rock. I should never have taken you there. People crouching in the ruins of a society — brutal, rigid, ignorant, superstitious — each one in a terrible solitude — and I let them make you into one of them!"

"You educated me," I said, and my voice began to tremble and my mouth to shake around the words, "and so does the school here, but my aunts educated me, and I want to finish my education." I was weeping, but I kept standing with my hands clenched. "I'm not a woman yet. I want to be a woman."

"But Ren, you will be! — ten times the woman you could ever be on Soro — you must try to understand, to believe me — "

"You have no power over me," I said, shutting my eyes and putting my hands over my ears. She came to me then and held me, but I stood stiff, enduring her touch, until she let me go.

The ship's crew had changed entirely while we were on-planet. The First Observers had gone on to other worlds; our backup was now a Gethenian archeologist named Arrem, a mild, watchful person, not young. Arrem had gone down on-planet only on the two desert continents, and welcomed the chance to talk with us, who had "lived with the living," as heshe said. I felt easy when I was with Arrem, who was so unlike anybody else. Arrem was not a man — I could not get used to having men around all the time — yet not a woman; and so not exactly an adult, yet not a child: a person, alone, like me. Heshe did not know my language well, but always tried to talk it with me. When this crisis came, Arrem came to my mother and took counsel with her, suggesting that she let me go back down on-planet. Borny was in on some of these talks, and told me about them.

"Arrem says if you go to Hain you'll probably die," he said. "Your soul will. Heshe says some of what we learned is like what they learn on Gethen, in their religion. That kind of stopped Mother from ranting about primitive superstition. . . . And Arrem says you could be useful to the Ekumen, if you stay and finish your education on Soro. You'll be an invaluable resource." Borny sniggered, and after a minute I did too. "They'll mine you like an asteroid," he said. Then he said, "You know, if you stay and I go, we'll be dead."

That was how the young people of the ships said it, when one was going to cross the lightyears and the other was going to stay. Goodbye, we're dead. It was the truth.

"I know," I said. I felt my throat get tight, and was afraid. I had never seen an adult at home cry, except when Sut's baby died. Sut howled all night. Howled like a dog, Mother said, but I had never seen or heard a dog; I heard a woman terribly crying. I was afraid of sounding like that. "If I can go home, when I finish making my soul, who knows, I might come to Hain for a while," I said, in Hainish.

"Scouting?" Borny said in my language, and laughed, and made me laugh again.

Nobody gets to keep a brother. I knew that. But Borny had come back from being dead to me, so I might come back from being dead to him; at least I could pretend I might.

My mother came to a decision. She and I would stay on the ship for another year while Borny went to Hain. I would keep going to school; if at the end of the year I was still determined to go back on-planet, I could do so. With me or without me, she would go on to Hain then and join Borny. If I ever wanted to see them again, I could follow them. It was a compromise that satisfied no one, but it was the best we could do, and we all consented.

When he left, Borny gave me his knife.

After he left, I tried not to be sick. I worked hard at learning everything they taught me in the ship school, and I tried to teach Arrem how to be aware and how to avoid witchcraft. We did slow walking together in the ship's garden, and the first hour of the Untrance movements from the Handdara of Karhide on Gethen. We agreed that they were alike.

The ship was staying in the Soro system not only because of my family, but because the crew was now mostly zoologists who had come to study a sea animal on Eleven-Soro, a kind of cephalopod that had mutated towards high intelligence, or maybe it already was highly intelligent; but there was a communication problem. "Almost as bad as with the local humans," said Steadiness, the zoologist who taught and teased us mercilessly. She took us down twice by lander to the uninhabited islands in the Northern Hemisphere where her station was. It was very strange to go down to my world and yet be a world away from my aunts and sisters and my soulmate; but I said nothing.

I saw the great, pale, shy creature come slowly up out of the deep waters with a running ripple of colors along its long coiling tentacles and a ringing shimmer of sound, all so quick it was over before you could follow the colors or hear the tune. The zoologist's machine produced a pink glow and a mechanically speeded-up twitter, tinny and feeble in the immensity of the sea. The cephalopod patiently responded in its beautiful silvery shadowy language. "CP," Steadiness said to us, ironic — Communication Problem. "We don't know what we're talking about."

I said, "I learned something in my education here. In one of the songs, it says," and I hesitated, trying to translate it into Hainish, "it says, thinking is one way of doing, and words are one way of thinking."

Steadiness stared at me, in disapproval I thought, but probably only because I had never said anything to her before except "Yes." Finally she said, "Are you suggesting that it doesn't speak in words?"

"Maybe it's not speaking at all. Maybe it's thinking."

Steadiness stared at me some more and then said, "Thank you." She looked as if she too might be thinking. I wished I could sink into the water, the way the cephalopod was doing.

The other young people on the ship were friendly and mannerly. Those are words that have no translation in my language. I was unfriendly and unmannerly, and they let me be. I was grateful. But there was no place to be alone on the ship. Of course we each had a room; though small, the *Heyho* was a Hainish-built explorer, designed to give its people room and privacy and comfort and variety and beauty while they hung around in a solar system for years on end. But it was designed. It was all human-made — everything was human. I had much more privacy than I had ever had at home in our one-room house; yet there I had been free and here I was in a trap. I felt the pressure of people all around me, all the time. People around me, people with me, people pressing on me, pressing me to be one of them, to be one of them, one of the people. How could I make my soul? I could barely cling to it. I was in terror that I would lose it altogether.

One of the rocks in my soulbag, a little ugly grey rock that I had picked up on a certain day in a certain place in the hills above the river in the Silver Time, a little piece of my world, that became my world. Every night I took it out and held it in my hand while I lay in bed waiting to sleep, thinking of the sunlight on the hills above the river, listening to the soft hushing of the ship's systems, like a mechanical sea.

The doctor hopefully fed me various tonics. Mother and I ate breakfast together every morning. She kept at work, making our notes from all the years on Eleven-Soro into her report to the Ekumen, but I knew the work did not go well. Her soul was in as much danger as mine was.

"You will never give in, will you, Ren?" she said to me one morning out of the silence of our breakfast. I had not intended the silence as a message. I had only rested in it.

"Mother, I want to go home and you want to go home," I said. "Can't we?"

Her expression was strange for a moment, while she misunderstood me; then it cleared to grief, defeat, relief.

"Will we be dead?" she asked me, her mouth twisting.

"I don't know. I have to make my soul. Then I can know if I can come."

"You know I can't come back. It's up to you."

"I know. Go see Borny," I said. "Go home. Here we're both dying." Then noises began to come out of me, sobbing, howling. Mother was crying. She came to me and held me, and I could hold my mother, cling to her and cry with her, because her spell was broken.

From the lander approaching I saw the oceans of Eleven-Soro, and in the greatness of my joy I thought that when I was grown and went out alone I would go to the sea shore and watch the sea-beasts shimmering their colors and tunes till I knew what they were thinking. I would listen, I would learn, till my soul was as large as the shining world. The scarred barrens whirled beneath us, ruins as wide as the continent, endless desolations. We touched down. I had my soulbag, and Borny's knife around my neck on its string, a communicator implant behind my right earlobe, and a medicine kit Mother had made for me. "No use dying of an infected finger, after all," she had said. The people on the lander said goodbye, but I forgot to. I set off out of the desert, home.

It was summer; the night was short and warm; I walked most of it. I got to the auntring about the middle of the second day. I went to my house cautiously, in case somebody had moved in while I was gone; but it was just as we had left it. The mattresses were moldy, and I put them and the bedding out in the sun, and started going over the garden to see what had kept growing by itself. The pigi had got small and seedy, but there were some good roots. A little boy came by and stared; he had to be Migi's baby. After a while Hyuru came by. She squatted down near me in the garden in the sunshine. I smiled when I saw her, and she smiled, but it took us a while to find something to say.

"Your mother didn't come back," she said.

"She's dead," I said.

"I'm sorry," Hyuru said.

She watched me dig up another root.

"Will you come to the singing circle?" she asked.

I nodded.

She smiled again. With her rose-brown skin and wide-set eyes, Hyuru had become very beautiful, but her smile was exactly the same as when we were little girls. "Hi, ya!" she sighed in deep contentment, lying down on the dirt with her chin on her arms. "This is good!"

I went on blissfully digging.

That year and the next two, I was in the singing circle with Hyuru and two other girls. Didsu still came to it often, and Han, a woman who settled in our auntring to have her first baby, joined it too. In the singing circle the older girls pass around the stories, songs, knowledge they learned from their own mother, and young women who have lived in other auntrings teach what they learned there; so women make each other's souls, learning how to make their children's souls.

Han lived in the house where old Dnemi had died. Nobody in the auntring except Sut's baby had died while my family lived there. My mother had complained that she didn't have any data on death and burial. Sut had gone away with her dead baby and never came back, and nobody talked about it. I think that turned my mother against the others more than anything else. She was angry and ashamed that she could not go and try to comfort Sut and that nobody else did. "It is not human," she said. "It is pure animal behavior. Nothing could be clearer evidence that this is a broken culture — not a society, but the remains of one. A terrible, an appalling poverty."

I don't know if Dnemi's death would have changed her mind. Dnemi was dying for a long time, of kidney failure I think; she turned a kind of dark orange color, jaundice. While she could get around, nobody helped her. When she didn't come out of her house for a day or two, the women would send the children in with water and a little food and firewood. It went on so through the winter; then one morning little Rashi told his mother Aunt Dnemi was "staring." Several of the women went to Dnemi's house, and entered it for the first and last time. They sent for all the girls in the singing circle, so that we could learn what to do. We took turns sitting by the body or in the porch of the house, singing soft songs, child-songs, giving the soul a day and a night to leave the body and the house; then the older women wrapped the body in the bedding, strapped it on a kind of litter, and set off with it towards the barren lands. There it would be given back, under a rock cairn or inside one of the ruins of the ancient city. "Those are the lands of the dead," Sadne said. "What dies stays there."

Han settled down in that house a year later. When her baby began to be born she asked Didsu to help her, and Hyuru and I stayed in the porch and watched, so that we could learn. It was a wonderful thing to see, and quite altered the course of my thinking, and Hyuru's too. Hyuru said, "I'd like to do that!" I said nothing, but thought, So do I, but not for a long time, because once you have a child you're never alone.

And though it is of the others, of relationships, that I write, the heart of my life has been my being alone.

I think there is no way to write about being alone. To write is to tell something to somebody, to communicate to others. CP, as Steadiness would say. Solitude is noncommunication, the absence of others, the presence of a self sufficient to itself.

A woman's solitude in the auntring is, of course, based firmly on the presence of others at a little distance. It is a contingent, and therefore human, solitude. The settled men are connected as stringently to the women, though not to one another; the settlement is an integral though distant element of the auntring. Even a scouting woman is part of the society — a moving part, connecting the settled parts. Only the isolation of a woman or man who chooses to live outside the settlements is absolute. They are outside the network altogether. There are worlds where such persons are called saints, holy people. Since isolation is a sure way to prevent magic, on my world the assumption is that they are sorcerers, outcast by others or by their own will, their conscience.

I knew I was strong with magic, how could I help it? and I began to long to get away. It would be so much easier and safer to be alone. But at the same time, and increasingly, I wanted to know something about the great harmless magic, the spells cast between men and women.

I preferred foraging to gardening, and was out on the hills a good deal; and these days, instead of keeping away from the man's-houses, I wandered by them, and looked at them, and looked at the men if they were outside. The men looked back. Downriver Lame Man's long, shining hair was getting a little white in it now, but when he sat singing his long, long songs I found myself sitting down and listening, as if my legs had lost their bones. He was very handsome. So was the man I remembered as a boy named Tret in the auntring, when I was little, Behyu's son. He had come back from the boygroup and from wandering, and had built a house and made a fine garden in the valley of Red Stone Creek. He had a big nose and big eyes, long arms and legs, long hands; he moved very quietly, almost like Arrem doing the Untrance. I went often to pick lowberries in Red Stone Creek valley.

He came along the path and spoke. "You were Borny's sister," he said. He had a low voice, quiet.

"He's dead," I said.

Red Stone Man nodded. "That's his knife."

In my world, I had never talked with a man. I felt extremely strange. I kept picking berries.

"You're picking green ones," Red Stone Man said.

His soft, smiling voice made my legs lose their bones again.

"I think nobody's touched you," he said. "I'd touch you gently. I think about it, about you, ever since you came by here early in the summer. Look, here's a bush full of ripe ones. Those are green. Come over here."

I came closer to him, to the bush of ripe berries.

When I was on the ship, Arrem told me that many languages have a single word for sexual desire and the bond between mother and child and the bond between soulmates and the feeling for one's home and worship of the sacred; they are all called love. There is no word that great in my language. Maybe my mother is right, and human greatness perished in my world with the people of the

Before Time, leaving only small, poor, broken things and thoughts. In my language, love is many different words. I learned one of them with Red Stone Man. We sang it together to each other.

We made a brush house on a little cove of the creek, and neglected our gardens, but gathered many, many sweet berries.

Mother had put a lifetime's worth of nonconceptives in the little medicine kit. She had no faith in Sorovian herbals. I did, and they worked.

But when a year or so later, in the Golden Time, I decided to go out scouting, I thought I might go places where the right herbs were scarce; and so I stuck the little noncon jewel on the back of my left earlobe. Then I wished I hadn't, because it seemed like witchcraft. Then I told myself I was being superstitious; the noncon wasn't any more witchcraft than the herbs were, it just worked longer. I had promised my mother in my soul that I would never be superstitious. The skin grew over the noncon, and I took my soulbag and Borny's knife and the medicine kit, and set off across the world.

I had told Hyuru and Red Stone Man I would be leaving. Hyuru and I sang and talked together all one night down by the river. Red Stone Man said in his soft voice, "Why do you want to go?" and I said, "To get away from your magic, sorcerer," which was true in part. If I kept going to him I might always go to him. I wanted to give my soul and body a larger world to be in.

Now to tell of my scouting years is more difficult than ever. CP! A woman scouting is entirely alone, unless she chooses to ask a settled man for sex, or camps in an auntring for a while to sing and listen with the singing circle. If she goes anywhere near the territory of a boygroup, she is in danger; and if she comes on a rogue she is in danger; and if she hurts herself or gets into polluted country, she is in danger. She has no responsibility except to herself, and so much freedom is very dangerous.

In my right earlobe was the tiny communicator; every forty days, as I had promised, I sent a signal to the ship that meant "all well." If

I wanted to leave, I would send another signal. I could have called for the lander to rescue me from a bad situation, but though I was in bad situations a couple of times I never thought of using it. My signal was the mere fulfilment of a promise to my mother and her people, the network I was no longer part of, a meaningless communication.

Life in the auntring, or for a settled man, is repetitive, as I said; and so it can be dull. Nothing new happens. The mind always wants new happenings. So for the young soul there is wandering and scouting, travel, danger, change. But of course travel and danger and change have their own dullness. It is finally always the same otherness over again; another hill, another river, another man, another day. The feet begin to turn in a long, long circle. The body begins to think of what it learned back home, when it learned to be still. To be aware. To be aware of the grain of dust beneath the sole of the foot, and the skin of the sole of the foot, and the touch and scent of the air on the cheek, and the fall and motion of the light across the air, and the color of the grass on the high hill across the river, and the thoughts of the body, of the soul, the shimmer and ripple of colors and sounds in the clear darkness of the depths, endlessly moving, endlessly changing, endlessly new.

So at last I came back home. I had been gone about four years.

Hyuru had moved into my old house when she left her mother's house. She had not gone scouting, but had taken to going to Red Stone Creek valley; and she was pregnant. I was glad to see her living there. The only house empty was an old half-ruined one too close to Hedimi's. I decided to make a new house. I dug out the circle as deep as my chest; the digging took most of the summer. I cut the sticks, braced and wove them, and then daubed the framework solidly with mud inside and out. I remembered when I had done that with my mother long, long ago, and how she had said, "That's right. That's good." I left the roof open, and the hot sun of late summer baked the mud into clay. Before the rains came, I thatched the house with reeds, a triple thatching, for I'd had enough of being wet all winter.

My auntring was more a string than a ring, stretching along the north bank of the river for about three kilos; my house lengthened the string a good bit, upstream from all the others. I could just see the smoke from Hyuru's fireplace. I dug the house into a sunny slope with good drainage. It is still a good house.

I settled down. Some of my time went to gathering and gardening and mending and all the dull, repetitive actions of primitive life, and some went to singing and thinking the songs and stories I had learned here at home and while scouting, and the things I had learned on the ship, also. Soon enough I found why women are glad to have children come to listen to them, for songs and stories are meant to be heard, listened to. "Listen!" I would say to the children. The children of the auntring came and went, like the little fish in the river, one or two or five of them, little ones, big ones. When they came, I sang or told stories to them. When they left, I went on in silence. Sometimes I joined the singing circle to give what I had learned travelling to the older girls. And that was all I did; except that I worked, always, to be aware of all I did.

By solitude the soul escapes from doing or suffering magic; it escapes from dullness, from boredom, by being aware. Nothing is boring if you are aware of it. It may be irritating, but it is not boring. If it is pleasant the pleasure will not fail so long as you are aware of it. Being aware is the hardest work the soul can do, I think.

I helped Hyuru have her baby, a girl, and played with the baby. Then after a couple of years I took the noncon out of my left earlobe. Since it left a little hole, I made the hole go all the way through with a burnt needle, and when it healed I hung in it a tiny jewel I had found in a ruin when I was scouting. I had seen a man on the ship with a jewel hung in his ear that way. I wore it when I went out foraging. I kept clear of Red Stone Valley. The man there behaved as if he had a claim on me, a right to me. I liked him still, but I did not like that smell of magic about him, his imagination of power over me. I went up into the hills, northward.

A pair of young men had settled in old North House about the time I came home. Often boys got through boygroup by pairing, and often they stayed paired when they left the Territory. It helped their chances of survival. Some of them were sexually paired, others weren't; some stayed paired, others didn't. One of this pair had gone off with another man last summer. The one that stayed wasn't a handsome man, but I had noticed him. He had a kind of solidness I liked. His body and hands were short and strong. I had courted him a little, but he was very shy. This day, a day in the Silver Time when the mist lay on the river, he saw the jewel swinging in my ear, and his eyes widened.

"It's pretty, isn't it?" I said.

He nodded.

"I wore it to make you look at me," I said.

He was so shy that I finally said, "If you only like sex with men, you know, just tell me." I really was not sure.

"Oh, no," he said, "no. No." He stammered and then bolted back down the path. But he looked back; and I followed him slowly, still not certain whether he wanted me or wanted to be rid of me.

He waited for me in front of a little house in a grove of redroot, a lovely little bower, all leaves outside, so that you would walk within arm's length of it and not see it. Inside he had laid sweet grass, deep and dry and soft, smelling of summer. I went in, crawling because the door was very low, and sat in the summer-smelling grass. He stood outside. "Come in," I said, and he came in very slowly.

"I made it for you," he said.

"Now make a child for me," I said.

And we did that; maybe that day, maybe another.

Now I will tell you why after all these years I called the ship, not knowing even if it was still there in the space between the planets, asking for the lander to meet me in the barren land.

When my daughter was born, that was my heart's desire and the fulfilment of my soul. When my son was born, last year, I knew there is no fulfilment. He will grow towards manhood, and go, and fight and endure, and live or die as a man must. My daughter, whose name is Yedneke, Leaf, like my mother, will grow to womanhood and go or stay as she chooses. I will live alone. This is as it should be, and my desire. But I am of two worlds; I am a person of this world, and a woman of my mother's people. I owe my knowledge to the children of her people. So I asked the lander to come, and spoke to the people on it. They gave me my mother's report to read, and I have written my story in their machine, making a record for those who want to learn one of the ways to make a soul. To them, to the children I say: Listen! Avoid magic! Be aware!

Old Music and the Slave Women

The chief intelligence officer of the Ekumenical embassy to Werel, a man who on his home world had the name Sohikelwenyanmurkeres Esdan, and who in Voe Deo was known by a nickname, Esdardon Aya or Old Music, was bored. It had taken a civil war and three years to bore him, but he had got to the point where he referred to himself in ansible reports to the Stabiles on Hain as the embassy's chief stupidity officer.

He had been able, however, to retain a few clandestine links with friends in the Free City even after the Legitimate Government sealed the embassy, allowing no one and no information to enter or leave it. In the third summer of the war, he came to the Ambassador with a request. Cut off from reliable communication with the embassy, Liberation Command had asked him (how? asked the Ambassador; through one of the men who delivered groceries, he explained) if the embassy would let one or two of its people slip across the lines and talk with them, be seen with them, offer proof that despite propaganda and disinformation, and though the embassy was stuck in

Jit City, its staff had not been co-opted into supporting the Legitimates, but remained neutral and ready to deal with rightful authority on either side.

"Jit City?" said the Ambassador. "Never mind. But how do you get there?"

"Always the problem with Utopia," Esdan said. "Well, I can pass with contact lenses, if nobody's looking closely. Crossing the Divide is the tricky bit."

Most of the great city was still physically there, the government buildings, factories and warehouses, the university, the tourist attractions: the Great Shrine of Tual, Theater Street, the Old Market with its interesting display rooms and lofty Hall of Auction, disused since the sale and rental of assets had been shifted to the electronic marketplace; the numberless streets, avenues, and boulevards, the dusty parks shaded by purple-flowered beya trees, the miles and miles of shops, sheds, mills, tracks, stations, apartment buildings, houses, compounds, the neighborhoods, the suburbs, the exurbs. Most of it still stood, most of its fifteen million people were still there, but its deep complexity was gone. Connections were broken. Interactions did not take place. A brain after a stroke.

The greatest break was a brutal one, an axe-blow right through the pons, a kilo-wide no-man's-land of blown-up buildings and blocked streets, wreckage and rubble. East of the Divide was Legitimate territory: downtown, government offices, embassies, banks, communications towers, the university, the great parks and wealthy neighborhoods, the roads out to the armory, barracks, airports, and spaceport. West of the Divide was Free City, Dustyville, Liberation territory: factories, union compounds, the rentspeople's quarters, the old gareot residential neighborhoods, endless miles of little streets petering out into the plains at last. Through both ran the great East–West highways, empty.

The Liberation people successfully smuggled him out of the embassy and almost across the Divide. He and they had had a lot of practice in the old days getting runaway assets out to Yeowe and freedom. He found it interesting to be the one smuggled instead of one of the smugglers, finding it far more frightening yet less stressful, since he was not responsible, the package not the postman. But somewhere in the connection there had been a bad link.

They made it on foot into the Divide and partway through it and stopped at a little derelict truck sitting on its wheel rims under a gutted apartment house. A driver sat at the wheel behind the cracked, crazed windshield, and grinned at him. His guide gestured him into the back. The truck took off like a hunting cat, following a crazy route, zigzagging through the ruins. They were nearly across the Divide, jolting across a rubbled stretch which might have been a street or a marketplace, when the truck veered, stopped, there were shouts, shots, the vanback was flung open and men plunged in at him. "Easy," he said, "go easy," for they were manhandling him, hauling him, twisting his arm behind his back. They yanked him out of the truck, pulled off his coat and slapped him down searching for weapons, frogmarched him to a car waiting beside the truck. He tried to see if his driver was dead but could not look around before they shoved him into the car.

It was an old government state-coach, dark red, wide and long, made for parades, for carrying great estate owners to the Council and ambassadors from the spaceport. Its main section could be curtained to separate men from women passengers, and the driver's compartment was sealed off so the passengers wouldn't be breathing in what a slave breathed out.

One of the men had kept his arm twisted up his back until he shoved him headfirst into the car, and all he thought as he found himself sitting between two men and facing three others and the car starting up was, "I'm getting too old for this."

He held still, letting his fear and pain subside, not ready yet to move even to rub his sharply hurting shoulder, not looking into faces nor too obviously at the streets. Two glances told him they were passing Rei Street, going east, out of the city. He realised then he had been hoping they were taking him back to the embassy. What a fool.

They had the streets to themselves, except for the startled gaze of people on foot as they flashed by. Now they were on a wide boulevard, going very fast, still going east. Although he was in a very bad situation, he still found it absolutely exhilarating just to be out of the embassy, out in the air, in the world, and moving, going fast.

Cautiously he raised his hand and massaged his shoulder. As cautiously, he glanced at the men beside him and facing him. All were dark-skinned, two blue-black. Two of the men facing him were young. Fresh, stolid faces. The third was a veot of the third rank, an oga. His face had the quiet inexpressiveness in which his caste was trained. Looking at him, Esdan caught his eye. Each looked away instantly.

Esdan liked veots. He saw them, soldiers as well as slaveholders, as part of the old Voe Deo, members of a doomed species. Businessmen and bureaucrats would survive and thrive in the Liberation and no doubt find soldiers to fight for them, but the military caste would not. Their code of loyalty, honor, and austerity was too like that of their slaves, with whom they shared the worship of Kamye, the Swordsman, the Bondsman. How long would that mysticism of suffering survive the Liberation? Veots were intransigent vestiges of an intolerable order. He trusted them, and had seldom been disappointed in his trust.

The oga was very black, very handsome, like Teyeo, a veot Esdan had particularly liked. He had left Werel long before the war, off to Terra and Hain with his wife, who would be a Mobile of the Ekumen one of these days. In a few centuries. Long after the war was over, long after Esdan was dead. Unless he chose to follow them, went back, went home.

Idle thoughts. During a revolution you don't choose. You're carried, a bubble in a cataract, a spark in a bonfire, an unarmed man in a car with seven armed men driving very fast down the broad, blank East Arterial Highway. . . . They were leaving the city. Heading for the East Provinces. The Legitimate Government of Voe Deo was now reduced to half the capital city and two provinces, in which seven out of eight people were what the eighth person, their owner, called assets.

The two men up in the front compartment were talking, though they couldn't be heard in the owner compartment. Now the bullet-headed man to Esdan's right asked a muttered question to the oga facing him, who nodded.

"Oga," Esdan said.

The veot's expressionless eyes met his.

"I need to piss."

The man said nothing and looked away. None of them said anything for a while. They were on a bad stretch of the highway, torn up by fighting during the first summer of the Uprising or merely not maintained since. The jolts and shocks were hard on Esdan's bladder.

"Let the fucking white-eyes piss himself," said one of the two young men facing him to the other, who smiled tightly.

Esdan considered possible replies, good-humored, joking, not offensive, not provocative, and kept his mouth shut. They only wanted an excuse, those two. He closed his eyes and tried to relax, to be aware of the pain in his shoulder, the pain in his bladder, merely aware.

The man to his left, whom he could not see clearly, spoke: "Driver. Pull off up there." He used a speakerphone. The driver nodded. The car slowed, pulled off the road, jolting horribly. They all got out of the car. Esdan saw that the man to his left was also a veot, of the second rank, a zadyo. One of the young men grabbed Esdan's arm as he got out, another shoved a gun against his liver. The others all stood on the dusty roadside and pissed variously on the dust, the gravel, the roots of a row of scruffy trees. Esdan managed to get his fly open but his legs were so cramped and shaky he could barely stand, and the young man with the gun had come around and now stood directly in front of him with the gun aimed at his penis. There was a knot of pain somewhere between his bladder and his cock. "Back up a little," he said with plaintive irritability. "I don't want to wet your shoes." The young man stepped forward instead, bringing his gun right against Esdan's groin.

The zadyo made a slight gesture. The young man backed off a step. Esdan shuddered and suddenly pissed out a fountain. He was pleased, even in the agony of relief, to see he'd driven the young man back two more steps.

"Looks almost human," the young man said.

Esdan tucked his brown alien cock away with discreet promptness and slapped his trousers shut. He was still wearing lenses that hid the whites of his eyes, and was dressed as a rentsman in loose, coarse clothes of dull yellow, the only dye color that had been permitted to urban slaves. The banner of the Liberation was that same dull yellow. The wrong color, here. The body inside the clothes was the wrong color too.

Having lived on Werel for thirty-three years, Esdan was used to being feared and hated, but he had never before been entirely at the mercy of those who feared and hated him. The aegis of the Ekumen had sheltered him. What a fool, to leave the embassy where at least he'd been harmless, and let himself be got hold of by these desperate defenders of a lost cause, who might do a good deal of harm not only to but with him. How much resistance, how much endurance, was he capable of? Fortunately they couldn't torture any information about Liberation plans from him, since he didn't know a damned thing about what his friends were doing. But still, what a fool.

Back in the car, sandwiched in the seat with nothing to see but the young men's scowls and the oga's watchful nonexpression, he shut his eyes again. The highway was smooth here. Rocked in speed and silence he slipped into a post-adrenaline doze.

When he came fully awake the sky was gold, two of the little moons glittering above a cloudless sunset. They were jolting along on a side road, a driveway that wound past fields, orchards, plantations of trees and building-cane, a huge field-worker compound, more fields, another compound. They stopped at a checkpoint guarded by a single armed man, were checked briefly and waved through. The road went through an immense, open, rolling park. Its familiarity troubled him. Lacework of trees against the sky, the swing of the road among groves and glades. He knew the river was over that long hill.

"This is Yaramera," he said aloud.

None of the men spoke.

Years ago, decades ago, when he'd been on Werel only a year or so, they'd invited a party from the embassy down to Yaramera, the greatest estate in Voe Deo. The Jewel of the East. The model of efficient slavery. Thousands of assets working the fields, mills, factories of the estate, living in enormous compounds, walled towns. Everything clean, orderly, industrious, peaceful. And the house on the hill above the river, a palace, three hundred rooms, priceless furnishings, paintings, sculptures, musical instruments — he remembered a private concert hall with walls of gold-backed glass mosaic, a Tualite shrine-room that was one huge flower carved of scented wood.

They were driving up to that house now. The car turned. He caught only a glimpse, jagged black spars against the sky.

The two young men were allowed to handle him again, haul him out of the car, twist his arm, push and shove him up the steps. Trying not to resist, not to feel what they were doing to him, he kept looking about him. The center and the south wing of the immense house were roofless, ruinous. Through the black outline of a window shone the blank clear yellow of the sky. Even here in the heartland of the Law, the slaves had risen. Three years ago, now, in that first terrible summer when thousands of houses had burned, compounds, towns, cities. Four million dead. He had not known the Uprising had reached even to Yaramera. No news came up the river. What toll among the Jewel's slaves for that night of burning? Had the owners been slaughtered, or had they survived to deal out punishment? No news came up the river.

All this went through his mind with unnatural rapidity and clarity as they crowded him up the shallow steps towards the north wing of the house, guarding him with drawn guns as if they thought a man of sixty-two with severe leg cramps from sitting motionless for hours was going to break and run for it, here, three hundred kilos inside their own territory. He thought fast and noticed everything.

This part of the house, joined to the central house by a long arcade, had not burned down. The walls still bore up the roof, but he saw as they came into the front hall that they were bare stone, their carved panelling burnt away. Dirty sheetflooring replaced parquet or covered painted tile. There was no furniture at all. In its ruin and dirt the high hall was beautiful, bare, full of clear evening light. Both veots had left his group and were reporting to some men in the doorway of what had been a reception room. He felt the veots as a safeguard and hoped they would come back, but they did not. One of the young men kept his arm twisted up his back. A heavy-set man came towards him, staring at him.

"You're the alien called Old Music?"

"I am Hainish, and use that name here."

"Mr. Old Music, you're to understand that by leaving your embassy in violation of the protection agreement between your Ambassador and the Government of Voe Deo, you've forfeited diplomatic immunity. You may be held in custody, interrogated, and duly punished for any infractions of civil law or crimes of collusion with insurgents and enemies of the State you're found to have committed."

"I understand that this is your statement of my position," Esdan said. "But you should know, sir, that the Ambassador and the Stabiles of the Ekumen of the Worlds consider me protected both by diplomatic immunity and the laws of the Ekumen."

No harm trying, but his wordy lies weren't listened to. Having recited his litany the man turned away, and the young men grabbed Esdan again. He was hustled through doorways and corridors that he was now in too much pain to see, down stone stairs, across a wide, cobbled courtyard, and into a room where with a final agonising jerk on his arm and his feet knocked from under him so that he fell sprawling, they slammed the door and left him belly-down on stone in darkness.

He dropped his forehead onto his arm and lay shivering, hearing his breath catch in a whimper again and again.

Later on he remembered that night, and other things from the next days and nights. He did not know, then or later, if he was tortured in order to break him down or was merely the handy object of aimless brutality and spite, a sort of plaything for the boys. There were kicks, beatings, a great deal of pain, but none of it was clear in his memory later except the crouchcage.

He had heard of such things, read about them. He had never seen one. He had never been inside a compound. Foreigners, visitors, were not taken into slave quarters on the estates of Voe Deo. They were served by house-slaves in the houses of the owners.

This was a small compound, not more than twenty huts on the women's side, three longhouses on the gateside. It had housed the staff of a couple of hundred slaves who looked after the house and the immense gardens of Yaramera. They would have been a privileged set compared to the fieldhands. But not exempt from punishment. The whipping post still stood near the high gate that sagged open in the high walls.

"There?" said Nemeo, the one who always twisted his arm, but the other one, Alatual, said, "No, come on, it's over here," and ran ahead, excited, to winch the crouchcage down from where it hung below the main sentry station, high up on the inside of the wall.

It was a tube of coarse, rusty steel mesh sealed at one end and closable at the other. It hung suspended by a single hook from a chain. Lying on the ground it looked like a trap for an animal, not a very big animal. The two young men stripped off his clothes and goaded him to crawl into it headfirst, using the fieldhandlers, electric prods to stir up lazy slaves, which they had been playing with the last couple of days. They screamed with laughter, pushing him and jabbing the prods in his anus and scrotum. He writhed into the cage until he was crouching in it head-down, his arms and legs bent and jammed up into his body. They slammed the trap end shut, catching his naked foot between the wires and causing a pain that blinded him while they hoisted the cage back up. It swung about wildly and he clung to the wires with his cramped hands. When he opened his eyes he saw the ground swinging about seven or eight meters below him. After a while the lurching and circling stopped. He could not move his head at all. He could see what was below the crouchcage, and by straining his eyes round he could see most of the inside of the compound.

In the old days there had been people down there to see the moral spectacle, a slave in the crouchcage. There had been children to learn the lesson of what happens to a housemaid who shirked a job, a gardener who spoiled a cutting, a hand who talked back to a boss. Nobody was there now. The dusty ground was bare. The dried-up garden plots, the little graveyard at the far edge of the women's side, the ditch between the two sides, the pathways, a vague circle of greener grass right underneath him, all were deserted. His torturers stood around for a while laughing and talking, got bored, went off.

He tried to ease his position but could move only very slightly. Any motion made the cage rock and swing so that he grew sick and increasingly fearful of falling. He did not know how securely the cage was balanced on that single hook. His foot, caught in the cage-closure, hurt so sharply that he longed to faint, but though his head swam he kept conscious. He tried to breathe as he had learned how to breathe a long time ago on another world, quietly, easily. He could not do it here now in this world in this cage. His lungs were squeezed in his ribcage so that each breath was extremely difficult. He tried not to suffocate. He tried not to panic. He tried to be aware, only to be aware, but awareness was unendurable.

When the sun came around to that side of the compound and shone full on him, the dizziness turned to sickness. Sometimes then he fainted for a while.

There was night and cold and he tried to imagine water, but there was no water.

He thought later he had been in the crouchcage two days. He could remember the scraping of the wires on his sunburned naked flesh when they pulled him out, the shock of cold water played over him from a hose. He had been fully aware for a moment then, aware of himself, like a doll, lying small, limp, on dirt, while men above him talked and shouted about something. Then he must have been carried back to the cell or stable where he was kept, for there was dark and silence, but also he was still hanging in the crouchcage roasting in the icy fire of the sun, freezing in his burning body, fitted tighter and tighter into the exact mesh of the wires of pain.

At some point he was taken to a bed in a room with a window, but he was still in the crouchcage, swinging high above the dusty ground, the dusties' ground, the circle of green grass.

The zadyo and the heavy-set man were there, were not there. A bondswoman, whey-faced, crouching and trembling, hurt him trying to put salve on his burned arm and leg and back. She was there and not there. The sun shone in the window. He felt the wire snap down on his foot again, and again.

Darkness eased him. He slept most of the time. After a couple of days he could sit up and eat what the scared bondswoman brought him. His sunburn was healing and most of his aches and pains were milder. His foot was swollen hugely; bones were broken; that didn't matter till he had to get up. He dozed, drifted. When Rayaye walked into the room, he recognised him at once.

They had met several times, before the Uprising. Rayaye had been Minister of Foreign Affairs under President Oyo. What position he had now, in the Legitimate Government, Esdan did not know. Rayaye was short for a Werelian but broad and solid, with a blue-black polished-looking face and greying hair, a striking man, a politician.

"Minister Rayaye," Esdan said.

"Mr. Old Music. How kind of you to recall me! I'm sorry you've been unwell. I hope the people here are looking after you satisfactorily?"

"Thank you."

"When I heard you were unwell I inquired for a doctor, but there's no one here but a veterinarian. No staff at all. Not like the old days! What a change! I wish you'd seen Yaramera in its glory."

"I did." His voice was rather weak, but sounded quite natural. "Thirty-two or -three years ago. Lord and Lady Aneo entertained a party from our embassy."

"Really? Then you know what it was," said Rayaye, sitting down in the one chair, a fine old piece missing one arm. "Painful to see it like this, isn't it! The worst of the destruction was here in the house. The whole women's wing and the great rooms burned. But the gardens were spared, may the Lady be praised. Laid out by Meneya himself, you know, four hundred years ago. And the fields are still being worked. I'm told there are still nearly three thousand assets attached to the property. When the trouble's over, it'll be far easier to restore Yaramera than many of the great estates." He gazed out the window. "Beautiful, beautiful. The Aneos' housepeople were famous for their beauty, you know. And training. It'll take a long time to build up to that kind of standard again."

"No doubt."

The Werelian looked at him with bland attentiveness. "I expect you're wondering why you're here."

"Not particularly," Esdan said pleasantly.

"Oh?"

"Since I left the embassy without permission, I suppose the Government wanted to keep an eye on me."

"Some of us were glad to hear you'd left the embassy. Shut up there — a waste of your talents."

"Oh, my talents," Esdan said with a deprecatory shrug, which hurt his shoulder. He would wince later. Just now he was enjoying himself. He liked fencing.

"You're a very talented man, Mr. Old Music. The wisest, canniest alien on Werel, Lord Mehao called you once. You've worked with us — and against us, yes — more effectively than any other offworlder. We understand one another. We can talk. It's my belief that you genuinely wish my people well, and that if I offered you a way of serving them — a hope of bringing this terrible conflict to an end — you'd take it."

"I would hope to be able to."

"Is it important to you that you be identified as a supporter of one side of the conflict, or would you prefer to remain neutral?"

"Any action can bring neutrality into question."

"To have been kidnapped from the embassy by the rebels is no evidence of your sympathy for them."

"It would seem not."

"Rather the opposite."

"It could be so perceived."

"It can be. If you like."

"My preferences are of no weight, Minister."

"They're of very great weight, Mr. Old Music. But here. You've been ill, I'm tiring you. We'll continue our conversation tomorrow, eh? If you like."

"Of course, Minister," Esdan said, with a politeness edging on submissiveness, a tone that he knew suited men like this one, more accustomed to the attention of slaves than the company of equals. Never having equated incivility with pride, Esdan, like most of his people, was disposed to be polite in any circumstance that allowed it, and disliked circumstances that did not. Mere hypocrisy did not trouble him. He was perfectly capable of it himself. If Rayaye's men had tortured him and Rayaye pretended ignorance of the fact, Esdan had nothing to gain by insisting on it.

He was glad, indeed, not to be obliged to talk about it, and hoped not to think about it. His body thought about it for him, remembered it precisely, in every joint and muscle, now. The rest of his thinking about it he would do as long as he lived. He had learned things he had not known. He had thought he understood what it was to be helpless. Now he knew he had not understood.

When the scared woman came in, he asked her to send for the veterinarian. "I need a cast on my foot," he said.

"He does mend the hands, the bondsfolk, master," the woman whispered, shrinking. The assets here spoke an archaic-sounding dialect that was sometimes hard to follow.

"Can he come into the house?"

She shook her head.

"Is there anybody here who can look after it?"

"I will ask, master," she whispered.

An old bondswoman came in that night. She had a wrinkled, seared, stern face, and none of the crouching manner of the other. When she first saw him she whispered, "Mighty Lord!" But she performed the reverence stiffly, and then examined his swollen foot, impersonal as any doctor. She said, "If you do let me bind that, master, it will heal."

"What's broken?"

"These toes. There. Maybe a little bone in here too. Lotsalot bones in feet."

"Please bind it for me."

She did so, firmly, binding cloths round and round until the wrapping was quite thick and kept his foot immobile at one angle. She said, "You do walk, then you use a stick, sir. You put down only that heel to the ground."

He asked her name.

"Gana," she said. Saying her name she shot a sharp glance right at him, full-face, a daring thing for a slave to do. She probably wanted to get a good look at his alien eyes, having found the rest of him, though a strange color, pretty commonplace, bones in the feet and all.

"Thank you, Gana. I'm grateful for your skill and kindness."

She bobbed, but did not reverence, and left the room. She herself walked lame, but upright. "All the grandmothers are rebels," somebody had told him long ago, before the Uprising.

The next day he was able to get up and hobble to the broken-armed chair. He sat for a while looking out the window.

The room looked out from the second floor over the gardens of Yaramera, terraced slopes and flowerbeds, walks, lawns, and a series of ornamental lakes and pools that descended gradually to the river: a vast pattern of curves and planes, plants and paths, earth and still water, embraced by the broad living curve of the river. All the plots and walks and terraces formed a soft geometry centered very subtly on an enormous tree down at the riverside. It must have been a great tree when the garden was laid out four hundred years ago. It stood above and well back from the bank, but its branches reached far out over the water and a village could have been built in its shade. The grass of the terraces had dried to soft gold. The river and the lakes and pools were all the misty blue of the summer sky. The flowerbeds and shrubberies were untended, overgrown, but not yet gone wild. The gardens of Yaramera were utterly beautiful in their desolation. Desolate, forlorn, forsaken, all such romantic words befitted them, yet they were also rational and noble, full of peace. They had been built by the labor of slaves. Their dignity and peace were founded on cruelty, misery, pain. Esdan was Hainish, from a very old people, people who had built and destroyed Yaramera a thousand times. His mind contained the beauty and the terrible grief of the place, assured that the existence of one cannot justify the other, the destruction of one cannot destroy the other. He was aware of both, only aware.

And aware also, sitting in some comfort of body at last, that the lovely sorrowful terraces of Yaramera may contain within them the terraces of Darranda on Hain, roof below red roof, garden below green garden, dropping steep down to the shining harbor, the promenades and piers and sailboats. Out past the harbor the sea rises up, stands up as high as his house, as high as his eyes. Esi knows that books say the sea lies down. "The sea lies calm tonight," says the poem, but he knows better. The sea stands, a wall, the blue-grey wall at the end of the world. If you sail out on it it will seem flat, but if you see it truly it's as tall as the hills of Darranda, and if you sail truly on it you will sail through that wall to the other side, beyond the end of the world.

The sky is the roof that wall holds up. At night the stars shine through the glass air roof. You can sail to them, too, to the worlds beyond the world.

"Esi," somebody calls from indoors, and he turns away from the sea and the sky, leaves the balcony, goes in to meet the guests, or for his music lesson, or to have lunch with the family. He's a nice little boy, Esi: obedient, cheerful, not talkative but quite sociable, interested in people. With very good manners, of course; after all he's a Kelwen and the older generation wouldn't stand for anything less in a child of the family, but good manners come easy to him, perhaps because he's never seen any bad ones. Not a dreamy child. Alert, present, noticing. But thoughtful, and given to explaining things to himself, such as the wall of the sea and the roof of the air. Esi isn't as clear and close to Esdan as he used to be; he's a little boy a long time ago and very far away, left behind, left at home. Only rarely now does Esdan see through his eyes, or breathe the marvelous intricate smell of the house in Darranda — wood, the resinous oil used to polish the wood, sweetgrass matting, fresh flowers, kitchen herbs, the sea wind — or hear his mother's voice: "Esi? Come on in now, love. The cousins are here from Dorased!"

Esi runs in to meet the cousins, old Iliawad with crazy eyebrows and hair in his nostrils, who can do magic with bits of sticky tape, and Tuitui who's better at catch than Esi even though she's younger, while Esdan falls asleep in the broken chair by the window looking out on the terrible, beautiful gardens.

Further conversations with Rayaye were deferred. The zadyo came with his apologies. The Minister had been called back to speak with the President, would return within three or four days. Esdan realised he had heard a flyer take off early in the morning, not far away. It was a reprieve. He enjoyed fencing, but was still very tired, very shaken, and welcomed the rest. No one came into his room but the scared woman, Heo, and the zadyo who came once a day to ask if he had all he needed.

When he could he was permitted to leave his room, go outside if he wished. By using a stick and strapping his bound foot onto a stiff old sandal-sole Gana brought him, he could walk, and so get out into the gardens and sit in the sun, which was growing milder daily as the summer grew old. The two veots were his guards, or more exactly guardians. He saw the two young men who had tortured him; they kept at a distance, evidently under orders not to approach him. One of the veots was usually in view, but never crowded him.

He could not go far. Sometimes he felt like a bug on a beach. The part of the house that was still usable was huge, the gardens were vast, the people were very few. There were the six men who had brought him, and five or six more who had been here, commanded by the heavy-set man Tualenem. Of the original asset population of the house and estate there were ten or twelve, a tiny remnant of the house-staff of cooks, cooks' helpers, washwomen, chambermaids, ladies' maids, bodyservants, shoe-polishers, window-cleaners, gardeners, path-rakers, waiters, footmen, errandboys, stablemen, drivers, usewomen and useboys who had served the owners and their guests in the old days. These few were no longer locked up at night in the old house-asset compound where the crouchcage was, but slept in the courtyard warren of stables for horses and people where he had been kept at first, or in the complex of rooms around the kitchens. Most of these remaining few were women, two of them young, and two or three old, frail-looking men.

He was cautious of speaking to any of them at first lest he get them into trouble, but his captors ignored them except to give orders, evidently considering them trustworthy, with good reason. Troublemakers, the assets who had broken out of the compounds, burned the great house, killed the bosses and owners, were long gone: dead, escaped, or re-enslaved with a cross branded deep on both cheeks. These were good dusties. Very likely they had been loyal all along. Many bondspeople, especially personal slaves, as terrified by the Uprising as their owners, had tried to defend them or had fled with them. They were no more traitors than were owners who had freed their assets and fought on the Liberation side. As much, and no more.

Girls, young fieldhands, were brought in one at a time as usewomen for the men. Every day or two the two young men who had tortured him drove a landcar off in the morning with a used girl and came back with a new one.

Of the two younger house bondswomen, the one called Kamsa always carried her little baby around with her, and the men ignored her. The other, Heo, was the scared one who had waited on him. Tualenem used her every night. The other men kept hands off.

When they or any of the bondspeople passed Esdan in the house or outdoors they dropped their hands to their sides, chin to the chest, looked down, and stood still: the formal reverence expected of personal assets facing an owner.

"Good morning, Kamsa."

Her reply was the reverence.

It had been years now since he had been with the finished product of generations of slavery, the kind of slave described as "perfectly trained, obedient, selfless, loyal, the ideal personal asset," when they were put up for sale. Most of the assets he had known, his friends and colleagues, had been city rentspeople, hired out by their owners to companies and corporations to work in factories or shops or at skilled trades. He had also known a good many fieldhands. Fieldhands seldom had any contact with their owners; they worked under gareot bosses and their compounds were run by cutfrees, eunuch assets. The ones he knew had mostly been runaways protected by the Hame, the underground railroad, on their way to independence in Yeowe. None of them had been as utterly deprived of education, options, any imagination of freedom, as these bondspeople were. He had forgotten what a good dusty was like. He had forgotten the utter impenetrability of the person who has no private life, the intactness of the wholly vulnerable.

Kamsa's face was smooth, serene, and showed no feeling, though he heard her sometimes talking and singing very softly to her baby, a joyful, merry little noise. It drew him. He saw her one afternoon sitting at work on the coping of the great terrace, the baby in its sling on her back. He limped over and sat down nearby. He could not prevent her from setting her knife and board aside and standing head and hands and eyes down in reverence as he came near.

"Please sit down, please go on with your work," he said. She obeyed. "What's that you're cutting up?"

"Dueli, master," she whispered.

It was a vegetable he had often eaten and enjoyed. He watched her work. Each big, woody pod had to be split along a sealed seam, not an easy trick; it took a careful search for the opening-point and hard, repeated twists of the blade to open the pod. Then the fat edible seeds had to be removed one by one and scraped free of a stringy, clinging matrix.

"Does that part taste bad?" he asked.

"Yes, master."

It was a laborious process, requiring strength, skill, and patience. He was ashamed. "I never saw raw dueli before," he said.

"No, master."

"What a good baby," he said, a little at random. The tiny creature in its sling, its head lying on her shoulder, had opened large bluish-black eyes and was gazing vaguely at the world. He had never heard it cry. It seemed rather unearthly to him, but he had not had much to do with babies.

She smiled.

"A boy?"

"Yes, master."

He said, "Please, Kamsa, my name is Esdan. I'm not a master. I'm a prisoner. Your masters are my masters. Will you call me by my name?"

She did not answer.

"Our masters would disapprove."

She nodded. The Werelian nod was a tip back of the head, not a bob down. He was completely used to it after all these years. It was the way he nodded himself. He noticed himself noticing it now. His captivity, his treatment here, had displaced, disoriented him. These last few days he had thought more about Hain than he had for years, decades. He had been at home on Werel, and now was not. Inappropriate comparisons, irrelevant memories. Alienated.

"They put me in the cage," he said, speaking as low as she did and hesitating on the last word. He could not say the whole word, crouchcage.

Again the nod. This time, for the first time, she looked up at him, the flick of a glance. She said soundlessly, "I know," and went on with her work.

He found nothing more to say.

"I was a pup, then I did live there," she said, with a glance in the direction of the compound where the cage was. Her murmuring voice was profoundly controlled, as were all her gestures and movements. "Before that time the house burned. When the masters did live here. They did often hang up the cage. Once, a man for until he did die there. In that. I saw that."

Silence between them.

"We pups never did go under that. Never did run there."

"I saw the . . . the ground was different, underneath," Esdan said, speaking as softly and with a dry mouth, his breath coming short. "I saw, looking down. The grass. I thought maybe . . . where they . . ." His voice dried up entirely.

"One grandmother did take a stick, long, a cloth on the end of that, and wet it, and hold it up to him. The cutfrees did look away. But he did die. And rot some time."

"What had he done?"

"*Enna,*" she said, the one-word denial he'd often heard assets use — I don't know, I didn't do it, I wasn't there, it's not my fault, who knows. . . .

He'd seen an owner's child who said "enna" be slapped, not for the cup she broke but for using a slave word.

"A useful lesson," he said. He knew she'd understand him. Underdogs know irony like they know air and water.

"They did put you in that, then I did fear," she said.

"The lesson was for me, not you, this time," he said.

She worked, carefully, ceaselessly. He watched her work. Her downcast face, clay-color with bluish shadows, was composed, peaceful. The baby was darker-skinned than she. She had not been bred to a bondsman, but used by an owner. They called rape "use." The baby's eyes closed slowly, translucent bluish lids like little shells.

It was small and delicate, probably only a month or two old. Its head lay with infinite patience on her stooping shoulder.

No one else was out on the terraces. A slight wind stirred in the flowering trees behind them, streaked the distant river with silver.

"Your baby, Kamsa, you know, he will be free," Esdan said.

She looked up, not at him, but at the river and across it. She said, "Yes. He will be free." She went on working.

It heartened him, her saying that to him. It did him good to know she trusted him. He needed someone to trust him, for since the cage he could not trust himself. With Rayaye he was all right; he could still fence; that wasn't the trouble. It was when he was alone, thinking, sleeping. He was alone most of the time. Something in his mind, deep in him, was injured, broken, had not mended, could not be trusted to bear his weight.

He heard the flyer come down in the morning. That night Rayaye invited him down to dinner. Tualenem and the two veots ate with them and excused themselves, leaving him and Rayaye with a half-bottle of wine at the makeshift table set up in one of the least damaged downstairs rooms. It had been a hunting-lodge or trophy-room, here in this wing of the house that had been the azade, the men's side, where no women would ever have come; female assets, servants and usewomen, did not count as women. The head of a huge packdog snarled above the mantel, its fur singed and dusty and its glass eyes gone dull. Crossbows had been mounted on the facing wall. Their pale shadows were clear on the dark wood. The electric chandelier flickered and dimmed. The generator was uncertain. One of the old bondsmen was always tinkering at it.

"Going off to his usewoman," Rayaye said, nodding towards the door Tualenem had just closed with assiduous wishes for the Minister to have a good night. "Fucking a white. Like fucking turds. Makes my skin crawl. Sticking his cock into a slave cunt. When the war's over there'll be no more of that kind of thing. Halfbreeds are the root of this revolution. Keep the races separate. Keep the ruler blood clean. It's the only answer." He spoke as if expecting complete accord, but did not wait to receive any sign of it. He poured Esdan's glass full and went in his resonant politician's voice, kind host, lord of the manor, "Well, Mr. Old Music, I hope you've been having a pleasant stay at Yaramera, and that your health's improved."

A civil murmur.

"President Oyo was sorry to hear you'd been unwell and sends his wishes for your full recovery. He's glad to know you're safe from any further mistreatment by the insurgents. You can stay here in safety as long as you like. However, when the time is right, the President and his cabinet are looking forward to having you in Bellen."

Civil murmur.

Long habit prevented Esdan from asking questions that would reveal the extent of his ignorance. Rayaye like most politicians loved his own voice, and as he talked Esdan tried to piece together a rough sketch of the current situation. It appeared that the Legitimate Government had moved from the city to a town, Bellen, northeast of Yaramera, near the eastern coast. Some kind of command had been left in the city. Rayaye's references to it made Esdan wonder if the city was in fact semi-independent of the Oyo government, governed by a faction, perhaps a military faction.

When the Uprising began, Oyo had at once been given extraordinary powers; but the Legitimate Army of Voe Deo, after their stunning defeats in the west, had been restive under his command, wanting more autonomy in the field. The civilian government had demanded retaliation, attack, and victory. The army wanted to contain the insurrection. Rega-General Aydan had established the Divide in the city and tried to establish and hold a border between the new Free State and the Legitimate Provinces. Veots who had gone over to the Uprising with their asset troops had similarly urged a border truce to the Liberation Command. The army sought armistice, the warriors sought peace. But "So long as there is one slave I am not free," cried Nekam-Anna, Leader of the Free State, and President Oyo thundered, "The nation will not be divided! We will defend legitimate property with the last drop of blood in our veins!" The Rega-General had suddenly been replaced by a new Commander-in-Chief. Very soon after that the embassy was sealed, its access to information cut.

Esdan could only guess what had happened in the half year since. Rayaye talked of "our victories in the south" as if the Legitimate Army had been on the attack, pushing back into the Free State across the Devan River, south of the city. If so, if they had regained territory, why had the government pulled out of the city and dug in down at Bellen? Rayaye's talk of victories might be translated to mean that the Army of the Liberation had been trying to cross the river in the south and the Legitimates had been successful in holding them off. If they were willing to call that a victory, had they finally given up the dream of reversing the revolution, retaking the whole country, and decided to cut their losses?

"A divided nation is not an option," Rayaye said, squashing that hope. "You understand that, I think."

Civil assent.

Rayaye poured out the last of the wine. "But peace is our goal. Our very strong and urgent goal. Our unhappy country has suffered enough."

Definite assent.

"I know you to be a man of peace, Mr. Old Music. We know the Ekumen fosters harmony among and within its member states. Peace is what we all desire with all our hearts."

Assent, plus faint indication of inquiry.

"As you know, the Government of Voe Deo has always had the power to end the insurrection. The means to end it quickly and completely."

No response but alert attention.

"And I think you know that it is only our respect for the policies of the Ekumen, of which my nation is a member, that has prevented us from using that means."

Absolutely no response or acknowledgment.

"You do know that, Mr. Old Music."

"I assumed you had a natural wish to survive."

Rayaye shook his head as if bothered by an insect. "Since we joined the Ekumen — and long before we joined it, Mr. Old Music — we have loyally followed its policies and bowed to its theories. And so we lost Yeowe! And so we lost the West! Four million dead, Mr. Old Music. Four million in the first Uprising. Millions since. Millions. If we had contained it then, many, many fewer would have died. Assets as well as owners."

"Suicide," Esdan said in a soft mild voice, the way assets spoke.

"The pacifist sees all weapons as evil, disastrous, suicidal. For all the age-old wisdom of your people, Mr. Old Music, you have not the experiential perspective on matters of war we younger, cruder peoples are forced to have. Believe me, we are not suicidal. We want our people, our nation, to survive. We are determined that it shall. The bibo was fully tested, long before we joined the Ekumen. It is controllable, targetable, containable. It is an exact weapon, a precise tool of war. Rumor and fear have wildly exaggerated its capacities and nature. We know how to use it, how to limit its effects. Nothing but the response of the Stabiles through your Ambassador prevented us from selective deployment in the first summer of the insurrection."

"I had the impression the high command of the Army of Voe Deo was also opposed to deploying that weapon."

"Some generals were. Many veots are rigid in their thinking, as you know."

"That decision has been changed?"

"President Oyo has authorised deployment of the bibo against forces massing to invade this province from the west."

Such a cute word, bibo. Esdan closed his eyes for a moment.

"The destruction will be appalling," Rayaye said.

Assent.

"It is possible," Rayaye said, leaning forward, black eyes in black face, intense as a hunting cat, "that if the insurgents were warned, they might withdraw. Be willing to discuss terms. If they withdraw, we will not attack. If they will talk, we will talk. A holocaust can be prevented. They respect the Ekumen. They respect you personally, Mr. Old Music. They trust you. If you were to speak to them on the net, or if their leaders will agree to a meeting, they will listen to you, not as their enemy, their oppressor, but as the voice of a benevolent, peace-loving neutrality, the voice of wisdom, urging them to save themselves while there is yet time. This is the opportunity I offer you, and the Ekumen. To spare your friends among the rebels, to spare this world untold suffering. To open the way to lasting peace."

"I am not authorised to speak for the Ekumen. The Ambassador — "

"Will not. Cannot. Is not free to. You are. You are a free agent, Mr. Old Music. Your position on Werel is unique. Both sides respect you. Trust you. And your voice carries infinitely more weight among the whites than his. He came only a year before the insurrection. You are, I may say, one of us."

"I am not one of you. I neither own nor am owned. You must redefine yourselves to include me."

Rayaye, for a moment, had nothing to say. He was taken aback, and would be angry. Fool, Esdan said to himself, old fool, to take the moral high ground! But he did not know what ground to stand on.

It was true that his word would carry more weight than the Ambassador's. Nothing else Rayaye had said made sense. If President Oyo wanted the Ekumen's blessing on his use of this weapon and seriously thought Esdan would give it, why was he working through Rayaye, and keeping Esdan hidden at Yaramera? Was Rayaye working with Oyo, or was he working for a faction that favored using the bibo, while Oyo still refused?

Most likely the whole thing was a bluff. There was no weapon. Esdan's pleading was to lend credibility to it, while leaving Oyo out of the loop if the bluff failed.

The biobomb, the bibo, had been a curse on Voe Deo for decades, centuries. In panic fear of alien invasion after the Ekumen first contacted them almost four hundred years ago, the Werelians had put all their resources into developing space flight and weaponry. The scientists who invented this particular device repudiated it, informing their government that it could not be contained; it would destroy all human and animal life over an enormous area and cause profound and permanent genetic damage worldwide as it spread throughout the water and the atmosphere. The government never used the weapon but was never willing to destroy it, and its existence had kept Werel from membership in the Ekumen as long as the Embargo was in force. Voe Deo insisted it was their guarantee against extraterrestrial invasion and perhaps believed it would prevent revolution. Yet they had not used it when their slave-planet Yeowe rebelled. Then, after the Ekumen no longer observed the Embargo, they announced that they had destroyed the stockpiles. Werel joined the Ekumen. Voe Deo invited inspection of the weapon sites. The Ambassador politely declined, citing the Ekumenical policy of trust. Now the bibo existed again. In fact? In Rayaye's mind? Was he desperate? A hoax, an attempt to use the Ekumen to back a bogey threat to scare off an invasion: the likeliest scenario, yet it was not quite convincing.

"This war must end," Rayaye said.

"I agree."

"We will never surrender. You must understand that." Rayaye had dropped his blandishing, reasonable tone. "We will restore the holy order of the world," he said, and now he was fully credible. His eyes, the dark Werelian eyes that had no whites, were fathomless in the dim light. He drank down his wine. "You think we fight for our property. To keep what we own. But I tell you, we fight to defend our Lady. In that fight is no surrender. And no compromise."

"Your Lady is merciful."

"The Law is her mercy."

Esdan was silent.

"I must go again tomorrow to Bellen," Rayaye said after a while, resuming his masterful, easy tone. "Our plans for moving on the southern front must be fully coordinated. When I come back, I'll need to know if you will give us the help I've asked you for. Our response will depend largely on that. On your voice. It is known that you're here in the East Provinces — known to the insurgents, I mean, as well as our people — though your exact location is of course kept hidden for your own safety. It is known that you may be preparing a statement of a change in the Ekumen's attitude toward the conduct of the civil war. A change that could save millions of lives and bring a just peace to our land. I hope you'll employ your time here in doing so."

He is a factionalist, Esdan thought. He's not going to Bellen, or if he is, that's not where Oyo's government is. This is some scheme of his own. Crackbrained. It won't work. He doesn't have the bibo. But he has a gun. And he'll shoot me.

"Thank you for a pleasant dinner, Minister," he said.

Next morning he heard the flyer leave at dawn. He limped out into the morning sunshine after breakfast. One of his veot guards watched him from a window and then turned away. In a sheltered nook just under the balustrade of the south terrace, near a planting of great bushes with big, blowsy, sweet-smelling white flowers, he saw Kamsa with her baby and Heo. He made his way to them, dot-and-go-one. The distances at Yaramera, even inside the house, were daunting to a lamed man. When he finally got there he said, "I am lonely. May I sit with you?"

The women were afoot, of course, reverencing, though Kamsa's reverence had become pretty sketchy. He sat on a curved bench splotched all over with fallen flowers. They sat back down on the flagstone path with the baby. They had unwrapped the little body to the mild sunshine. It was a very thin baby, Esdan thought. The joints in the bluish-dark arms and legs were like the joints in flowerstems, translucent knobs. The baby was moving more than he had ever seen it move, stretching its arms and turning its head as if enjoying the feel of the air. The head was large for the neck, again like a flower, too large a flower on too thin a stalk. Kamsa dangled one of the real flowers over the baby. His dark eyes gazed up at it. His eyelids and eyebrows were exquisitely delicate. The sunlight shone through his fingers. He smiled. Esdan caught his breath. The baby's smile at the flower was the beauty of the flower, the beauty of the world.

"What is his name?"

"Rekam."

Grandson of Kamye. Kamye the Lord and slave, huntsman and husbandman, warrior and peacemaker.

"A beautiful name. How old is he?"

In the language they spoke that was, "How long has he lived?" Kamsa's answer was strange. "As long as his life," she said, or so he understood her whisper and her dialect. Maybe it was bad manners or bad luck to ask a child's age.

He sat back on the bench. "I feel very old," he said. "I haven't seen a baby for a hundred years."

Heo sat hunched over, her back to him; he felt that she wanted to cover her ears. She was terrified of him, the alien. Life had not left much to Heo but fear, he guessed. Was she twenty, twenty-five? She looked forty. Maybe she was seventeen. Usewomen, ill-used, aged fast. Kamsa he guessed to be not much over twenty. She was thin and plain, but there was bloom and juice in her as there was not in Heo.

"Master did have children?" Kamsa asked, lifting up her baby to her breast with a certain discreet pride, shyly flaunting.

"No."

"A *yera yera*," she murmured, another slave word he had often heard in the urban compounds: O pity, pity.

"How you get to the center of things, Kamsa," he said. She glanced his way and smiled. Her teeth were bad but it was a good smile. He thought the baby was not sucking. It lay peacefully in the crook of her arm. Heo remained tense and jumped whenever he spoke, so he said no more. He looked away from them, past the bushes, out over the wonderful view that arranged itself, wherever you walked or sat, into a perfect balance: the levels of flagstone, of dun grass and blue water, the curves of the avenues, the masses and lines of shrubbery, the great old tree, the misty river and its green far bank. Presently the women began talking softly again. He did not listen to what they said. He was aware of their voices, aware of sunlight, aware of peace.

Old Gana came stumping across the upper terrace towards them, bobbed to him, said to Kamsa and Heo, "Choyo does want you. Leave me that baby." Kamsa set the baby down on the warm stone again. She and Heo sprang up and went off, thin, light women moving with easy haste. The old woman settled down piece by piece and with groans and grimaces onto the path beside Rekam. She immediately covered him up with a fold of his swaddling-cloth, frowning and muttering at the foolishness of his mother. Esdan watched her careful movements, her gentleness when she picked the child up, supporting that heavy head and tiny limbs, her tenderness cradling him, rocking her body to rock him.

She looked up at Esdan. She smiled, her face wrinkling up into a thousand wrinkles. "He is my great gift," she said.

He whispered, "Your grandson?"

The backward nod. She kept rocking gently. The baby's eyes were closed, his head lay softly on her thin, dry breast. "I think now he'll die not long now."

After a while Esdan said, "Die?"

The nod. She still smiled. Gently, gently rocking. "He is two years of age, master."

"I thought he was born this summer," Esdan said in a whisper.

The old woman said, "He did come to stay a little while with us."

"What is wrong?"

"The wasting."

Esdan had heard the term. He said, "Avo?" the name he knew for it, a systemic viral infection common among Werelian children, frequently epidemic in the asset compounds of the cities.

She nodded.

"But it's curable!"

The old woman said nothing.

Avo was completely curable. Where there were doctors. Where there was medicine. Avo was curable in the city not the country. In the great house not the asset quarters. In peacetime not in wartime. Fool!

Maybe she knew it was curable, maybe she did not, maybe she did not know what the word meant. She rocked the baby, crooning in a whisper, paying no attention to the fool. But she had heard him, and answered him at last, not looking at him, watching the baby's sleeping face.

"I was born owned," she said, "and my daughters. But he was not. He is the gift. To us. Nobody can own him. The gift of the Lord Kamye of himself. Who could keep that gift?"

Esdan bowed his head down.

He had said to the mother, "He will be free." And she had said, "Yes."

He said at last, "May I hold him?"

The grandmother stopped rocking and held still a while. "Yes," she said. She raised herself up and very carefully transferred the sleeping baby into Esdan's arms, onto his lap.

"You do hold my joy," she said.

The child weighed nothing — six or seven pounds. It was like holding a warm flower, a tiny animal, a bird. The swaddling-cloth trailed down across the stones. Gana gathered it up and laid it softly around the baby, hiding his face. Tense and nervous, jealous, full of pride, she knelt there. Before long she took the baby back against her heart. "There," she said, and her face softened into happiness.

That night Esdan sleeping in the room that looked out over the terraces of Yaramera dreamed that he had lost a little round, flat stone that he always carried with him in a pouch. The stone was from the pueblo. When he held it in his palm and warmed it, it was able to speak, to talk with him. But he had not talked with it for a long time. Now he realised he did not have it. He had lost it, left it somewhere. He thought it was in the basement of the embassy. He tried to get into the basement, but the door was locked, and he could not find the other door.

He woke. Early morning. No need to get up. He should think about what to do, what to say, when Rayaye came back. He could not. He thought about the dream, the stone that talked. He wished he had heard what it said. He thought about the pueblo. His father's brother's family had lived in Arkanan Pueblo in the Far South Highlands. In his boyhood, every year in the heart of the northern winter, Esi had flown down there for forty days of summer. With his parents at first, later on alone. His uncle and aunt had grown up in Darranda and were not pueblo people. Their children were. They had grown up in Arkanan and belonged to it entirely. The eldest, Suhan, fourteen years older than Esdan, had been born with irreparable brain and neural defects, and it was for his sake that his parents had settled in a pueblo. There was a place for him there. He became a herdsman. He went up on the mountains with the yama, animals the South Hainish had brought over from O a millennium or so ago. He looked after the animals. He came back to live in the pueblo only in winter. Esi saw him seldom, and was glad of it, finding Suhan a fearful figure — big, shambling, foul-smelling, with a loud braying voice, mouthing incomprehensible words. Esi could not understand why Suhan's parents and sisters loved him. He thought they pretended to. No one could love him.

To adolescent Esdan it was still a problem. His cousin Noy,

Suhan's sister, who had become the Water Chief of Arkanan, told him it was not a problem but a mystery. "You see how Suhan is our guide?" she said. "Look at it. He led my parents here to live. So my sister and I were born here. So you come to stay with us here. So you've learned to live in the pueblo. You'll never be just a city man. Because Suhan guided you here. Guided us all. Into the mountains."

"He didn't really guide us," the fourteen-year-old argued.

"Yes, he did. We followed his weakness. His incompleteness. Failure's open. Look at water, Esi. It finds the weak places in the rock, the openings, the hollows, the absences. Following water we come where we belong." Then she had gone off to arbitrate a dispute over the usage-rights to an irrigation system outside town, for the east side of the mountains was very dry country, and the people of Arkanan were contentious, though hospitable, and the Water Chief stayed busy.

But Suhan's condition had been irreparable, his weakness inaccesible even to the wondrous medical skills of Hain. This baby was dying of a disease that could be cured by a mere series of injections. It was wrong to accept his illness, his death. It was wrong to let him be cheated out of his life by circumstance, bad luck, an unjust society, a fatalistic religion. A religion that fostered and encouraged the terrible passivity of the slaves, that told these women to do nothing, to let the child waste away and die.

He should interfere, he should do something, what could be done?

"How long has he lived?"

"As long as his life."

There was nothing they could do. Nowhere to go. No one to turn to. A cure for avo existed, in some places, for some children. Not in this place, not for this child. Neither anger nor hope served any purpose. Nor grief. It was not the time for grief yet. Rekam was here with them, and they would delight in him as long as he was here. As long as his life. *He is my great gift. You do hold my joy.*

This was a strange place to come to learn the quality of joy. Water is my guide, he thought. His hands still felt what it had been like to hold the child, the light weight, the brief warmth.

He was out on the terrace late the next morning, waiting for Kamsa and the baby to come out as they usually did, but the older veot came instead. "Mr. Old Music, I must ask you to stay indoors for a time," he said.

"Zadyo, I'm not going to run away," Esdan said, sticking out his swathed lump of a foot.

"I'm sorry, sir."

He stumped crossly indoors after the veot and was locked into a downstairs room, a windowless storage space behind the kitchens. They had fixed it up with a cot, a table and chair, a pisspot, and a battery lamp for when the generator failed, as it did for a while most days. "Are you expecting an attack, then?" he said when he saw these preparations, but the veot replied only by locking the door. Esdan sat on the cot and meditated, as he had learned to do in Arkanan Pueblo. He cleared distress and anger from his mind by going through the long repetitions: health and good work, courage, patience, peace, for himself, health and good work, courage, patience, peace for the zadyo . . . for Kamsa, for baby Rekam, for Rayaye, for Heo, for Tualenem, for the oga, for Nemeo who had put him in the crouch-cage, for Alatual who had put him in the crouchcage, for Gana who had bound his foot and blessed him, for people he knew in the embassy, in the city, health and good work, courage, patience, peace. . . . That went well, but the meditation itself was a failure. He could not stop thinking. So he thought. He thought about what he could do. He found nothing. He was weak as water, helpless as the baby. He imagined himself speaking on the holonet with a script saying that the Ekumen reluctantly approved the limited use of biological weapons in order to end the civil war. He imagined himself on the holonet dropping the script and saying that the Ekumen would never approve the use of biological weapons for any reason. Both imaginings were fantasies. Rayaye's schemes were fantasies. Seeing that his hostage was useless Rayaye would have him shot. How long has he lived? As long as sixty-two years. A much fairer share of time than Rekam was getting. His mind went on past thinking.

The zadyo opened the door and told him he could come out.

"How close is the Liberation Army, zadyo?" he asked. He expected no answer. He went out onto the terrace. It was late afternoon. Kamsa was there, sitting with the baby at her breast. Her nipple was in his mouth but he was not sucking. She covered her breast. Her face as she did so looked sad for the first time.

"Is he asleep? May I hold him?" Esdan said, sitting by her.

She shifted the little bundle over to his lap. Her face was still troubled. Esdan thought the child's breathing was more difficult, harder work. But he was awake, and looked up into Esdan's face with his big eyes. Esdan made faces, sticking out his lips and blinking. He won a soft little smile.

"The hands say, that army do come," Kamsa said in her very soft voice.

"The Liberation?"

"Enna. Some army."

"From across the river?"

"I think."

"They're assets — freedmen. They're your own people. They won't hurt you." Maybe.

She was frightened. Her control was perfect, but she was frightened. She had seen the Uprising, here. And the reprisals.

"Hide out, if you can, if there's bombing or fighting," he said. "Underground. There must be hiding places here."

She thought and said, "Yes."

It was peaceful in the gardens of Yaramera. No sound but the wind rustling leaves and the faint buzz of the generator. Even the burned, jagged ruins of the house looked mellowed, ageless. The worst has happened, said the ruins. To them. Maybe not to Kamsa and Heo, Gana and Esdan. But there was no hint of violence in the summer air. The baby smiled its vague smile again, nestling in Esdan's arms. He thought of the stone he had lost in his dream.

He was locked into the windowless room for the night. He had no way to know what time it was when he was roused by noise, brought stark awake by a series of shots and explosions, gunfire or handbombs. There was silence, then a second series of bangs and cracks, fainter. Silence again, stretching on and on. Then he heard a flyer right over the house as if circling, sounds inside the house: a shout, running. He lighted the lamp, struggled into his trousers, hard to pull on over the swathed foot. When he heard the flyer coming back and an explosion, he leapt in panic for the door, knowing nothing but that he had to get out of this deathtrap room. He had always feared fire, dying in fire. The door was solid wood, solidly bolted into its solid frame. He had no hope at all of breaking it down and knew it even in his panic. He shouted once, "Let me out of here!" then got control of himself, returned to the cot, and after a minute sat down on the floor between the cot and the wall, as sheltered a place as the room afforded, trying to imagine what was going on. A Liberation raid and Rayaye's men shooting back, trying to bring the flyer down, was what he imagined.

Dead silence. It went on and on.

His lamp flickered.

He got up and stood at the door.

"Let me out!"

No sound.

A single shot. Voices again, running feet again, shouting, calling. After another long silence, distant voices, the sound of men coming down the corridor outside the room. A man said, "Keep them out there for now," a flat, harsh voice. He hesitated and nerved himself and shouted out, "I'm a prisoner! In here!"

A pause.

"Who's in there?"

It was no voice he had heard. He was good at voices, faces, names, intentions.

"Esdardon Aya of the embassy of the Ekumen."

"Mighty Lord!" the voice said.

"Get me out of here, will you?"

There was no reply, but the door was rattled vainly on its massive hinges, was thumped; more voices outside, more thumping and banging. "Axe," somebody said. "Find the key," somebody else said; they went off. Esdan waited. He fought down a repeated impulse to laugh, afraid of hysteria, but it was funny, stupidly funny, all the shouting through the door and seeking keys and axes, a farce in the middle of a battle. What battle?

He had had it backwards. Liberation men had entered the house and killed Rayaye's men, taking most of them by surprise. They had been waiting for Rayaye's flyer when it came. They must have had contacts among the fieldhands, informers, guides. Sealed in his room, he had heard only the noisy end of the business. When he was let out, they were dragging out the dead. He saw the horribly maimed body of one of the young men, Alatual or Nemeo, come apart as they dragged it, ropy blood and entrails stretching out along the floor, the legs left behind. The man dragging the corpse was nonplussed and stood there holding the shoulders of the torso. "Well, shit," he said, and Esdan stood gasping, again trying not to laugh, not to vomit.

"Come on," said the men with him, and he came on.

Early morning light slanted through broken windows. Esdan kept looking around, seeing none of the house people. The men took him into the room with the packdog head over the mantel. Six or seven men were gathered around the table there. They wore no uniforms, though some had the yellow knot or ribbon of the Liberation on their cap or sleeve. They were ragged, tough, hard. Some were dark, some had beige or clayey or bluish skin, all of them looked edgy and dangerous. One of those with him, a thin, tall man, said in the harsh voice that had said "Mighty Lord" outside the door: "This is him."

"I'm Esdardon Aya, Old Music, of the embassy of the Ekumen," he said again, as easily as he could. "I was being held here. Thank you for liberating me."

Several of them stared at him the way people who had never seen an alien stared, taking in his red-brown skin and deep-set, white-cornered eyes and the subtler differences of skull structure and features. One or two stared more aggressively, as if to test his assertion, show they'd believe he was what he said he was when he proved it. A big, broad-shouldered man, white-skinned and with brownish hair, pure dusty, pure blood of the ancient conquered race, looked at Esdan a long time. "We came to do that," he said.

He spoke softly, the asset voice. It might take them a generation or more to learn to raise their voices, to speak free.

"How did you know I was here? The fieldnet?"

It was what they had called the clandestine system of information passed from voice to ear, field to compound to city and back again, long before there was a holonet. The Hame had used the fieldnet and it had been the chief instrument of the Uprising.

A short, dark man smiled and nodded slightly, then froze his nod as he saw that the others weren't giving out any information.

"You know who brought me here, then — Rayaye. I don't know who he was acting for. What I can tell you, I will." Relief had made him stupid, he was talking too much, playing hands-around-the-flowerbed while they played tough guy. "I have friends here," he went on in a more neutral voice, looking at each of their faces in turn, direct but civil. "Bondswomen, house people. I hope they're all right."

"Depends," said a grey-haired, slight man who looked very tired.

"A woman with a baby, Kamsa. An old woman, Gana."

A couple of them shook their heads to signify ignorance or indifference. Most made no response at all. He looked around at them again, repressing anger and irritation at this pomposity, this tight-lipped stuff.

"We need to know what you were doing here," the brown-haired man said.

"A Liberation Army contact in the city was taking me from the embassy to Liberation Command, about fifteen days ago. We were intercepted in the Divide by Rayaye's men. They brought me here. I spent some time in a crouchcage," Esdan said in the same neutral voice. "My foot was hurt and I can't walk much. I talked twice with Rayaye. Before I say anything else I think you can understand that I need to know who I'm talking to."

The tall thin man who had released him from the locked room went around the table and conferred briefly with the grey-haired man. The brown-haired one listened, consented. The tall thin one spoke to Esdan in his uncharacteristically harsh, flat voice: "We are a special mission of the Advance Army of the World Liberation. I am Marshal Metoy." The others all said their names. The big brown-haired man was General Banarkamye, the tired older man was General Tueyo. They said their rank with their name, but didn't use it addressing one another, nor did they call him Mister. Before Liberation, rentspeople had seldom used any titles to one another but those of parentage: father, sister, aunty. Titles were something that went in front of an owner's name: Lord, Master, Mister, Boss. Evidently the Liberation had decided to do without them. It pleased him to find an army that didn't click its heels and shout Sir! But he wasn't certain what army he'd found.

"They kept you in that room?" Metoy asked him. He was a strange man, a flat, cold voice, a pale, cold face, but he wasn't as jumpy as the others. He seemed sure of himself, used to being in charge.

"They locked me in there last night. As if they'd had some kind of warning of trouble coming. Usually I had a room upstairs."

"You may go there now," Metoy said. "Stay indoors."

"I will. Thank you again," he said to them all. "Please, when you have word of Kamsa and Gana — ?" He did not wait to be snubbed, but turned and went out.

One of the younger men went with him. He had named himself Zadyo Tema. The Army of the Liberation was using the old veot ranks, then. There were veots among them, Esdan knew, but Tema was not one. He was light-skinned and had the city-dusty accent, soft, dry, clipped. Esdan did not try to talk to him. Tema was extremely nervous, spooked by the night's work of killing at close quarters or by something else; there was an almost constant tremor in his shoulders, arms, and hands, and his pale face was set in a painful scowl. He was not in a mood for chitchat with an elderly civilian alien prisoner.

In war everybody is a prisoner, the historian Henennemores had written.

Esdan had thanked his new captors for liberating him, but he knew where, at the moment, he stood. It was still Yaramera.

Yet there was some relief in seeing his room again, sitting down in the one-armed chair by the window to look out at the early sunlight, the long shadows of trees across the lawns and terraces.

None of the housepeople came out as usual to go about their work or take a break from it. Nobody came to his room. The morning wore on. He did what exercises of the tanhai he could do with his foot as it was. He sat aware, dozed off, woke up, tried to sit aware, sat restless, anxious, working over words: *A special mission of the Advance Army of World Liberation.*

The Legitimate Government called the enemy army "insurgent forces" or "rebel hordes" on the holonews. It had started out calling itself the Army of the Liberation, nothing about World Liberation; but he had been cut off from any coherent contact with the freedom fighters ever since the Uprising, and cut off from all information of any kind since the embassy was sealed — except for information from other worlds light years away, of course, there'd been no end of that, the ansible was full of it, but of what was going on two streets away, nothing, not a word. In the embassy he'd been ignorant, useless, helpless, passive. Exactly as he was here. Since the war began he'd been, as Henennemores had said, a prisoner. Along with everybody else on Werel. A prisoner in the cause of liberty.

He feared that he would come to accept his helplessness, that it would persuade his soul. He must remember what this war was about. But let the Liberation come soon, he thought, come set me free!

In the middle of the afternoon the young zadyo brought him a plate of cold food, obviously scraps and leftovers they'd found in the kitchens, and a bottle of beer. He ate and drank gratefully. But it was clear that they had not released the housepeople. Or had killed them. He would not let his mind stay on that.

After sunset the zadyo came back and brought him downstairs to the packdog room. The generator was off, of course; nothing had kept it going but old Saka's eternal tinkering. Men carried electric torches, and in the packdog room a couple of big oil lamps burned on the table, putting a romantic, golden light on the faces round it, throwing deep shadows behind them.

"Sit down," said the brown-haired general, Banarkamye — Read-bible, his name could be translated. "We have some questions to ask you."

Silent but civil assent.

They asked how he had got out of the embassy, who his contacts with the Liberation had been, where he had been going, why he had tried to go, what happened during the kidnapping, who had brought him here, what they had asked him, what they had wanted from him. Having decided during the afternoon that candor would serve him best, he answered all the questions directly and briefly until the last one.

"I personally am on your side of this war," he said, "but the Ekumen is necessarily neutral. Since at the moment I'm the only alien on Werel free to speak, whatever I say may be taken, or mistaken, as coming from the embassy and the Stabiles. That was my value to Rayaye. It may be my value to you. But it's a false value. I can't speak for the Ekumen. I have no authority."

"They wanted you to say the Ekumen supports the Jits," the tired man, Tueyo, said.

Esdan nodded.

"Did they talk about using any special tactics, weapons?" That was Banarkamye, grim, trying not to weight the question.

"I'd rather answer that question when I'm behind your lines, General, talking to people I know in Liberation Command."

"You're talking to the World Liberation Army Command. Refusal to answer can be taken as evidence of complicity with the enemy." That was Metoy, glib, hard, harsh-voiced.

"I know that, Marshal."

They exchanged a glance. Despite his open threat, Metoy was the one Esdan felt inclined to trust. He was solid. The others were nervy, unsteady. He was sure now that they were factionalists. How big their faction was, how much at odds with Liberation Command it was, he could learn only by what they might let slip.

"Listen, Mr. Old Music," Tueyo said. Old habits die hard. "We know you worked for the Hame. You helped send people to Yeowe. You backed us then." Esdan nodded. "You must back us now. We are speaking to you frankly. We have information that the Jits are planning a counterattack. What that means, now, it means that they're going to use the bibo. It can't mean anything else. That can't happen. They can't be let do that. They have to be stopped."

"You say the Ekumen is neutral," Banarkamye said. "That is a lie. A hundred years the Ekumen wouldn't let this world join them, because we had the bibo. Had it, didn't use it, just had it was enough. Now they say they're neutral. Now when it matters! Now when this world is part of them! They have got to act. To act against that weapon. They have got to stop the Jits from using it."

"If the Legitimates did have it, if they did plan to use it, and if I could get word to the Ekumen — what could they do?"

"You speak. You tell the Jit President: the Ekumen says stop there. The Ekumen will send ships, send troops. You back us! If you aren't with us, you are with them!"

"General, the nearest ship is light years away. The Legitimates know that."

"But you can call them, you have the transmitter."

"The ansible in the embassy?"

"The Jits have one of them too."

"The ansible in the foreign ministry was destroyed in the Uprising. In the first attack on the government buildings. They blew the whole block up."

"How do we know that?"

"Your own forces did it. General, do you think the Legitimates have an ansible link with the Ekumen that you don't have? They don't. They could have taken over the embassy and its ansible, but in so doing they'd have lost what credibility they have with the Ekumen. And what good would it have done them? The Ekumen has no troops to send," and he added, because he was suddenly not sure Banarkamye knew it, "as you know. If it did, it would take them years to get here. For that reason and many others, the Ekumen has no army and fights no wars."

He was deeply alarmed by their ignorance, their amateurishness, their fear. He kept alarm and impatience out of his voice, speaking quietly and looking at them unworriedly, as if expecting understanding and agreement. The mere appearance of such confidence sometimes fulfills itself. Unfortunately, from the looks of their faces, he was telling the two generals they'd been wrong and telling Metoy he'd been right. He was taking sides in a disagreement.

Banarkamye said, "Keep all that a while yet," and went back over the first interrogation, repeating questions, asking for more details, listening to them expressionlessly. Saving face. Showing he distrusted the hostage. He kept pressing for anything Rayaye had said concerning an invasion or a counterattack in the south. Esdan repeated several times that Rayaye had said President Oyo was expecting a Liberation invasion of this province, downriver from here. Each time he added, "I have no idea whether anything Rayaye told me was the truth." The fourth or fifth time round he said, "Excuse me, General. I must ask again for some word about the people here — "

"Did you know anybody at this place before you came here?" a younger man asked sharply.

"No. I'm asking about housepeople. They were kind to me. Kamsa's baby is sick, it needs care. I'd like to know they're being looked after."

The generals were conferring with each other, paying no attention to this diversion.

"Anybody stayed here, a place like this, after the Uprising, is a collaborator," said the zadyo, Tema.

"Where were they supposed to go?" Esdan asked, trying to keep his tone easy. "This isn't liberated country. The bosses still work these fields with slaves. They still use the crouchcage here." His voice shook a little on the last words, and he cursed himself for it.

Banarkamye and Tueyo were still conferring, ignoring his question. Metoy stood up and said, "Enough for tonight. Come with me."

Esdan limped after him across the hall, up the stairs. The young zadyo followed, hurrying, evidently sent by Banarkamye. No private conversations allowed. Metoy, however, stopped at the door of Esdan's room and said, looking down at him, "The housepeople will be looked after."

"Thank you," Esdan said with warmth. He added, "Gana was caring for this injury. I need to see her." If they wanted him alive and undamaged, no harm using his ailments as leverage. If they didn't, no use in anything much.

He slept little and badly. He had always thrived on information and action. It was exhausting to be kept both ignorant and helpless, crippled mentally and physically. And he was hungry.

Soon after sunrise he tried his door and found it locked. He knocked and shouted a while before anybody came, a young fellow looking scared, probably a sentry, and then Tema, sleepy and scowling, with the door key.

"I want to see Gana," Esdan said, fairly peremptory. "She looks after this," gesturing to his swaddled foot. Tema shut the door without saying anything. After an hour or so, the key rattled in the lock again and Gana came in. Metoy followed her. Tema followed him.

Gana stood in the reverence to Esdan. He came forward quickly and put his hands on her arms and laid his cheek against hers. "Lord Kamye be praised I see you well!" he said, words that had often been said to him by people like her. "Kamsa, the baby, how are they?"

She was scared, shaky, her hair unkempt, her eyelids red, but she recovered herself pretty well from his utterly unexpected brotherly greeting. "They are in the kitchen now, sir," she said. "The army men, they said that foot do pain you."

"That's what I said to them. Maybe you'd re-bandage it for me."

He sat down on the bed and she got to work unwrapping the cloths.

"Are the other people all right? Heo? Choyo?"

She shook her head once.

"I'm sorry," he said. He could not ask her more.

She did not do as good a job bandaging his foot as before. She had little strength in her hands to pull the wrappings tight, and she hurried her work, unnerved by the strangers watching.

"I hope Choyo's back in the kitchen," he said, half to her half to them. "Somebody's got to do some cooking here."

"Yes, sir," she whispered.

Not sir, not master! he wanted to warn her, fearing for her. He looked up at Metoy, trying to judge his attitude, and could not.

Gana finished her job. Metoy sent her off with a word, and sent the zadyo after her. Gana went gladly, Tema resisted. "General Banarkamye —" he began. Metoy looked at him. The young man hesitated, scowled, obeyed.

"I will look after these people," Metoy said. "I always have. I was a compound boss." He gazed at Esdan with his cold black eyes. "I'm a cutfree. Not many like me left, these days."

Esdan said after a moment, "Thanks, Metoy. They need help. They don't understand."

Metoy nodded.

"I don't understand either," Esdan said. "Does the Liberation plan to invade? Or did Rayaye invent that as an excuse for talking about deploying the bibo? Does Oyo believe it? Do you believe it? Is the Liberation Army across the river there? Did you come from it? Who are you? I don't expect you to answer."

"I won't," the eunuch said.

If he was a double agent, Esdan thought after he left, he was working for Liberation Command. Or he hoped so. Metoy was a man he wanted on his side.

But I don't know what my side is, he thought, as he went back to his chair by the window. The Liberation, of course, yes, but what is the Liberation? Not an ideal, the freedom of the enslaved. Not now. Never again. Since the Uprising, the Liberation is an army, a political body, a great number of people and leaders and would-be leaders, ambitions and greed clogging hopes and strength, a clumsy amateur semi-government lurching from violence to compromise, ever more complicated, never again to know the beautiful simplicity of the ideal, the pure idea of liberty. And that's what I wanted, what I worked for, all these years. To muddle the nobly simple structure of the hierarchy of caste by infecting it with the idea of justice. And then to confuse the nobly simple structure of the ideal of human equality by trying to make it real. The monolithic lie frays out into a thousand incompatible truths, and that's what I wanted. But I am caught in the insanity, the stupidity, the meaningless brutality of the event.

They all want to use me, but I've outlived my usefulness, he thought; and the thought went through him like a shaft of clear light. He had kept thinking there was something he could do. There wasn't.

It was a kind of freedom.

No wonder he and Metoy had understood each other wordlessly and at once.

The zadyo Tema came to his door to conduct him downstairs. Back to the packdog room. All the leader-types were drawn to that room, its dour masculinity. Only five men were there this time, Metoy, the two generals, the two who used the rank of rega. Banarkamye dominated them all. He was through asking questions and was in the order-giving vein. "We leave here tomorrow," he said to Esdan. "You with us. We will have access to the Liberation holonet. You will speak for us. You will tell the Jit goverment that the Ekumen knows they are planning to deploy banned weapons and warns them that if they do, there will be instant and terrible retaliation."

Esdan was light-headed with hunger and sleeplessness. He stood still — he had not been invited to sit down — and looked down at the floor, his hands at his sides. He murmured barely audibly, "Yes, master."

Banarkamye's head snapped up, his eyes flashed. "What did you say?"

"Enna."

"Who do you think you are?"

"A prisoner of war."

"You can go."

Esdan left. Tema followed him but did not stop or direct him. He made his way straight to the kitchen, where he heard the rattle of pans, and said, "Choyo, please, give me something to eat!" The old man, cowed and shaky, mumbled and apologised and fretted, but produced some fruit and stale bread. Esdan sat at the worktable and devoured it. He offered some to Tema, who refused stiffly. Esdan ate it all. When he was done he limped on out through the kitchen exitways to a side door leading to the great terrace. He hoped to see Kamsa there, but none of the housepeople were out. He sat on a bench in the balustrade that looked down on the long reflecting pool. Tema stood nearby, on duty.

"You said the bondspeople on a place like this, if they didn't join the Uprising, were collaborators," Esdan said.

Tema was motionless, but listening.

"You don't think any of them might just not have understood what was going on? And still don't understand? This is a benighted place, zadyo. Hard to even imagine freedom, here."

The young man resisted answering for a while, but Esdan talked on, trying to make some contact with him, get through to him. Suddenly something he said popped the lid.

"Usewomen," Tema said. "Get fucked by blacks, every night. All they are, fucks. Jits' whores. Bearing their black brats, yesmaster yesmaster. You said it, they don't know what freedom is. Never will. Can't liberate anybody lets a black fuck 'em. They're foul. Dirty, can't get clean. They got black jizz through and through 'em. Jitjizz!" He spat on the terrace and wiped his mouth.

Esdan sat still, looking down over the still water of the pool to the lower terraces, the big tree, the misty river, the far green shore. *May he be well and work well, have patience, compassion, peace. What use was I, ever? All I did. It never was any use. Patience, compassion, peace. They are your own people. . . .* He looked down at the thick blob of spittle on the yellow sandstone of the terrace. *Fool, to leave his own people a lifetime behind him and come to meddle* with another world. Fool, to think you could give anybody freedom. That was what death was for. To get us out of the crouchcage.

He got up and limped towards the house in silence. The young man followed him.

The lights came back on just as it was getting dark. They must have let old Saka go back to his tinkering. Preferring twilight, Esdan turned the room light off. He was lying on his bed when Kamsa knocked and came in, carrying a tray. "Kamsa!" he said, struggling up, and would have hugged her, but the tray prevented him. "Rekam is — ?"

"With my mother," she murmured.

"He's all right?"

The backward nod. She set the tray down on the bed, as there was no table.

"You're all right? Be careful, Kamsa. I wish I — They're leaving tomorrow, they say. Stay out of their way if you can."

"I do. Do you be safe, sir," she said in her soft voice. He did not know if it was a question or a wish. He made a little rueful gesture, smiling. She turned to leave.

"Kamsa, is Heo — ?"

"She was with that one. In his bed."

After a pause he said, "Is there anywhere you can hide out?" He was afraid that Banarkamye's men might execute these people when they left, as "collaborators" or to hide their own tracks.

"We got a hole to go to, like you said," she said.

"Good. Go there, if you can. Vanish! Stay out of sight."

She said, "I will hold fast, sir."

She was closing the door behind her when the sound of a flyer approaching buzzed the windows. They both stood still, she in the doorway, he near the window. Shouts downstairs, outside, men running. There was more than one flyer, approaching from the southeast. "Kill the lights!" somebody shouted. Men were running out to the flyers parked on the lawn and terrace. The window flared up with light, the air with a shattering explosion.

"Come with me," Kamsa said, and took his hand and pulled him after her, out the door, down the hall and through a service door he had never even seen. He hobbled with her as fast as he could down ladderlike stone stairs, through a back passage, out into the stable warren. They came outdoors just as a series of explosions rocked everything around them. They hurried across the courtyard through overwhelming noise and the leap of fire, Kamsa still pulling him along with complete sureness of where she was going, and ducked into one of the storerooms at the end of the stables. Gana was there and one of the old bondsmen, opening up a trap door in the floor. They went down, Kamsa with a leap, the others slow and awkward on the wooden ladder, Esdan most awkward, landing badly on his broken foot. The old man came last and pulled the trap shut over them. Gana had a battery lamp, but kept it on only briefly, showing a big, low, dirt-floored cellar, shelves, an archway to another room, a heap of wooden crates, five faces: the baby awake, gazing silent as ever from its sling on Gana's shoulder. Then darkness. And for some time silence.

They groped at the crates, set them down for seats at random in the darkness.

A new series of explosions, seeming far away, but the ground and the darkness shivered. They shivered in it. "O Kamye," one of them whispered.

Esdan sat on the shaky crate and let the jab and stab of pain in his foot sink into a burning throb.

Explosions: three, four.

Darkness was a substance, like thick water.

"Kamsa," he murmured.

She made some sound that located her near him.

"Thank you."

"You said hide, then we did talk of this place," she whispered.

The old man breathed wheezily and cleared his throat often. The baby's breathing was also audible, a small uneven sound, almost panting.

"Give me him." That was Gana. She must have transferred the baby to his mother.

Kamsa whispered, "Not now."

The old man spoke suddenly and loudly, startling them all: "No water in this!"

Kamsa shushed him and Gana hissed, "Don't shout, fool man!"

"Deaf," Kamsa murmured to Esdan, with a hint of laughter.

If they had no water, their hiding time was limited; the night, the next day; even that might be too long for a woman nursing a baby. Kamsa's mind was running on the same track as Esdan's. She said, "How do we know, should we come out?"

"Chance it, when we have to."

There was a long silence. It was hard to accept that one's eyes did not adjust to the darkness, that however long one waited one would see nothing. It was cave-cool. Esdan wished his shirt were warmer.

"You keep him warm," Gana said.

"I do," Kamsa murmured.

"Those men, they were bondsfolk?" That was Kamsa whispering to him. She was quite near him, to his left.

"Yes. Freed bondsfolk. From the north."

She said, "Lotsalot different men come here, since the old Owner did die. Army soldiers, some. But no bondsfolk before. They shot Heo. They shot Vey and old Seneo. He didn't die but he's shot."

"Somebody from the field compound must have led them, showed them where the guards were posted. But they couldn't tell the bondsfolk from the soldiers. Where were you when they came?"

"Sleeping, back of the kitchen. All us housefolk. Six. That man did stand there like a risen dead. He said, Lie down there! Don't stir a hair! So we did that. Heard them shooting and shouting all over the house. Oh, mighty Lord! I did fear! Then no more shooting, and that man did come back to us and hold his gun at us and take us out to the old house-compound. They did get that old gate shut on us. Like old days."

"For what did they do that if they are bondsfolk?" Gana's voice said from the darkness.

"Trying to get free," Esdan said dutifully.

"How free? Shooting and killing? Kill a girl in the bed?"

"They do all fight all the others, mama," Kamsa said.

"I thought all that was done, back three years," the old woman said. Her voice sounded strange. She was in tears. "I thought that was freedom then."

"They did kill the master in his bed!" the old man shouted out at the top of his voice, shrill, piercing. "What can come of that!"

There was a bit of a scuffle in the darkness. Gana was shaking the old fellow, hissing at him to shut up. He cried, "Let me go!" but quieted down, wheezing and muttering.

"Mighty Lord," Kamsa murmured, with that desperate laughter in her voice.

The crate was increasingly uncomfortable, and Esdan wanted to get his aching foot up or at least level. He lowered himself to the ground. It was cold, gritty, unpleasant to the hands. There was nothing to lean against. "If you made a light for a minute, Gana," he said, "we might find sacks, something to lie down on."

The world of the cellar flashed into being around them, amazing in its intricate precision. They found nothing to use but the loose board shelves. They set down several of these, making a kind of platform, and crept onto it as Gana switched them back into formless simple night. They were all cold. They huddled up against one another, side to side, back to back.

After a long time, an hour or more, in which the utter silence of the cellar was unbroken by any noise, Gana said in an impatient whisper, "Everybody up there did die, I think."

"That would simplify things for us," Esdan murmured.

"But we are the buried ones," said Kamsa.

Their voices roused the baby and he whimpered, the first complaint Esdan had ever heard him make. It was a tiny, weary grizzling or fretting, not a cry. It roughened his breathing and he gasped between his frettings. "Oh, baby, baby, hush now, hush," the mother murmured, and Esdan felt her rocking her body, cradling the baby close to keep him warm. She sang almost inaudibly, *"Suna meya, suna na . . . Sura rena, sura na . . ."* Monotonous, rhythmic, buzzy, purring, the sound made warmth, made comfort.

He must have dozed. He was lying curled up on the planks. He had no idea how long they had been in the cellar.

I have lived here forty years desiring freedom, his mind said to him. That desire brought me here. It will bring me out of here. I will hold fast.

He asked the others if they had heard anything since the bombing raid. They all whispered no.

He rubbed his head. "What do you think, Gana?" he said.

"I think the cold air does harm that baby," she said in almost her normal voice, which was always low.

"You do talk? What do you say?" the old man shouted. Kamsa, next to him, patted him and quieted him.

"I'll go look," Gana said.

"I'll go."

"You got one foot on you," the old woman said in a disgusted tone. She grunted and leaned hard on Esdan's shoulder as she stood up. "Now be still." She did not turn on the light, but felt her way over to the ladder and climbed it, with a little whuff of breath at each step up. She pushed, heaved at the trap door. An edge of light showed. They could dimly see the cellar and each other and the dark blob of Gana's head up in the light. She stood there a long time, then let the trap down. "Nobody," she whispered from the ladder. "No noise. Looks like first morning."

"Better wait," Esdan said.

She came back and lowered herself down among them again. After a time she said, "We go out, it's strangers in the house, some other army soldiers. Then where?"

"Can you get to the field compound?" Esdan suggested.

"It's a long road."

After a while he said, "Can't know what to do till we know who's up there. All right. But let me go out, Gana."

"For what?"

"Because I'll know who they are," he said, hoping he was right.

"And they too," Kamsa said, with that strange little edge of laughter. "No mistaking you, I guess."

"Right," he said. He struggled to his feet, found his way to the ladder, and climbed it laboriously. "I'm too old for this," he thought again. He pushed up the trap and looked out. He listened for a long time. At last he whispered to those below him in the dark, "I'll be back as soon as I can," and crawled out, scrambling awkwardly to his feet. He caught his breath: the air of the place was thick with burning. The light was strange, dim. He followed the wall till he could peer out of the storeroom doorway.

What had been left of the old house was down like the rest of it, blown open, smouldering and masked in stinking smoke. Black embers and broken glass covered the cobbled yard. Nothing moved except the smoke. Yellow smoke, grey smoke. Above it all was the even, clear blue of dawn.

He went around onto the terrace, limping and stumbling, for his foot shot blinding pains up his leg. Coming to the balustrade he saw the blackened wrecks of the two flyers. Half the upper terrace was a raw crater. Below it the gardens of Yaramera stretched beautiful and serene as ever, level below level, to the old tree and the river. A man lay across the steps that went down to the lower terrace; he lay easily, restfully, his arms outflung. Nothing moved but the creeping smoke and the white-flowered bushes nodding in a breath of wind.

The sense of being watched from behind, from the blank windows of the fragments of the house that still stood, was intolerable. "Is anybody here?" Esdan suddenly called out.

Silence.

He shouted again, louder.

There was an answer, a distant call, from around in front of the house. He limped his way down onto the path, out in the open, not seeking to conceal himself; what was the use? Men came around from the front of the house, three men, then a fourth — a woman. They were assets, roughly clothed, fieldhands they must be, come down from their compound. "I'm with some of the housepeople," he said, stopping when they stopped, ten meters apart. "We hid out in a cellar. Is anybody else around?"

"Who are you?" one of them said, coming closer, peering, seeing the wrong color skin, the wrong kind of eyes.

"I'll tell you who I am. But is it safe for us to come out? There's old people, a baby. Are the soldiers gone?"

"They are dead," the woman said, a tall, pale-skinned, bony-faced woman.

"One we found hurt," said one of the men. "All the housepeople dead. Who did throw those bombs? What army?"

"I don't know what army," Esdan said. "Please, go tell my people they can come up. Back there, in the stables. Call out to them. Tell them who you are. I can't walk." The wrappings on his foot had worked loose, and the fractures had moved; the pain began to take away his breath. He sat down on the path, gasping. His head swam. The gardens of Yaramera grew very bright and very small and drew away and away from him, farther away than home.

He did not quite lose consciousness, but things were confused in his mind for a good while. There were a lot of people around, and they were outdoors, and everything stank of burnt meat, a smell that clung in the back of his mouth and made him retch. There was Kamsa, the tiny bluish shadowy sleeping face of the baby on her shoulder. There was Gana, saying to other people, "He did befriend us." A young man with big hands talked to him and did something to his foot, bound it up again, tighter, causing terrible pain and then the beginning of relief.

He was lying down on his back on grass. Beside him a man was lying down on his back on grass. It was Metoy, the eunuch. Metoy's scalp was bloody, the black hair burned short and brown. The dust-colored skin of his face was pale, bluish, like the baby's. He lay quietly, blinking sometimes.

The sun shone down. People were talking, a lot of people, somewhere nearby, but he and Metoy were lying on the grass and nobody bothered them.

"Were the flyers from Bellen, Metoy?" Esdan said.

"Came from the east." Metoy's harsh voice was weak and hoarse. "I guess they were." After a while he said, "They want to cross the river."

Esdan thought about this for a while. His mind still did not work well at all. "Who does?" he said finally.

"These people. The fieldhands. The assets of Yaramera. They want to go meet the Army."

"The Invasion?"

"The Liberation."

Esdan propped himself up on his elbows. Raising his head seemed to clear it, and he sat up. He looked over at Metoy. "Will they find them?" he asked.

"If the Lord so wills," said the eunuch.

Presently Metoy tried to prop himself up like Esdan, but failed. "I got blown up," he said, short of breath. "Something hit my head. I see two for one."

"Probably a concussion. Lie still. Stay awake. Were you with Banarkamye, or observing?"

"I'm in your line of work."

Esdan nodded, the backward nod.

"Factions will be the death of us," Metoy said faintly.

Kamsa came and squatted down beside Esdan. "They say we must go cross the river," she told him in her soft voice. "To where the people-army will keep us safe. I don't know."

"Nobody knows, Kamsa."

"I can't take Rekam cross a river," she whispered. Her face clenched up, her lips drawing back, her brows down. She wept, without tears and in silence. "The water is cold."

"They'll have boats, Kamsa. They'll look after you and Rekam. Don't worry. It'll be all right." He knew his words were meaningless.

"I can't go," she whispered.

"Stay here then," Metoy said.

"They said that other army will come here."

"It might. More likely ours will."

She looked at Metoy. "You are the cutfree," she said. "With those others." She looked back at Esdan. "Choyo got killed. All the kitchen is blown in pieces burning." She hid her face in her arms.

Esdan sat up and reached out to her, stroking her shoulder and arm. He touched the baby's fragile head with its thin, dry hair.

Gana came and stood over them. "All the fieldhands are going cross the river," she said. "To be safe."

"You'll be safer here. Where there's food and shelter." Metoy spoke in short bursts, his eyes closed. "Than walking to meet an invasion."

"I can't take him, mama," Kamsa whispered. "He has got to be warm. I can't, I can't take him."

Gana stooped and looked into the baby's face, touching it very softly with one finger. Her wrinkled face closed like a fist. She straightened up, but not erect as she used to stand. She stood bowed. "All right," she said. "We'll stay."

She sat down on the grass beside Kamsa. People were on the move around them. The woman Esdan had seen on the terrace stopped by Gana and said, "Come on, grandmother. Time to go. The boats are ready waiting."

"Staying," Gana said.

"Why? Can't leave that old house you worked in?" the woman said, jeering, humoring. "It's all burned up, grandmother! Come on now. Bring that girl and her baby." She looked at Esdan and Metoy, a flick-glance. They were not her concern. "Come on," she repeated. "Get up now."

"Staying," Gana said.

"You crazy housefolk," the woman said, turned away, turned back, gave it up with a shrug, and went on.

A few others stopped, but none for more than a question, a moment. They streamed on down the terraces, the sunlit paths beside the quiet pools, down towards the boathouses beyond the great tree. After a while they were all gone.

The sun had grown hot. It must be near noon. Metoy was whiter than ever, but he sat up, saying he could see single, most of the time.

"We should get into the shade, Gana," Esdan said. "Metoy, can you get up?"

He staggered and shambled, but walked without help, and they got to the shade of a garden wall. Gana went off to look for water. Kamsa was carrying Rekam in her arms, close against her breast, sheltered from the sun. She had not spoken for a long time. When they had settled down she said, half questioning, looking around dully, "We are all alone here."

"There'll be others stayed. In the compounds," Metoy said. "They'll turn up."

Gana came back; she had no vessel to carry water in, but had soaked her scarf, and laid the cold wet cloth on Metoy's head. He shuddered. "You can walk better, then we can go to the house-compound, cutfree," she said. "Places we can live in, there."

"House-compound is where I grew up, grandmother," he said.

And presently, when he said he could walk, they made their halt and lame way down a road which Esdan vaguely remembered, the road to the crouchcage. It seemed a long road. They came to the high compound wall and the gate standing open.

Esdan turned to look back at the ruins of the great house for a moment. Gana stopped beside him.

"Rekam died," she said under her breath.

He caught his breath. "When?"

She shook her head. "I don't know. She wants to hold him. She's done with holding him, then she will let him go." She looked in the open gateway at the rows of huts and longhouses, the dried-up garden patches, the dusty ground. "Lotsalot little babies are in there," she said. "In that ground. Two of my own. Her sisters." She went in, following Kamsa. Esdan stood a while longer in the gateway, and then he went in to do what there was for him to do: dig a grave for the child, and wait with the others for the Liberation.

THE BIRTHDAY OF THE WORLD

Tazu was having a tantrum, because he was three. After the birthday of the world, tomorrow, he would be four and would not have tantrums.

He had left off screaming and kicking and was turning blue from holding his breath. He lay on the ground stiff as a corpse, but when Haghag stepped over him as if he wasn't there, he tried to bite her foot.

"This is an animal or a baby," Haghag said, "not a person." She glanced may-I-speak-to-you and I glanced yes. "Which does God's daughter think it is," she asked, "an animal or a baby?"

"An animal. Babies suck, animals bite," I said. All the servants of God laughed and tittered, except the new barbarian, Ruaway, who never smiled. Haghag said, "God's daughter must be right. Maybe somebody ought to put the animal outside. An animal shouldn't be in the holy house."

"I'm not an aminal!" Tazu screamed, getting up, his fists clenched and his eyes as red as rubies. "I'm God's son!"

"Maybe," Haghad said, looking him over. "This doesn't look so much like an animal now. Do you think this might be God's son?" she asked the holy women and men, and they all nodded their bodies, except the wild one, who stared and said nothing.

"I am, I am God's son!" Tazu shouted. "Not a baby! Arzi is the baby!" Then he burst into tears and ran to me, and I hugged him and began crying because he was crying. We cried till Haghag took us both on her lap and said it was time to stop crying, because God Herself was coming. So we stopped, and the bodyservants wiped the tears and snot from our faces and combed our hair, and Lady Clouds brought our gold hats, which we put on to see God Herself.

She came with her mother, who used to be God Herself a long time ago, and the new baby, Arzi, on a big pillow carried by the idiot. The idiot was a son of God too. There were seven of us: Omimo, who was fourteen and had gone to live with the army, then the idiot, who was twelve, and had a big round head and small eyes and liked to play with Tazu and the baby, then Goïz, and another Goïz, who were called that because they had died and were in the ash-house where they ate spirit food, then me and Tazu, who would get married and be God, and then Babam Arzi, Lord Seven. I was important because I was the only daughter of God. If Tazu died I could marry Arzi, but if I died everything would be bad and difficult, Haghag said. They would have to act as if Lady Clouds' daughter Lady Sweetness was God's daughter and marry her to Tazu, but the world would know the difference. So my mother greeted me first, and Tazu second. We knelt and clasped our hands and touched our foreheads to our thumbs. Then we stood up, and God asked me what I had learned that day.

I told her what words I had learned to read and write.

"Very good," God said. "And what have you to ask, daughter?"

"I have nothing to ask, I thank you, Lady Mother," I said. Then I remembered I did have a question, but it was too late.

"And you, Tazu? What have you learned this day?"

THE BIRTHDAY OF THE WORLD | 215

"I tried to bite Haghag."

"Did you learn that was a good thing to do, or a bad thing?"

"Bad," Tazu said, but he smiled, and so did God, and Haghag laughed.

"And what have you to ask, son?"

"Can I have a new bath maid because Kig washes my head too hard?"

"If you have a new bath maid where will Kig go?"

"Away."

"This is her house. What if you asked Kig to wash your head more gently?"

Tazu looked unhappy, but God said, "Ask her, son." Tazu mumbled something to Kig, who dropped on her knees and thumbed her forehead. But she grinned the whole time. Her fearlessness made me envious. I whispered to Haghag, "If I forgot a question to ask can I ask if I can ask it?"

"Maybe," said Haghag, and thumbed her forehead to God for permission to speak, and when God nodded, Haghag said, "The daughter of God asks if she may ask a question."

"Better to do a thing at the time for doing it," God said, "but you may ask, daughter."

I rushed into the question, forgetting to thank her. "I wanted to know why I can't marry Tazu and Omimo both, because they're both my brothers."

Everybody looked at God, and seeing her smile a little, they all laughed, some of them loudly. My ears burned and my heart thumped.

"Do you want to marry all your brothers, child?"

"No, only Tazu and Omimo."

"Is Tazu not enough?"

Again they all laughed, especially the men. I saw Ruaway staring at us as if she thought we were all crazy.

"Yes, Lady Mother, but Omimo is older and bigger."

Now the laughter was even louder, but I had stopped caring, since God was not displeased. She looked at me thoughtfully and said, "Understand, my daughter. Our eldest son will be a soldier. That's his road. He'll serve God, fighting barbarians and rebels. The day he was born, a tidal wave destroyed the towns of the outer coast. So his name is Babam Omimo, Lord Drowning. Disaster serves God, but is not God."

I knew that was the end of the answer, and thumbed my forehead. I kept thinking about it after God left. It explained many things. All the same, even if he had been born with a bad omen, Omimo was handsome, and nearly a man, and Tazu was a baby that had tantrums. I was glad it would be a long time till we were married.

I remember that birthday because of the question I asked. I remember another birthday because of Ruaway. It must have been a year or two later. I ran into the water room to piss and saw her hunched up next to the water tank, almost hidden.

"What are you doing there?" I said, loud and hard, because I was startled. Ruaway shrank and said nothing. I saw her clothes were torn and there was blood dried in her hair.

"You tore your clothes," I said.

When she didn't answer, I lost patience and shouted, "Answer me! Why don't you talk?"

"Have mercy," Ruaway whispered so low I had to guess what she said.

"You talk all wrong when you do talk. What's wrong with you? Are they animals where you come from? You talk like an animal, brr-grr, grr-gra! Are you an idiot?"

When Ruaway said nothing, I pushed her with my foot. She looked up then and I saw not fear but killing in her eyes. That made me like her better. I hated people who were afraid of me. "Talk!" I said. "Nobody can hurt you. God the Father put his penis in you when he was conquering your country, so you're a holy woman. Lady Clouds told me. So what are you hiding for?"

Ruaway showed her teeth and said, "Can hurt me." She showed me places on her head where there was dried blood and fresh blood. Her arms were darkened with bruises.

"Who hurt you?"

"Holy women," she said with a snarl.

"Kig? Omery? Lady Sweetness?"

She nodded her body at each name.

"They're shit," I said. "I'll tell God Herself."

"No tell," Ruaway whispered. "Poison."

I thought about it and understood. The girls hurt her because she was a stranger, powerless. But if she got them in trouble they would cripple or kill her. Most of the barbarian holy women in our house were lame, or blind, or had had root-poison put in their food so that their skin was scabbed with purplish sores.

"Why don't you talk right, Ruaway?"

She said nothing.

"You still don't know how to talk?"

She looked up at me and suddenly said a whole long speech I did not understand. "How I talk," she said at the end, still looking at me, right in the eyes. That was nice; I liked it. Mostly I saw only eyelids. Ruaway's eyes were clear and beautiful, though her face was dirty and blood-smeared.

"But it doesn't mean anything," I said.

"Not here."

"Where does it mean anything?"

Ruaway said some more gra-gra and then said, "My people."

"Your people are Teghs. They fight God and get beaten."

"Maybe," Ruaway said, sounding like Haghag. Her eyes looked into mine again, without killing in them but without fear. Nobody looked at me, except Haghag and Tazu and of course God. Everybody else put their forehead on their thumbs so I couldn't tell what they were thinking. I wanted to keep Ruaway with me, but if I favored her, Kig and the others would torment and hurt her. I remembered that when Lord Festival began sleeping with Lady Pin, the men who had insulted Lady Pin became oily and sugary with her and the bodymaids stopped stealing her earrings. I said, "Sleep with me tonight," to Ruaway.

She looked stupid.

"But wash first," I said.

She still looked stupid.

"I don't have a penis!" I said, impatient with her. "If we sleep together Kig will be afraid to touch you."

After a while Ruaway reached out and took my hand and put her forehead against the back of it. It was like thumbing the forehead only it took two people to do it. I liked that. Ruaway's hand was warm, and I could feel the feather of her eyelashes on my hand.

"Tonight," I said. "You understand?" I had understood that Ruaway didn't always understand. Ruaway nodded her body, and I ran off.

I knew nobody could stop me from doing anything, being God's only daughter, but there was nothing I could do except what I was supposed to do, because everybody in the house of God knew everything I did. If sleeping with Ruaway was a thing I wasn't supposed to do, I couldn't do it. Haghag would tell me. I went to her and asked her.

Haghag scowled. "Why do you want that woman in your bed? She's a dirty barbarian. She has lice. She can't even talk."

Haghag was saying yes. She was jealous. I came and stroked her hand and said, "When I'm God I'll give you a room full of gold and jewels and dragon crests."

"You are my gold and jewels, little holy daughter," Haghag said.

Haghag was only a common person, but all the holy men and women in God's house, relatives of God or people touched by God, had to do what Haghag said. The nurse of God's children was always a common person, chosen by God Herself. Haghag had been chosen to be Omimo's nurse when her own children were grown up, so when I first remember her she was quite old. She was always the same, with strong hands and a soft voice, saying, "Maybe." She liked to laugh and eat. We were in her heart, and she was in mine. I thought I was her favorite, but when I told her so she said, "After Didi." Didi is what the idiot called himself. I asked her why he was deepest in her heart and she said, "Because he's foolish. And you because you're wise," she said, laughing at me because I was jealous of Lord Idiot.

So now I said, "You fill my heart," and she, knowing it, said hmph.

I think I was eight that year. Ruaway had been thirteen when God the Father put his penis into her after killing her father and mother in the war with her people. That made her sacred, so she had to come live in God's house. If she had conceived, the priests would have strangled her after she had the baby, and the baby would have been nursed by a common woman for two years and then brought back to God's house and trained to be a holy woman, a servant of God. Most of the bodyservants were God's bastards. Such people were holy, but had no title. Lords and ladies were God's relations, descendants of the ancestors of God. God's children were called lord and lady too, except the two who were betrothed. We were just called Tazu and Ze until we became God. My name is what the divine mother is called, the name of the sacred plant that feeds the people of God. Tazu means "great root," because when he was being born our father drinking smoke in the childbirth rituals saw a big tree blown over by a storm, and its roots held thousands of jewels in their fingers.

When God saw things in the shrine or in sleep, with the eyes in the back of their head, they told the dream priests. The priests would ponder these sights and say whether the oracle foretold what would happen or told what should be done or not done. But never had the priests seen the same things God saw, together with God, until the birthday of the world that made me fourteen years old and Tazu eleven.

Now, in these years, when the sun stands still over Mount Kanaghadwa people still call it the birthday of the world and count themselves a year older, but they no longer know and do all the rituals and ceremonies, the dances and songs, the blessings; and there is no feasting in the streets, now.

All my life used to be rituals, ceremonies, dances, songs, blessings, lessons, feasts, and rules. I knew and I know now on which day of God's year the first perfect ear of ze is to be brought by an angel from the ancient field up by Wadana where God set the first seed of the ze. I knew and know whose hand is to thresh it, and whose hand is to grind the grain, and whose lips are to taste the meal, at what hour, in what room of the house of God, with what priests officiating. There were a thousand rules, but they only seem complicated when I write them here. We knew them and followed them and only thought about them when we were learning them or when they were broken.

I had slept all these years with Ruaway in my bed. She was warm and comfortable. When she began to sleep with me I stopped having bad sights at night as I used to do, seeing huge white clouds whirling in the dark, and toothed mouths of animals, and strange faces that came and changed themselves. When Kig and the other ill-natured holy people saw Ruaway stay in my bedroom with me every night, they dared not lay a finger or a breath on her. Nobody was allowed to touch me except my family and Haghag and the bodyservants, unless I told them to. And after I was ten, the punishment for touching me was death. All the rules had their uses.

The feast after the birthday of the world used to go on for four days and nights. All the storehouses were open and people could take what they needed. The servants of God served out food and beer in the streets and squares of the city of God and every town and village of God's country, and common people and holy people ate together. The lords and ladies and God's sons went down into the streets to join the feast; only God and I did not. God came out on the balcony of the house to hear the histories and see the dances, and I came with them. Singing and dancing priests entertained everyone in the Glittering Square, and drumming priests, and story priests, and history priests. Priests were common people, but what they did was holy.

But before the feast, there were many days of rituals, and on the day itself, as the sun stopped above the right shoulder of Kanaghadwa, God Himself danced the Dance that Turns, to bring the year back round.

He wore a gold belt and the gold sun mask, and danced in front of our house on the Glittering Square, which is paved with stones full of mica that flash and sparkle in the sunlight. We children were on the long south balcony to see God dance.

Just as the dance was ending a cloud came across the sun as it stood still over the right shoulder of the mountain, one cloud in the clear blue summer sky. Everybody looked up as the light dimmed. The glittering died out of the stones. All the people in the city made a sound, "Oh," drawing breath. God Himself did not look up, but his step faltered.

He made the last turns of the dance and went into the ash house, where all the Goïz are in the walls, with the bowls where their food is burned in front of each of them, full of ashes.

There the dream priests were waiting for him, and God Herself had lighted the herbs to make the smoke to drink. The oracle of the birthday was the most important one of the year. Everybody waited in the squares and streets and on the balconies for the priests to come out and tell what God Himself had seen over his shoulder and interpret it to guide us in the new year. After that the feasting would begin.

Usually it took till evening or night for the smoke to bring the seeing and for God to tell it to the priests and for them to interpret it and tell us. People were settling down to wait indoors or in shady places, for when the cloud had passed it became very hot. Tazu and

Arzi and the idiot and I stayed out on the long balcony with Haghag and some of the lords and ladies, and Omimo, who had come back from the army for the birthday.

He was a grown man now, tall and strong. After the birthday he was going east to command the army making war on the Tegh and Chasi peoples. He had hardened the skin of his body the way soldiers did by rubbing it with stones and herbs until it was thick and tough as the leather of a ground-dragon, almost black, with a dull shine. He was handsome, but I was glad now that I was to marry Tazu, not him. An ugly man looked out of his eyes.

He made us watch him cut his arm with his knife to show how the thick skin was cut deep yet did not bleed. He kept saying he was going to cut Tazu's arm to show how quickly Tazu would bleed. He boasted about being a general and slaughtering barbarians. He said things like "I'll walk across the river on their corpses. I'll drive them into the jungles and burn the jungles down." He said the Tegh people were so stupid they called a flying lizard God. He said that they let their women fight in wars, which was such an evil thing that when he captured such women he would cut open their bellies and trample their wombs. I said nothing. I knew Ruaway's mother had been killed fighting beside her father. They had led a small army which God Himself had easily defeated. God made war on the barbarians not to kill them but to make them people of God, serving and sharing like all people in God's country. I knew no other good reason for war. Certainly Omimo's reasons were not good.

Since Ruaway slept with me she had learned to speak well, and also I learned some words of the way she talked. One of them was *techeg.* Words like it are: companion, fights-beside-me, countrywoman or countryman, desired, lover, known-a-long-time; of all our words the one most like techeg is our word in-my-heart. Their name Tegh was the same word as techeg; it meant they were all in one another's heart. Ruaway and I were in each other's heart. We were techeg.

Ruaway and I were silent when Omimo said, "The Tegh are filthy insects. I'll crush them."

"Ogga! ogga! ogga!" the idiot said, imitating Omimo's boastful voice. I burst out laughing. In that moment, as I laughed at my brother, the doors of the ash house flew open wide and all the priests hurried out, not in procession with music, but in a crowd, wild, disordered, crying out aloud —

"The house burns and falls!"

"The world dies!"

"God is blind!"

There was a moment of terrible silence in the city and then people began to wail and call out in the streets and from the balconies.

God came out of the ash house, Herself first, leading Himself, who walked as if drunk and sun-dazzled, as people walk after drinking smoke. God came among the staggering, crying priests and silenced them. Then she said, "Hear what I have seen coming behind me, my people!"

In the silence he began speaking in a weak voice. We could not hear all his words, but she said them again in a clear voice after he said them: "God's house falls down to the ground burning, but is not consumed. It stands by the river. God is white as snow. God's face has one eye in the center. The great stone roads are broken. War is in the east and north. Famine is in the west and south. The world dies."

He put his face in his hands and wept aloud. She said to the priests, "Say what God has seen!"

They repeated the words God had said.

She said, "Go tell these words in the quarters of the city and to God's angels, and let the angels go out into all the country to tell the people what God has seen."

The priests put their foreheads to their thumbs and obeyed.

When Lord Idiot saw God weeping, he became so distressed and frightened that he pissed, making a pool on the balcony. Haghag, terribly upset, scolded and slapped him. He roared and sobbed. Omimo shouted that a foul woman who struck God's son should be put to death. Haghag fell on her face in Lord Idiot's pool of urine to beg mercy. I told her to get up and be forgiven. I said, "I am God's daughter and I forgive you," and I looked at Omimo with eyes that told him he could not speak. He did not speak.

When I think of that day, the day the world began dying, I think of the trembling old woman standing there sodden with urine, while the people down in the square looked up at us.

Lady Clouds sent Lord Idiot off with Haghag to be bathed, and some of the lords took Tazu and Arzi off to lead the feasting in the city streets. Arzi was crying and Tazu was keeping from crying. Omimo and I stayed among the holy people on the balcony, watching what happened down in Glittering Square. God had gone back into the ash house, and the angels had gathered to repeat together their message, which they would carry word for word, relay by relay, to every town and village and farm of God's country, running day and night on the great stone roads.

All that was as it should be; but the message the angels carried was not as it should be.

Sometimes when the smoke is thick and strong the priests also see things over their shoulder as God does. These are lesser oracles. But never before had they all seen the same thing God saw, speaking the same words God spoke.

And they had not interpreted or explained the words. There was no guidance in them. They brought no understanding, only fear.

But Omimo was excited: "War in the east and north," he said. "My war!" He looked at me, no longer sneering or sullen, but right at me, eye in eye, the way Ruaway looked at me. He smiled. "Maybe the idiots and crybabies will die," he said. "Maybe you and I will be God." He spoke low, standing close to me, so no one else heard. My heart gave a great leap. I said nothing.

· · ·

Soon after that birthday, Omimo went back to lead the army on the eastern border.

All year long people waited for our house, God's house in the center of the city, to be struck by lightning, though not destroyed, since that is how the priests interpreted the oracle once they had time to talk and think about it. When the seasons went on and there was no lightning or fire, they said the oracle meant that the sun shining on the gold and copper roof-gutters was the unconsuming fire, and that if there was an earthquake the house would stand.

The words about God being white and having one eye they interpreted as meaning that God was the sun and was to be worshipped as the all-seeing giver of light and life. This had always been so.

There was war in the east, indeed. There had always been war in the east, where people coming out of the wilderness tried to steal our grain, and we conquered them and taught them how to grow it. General Lord Drowning sent angels back with news of his conquests all the way to the Fifth River.

There was no famine in the west. There had never been famine in God's country. God's children saw to it that crops were properly sown and grown and saved and shared. If the ze failed in the western lands, our carters pulled two-wheeled carts laden with grain on the great stone roads over the mountains from the central lands. If crops failed in the north, the carts went north from the Four Rivers land. From west to east carts came laden with smoked fish, from the Sunrise peninsula they came west with fruit and seaweed. The granaries and storehouses of God were always stocked and open to people in need. They had only to ask the administrators of the stores; what was needed was given. No one went hungry. Famine was a word that belonged to those we had brought into our land, people like the Tegh, the Chasi, the North Hills people. The hungry people, we called them.

The birthday of the world came again, and the most fearful words of the oracle — *the world dies* — were remembered. In public the priests rejoiced and comforted the common people, saying that God's mercy had spared the world. In our house there was little comfort. We all knew that God Himself was ill. He had hidden himself away more and more throughout the year, and many of the ceremonies took place without the divine presence, or only Herself was there. She seemed always quiet and untroubled. My lessons were mostly with her now, and with her I always felt that nothing had changed or could change and all would be well.

God danced the Dance that Turns as the sun stood still above the shoulder of the sacred mountain. He danced slowly, missing many steps. He went into the ash house. We waited, everybody waited, all over the city, all over the country. The sun went down behind Kanaghadwa. All the snow peaks of the mountains from north to south, Kayewa, Korosi, Aghet, Enni, Aziza, Kanaghadwa, burned gold, then fiery red, then purple. The light went up them and went out, leaving them white as ashes. The stars came out above them. Then at last the drums beat and the music sounded down in the Glittering Square, and torches made the pavement sparkle and gleam. The priests came out of the narrow doors of the ash house in order, in procession. They stopped. In the silence the oldest dream priest said in her thin, clear voice, "Nothing was seen over the shoulder of God."

Onto the silence ran a buzzing and whispering of people's voices, like little insects running over sand. That died out.

The priests turned and went back into the ash house in procession, in due order, in silence.

The ranks of angels waiting to carry the words of the oracle to the countryside stood still while their captains spoke in a group. Then the angels all moved away in groups by the five streets that start at the Glittering Square and lead to the five great stone roads that go out from the city across the lands. As always before, when the angels entered the streets they began to run, to carry God's word swiftly to the people. But they had no word to carry.

Tazu came to stand beside me on the balcony. He was twelve years old that day. I was fifteen.

He said, "Ze, may I touch you?"

I looked yes, and he put his hand in mine. That was comforting. Tazu was a serious, silent person. He tired easily, and often his head and eyes hurt so badly he could hardly see, but he did all the ceremonies and sacred acts faithfully, and studied with our teachers of history and geography and archery and dancing and writing, and with our mother studied the sacred knowledge, learning to be God. Some of our lessons he and I did together, helping each other. He was a kind brother and we were in each other's heart.

As he held my hand he said, "Ze, I think we'll be married soon."

I knew what his thoughts were. God our father had missed many steps of the dance that turns the world. He had seen nothing over his shoulder, looking into the time to come.

But what I thought in that moment was how strange it was that in the same place on the same day one year it was Omimo who said we should be married, and the next year it was Tazu.

"Maybe," I said. I held his hand tight, knowing he was frightened at being God. So was I. But there was no use being afraid. When the time came, we would be God.

If the time came. Maybe the sun had not stopped and turned back above the peak of Kanaghadwa. Maybe God had not turned the year.

Maybe there would be no more time — no time coming behind our backs, only what lay before us, only what we could see with mortal eyes. Only our own lives and nothing else.

That was so terrible a thought that my breath stopped and I shut my eyes, squeezing Tazu's thin hand, holding on to him, till I could steady my mind with the thought that there was still no use being afraid.

This year past, Lord Idiot's testicles had ripened at last, and he had begun trying to rape women. After he hurt a young holy girl and attacked others, God had him castrated. Since then he had been quiet again, though he often looked sad and lonely. Seeing Tazu and me holding hands, he seized Arzi's hand and stood beside him as Tazu and I were standing. "God, God!" he said, smiling with pride. But Arzi, who was nine, pulled his hand away and said, "You won't ever be God, you can't be, you're an idiot, you don't know anything!" Old Haghag scolded Arzi wearily and bitterly. Arzi did not cry, but Lord Idiot did, and Haghag had tears in her eyes.

The sun went north as in any year, as if God had danced the steps of the dance rightly. And on the dark day of the year, it turned back southward behind the peak of great Enni, as in any year. On that day, God Himself was dying, and Tazu and I were taken in to see him and be blessed. He lay all gone to bone in a smell of rot and sweet herbs burning. God my mother lifted his hand and put it on my head, then on Tazu's, while we knelt by the great bed of leather and bronze with our thumbs to our foreheads. She said the words of blessing. God my father said nothing, until he whispered, "Ze, Ze!" He was not calling to me. The name of God Herself is always Ze. He was calling to his sister and wife while he died.

Two nights later I woke in darkness. The deep drums were beating all through the house. I heard other drums begin to beat in the temples of worship and the squares farther away in the city, and then others yet farther away. In the countryside under the stars they would hear those drums and begin to beat their own drums, up in the hills, in the mountain passes and over the mountains to the western sea, across the fields eastward, across the four great rivers, from town to town clear to the wilderness. That same night, I thought, my brother Omimo in his camp under the North Hills would hear the drums saying God is dead.

A son and daughter of God, marrying, became God. This marriage could not take place till God's death, but always it took place within a few hours, so that the world would not be long bereft. I knew this from all we had been taught. It was ill fate that my mother delayed my marriage to Tazu. If we had been married at once, Omimo's claim would have been useless; not even his soldiers would have dared follow him. In her grief she was distraught. And she did not know or could not imagine the measure of Omimo's ambition, driving him to violence and sacrilege.

Informed by the angels of our father's illness, he had for days been marching swiftly westward with a small troop of loyal soldiers. When the drums beat, he heard them not in the far North Hills, but in the fortress on the hill called Ghari that stands north across the valley in sight of the city and the house of God.

The preparations for burning the body of the man who had been God were going forward; the ash priests saw to that. Preparations for our wedding should have been going forward at the same time, but our mother, who should have seen to them, did not come out of her room.

Her sister Lady Clouds and other lords and ladies of the household talked of the wedding hats and garlands, of the music priests who should come to play, of the festivals that should be arranged in the city and the villages. The marriage priest came anxiously to them, but they dared do nothing and he dared do nothing until my mother allowed them to act. Lady Clouds knocked at her door but she did not answer. They were so nervous and uneasy, waiting for her all day long, that I thought I would go mad staying with them. I went down into the garden court to walk.

I had never been farther outside the walls of our house than the balconies. I had never walked across the Glittering Square into the streets of the city. I had never seen a field or a river. I had never walked on dirt.

God's sons were carried in litters into the streets to the temples for rituals, and in summer after the birthday of the world they were always taken up into the mountains to Chimlu, where the world began, at the springs of the River of Origin. Every year when he came back from there, Tazu would tell me about Chimlu, how the mountains went up all around the ancient house there, and wild dragons flew from peak to peak. There God's sons hunted dragons and slept under the stars. But the daughter of God must keep the house.

The garden court was in my heart. It was where I could walk under the sky. It had five fountains of peaceful water, and flowering trees in great pots; plants of sacred ze grew against the sunniest wall in containers of copper and silver. All my life, when I had a time free of ceremonies and lessons, I went there. When I was little, I pretended the insects there were dragons and hunted them. Later I played throwbone with Ruaway, or sat and watched the water of the fountains well and fall, well and fall, till the stars came out in the sky above the walls.

This day as always, Ruaway came with me. Since I could not go anywhere alone but had to have a companion, I had asked God Herself to make her my chief companion.

I sat down by the center fountain. Ruaway knew I wanted silence and went off to the corner under the fruit trees to wait. She could sleep anywhere at any time. I sat thinking how strange it would be to have Tazu always as my companion, day and night, instead of Ruaway. But I could not make my thoughts real.

The garden court had a door that opened on the street. Sometimes when the gardeners opened it to let each other in and out, I had looked out of it to see the world outside my house. The door was always locked on both sides, so that two people had to open it. As I sat by the fountain, I saw a man who I thought was a gardener cross the court and unbolt the door. Several men came in. One was my brother Omimo.

I think that door had been only his way to come secretly into the house. I think he had planned to kill Tazu and Arzi so that I would have to marry him. That he found me there in the garden as if waiting for him was the chance of that time, the fate that was on us.

"Ze!" he said as he came past the fountain where I sat. His voice was like my father's voice calling to my mother.

"Lord Drowning," I said, standing up. I was so bewildered that I said, "You're not here!" I saw that he had been wounded. His right eye was closed with a scar.

He stood still, staring at me from his one eye, and said nothing, getting over his own surprise. Then he laughed.

"No, sister," he said, and turning to his men gave them orders. There were five of them, I think, soldiers, with hardened skin all over their bodies. They wore angel's shoes on their feet, and belts around their waists and necks to support the sheaths for their penis and sword and daggers. Omimo looked like them, but with gold sheaths and the silver hat of a general. I did not understand what he said to the men. They came close to me, and Omimo came closer, so that I said, "Don't touch me," to warn them of their danger, for common men who touched me would be burned to death by the priests of the law, and even Omimo if he touched me without my permission would have to do penance and fast for a year. But he laughed again, and as I drew away, he took hold of my arm suddenly, putting his hand over my mouth. I bit down as hard as I could on his hand. He pulled it away and then slapped it again so hard on my mouth and nose that my head fell back and I could not breathe. I struggled and fought, but my eyes kept seeing blackness and flashes. I felt hard hands holding me, twisting my arms, pulling me up in the air, carrying me, and the hand on my mouth and nose tightened its grip till I could not breathe at all.

Ruaway had been drowsing under the trees, lying on the pavement among the big pots. They did not see her, but she saw them. She knew at once if they saw her they would kill her. She lay still. As soon as they had carried me out the gate into the street, she ran into the house to my mother's room and threw open the door. This was sacrilege, but, not knowing who in the household might be in sympathy with Omimo, she could trust only my mother.

"Lord Drowning has carried Ze off," she said. She told me later that my mother sat there silent and desolate in the dark room for so long that Ruaway thought she had not heard. She was about to speak again, when my mother stood up. Grief fell away from her. She said, "We cannot trust the army," her mind leaping at once to see what must be done, for she was one who had been God. "Bring Tazu here," she said to Ruaway.

Ruaway found Tazu among the holy people, called him to her with her eyes, and asked him to go to his mother at once. Then she went out of the house by the garden door that still stood unlocked and unwatched. She asked people in the Glittering Square if they had seen some soldiers with a drunken girl. Those who had seen us told her to take the northeast street. And so little time had passed that when she came out the northern gate of the city she saw Omimo and his men climbing the hill road towards Ghari, carrying me up to the old fort. She ran back to tell my mother this.

Consulting with Tazu and Lady Clouds and those people she most trusted, my mother sent for several old generals of the peace, whose soldiers served to keep order in the countryside, not in war on the frontiers. She asked for their obedience, which they promised her, for though she was not God she had been God, and was daughter and mother of God. And there was no one else to obey.

She talked next with the dream priests, deciding with them what messages the angels should carry to the people. There was no doubt that Omimo had carried me off to try to make himself God by marrying me. If my mother announced first, in the voices of the angels, that his act was not a marriage performed by the marriage priest, but was rape, then it might be the people would not believe he and I were God.

So the news went out on swift feet, all over the city and the countryside.

Omimo's army, now following him west as fast as they could march, were loyal to him. Some other soldiers joined him along the way. Most of the peacekeeping soldiers of the center land supported my mother. She named Tazu their general. He and she put up a brave and resolute front, but they had little true hope, for there was no God, nor could there be so long as Omimo had me in his power to rape or kill.

All this I learned later. What I saw and knew was this: I was in a low room without windows in the old fortress. The door was locked from outside. Nobody was with me and no guards were at the door, since nobody was in the fort but Omimo's soldiers. I waited there not knowing if it was day or night. I thought time had stopped, as I had feared it would. There was no light in the room, an old store-room under the pavement of the fortress. Creatures moved on the dirt floor. I walked on dirt then. I sat on dirt and lay on it.

The bolt of the door was shot. Torches flaring in the doorway dazzled me. Men came in and stuck a torch in the sconce on the wall. Omimo came through them to me. His penis stood upright and he came to me to rape me. I spat in his half-blind face and said, "If you touch me your penis will burn like that torch!" He showed his teeth as if he was laughing. He pushed me down and pushed my legs apart, but he was shaking, frightened of my sacred being. He tried to push his penis into me with his hands but it had gone soft. He could not rape me. I said, "You can't, look, you can't rape me!"

His soldiers watched and heard all this. In his humiliation, Omimo pulled his sword from its gold sheath to kill me, but the soldiers held his hands, preventing him, saying, "Lord, Lord, don't kill her, she must be God with you!" Omimo shouted and fought them as I had fought him, and so they all went out, shouting and struggling with him. One of them seized the torch, and the door clashed behind them. After a little while I felt my way to the door and tried it, thinking they might have forgotten to bolt it, but it was bolted. I crawled back to the corner where I had been and lay on the dirt in the dark.

Truly we were all on the dirt in the dark. There was no God. God was the son and daughter of God joined in marriage by the marriage priest. There was no other. There was no other way to go. Omimo did not know what way to go, what to do. He could not marry me without the marriage priest's words. He thought by raping me he would be my husband, and maybe it would have been so: but he could not rape me. I made him impotent.

The only thing he saw to do was attack the city, take the house of God and its priests captive, and force the marriage priest to say the words that made God. He could not do this with the small force he had with him, so he waited for his army to come from the east.

Tazu and the generals and my mother gathered soldiers into the city from the center land. They did not try to attack Ghari. It was a strong fort, easy to defend, hard to attack, and they feared that if they besieged it, they would be caught between it and Omimo's great army coming from the east.

So the soldiers that had come with him, about two hundred of them, garrisoned the fort. As the days passed, Omimo provided women for them. It was the policy of God to give village women extra grain or tools or crop-rows for going to fuck with the soldiers at army camps and stations. There were always women glad to oblige the soldiers and take the reward, and if they got pregnant of course they received more reward and support. Seeking to ease and placate his men, Omimo sent officers down to offer gifts to girls in the villages near Ghari. A group of girls agreed to come; for the common people understood very little of the situation, not believing that anyone could revolt against God. With these village women came Ruaway.

The women and girls ran about the fort, teasing and playing with the soldiers off duty. Ruaway found where I was by fate and courage, coming down into the dark passages under the pavement and trying the doors of the storerooms. I heard the bolt move in the lock. She said my name. I made some sound. "Come!" she said. I crawled to the door. She took my arm and helped me stand and walk. She shot the bolt shut again, and we felt our way down the black passage till we saw light flicker on stone steps. We came out into a torchlit court-yard full of girls and soldiers. Ruaway at once began to run through them, giggling and chattering nonsense, holding tight to my arm so that I ran with her. A couple of soldiers grabbed at us, but Ruaway dodged them, saying, "No, no, Tuki's for the Captain!" We ran on, and came to the side gate, and Ruaway said to the guards, "Oh, let us out, Captain, Captain, I have to take her back to her mother, she's vomiting sick with fever!" I was staggering and covered with dirt and filth from my prison. The guards laughed at me and said foul words about my foulness and opened the gate a crack to let us out. And we ran on down the hill in the starlight.

To escape from a prison so easily, to run through locked doors, people have said, I must have been God indeed. But there was no God then, as there is none now. Long before God, and long after also, is the way things are, which we call chance, or luck, or fortune, or fate; but those are only names.

And there is courage. Ruaway freed me because I was in her heart.

As soon as we were out of sight of the guards at the gate we left the road, on which there were sentries, and cut across country to the city. It stood mightily on the great slope before us, its stone walls starlit. I had never seen it except from the windows and balconies of the house at the center of it.

I had never walked far, and though I was strong from the exer-cises I did as part of our lessons, my soles were as tender as my palms. Soon I was grunting and tears kept starting in my eyes from the shocks of pain from rocks and gravel underfoot. I found it harder and harder to breathe. I could not run. But Ruaway kept hold of my hand, and we went on.

We came to the north gate, locked and barred and heavily guarded by soldiers of the peace. Then Ruaway cried out, "Let God's daughter enter the city of God!"

I put back my hair and held myself up straight, though my lungs were full of knives, and said to the captain of the gate, "Lord Captain, take us to my mother Lady Ze in the house in the center of the world."

He was old General Rire's son, a man I knew, and he knew me. He stared at me once, then quickly thumbed his forehead, and roared out orders, and the gates opened. So we went in and walked the northeast street to my house, escorted by soldiers, and by more and more people shouting in joy. The drums began to beat, the high, fast beat of the festivals.

That night my mother held me in her arms, as she had not done since I was a suckling baby.

That night Tazu and I stood under the garland before the marriage priest and drank from the sacred cups and were married into God.

That night also Omimo, finding I was gone, ordered a death priest of the army to marry him to one of the village girls who came to fuck with the soldiers. Since nobody outside my house, except a few of his men, had ever seen me up close, any girl could pose as me. Most of his soldiers believed the girl was me. He proclaimed that he had married the daughter of the Dead God and that she and he were now God. As we sent out angels to tell of our marriage, so he sent runners to say that the marriage in the house of God was false, since his sister Ze had run away with him and married him at Ghari, and she and he were now the one true God. And he showed himself to the people wearing a gold hat, with white paint on his face, and his blinded eye, while the army priests cried out, "Behold! The oracle is fulfilled! God is white and has one eye!"

Some believed his priests and messengers. More believed ours. But all were distressed or frightened or made angry by hearing messengers proclaim two Gods at one time, so that instead of knowing the truth, they had to choose to believe.

Omimo's great army was now only four or five days' march away.

Angels came to us saying that a young general, Mesiwa, was bringing a thousand soldiers of the peace up from the rich coasts south of the city. He told the angels only that he came to fight for "the one true God." We feared that meant Omimo. For we added no words to our name, since the word itself means the only truth, or else it means nothing.

We were wise in our choice of generals, and decisive in acting on their advice. Rather than wait for the city to be besieged, we resolved to send a force to attack the eastern army before it reached Ghari, meeting it in the foothills above the River of Origin. We would have to fall back as their full strength came up, but we could strip the country as we did so, and bring the country people into the city. Meanwhile we sent carts to and from all the storehouses on the southern and western roads to fill the city's granaries. If the war did not end quickly, said the old generals, it would be won by those who could keep eating.

"Lord Drowning's army can feed themselves from the storehouses along the east and north roads," said my mother, who attended all our councils.

"Destroy the roads," Tazu said.

I heard my mother's breath catch, and remembered the oracle: The roads will be broken.

"That would take as long to do as it took to make them," said the oldest general, but the next oldest general said, "Break down the stone bridge at Almoghay." And so we ordered. Retreating from its delaying battle, our army tore down the great bridge that had stood a thousand years. Omimo's army had to go around nearly a hundred miles farther, through forests, to the ford at Domi, while our army and our carters brought the contents of the storehouses in to the city. Many country people followed them, seeking the protection of God, and so the city grew very full. Every grain of ze came with a mouth to eat it.

All this time Mesiwa, who might have come against the eastern army at Domi, waited in the passes with his thousand men. When we commanded him to come help punish sacrilege and restore peace, he sent our angel back with meaningless messages. It seemed certain that he was in league with Omimo. "Mesiwa the finger, Omimo the thumb," said the oldest general, pretending to crack a louse.

"God is not mocked," Tazu said to him, deadly fierce. The old general bowed his forehead down on his thumbs, abashed. But I was able to smile.

Tazu had hoped the country people would rise up in anger at the sacrilege and strike the Painted God down. But they were not soldiers and had never fought. They had always lived under the protection of the soldiers of peace and under our care. As if our doings now were like the whirlwind or the earthquake, they were paralyzed by them and could only watch and wait till they were over, hoping to survive. Only the people of our household, whose livelihood depended directly upon us and whose skills and knowledge were at our service, and the people of the city in whose heart we were, and the soldiers of the peace, would fight for us.

The country people had believed in us. Where no belief is, no God is. Where doubt is, foot falters and hand will not take hold.

The wars at the borders, the wars of conquest, had made our land too large. The people in the towns and villages knew no more who I was than I knew who they were. In the days of the origin, Babam Kerul and Bamam Ze came down from the mountain and walked the fields of the center lands beside the common people. The common people who laid the first stones of the great roads and the huge base stones of the old city wall had known the face of their God, seeing it daily.

After I spoke of this to our councils, Tazu and I went out into the streets, sometimes carried in litters, sometimes walking. We were surrounded by the priests and guards who honored our divinity, but we went among the people, meeting their eyes. They fell on their knees and put their foreheads to their thumbs, and many wept

THE BIRTHDAY OF THE WORLD | 239

when they saw us. They called out from street to street, and little children cried out, "There's God!"

"You walk in their hearts," my mother said.

But Omimo's army had come to the River of Origin, and one day's march brought the vanguard to Ghari.

That evening we stood on the north balcony looking towards Ghari hill, which was swarming with men, as when a nest of insects swarms. To the west the light was dark red on the mountains in their winter snow. From Korosi a vast plume of smoke trailed, blood color.

"Look," Tazu said, pointing northwest. A light flared in the sky, like the sheet lightning of summer. "A falling star," he said, and I said, "An eruption."

In the dark of the night, angels came to us. "A great house burned and fell from the sky," one said, and the other said, "It burned but it stands, on the bank of the river."

"The words of God spoken on the birthday of the world," I said.

The angels knelt down hiding their faces.

What I saw then is not what I see now looking far off to the distant past; what I knew then is both less and more than I know now. I try to say what I saw and knew then.

That morning I saw coming down the great stone road to the northern gate a group of beings, two-legged and erect like people or lizards. They were the height of giant desert lizards, with monstrous limbs and feet, but without tails. They were white all over and hairless. Their heads had no mouth or nose and one huge single staring shining lidless eye.

They stopped outside the gate.

Not a man was to be seen on Ghari Hill. They were all in the fortress or hidden in the woods behind the hill.

We were standing up on the top of the northern gate, where a wall runs chest-high to protect the guards.

There was a little sound of frightened weeping on the roofs and balconies of the city, and people called out to us, "God! God, save us!"

Tazu and I had talked all night. We listened to what our mother and other wise people said, and then we sent them away to reach out our minds together, to look over our shoulder into the time that was coming. We saw the death and the birth of the world, that night. We saw all things changed.

The oracle had said that God was white and had one eye. This was what we saw now. The oracle had said that the world died. With it died our brief time of being God. This was what we had to do now: to kill the world. The world must die so that God may live. The house falls so that it may stand. Those who have been God must make God welcome.

Tazu spoke welcome to God, while I ran down the spiral stairs inside the wall of the gate and unbolted the great bolts — the guards had to help me — and swung the door open. "Enter in!" I said to God, and put my forehead to my thumbs, kneeling.

They came in, hesitant, moving slowly, ponderously. Each one turned its huge eye from side to side, unblinking. Around the eye was a ring of silver that flashed in the sun. I saw myself in one of those eyes, a pupil in the eye of God.

Their snow-white skin was coarse and wrinkled, with bright tattoos on it. I was dismayed that God could be so ugly.

The guards had shrunk back against the walls. Tazu had come down to stand with me. One of them raised a box towards us. A noise came out of the box, as if some animal was shut in it.

Tazu spoke to them again, telling them that the oracle had foretold their coming, and that we who had been God welcomed God.

They stood there, and the box made more noises. I thought it sounded like Ruaway before she learned to talk right. Was the language of God no longer ours? Or was God an animal, as Ruaway's people believed? I thought they seemed more like the monstrous lizards of the desert that lived in the zoo of our house than they seemed like us.

One raised its thick arm and pointed at our house, down at the end of the street, taller than other houses, its copper gutters and goldleaf carvings shining in the bright winter sunlight.

"Come, Lord," I said, "come to your house." We led them to it and brought them inside.

When we came into the low, long, windowlesss audience room, one of them took off its head. Inside it was a head like ours, with two eyes, nose, mouth, ears. The others did the same.

Then, seeing their head was a mask, I saw that their white skin was like a shoe that they wore not just on the foot but all over their body. Inside this shoe they were like us, though the skin of their faces was the color of clay pots and looked very thin, and their hair was shiny and lay flat.

"Bring food and drink," I said to the children of God cowering outside the door, and they ran to bring trays of ze-cakes and dried fruit and winter beer. God came to the tables where the food was set. Some of them pretended to eat. One, watching what I did, touched the ze-cake to its forehead first, and then bit into it and chewed and swallowed. It spoke to the others, gre-gra, gre-gra.

This one was also the first to take off its body-shoe. Inside it other wrappings and coverings hid and protected most of its body, but this was understandable, because even the body skin was pale and terribly thin, soft as a baby's eyelid.

In the audience room, on the east wall over the double seat of God, hung the gold mask which God Himself wore to turn the sun back on its way. The one who had eaten the cake pointed at the mask. Then it looked at me — its own eyes were oval, large, and beautiful — and pointed up to where the sun was in the sky. I nodded my body. It pointed its finger here and there all about the mask, and then all about the ceiling.

"There must be more masks made, because God is now more than two," Tazu said.

I had thought the gesture might signify the stars, but I saw that Tazu's interpretation made more sense.

"We will have masks made," I told God, and then ordered the hat priest to go fetch the gold hats which God wore during ceremonies and festivals. There were many of these hats, some jewelled and ornate, others plain, all very ancient. The hat priest brought them in due order two by two until they were all set out on the great table of polished wood and bronze where the ceremonies of First Ze and Harvest were celebrated.

Tazu took off the gold hat he wore, and I took off mine. Tazu put his hat on the head of the one who had eaten the cake, and I chose a short one and reached up and put my hat on its head. Then, choosing ordinary-day hats, not those of the sacred occasions, we put a hat on each of the heads of God, while they stood and waited for us to do so.

Then we knelt bareheaded and put our foreheads against our thumbs.

God stood there. I was sure they did not know what to do. "God is grown, but new, like a baby," I said to Tazu. I was sure they did not understand what we said.

All at once the one I had put my hat on came to me and put its hands on my elbows to raise me up from kneeling. I pulled back at first, not being used to being touched; then I remembered I was no longer very sacred, and let God touch me. It talked and gestured. It gazed into my eyes. It took off the gold hat and tried to put it back on my head. At that I did shrink away, saying, "No, no!" It seemed blasphemy, to say No to God, but I knew better.

God talked among themselves then for a while, and Tazu and our mother and I were able to talk among ourselves. What we understood was this: the oracle had not been wrong, of course, but it had been subtle. God was not truly one-eyed nor blind, but did not know how to see. It was not God's skin that was white, but their mind that was blank and ignorant. They did not know how to talk, how to act, what to do. They did not know their people.

Yet how could Tazu and I, or our mother and our old teachers, teach them? The world had died and a new world was coming to be. Everything in it might be new. Everything might be different. So it was not God, but we, who did not know how to see, what to do, how to speak.

I felt this so strongly that I knelt again and prayed to God, "Teach us!"

They looked at me and talked to each other, brr-grr, gre-gra.

I sent our mother and the others to talk with our generals, for angels had come with reports about Omimo's army. Tazu was very tired from lack of sleep. We two sat down on the floor together and talked quietly. He was concerned about God's seat. "How can they all sit on it at once?" he said.

"They'll have more seats added," I said. "Or now two will sit on it, and then another two. They're all God, the way you and I were, so it doesn't matter."

"But none of them is a woman," Tazu said.

I looked at God more carefully and saw that he was right. This disturbed me slowly, but very deeply. How could God be only half human?

In my world, a marriage made God. In this world coming to be, what made God?

I thought of Omimo. White clay on his face and a false marriage had made him a false God, but many people believed he was truly God. Would the power of their belief make him God, while we gave our power to this new, ignorant God?

If Omimo found out how helpless they appeared to be, not knowing how to speak, not even knowing how to eat, he would fear their divinity even less than he had feared ours. He would attack. And would our soldiers fight for this God?

I saw clearly that they would not. I saw from the back of my head, with the eyes that see what is coming. I saw the misery that was coming to my people. I saw the world dead, but I did not see it being born. What world could be born of a God who was male? Men do not give birth.

Everything was wrong. It came very strongly into my mind that we should have our soldiers kill God now, while they were still new in the world, and weak.

And then? If we killed God there would be no God. We could pretend to be God again, the way Omimo pretended. But godhead is not pretense. Nor is it put on and off like a golden hat.

The world had died. That was fated and foretold. The fate of these strange men was to be God, and they would have to live their fate as we lived ours, finding out what it was to be as it came to be, unless they could see over their shoulders, which is one of the gifts of God.

I stood up again, taking Tazu's hand so that he stood beside me. "The city is yours," I said to them, "and the people are yours. The world is yours, and the war is yours. All praise and glory to you, our God!" And we knelt once more and bowed our foreheads deeply to our thumbs, and left them.

"Where are we going?" Tazu said. He was twelve years old and no longer God. There were tears in his eyes.

"To find Mother and Ruaway," I said, "and Arzi and Lord Idiot and Haghag, and any of our people who want to come with us." I had begun to say "our children," but we were no longer their mother and father.

"Come where?" Tazu said.

"To Chimlu."

"Up in the mountains? Run and hide? We should stay and fight Omimo."

"What for?" I said.

That was sixty years ago.

I have written this to tell how it was to live in the house of God before the world ended and began again. To tell it I have tried to write with the mind I had then. But neither then nor now do I fully understand the oracle which my father and all the priests saw and spoke. All of it came to pass. Yet we have no God, and no oracles to guide us.

None of the strange men lived a long life, but they all lived longer than Omimo.

We were on the long road up into the mountains when an angel caught up with us to tell us that Mesiwa had joined Omimo, and the two generals had brought their great army against the house of the strangers, which stood like a tower in the fields near Soze River, with a waste of burned earth around it. The strangers warned Omimo and his army clearly to withdraw, sending lightning over their heads that set distant trees afire. Omimo would not heed. He could prove he was God only by killing God. He commanded his army to rush at the tall house. He and Mesiwa and a hundred men around him were destroyed by a single bolt of lightning. They were burned to ash. His army fled in terror.

"They are God! They are God indeed!" Tazu said when he heard the angel tell us that. He spoke joyfully, for he was as unhappy in his doubt as I was. And for a while we could all believe in them, since they could wield the lightning. Many people called them God as long as they lived.

My belief is that they were not God in any sense of the word I understand, but were otherworldly, supernatural beings, who had great powers, but were weak and ignorant of our world, and soon sickened of it and died.

There were fourteen of them in all. Some of them lived more than ten years. These learned to speak as we do. One of them came up into the mountains to Chimlu, along with some of the pilgrims who still wanted to worship Tazu and me as God. Tazu and I and this man talked for many days, learning from each other. He told us that their house moved in the air, flying like a dragon-lizard, but its wings were broken. He told us that in the land they came from the sunlight is very weak, and it was our strong sunlight that made them sick. Though they covered their bodies with weavings, still their thin skins let the sunlight in, and they would all die soon. He told us they were sorry they had come. I said, "You had to come. God saw you coming. What use is it to be sorry?"

He agreed with me that they were not God. He said that God lived in the sky. That seemed to us a useless place for God to live. Tazu said they had indeed been God when they came, since they fulfilled the oracle and changed the world; but now, like us, they were common people.

Ruaway took a liking to this stranger, maybe because she had been a stranger, and when he was at Chimlu they slept together. She said he was like any man under his weavings and coverings. He told her he could not impregnate her, as his seed would not ripen in our earth. Indeed the strangers left no children.

This stranger told us his name, Bin-yi-zin. He came back up to Chimlu several times, and was the last of them to die. He left with Ruaway the dark crystals he wore before his eyes, which make things look larger and clearer for her, though to my eyes they make things dim. To me he gave his own record of his life, in a beautiful writing made of lines of little pictures, which I keep in the box with this writing I make.

When Tazu's testicles ripened we had to decide what to do, for brothers and sisters among the common people do not marry. We asked the priests and they advised us that our marriage being divine could not be unmade, and that though no longer God we were husband and wife. Since we were in each other's heart, this pleased us, and often we slept together. Twice I conceived, but the conceptions aborted, one very early and one in the fourth month, and I did not conceive again. This was a grief to us, and yet fortunate, for had we had children, the people might have tried to make them be God.

It takes a long time to learn to live without God, and some people never do. They would rather have a false God than none at all. All through the years, though seldom now, people would climb up to Chimlu to beg Tazu and me to come back down to the city and be God. And when it became clear that the strangers would not rule the country as God, either under the old rules or with new ones, men began to imitate Omimo, marrying ladies of our lineage and claiming to be a new God. They all found followers and they all made wars, fighting each other. None of them had Omimo's terrible courage, or the loyalty of a great army to a successful general. They have all come to wretched ends at the hands of angry, disappointed, wretched people.

For my people and my land have fared no better than I feared and saw over my shoulder on the night the world ended. The great stone roads are not maintained. In places they are already broken. Almoghay bridge was never rebuilt. The granaries and storehouses are empty and falling down. The old and sick must beg from neighbors, and a pregnant girl has only her mother to turn to, and an orphan has no one. There is famine in the west and south. We are the hungry people, now. The angels no longer weave the net of government, and one part of the land knows nothing of the others. They say barbarians have brought back the wilderness across the Fourth River, and ground dragons spawn in the fields of grain. Little generals and painted gods raise armies to waste lives and goods and spoil the sacred earth.

The evil time will not last forever. No time does. I died as God a long time ago. I have lived as a common woman a long time. Each year I see the sun turn back from the south behind great Kanaghadwa. Though God does not dance on the glittering pavement, yet I see the birthday of the world over the shoulder of my death.

PARADISES LOST

This shaking keeps me steady. I should know.
What falls away is always. And is near.
I wake to sleep, and take my waking slow.
I learn by going where I have to go.

Theodore Roethke: *The Waking*

THE DIRTBALL

The blue parts were lots of water, like the hydro tanks only deeper, and the other-colored parts were dirt, like the earth gardens only bigger. Sky was what she couldn't understand. Sky was another ball that fit around the dirtball, Father said, but they couldn't show it in the model globe, because you couldn't see it. It was transparent, like air. It was air. But blue. A ball of air, and it looked blue from under-neath, and it was outside the dirtball. Air outside. That was really strange. Was there air inside the dirtball? No, Father said, just earth. You lived on the outside of the dirtball, like evamen doing eva, only you didn't have to wear a suit. You could breathe the blue air, just like you were inside. In nighttime you'd see black and stars, like if you were doing eva, Father said, but in daytime you'd see only blue. She asked why. Because the light was brighter than the stars, he said. Blue light? No; the star that made it was yellow, but there was so much air it looked blue. She gave up. It was all so hard and so long ago. And it didn't matter.

Of course they would "land" on some other dirtball, but that wasn't going to happen till she was very old, nearly dead, sixty-five years old. By then, if it mattered, she'd understand.

PRIVATIVE DEFINITION

Alive in the world are human beings, plants, and bacteria.

The bacteria live in and on the human beings and the plants and the soils and other things, and are alive but not visible. The activity even of great numbers of bacteria is not often visible, or appears to be simply a property of their host. Their life is on another order. Orders, as a rule, cannot perceive one another except with instruments which allow perception of a different scale. With such an instrument one gazes in wonder at the world revealed. But the instrument has not revealed one's larger-order world to that smaller-order world, which continues orderly, undisturbed and unaware, until the drop dries suddenly on the glass slide. Reciprocity is a rare thing.

The smaller-order world revealed here is an austere one. No amoeba oozing along, or graceful paisley-paramecium, or vacuum-cleaning rotifer; no creature larger than bacteria, juddering endlessly under the impacts of molecules.

And only certain bacteria. No molds, no wild yeasts. No virus (down another order). Nothing that causes disease in human beings or in plants. Nothing but the necessary bacteria, the house-cleaners, the digesters, the makers of dirt — clean dirt. There is no gangrene in the world, no blood poisoning. No colds in the head, no flu, no measles, no plague, no typhus or typhoid or tuberculosis or AIDS or dengue or cholera or yellow fever or Ebola or syphilis or poliomyelitis or leprosy or bilharzia or herpes, no chickenpox, no cold sores, no shingles. No Lyme disease. No ticks. No malaria. No mosquitoes. No fleas or flies, no roaches or spiders, no weevils or worms. Nothing in the world has more or less than two legs. Nothing has wings.

Nothing sucks blood. Nothing hides in tiny crevices, waves tendrils, scuttles into shadows, lays eggs, washes its fur, clicks its mandibles, or turns around three times before it lies down with its nose on its tail. Nothing has a tail. Nothing in the world has tentacles or fins or paws or claws. Nothing in the world soars. Nothing swims. Nothing purrs, barks, growls, roars, chitters, trills, or cries repeatedly two notes, a descending fourth, for three months of the year. There are no months of the year. There is no moon. There is no year. There is no sun. Time is divided into lightcycles, darkcycles, and tendays. Every 365.25 cycles there is a celebration and a number called The Year is changed. This Year is 141. It says so on the schoolroom clock.

THE TIGER

Of course there are pictures of moons and suns and animals, all labelled with names. In the Library on the bookscreens you can watch big things running on all fours over some kind of hairy carpet and the voices say, "horses in wyoming," or "llamas in peru." Some of the pictures are funny. Some of them you wish you could touch. Some are frightening. There's one with bright hair all gold and dark, with terrible clear eyes that stare at you without liking you, without knowing you at all. "Tiger in zoo," the voice says. Then children are playing with some little "kittens" that climb on them and the children giggle and the kittens are cute, like dolls or babies, until one of them looks right at you and there are the same eyes, the round, clear eyes that do not know your name.

"I am Hsing," Hsing said loudly to the kitten-picture on the bookscreen. The picture turned its head away, and Hsing burst into tears.

Teacher was there, full of comfort and queries. "I hate it, I hate it!" the five-year-old wailed.

"It's only a movie. It can't hurt you. It isn't real," said the twenty-five-year-old.

Only people are real. Only people are alive. Father's plants are alive, he says so, but people are really alive. People know you. They know your name. They like you. Or if they don't, like Alida's cousin's little boy from School Four, you tell them who you are and then they know you.

"I'm Hsing."

"Shing," the little boy said, and she tried to teach him the difference between saying Hsing and saying Shing, but the difference didn't matter unless you were talking Chinese, and it didn't matter anyway, because they were going to play Follow-the-Leader with Rosie and Lena and all the others. And Luis, of course.

IF NOTHING IS VERY DIFFERENT FROM YOU, WHAT IS A LITTLE DIFFERENT FROM YOU IS VERY DIFFERENT FROM YOU

Luis was very different from Hsing. For one thing, she had a vulva and he had a penis. As they were comparing the two one day, Luis remarked that he liked the word vulva because it sounded warm and soft and round. And vagina sounded rather grand. But "Penis, peee-niss," he said mincingly, "pee-piss! It sounds like a little dinky pissy sissy thing. It ought to have a better name." They made up names for it. Bobwob, said Hsing. Gowbondo! said Luis. Bobwob when it was lying down and Gowbondo when it stood up, they decided, aching with laughter. "Up, up, Gowbondo!" Luis cried, and it raised its head a little from his slender, silky thigh. "See, it knows its name! You call it." And she called it, and it answered, although Luis had to help it a little, and they laughed until not only Bobwob-Gowbondo but both of them were limp all over, rolling on the floor, there in Luis's room where they always went after school unless they went to Hsing's room.

PUTTING ON CLOTHES

She looked forward to it forever and couldn't sleep at all the night before, lying awake forever. But there was Father standing there suddenly, wearing his dress-up clothes, black long pants and his white silky kurta. "Wake up, sleepyhead, are you going to sleep through your Ceremony?" She leaped up from bed in terror, believing him, so that he said at once, seriously, "No, no, I was only joking. You have plenty of time. You don't have to get dressed, yet!" She saw the joke, but she was too bewildered and excited to laugh. "Help me comb my *hair!*" she wailed, tugging her comb into a knot in the thick black tangles. He knelt to help her.

By the time they got to the Temenos her excitement only made everything clearer than usual, bright, distinct. The huge room seemed even bigger than usual. Music was playing, cheery and dancy. Lots and lots of people were coming, naked children, each one with a parent in dress-up clothes, some of them with two parents, many with grandparents, a few with a little naked brother or sister or a big brother or sister in dress-up clothes. Luis's father was there, but he was only wearing workshorts and an old singlet, and she was sorry for Luis. Her mother Jael came through the big crowd of people. Jael's son Joel came with her from Quad Four, and both of them were wearing really, really dress-up clothes. Jael's had red zigzags and sparkles painted on, and Joel's shirt was purple with a gold zipper. They hugged and kissed, and Jael gave Father a package and said "For later," and Hsing knew what was in it, but didn't say anything. Father was hiding his package in one hand behind his back and she knew what was in it too.

The music was turning into the song they had all been learning, all the seven-year-olds in all four schools in the whole world: "I'm growing up! I'm growing up!" The parents pushed the children forward or led the shy ones by the hand, whispering, "Sing! Sing!" And all the little naked children, singing, came together in the center of the high round room. "I'm growing up! What a happy happy day!" they sang, and the grown-ups began to sing with them, so it got huge and loud and deep and made tears start in her eyes. "What a happy happy day!"

An old teacher talked a little while, and then a young teacher with a beautiful high clear voice said, "Now everyone sit down," and everyone sat down on the deck. "I will read each child's name. When I read your name, stand up. Your parent and relations will stand up too, and then you can go to them, and look at your clothes. But don't put them on till everybody in the world has their new clothes! I'll say when. So! Are you ready? So! 5-Adano Sita! Stand up and be clothed!"

A little tiny girl jumped up in the circle of sitting children. She was red in the face and looked around in terror for her mother, who stood up laughing and waving a beautiful red shirt. Little Sita ran headlong for her, and everybody laughed and clapped. "5-Alzs-Matteu Frans! Stand up and be clothed!" And so it went, till the clear voice said, "5-Liu Hsing! Stand up and be clothed!" and she stood up, her eyes fixed on Father, who was easy to see because of Jael and Joel glittering beside him. She ran to him and took something silky, something wonderful, into her arms, and the people from Peony Compound and Lotus Compound clapped specially hard. She turned and stood pressed against Father's legs, watching.

"5-Nova Luis! Stand up and be clothed," but he was up and over with his father almost before the words were said, so that people laughed again, and hardly had time to clap. Hsing tried to catch Luis's eye but he wouldn't look. He watched the rest of the Ceremony seriously, so she did too.

"These are the fifty-four seven-year-old children of the Fifth Generation," the teacher said when no more children were left in the center of the circle. "Let us welcome them to all the joys and responsibilities of growing up," and everybody cheered and clapped while the naked children, hurrying and inept, struggling with unfamiliar holes, getting things upside down, fumbling with buttons, put on their new clothes, their first clothes, and stood up again, resplendent.

Then all the teachers and grown-ups started singing "What a happy happy day" again and there was a lot more hugging and kissing. Hsing got enough of that pretty soon, but she noticed that Luis really liked it, and hugged back hard when grown-ups he hardly knew hugged him.

Ed had given Luis black shorts and a blue silky shirt, in which he looked absolutely different and absolutely himself. Rosa had all white clothes because her mother was an angel. Father had given Hsing dark blue shorts and a white shirt, and Jael's package was light blue pants and a blue shirt with white stars on it, to wear tomorrow. The cloth of the shorts rubbed her thighs when she moved and the shirt felt soft, soft on her shoulders and belly. She danced with joy, and Father took her hands and danced gravely with her. "So, my grown-up daughter!" he said, and his smile crowned the day.

LUIS BEING DIFFERENT

The penis-vulva difference was superficial. She had learned that word from Father not long ago, and found it useful. Luis wasn't different only from her or only because of that superficial difference. He was different from everybody. Nobody said "ought to" the way Luis did. He wanted the truth. Not to lie. He wanted honor. That was the word. That was the difference. He had more honor than the others. Honor is hard and clear and Luis was hard and clear. And at the same time and in exactly the same way he was tender, he was soft. He got asthma and couldn't breathe, he got big headaches that knocked him out for days, he was sick before exams and performances and ceremonies. He was like the knife that wounds, and like the wound. Everybody treated Luis with a difference, respectfully, liking him but not trying to get close to him. Only she knew that he was also the touch that heals the wound.

V

When they were ten and finally were allowed to enter what the teachers called Virtual Earth and the Chi-Ans called V-Dichew, Hsing was overwhelmed and disappointed. V-Dichew was exciting and tremendously complicated, yet thin. It was superficial. It was programs.

There were infinite things in it, but one stupid real thing, her old toothbrush, had more being in it than all the swarming rush of objects and sensations in City or Jungle or Countryside. In Countryside, she was always aware that although there was nothing overhead but the blue air, and she was walking along on grass-stuff that carpeted the uneven deck for impossible distances rising up into impossible shapes *(hills)*, and that the noises in her ears were air moving fast *(wind)* and a kind of high yit-yit sound sometimes *(birds)*, and that those things on all fours way off on the winds, no, on the hills, were animals *(cattle)*, all the same, all the time, she knew she was sitting in a chair in School Two V-Lab with some junk attached to her body, and her body refused to be fooled, insisting that no matter how strange and amazing and educational and important and historical V-Dichew was, it was a fake. Dreams could also be convincing, beautiful, frightening, important. But she didn't want to live in dreams. She wanted to be awake in her body touching true cloth, true metal, true skin.

THE POET

When she was fourteen, Hsing wrote a poem for an English assignment. She wrote it in both the languages she knew. In English it went:

In the Fifth Generation

My grandfather's grandfather walked under heaven.
That was another world.

When I am a grandmother, they say, I may walk under heaven
On another world.

But I am living my life now joyously in my world
Here in the middle of heaven.

She had been learning Chinese with her father since she was nine; they had read some of the classics together. He smiled when he read the Chinese poem, read the characters "under heaven" — "t'ien hsia." She saw his smile and it made her happy, proud of her erudition and enormously proud that Yao had recognised it, that they shared this almost secret, almost private understanding.

The teacher asked her to read her poem aloud in both languages at first-quarter Class Day for second-year high-schoolers. The next day the editor of *Q-4*, the most famous literary magazine in the world, called her up and asked if he could publish it. Her teacher had sent it to him. He wanted her to read it for the audio. "It needs your voice," he said. He was a big man with a beard, 4-Bass Abby, imperious and opinionated, a god. He was rude to everybody else but kind to her. When they made the recording and she fluffed it, he just said, "Back up and take it easy, poet," and she did.

Then it seemed for a while that everywhere she was she heard her own voice saying "When I am a grandmother, they say. . . ." on the speaker, and people she hardly knew at school said, "Hey I heard your poem, it was zazz." All the angels liked it specially and told her so.

She was going to be a poet, of course. She would be really great, like 2-Eli Ali. Only instead of little short weird obscure poems like Eli's, she would write a great narrative poem about — actually the problem was what should it be about. It could be a great historical epic about the Zero Generation. It would be called *Genesis*. For a week she was excited, thinking about it all the time. But to do it she'd really have to learn all the history that she was sort of gliding through in History, she'd have to read hundreds of books. And she'd have to really go into V-Dichew to feel what it had been like to live there. It would all take years before she could even start writing it.

Maybe she could write love poems. There were an awful lot of love poems in the World Lit anthology. She had a feeling that you didn't need to really be in love with a person to write a love poem. Maybe in fact if you were really seriously in love it would interfere with the poetry. A sort of yearning, undemanding adoration like she felt for Bass Abby, or for Rosa at school, maybe was a good place to start from. So she wrote quite a few love poems, but for one reason or another she was embarrassed about turning them in to her teacher, and only showed them to Luis. Luis had acted all along like he didn't think she was a poet. She had to show him.

"I like this one," he said. She peered to see which one.

> What is the sadness in you
> that I see only in your smile?
> I wish I could hold your sadness
> in my arms like a sleeping child.

She hadn't thought much of the poem, it was so short, but now it seemed better than she'd thought.

"It's about Yao, isn't it?" Luis said.

"About my *father?*" Hsing said, so shocked she felt her cheeks burning. "No! It's a *love* poem!"

"Well, who do you actually love a lot besides your father?" Luis asked in his horrible matter-of-fact way.

"A whole lot of people! And love is — There are different *kinds* — "

"Are there?" He glanced up at her. He pondered. "I didn't say it was a sex poem. I don't think it is a sex poem."

"Oh, you are so weird," Hsing said, abruptly and deftly snatching her writer back and closing the folder labelled *Original Poems by 5-Liu Hsing.* "What makes you think you know anything about poetry anyhow?"

"I know about as much about it as you do," said Luis with his pedantic fairness, "but I can't *do* it at all. You can. Sometimes."

"Nobody can write great poetry all the time!"

"Well," — her heart always sank when he said "Well" — "maybe not literally all the time, but the good ones have an amazingly high average. Shakespeare, and Li Po, and Yeats, and 2-Eli — "

"What's the use trying to be like *them?*" she wailed.

"I didn't mean you had to be like them," he said after a slight pause and in a different tone. He had realised that he might have hurt her. That made him unhappy. When he was unhappy he became gentle. She knew exactly how he felt, and why, and what he'd do, and she also knew the fierce, regretful tenderness for him that swelled up inside her, a sore tenderness, like a bruise. She said, "Oh, I don't care about all that anyway. Words are too sloppy, I like math. Let's go meet Lena at the gym."

As they jogged through the corridors it occurred to her that in fact the poem he had liked wasn't about Rosa, as she had thought, or about her father, as he had thought, but was about him, Luis. But it was all stupid anyhow and didn't matter. So she wasn't Shakespeare. But she loved quadratic equations.

4-LIU YAO

How sheltered they were, how protected! Safer than any guarded prince or pampered child of the rich had ever been; safer than any child had ever been on Earth.

No cold winds to shiver in or heavy heat to sweat in. No plagues or coughs or fevers or toothaches. No hunger. No wars. No weapons. No danger. No danger from anything in the world but the danger the world itself was in. But that was a constant, a condition of being, and therefore hard to think about, except sometimes in dream; the horrible images. The walls of the world deformed, bulging, shattering. The soundless explosion. A spray of bloody mist, a tiny smear of vapor in the starlight. They were all in danger all the time, surrounded by danger. That is the essence of safety, the heart of it: that the danger is outside.

They lived inside. Inside their world with its strong walls and strong laws, shaped and bulwarked to protect and surround them with strength. There they lived, and there was no threat unless they made it.

"People are a risky business," Liu Yao said, smiling. "Plants mostly don't go crazy."

Yao's profession was gardening. He worked in hydroponic engineering and maintenance and in plant-genetic quality and control. He was in the gardens every workday and many evenings. The 4-5-Liu homespace was full of pet plants — gourdvines in carboys of water, flowering shrubs in pots of dirt, epiphytes festooning the vents and light-fixtures. Many of them were experimentals, which usually died. Hsing believed that her father was sorry for these genetic errors, felt guilty about them, and brought them home to die in peace. Occasionally one of the experiments thrived under his patient attendance and went back to the plant labs in triumph, accompanied by Yao's faint, deprecating smile.

4-Liu Yao was a short, slender, handsome man with a shock of black hair early going grey. He did not have the bearing of a hand-some man. He was reserved, courteous, but shy. A good listener but a rare and low-voiced talker, when he was with more than one or two people he was almost entirely silent. With his mother 3-Liu Meiling or his friend 4-Wang Yuen or his daughter Hsing he would converse contentedly, unassertively. His passions were contained, restrained, powerful: the Chinese classics, his plants, his daughter. He thought a good deal and felt a good deal. He was mostly content to follow his thoughts and feelings alone, in silence, like a man going downstream in a small boat on a great river, sometimes steer-ing, more often drifting. Of boats and rivers, of cliffs and currents, Yao knew only images in pictures, words in poems. Sometimes he dreamed that he was in a boat on a river, but the dreams were vague. He knew dirt, though, knew it exactly, bodily. Dirt was what he worked in. And water and air he knew, the humble, transparent things, on whose clarity, invisibility, life depended, the miracles. A bubble of air and water floated in the dry black vacuum, reflecting starlight. He lived inside it.

3-Liu Meiling lived in the group of homespaces called Peony Compound, a corridor away from her son's homespace. She led an extremely active social life limited almost entirely to the Chinese-Ancestry population of Quadrant Two. Her profession was chem-istry; she worked in the fabric labs; she had never liked the work. As soon as she decently could she went on halftime and then retired. Didn't like any work, she said. Liked to look after babies in the baby-garden, play games, gamble for flower-cookies, talk, laugh, gossip, find out what was happening next door. She took great pleasure in her son and granddaughter and ran in and out of their homespace constantly, bringing dumplings, rice cakes, gossip. "You should move to Peony!" she said frequently, but knew they wouldn't, because Yao was unsociable, and that was fine, except she did hope that Hsing would stay with her own people when she decided to have a baby, which she also said frequently. "Hsing's mother is a fine woman, I like Jael," she told her son, "but I never will understand why you couldn't have had a baby from one of the Wong girls and then her mama would be right here in Quadrant Two, that would have been so nice for all of us. But I know you have to do things your way. And I must say even if Hsing is only half Chinese Ancestry nobody would ever know it, and what a beauty she's getting to be, so I suppose you did know what you were doing, if anyone ever does when it comes to falling in love or having a child, which I doubt. It's basically luck, is all it is. Young 5-Li has an eye on her, did you notice yesterday? He's twenty-three, a good solid boy. Here she is now! Hsing! How beautiful your hair is when it's long! You should let it grow longer!" The kind, practical, undemanding babble of his mother's talk was another stream on which Yao floated vaguely, peacefully, until all at once, in one moment, it was cut short. Silence. A bubble had burst. A bubble in an artery of the brain, the doctors said. For a few hours 3-Liu Meiling gazed in mute bewilder-ment at something no one else could see, and then died. She was only seventy. All life is in danger, from without, from within. People are a risky business.

THE FLOATING WORLD

The brief funeral was held in Peony Compound; then the body of 3-Liu Meiling was taken by her son and granddaughter and the technician to the Life Center to be recycled, a chemical process of breakdown and re-use with which as a chemist she had been per-fectly familiar. She would still be part of their world, not as a being but as an endless becoming. She would be part of the children Hsing would bear. They were all part of one another. All used and users, all eaters, all eaten.

Inside a bubble where there is so much air and no more, so

much water and no more, so much food and no more, so much energy and no more — in an aquarium, perfectly self-contained in its tiny balancing act: one catfish, two sticklebacks, three water-weeds, plenty of algae, three snails, maybe four, but no dragonfly larvae — inside a bubble, the population must be strictly controlled.

When Meiling dies she is replaced. But she is no more than replaced. Everybody can have a child. Some can't or won't or don't have children and some children die young, and so most of those who want two children can have two children. Four thousand isn't a great number. It is a carefully maintained number. Four thousand isn't a great gene pool, but it is a carefully selected and managed one. The anthrogeneticists are just as watchful and dispassionate as Yao in the plant labs. But they do not experiment. Sometimes they can catch a fault at the source, but they have not the resources to meddle with twists and recombinations. All such massive, elaborate technologies, supported by the continuous exploitation of the resources of a planet, were left behind by the Zero Generation. The anthrogeneticists have good tools and know their job, and their job is maintenance. They maintain the quality, literally, of life.

Everyone who wants to can have a child. One child, two at most. A woman has her motherchild. A man has his fatherchild.

The arrangement is unfair to men, who have to persuade a woman to bear a child for them. The arrangement is unfair to women, who are expected to spend three-quarters of a year of their life bearing somebody else's child. To women who want a child and cannot conceive or whose sexual life is with other women, so that they have to persuade both a man and a woman to get and give them a child, the arrangement is doubly unfair. The arrangement is, in fact, unfair. Sexuality and justice have little if anything in common. Love and friendship and conscience and kindness and obstinacy find ways to make the unfair arrangement work, though not without anxiety, not without anguish, and not always.

Marriage and linking are informal options, often chosen while the children are young, for many women find it hard to part with a fatherchild, and a homespace for four is luxuriously spacious.

Many women do not want to bear or bring up a child at all, many feel their fertility to be a privilege and obligation, and some pride themselves on it. Now and then there is a woman who boasts of the number of her fatherchildren, as of a basketball score.

4-Steinfeld Jael bore Hsing; she's Hsing's mother, but Hsing isn't her child. Hsing is 4-Liu Yao's child, his fatherdaughter. Jael's child is Joel, her motherson, six years older than his halfsister Hsing, two years younger than his halfbrother 4-Adami Seth.

Everybody has a homespace. A single is one and one half rooms; a room is a space of 960 cubic feet. The commonest shape is 10' x 12' x 8', but since the partitions are movable the proportions can be altered freely within the limits of the structural space. A double, like the 4-5 Lius', is usually arranged as two little sleepcells and a large sharespace: two privacies and a commonality. When people link, and if they each have one or two children, their homespace may get quite large. The 3-4-5-Steinman-Adamis, Jael and Joel and 3-Adami Manhattan, to whom she has been linked for years, and his fatherson Seth, have 3,840 cubic feet of homespace. They live in Quad Four, where a lot of Nor-Ans live, Northamerican and European Ancestry people. With her usual flair for the dramatic, Jael has found an area in the outer arc where there's room for ten-foot ceilings. "Like the sky!" she cries. She has painted the ceilings bright blue. "Feel the difference?" she says. "The sense of liberation — of freedom?" In fact, when she goes to stay with Jael on visits, Hsing finds the rooms rather disagreeable; they seem deep and cold, with all that waste space overhead. But Jael fills them with her warmth, her golden, inexhaustible voice, her bright clothing, her abundance of being.

When Hsing began menstruating and learning how to use prevention and brooding about sex, both Jael and Meiling told her that having a baby is a piece of luck. They were very different women, but they used the same word. "The best luck," Meiling said. "So interesting! Nothing else uses *all* of you." And Jael talked about how your relation to the baby in your womb and the newborn baby nursing was part of sex, an extension and completion of it that you were really lucky to know. Hsing listened with the modest, cynical reserve of the virgin. She'd make up her own mind about all that when the time came.

Many Chi-Ans had, more or less silently, disapproved of Yao's asking a woman of another quadrant and a different ancestry to bear his child. Many people of Jael's ancestry had asked her if she wanted an exotic experience or what. The fact was Jael and Yao had fallen desperately in love. They were old enough to realise that love was all they had in common. Jael had asked Yao if she could have his child. Moved to the heart, he had agreed. Hsing was born of an undying passion. Whenever Yao came to bring Hsing for a visit, Jael flung her arms about him crying "Oh Yao, it's you!" with such utter, ravished joy and delight that only a man as thoroughly satisfied and self-satisfied as Adami Manhattan could have escaped agonies of jealousy. Manhattan was a huge, hairy man. Perhaps being fifteen years older, eight inches taller, and a great deal hairier than Yao helped him to be unjealous of him.

Grandparents provided another way to increase the size of a homespace. Sometimes relatives, halfsibs, their parents, their children grouped together in still larger spaces. Next down the corridor from the 4-5 Lius' was the 3-4-5-Wangs' — Lotus Compound — eleven contiguous homespaces, the partitions arranged so as to provide a central atrium, the scene of ceaseless noise and activity. Peony Compound, where Meiling had lived all her life, always had from eight to eighteen homespaces. None of the other ancestries lived in such large groupings.

In fact by the fifth generation many people had lost any sense of what ancestry was, found it irrelevant, and disapproved of people who based their identity or their community on it. In Council, disapproval was frequently expressed of Chinese-Ancestry clannishness, referred to by its critics as "Quad Two separatism" or more darkly as "racism," and by those who practiced it as "keeping to our ways." The Chi-Ans protested the new Schools Administration policy of shifting teachers around from quad to quad, so that children would be taught by people from other ancestries, other communities; but they were outvoted in Council.

THE BUBBLE

Dangers, risks. In the glass bubble, the fragile world, the danger of schism, of conspiracy, the danger of aberrant behavior, madness, the violence of madness. No decision of any consequence at all was to be made by a single person acting without counsel. Nobody ever, since the beginning, had been allowed alone at any of the systems controls. Always a backup, a watcher. Yet there had been incidents. None had yet wreaked permanent damage.

But what of the merely normal, usual behavior of human beings? What is aberrant? Who's sane?

Read the histories, say the teachers. History tells us who we are, how we have behaved, therefore how we will behave.

Does it? The history in the bookscreens, Earth History, that appalling record of injustice, cruelty, enslavement, hatred, murder — that record, justified and glorified by every government and institution, of waste and misuse of human life, animal life, plant life, the air, the water, the planet? If that is who we are, what hope for us? History must be what we have escaped from. It is what we were, not what we are. History is what we need never do again.

The foam of the salt ocean has tossed up a bubble. It floats free.

To learn who we are, look not at history but at the arts, the record of our best, our genius. The elderly, sorrowful, Dutch faces gaze out of the darkness of a lost century. The mother's beautiful grave head is bowed above the dead son who lies across her lap. The old mad king cries over his murdered daughter, "Never, never, never, never, never!" With infinite gentleness the Compassionate One murmurs, "It does not last, it cannot satisfy, it has no being." "Sleep, sleep," say the cradle songs, and "Set me free" cry the yearning slave-songs. The symphonies rise, a glory out of darkness. And the poets, the crazy poets cry out, "A terrible beauty is born." But they're all crazy. They're all old and mad. All their beauty is terrible. Don't read the poets. They don't last, they can't satisfy, they have no being. They wrote about another world, the dirt world. That too, too solid world which the Zeroes made naught of.

Ti Chiu, Dichew, the dirt-ball. Earth. The "garbage" world. The "trash" planet.

These words are archaic, history-words, attached only to history-images: receptacles were filled with "dirty" "garbage" that was poured into vehicles which carried it to "trash dumps" to "throw away." What does that mean? Where is "away"?

ROXANA AND ROSA

When she was sixteen Hsing read the Diaries of 0-Fayez Roxana. That self-probing mind, forever questioning its own honesty, was attractive to the adolescent. Roxana was rather like Luis, Hsing thought, but a woman. Sometimes she needed to be with a woman's mind, not a man's, but Lena was obsessed with her basketball scores, and Rosa had gone totally angel, and Grandmother had died. Hsing read Roxana's Diaries.

She realised for the first time that the people of the Zero Generation, the worldmakers, had believed that they were imposing an immense sacrifice on their descendants. What the Zeroes gave up, what they lost in leaving Earth — Roxana always used the English word — was compensated to them by their mission, their hope, and (as Roxana was well aware) by the tremendous power they had wielded in creating the very fabric of life for thousands of people for generations to come. "We are the gods of *Discovery*," Roxana wrote. "May the true gods forgive us our arrogance!"

But when she speculated on the years to come, she did not write of her descendants as children of the gods, but as victims, seeing them with fear, guilt, and pity, helpless prisoners of their ancestor's will and desire. "How will *they* forgive us?" she mourned. "We who took the world from them before they were ever born — we who took the seas, the mountains, the meadowlands, the cities, the sunlight from them, all their birthright? We have left them trapped in a cage, a tin can, a specimen box, to live and die like laboratory rats and never see the moon, never run across a field, never know what freedom is!"

I don't know what cages or tin cans or specimen boxes are, Hsing thought with impatience, but whatever a laboratory rat is, I'm not. I've run across a v-field in Countryside. You don't need fields and hills and all that stuff to be free! Freedom's what your mind does, what your soul is. It has nothing to do with all that Dichew-stuff. Don't worry, Grandmother! she said to the long-dead writer. It all worked out just fine. You made a wonderful world. You were a very wise, kind god.

When Roxana got depressed about her poor deprived descendants she also tended to go on and on about Shindychew, which she called the destination planet or just the Destination. Sometimes it cheered her up to imagine what it might be like, but mostly she worried about it. Would it be habitable? Would there be life on it? What kind of life? What would "the settlers" find, how would they cope with what they found, would they send the information back to Earth? That was so important to her. It was funny, poor Roxana worrying about what kind of signals her great-great-great-grandchildren would send "back" in two hundred years to a place they'd never been! But the bizarre idea was a great consolation to her. It was her justification for what they had done. It was the reason. *Discovery* would build a vast and delicate rainbow bridge across Space, and across it the true gods would walk: information, knowledge. The rational gods. That was Roxana's recurring image, her solace.

Hsing found her god-imagery tiresome. People with a monotheist ancestry seemed unable to get over it. Roxana's lower-case metaphorical deities were preferable to the capitalised Gods and Fathers in History and Lit, but she had very little patience with any of them.

GETTING THE MESSAGE

Disappointed with Roxana, Hsing quarreled with her friend.

"Rosie, I wish you'd talk about other stuff," she said.

"I just want to share my happiness with you," Rosa said in her Bliss voice, soft, mild, and as flexible as a steel mainbeam.

"We used to be happy together without dragging in Bliss."

Rosa looked at her with a general lovingness that insulted Hsing obscurely but very deeply. We were *friends*, Rosie! she wanted to cry.

"Why do you think we're here, Hsing?"

Mistrusting the question, she pondered a bit before she answered. "If you mean that literally, we're here because the Zero Generation arranged that we should be here. If you mean it in some abstract sense, then I reject the question as loaded. To ask 'why' assumes purpose, a final cause. Zero Generation had a purpose: to send a ship to another planet. We're carrying it out."

"But where are we going?" Rosa asked with the intense sweetness, the sweet intensity, that made Hsing feel tight, sour, and defensive.

"To the Destination. Shindychew. And you and I will be old grannies when we get there!"

"Why are we going there?"

"To get information and send it back," Hsing said, having no answer ready except Roxana's, and then hesitated. She realised that it was a fair question, and that she had never really asked or answered it. "And to live there," she said. "To find out — about the universe. We are a — we are a voyage. Of discovery. The voyage of the *Discovery*."

She discovered the meaning of the name of the world as she said it.

"To discover — ?"

"Rosie, this leading-question bit belongs in babygarden. 'And what do we call *this* nice curly letter?' Come on. Talk to me, don't manipulate me!"

"Don't be afraid, angel," Rosa said, smiling at Hsing's anger. "Don't be afraid of joy."

"Don't call me angel. I liked you when you were just you, Rosa."

"I never had any idea who I was before I knew Bliss," Rosa said, no longer smiling, and with such simplicity that Hsing felt both awed and ashamed.

But when she left Rosa, she was bereft. She had lost her friend for years, her beloved for a while. They wouldn't link when they grew up, as she had dreamed. She was damned if she'd be an angel! But oh, Rosie, Rosie. She tried to write a poem. Only two lines came:

> We will always meet and never meet again.
> Our corridors lead us forever apart.

WHAT DOES APART MEAN IN A CLOSED WORLD?

It was Hsing's first real loss. Grandmother Meiling had been such a cheerful, kindly presence, her death had been so unexpected, so quietly abrupt, that Hsing had never been entirely aware that she was gone. It seemed as if she still lived down the corridor. To think of her was not to grieve, but to be comforted. But Rosa was lost.

Hsing brought all the vigor and passion of her youth to her first grief. She walked in shadow. Certain parts of her mind might have been darkened permanently. Her fierce resentment of the angels for taking Rosa from her led her to think that some of the older people of her ancestry were right: it was no use trying to understand other-ancestry people. They were different. They were best avoided. Keep to our own kind. Keep to the middle, keep to the way.

Even Yao, tired of fellow-workers in the plantlabs preaching Bliss, quoted Old Long-Ears — "They talk, they don't know. They know, they don't talk."

FOOLS

"So you know?" Luis said, when she repeated the line to him. "You Chi-Ans?"

"No. Nobody knows. I just don't like preaching!"

"Lots of people do, though," Luis said. "They like preaching and they like being preached to. All kinds of people."

Not us, she thought, but didn't say. After all, Luis wasn't Chinese Ancestry.

"Just because you have a flat face," he said, "you don't have to make a wall out of it."

"I don't have a flat face. That's racist."

"Yes you do. The Great Wall of China. Come on out, Hsing. It's me. Hybrid Luis."

"You aren't any more hybrid than I am."

"Much more."

"You don't think Jael is Chinese!" she jeered.

"No, she's pure Nor-An. But my birthmother's half Euro and half Indo and my father's one quarter each Southamerican and Afro and the other half Japanese, if I have it straight. Whatever it all means. What it means is I have no ancestry. Only ancestors. But you! You look like Yao and your grandmother, and you talk like them, and you learned Chinese from them, and you grew up here in the heart of an ancestry, and you're in process right now of doing the old Chi-An Exclusion Act. Your ancestry comes from the most racist people in history."

"Not so! The Japanese — the Euros — the Northamericans — "

They argued amicably for a while on sketchy data, and agreed that probably everybody on Dichew had been racist, as well as sexist, classist, and obsessed with money, that incomprehensible but omnipresent element of all the histories. They got sidetracked into economics, which they had been trying to understand in history class. They talked about money for a while, very stupidly.

If everybody has access to the same food, clothing, furniture, tools, education, information, work, and authority, and hoarding is useless because you can have for the asking, and gambling is an idle sport because there's nothing to lose, so that wealth and poverty have become mere metaphors — "rich in love," "poor in spirit" — how is one to understand the importance of money?

"Really they were awful fools," Hsing said, voicing the heresy all intelligent young people arrived at sooner or later.

"Then we are too," Luis said, maybe believing it, maybe not.

"Oh Luis," Hsing said with a long, deep sigh, looking up at the mural on the wall of the High School snackery, currently an abstract of soft curving pinks and golds, "I don't know what I'd do without you."

"Be an awful fool."

She nodded.

4-NOVA ED

Luis wasn't turning out the way his father intended. They both knew it. 4-Nova Ed was a kind man whose existence was centered in his genitals. Stimulation and relief was the pressing issue, but procreation was important to him too. He had wanted a son to carry his name and his genes into the future. He was glad to help make a child for any woman who asked him to, and did so three times; but he had looked long and carefully for the right woman to bear his fatherson. He studied every word of several compatibility charts and genetic mixmatches, though reading wasn't his favorite occupation; and when he finally decided he'd found the one, he made sure she was willing to control the gender. "A daughter would be fine if I had two, but if it's one it's a son, right?"

"A son you want, a son you get," said 4-Sandstrom Lakshmi, and bore him one. An active, athletic woman, she found the experience of pregnancy so uncomfortable and time-consuming that she never repeated it. "It was your big, brown, Goddam eyes, Ed," she said. "Never again. Here you are. He's all yours." Every now and then Lakshmi turned up at the 4-5 Nova homespace, always bringing a toy appropriate to Luis's age a year ago or five years from now. Usually she and Ed had what she called commemorative sex. After it she would say, "I wonder what the hell I thought I was doing. Never again! But I guess he's OK, isn't he?"

"The kid's OK!" his father said, heartily and without conviction. "Your brains, my plumbing."

She worked in Central Communications; Ed was a physical therapist, a good one, but as he said, his ideas were all in his hands. "It's why I'm such a good lover," he told his partners, and he was right. He was also a good parent for a baby. He knew how to hold the baby and handle him, and loved to do so. He lacked the fear of the infant, the squeamish dissociation which paralyses less manly men. The delicacy and vigor of the tiny body delighted him. He loved Luis as flesh of his flesh, wholeheartedly and happily, for the first couple of years, and less happily for the rest of his life. As the years went on the pure delight got covered over and buried under a lot of other stuff, a lot of hard feelings.

The child had a deep, silent will and temper. He would never give in and never take things easy. He had colic forever. Every tooth was a battle. He wheezed. He learned to talk before he could walk. By the time he was three he was saying things that left Ed staring. "Don't talk so Goddam fancy!" he told the child. He was disappointed in his son and ashamed of his disappointment. He had wanted a companion, a double, a kid to teach racquetball to. Ed had been Quad Two racquetball champion six years running.

Luis dutifully learned to play racquetball, never very well, and tried to teach his father a word game called Grammary, which drove Ed nuts. He did outstandingly well at school, and Ed tried to be proud of him. Instead of running around with the kidherd, Luis always brought a Chi-An kid over, a girl, Liu Hsing, and they shut the room door and played for hours, silently. Ed checked, of course. They weren't up to anything more than all herdkids got up to, but he was glad when they got to their Ceremony and started wearing clothes. In shorts and shirts they looked like little adults. In their nakedness they had been somehow slippery, elusive, mysterious.

As all the growing-up rules came into force, Luis obeyed them. He still preferred the girl Hsing over all the boys and they still saw each other all the time, but never alone together with the door shut. Which meant that when Ed was home he had to listen to them as they did their homework or talked. Talked, talked, shit, how they talked. Until the girl was twelve. Then her ancestry's rule was that she could only meet a boy in public places and with other people around. Ed found this an excellent idea. He hoped Luis would take up with other girls, maybe get into some boy activities. Luis and Hsing did go around with a group of the Quad Two teens. But the two of them always ended up somewhere, talking.

"When I was sixteen, I'd slept with three girls," Ed said. "And a couple of guys." It didn't come out the way he meant. He meant to confide in Luis, to encourage him, but it sounded like a boast or a reproach.

"I don't want to have sex yet," the boy said, sounding stuffy. Ed couldn't blame him.

"It's not really a big deal," Ed said.

"It is for you," Luis said. "So I guess it is for me."

"No, what I mean — " But Ed could not say what he meant. "It's not just fun," he said lamely.

A pause.

"Beats jerking off," Ed said.

Luis nodded, evidently in full agreement.

A pause.

"I just want to figure out how to, maybe, you know, how to find my own way, in all that," the boy said, not as fast with the words as usual.

"That's OK," the father said, and they parted with mutual relief. The boy might be slow, Ed thought, but at least he'd grown up in a homespace with plenty of healthy, open, happy sex as an example.

ON NATURE

It was interesting to know that Ed had slept with men; it must have been youthful experiment, for he'd never to Luis's knowledge brought a man home. But he brought women home. Probably every woman of his own generation, Luis thought, and now he was bringing home some of the older Fives. Luis knew the sound of his orgasms by heart — a harsh, increasing hah! hah! HAH! — and had heard every conceivable form of ecstatic female shriek, wail, howl, grunt, gasp, and bellow. The most notable bellower was 4-Yep Sosi, a physical therapist from Quad Three. She had been coming over every now and then ever since Luis could remember. She always brought star-cookies for Luis, even now. Sosi started out going aah, like a lot of them, but her aahs got louder and louder and more and more continuous, rising to a relentless, mindless ululation, so piercing that once Granny 2-Wong down the corridor thought it was an alarm siren and roused up everybody in the Wong compound. It didn't embarrass Ed at all. Nothing did. "It's perfectly natural," he said.

It was a favorite phrase of his. Anything to do with the body was "perfectly natural." Anything to do with the mind wasn't.

So, what was "nature"?

As far as Luis could think it through, and he thought about it a good deal his last year in high school, Ed was quite correct. In this world — on this ship, he corrected himself, for he was trying to train his mind in certain habits — on this ship, "nature" was the human body. And to some extent the plants, soils, and water in hydroponics; and the bacterial population. Those only to some extent, because they were so closely controlled by the techs, even more closely controlled than human bodies were.

"Nature," on the original planet, had meant what was not controlled by human beings. "Nature" was what was substantially previous to control, the raw material for control, or what had escaped from control. Thus the areas of Dichew where few people lived, quadrants that were undesirably dry or cold or steep, had been called "nature," "wilderness," or "nature preserves." In these areas lived the animals, which were also called "natural" or "wild." And all the "animal" functions of the human body were therefore "natural" — eating, drinking, pissing, shitting, sex, reflex, sleep, shouting, and going off like a siren when somebody licked your clitoris.

Control over these functions wasn't called unnatural, however, except possibly by Ed. It was called civilisation. Control started affecting the natural body as soon as it was born. And it really began to click in, Luis saw, at seven when you put on clothes and undertook to be a citizen instead of one of the kidherd, the wild bunch, the naked little savages.

Wonderful words! — wild — savage — civilisation — citizen —

No matter how you civilised it, the body remained somewhat wild, or savage, or natural. It had to keep up its animal functions, or die. It could never be fully tamed, fully controlled. Even plants, Luis learned from listening to Hsing's father, however manipulated to serve their symbiotic functions, were not totally predictable or obedient; and the bacteria populations came up constantly with "wild" breeds, possibly dangerous mutations. The only things that could be perfectly controlled were inanimate, the matter of the world, the elements and compounds, solid, liquid, or gas, and the artifacts made from them.

What about the controller, the civiliser itself, the mind? Was it civilised? Did it control itself?

There seemed to be no reason why it should not; yet its failures to do so constituted most of what was taught as History. But that was inevitable, Luis thought, because on Dichew "Nature" had been so huge and so strong. Nothing there was really, absolutely under control, except v-stuff.

Oddly enough he had learned that interesting fact from a virtual. He hacked his way through a tropical jungle buzzing with things that flew, bit, crawled, stung, snapped, and tormented the flesh, gasping for breath in a malodorous clinging heat that took his strength away, until he came to an open place where a horrible little group of humans deformed by disease, malnutrition, and self-mutilation rushed out of huts, screaming at the sight of him, and shot poisoned darts at him through blowguns. It was part of a lesson in Ethical Dilemmas, using the V-Dichew program Jungle. The words tropic, jungle, trees, insects, sting, huts, tattoos, darts had been in the Preliminary Vocabulary yesterday. But right now the Ethical Dilemma was pressing. Should he run away? try to parley? ask for mercy? shoot back? His v-persona carried a lethal weapon and wore a heavy garment, which might deflect the darts or might not.

It was an interesting lesson, and they had a good debate in class afterwards. But what stuck with Luis long after was the sheer, overwhelming enormity of that "jungle," that "wild nature" in which the savage human beings seemed so insignificant as to be accidental, and the civilised human being was completely foreign. He did not belong there. No sane person did. No wonder the subzero generations had had trouble maintaining civilisation and self-control, against odds like that.

A CONTROLLED EXPERIMENT

Although he found the arguments of the angels both rather silly and rather disturbing, he thought that they might be right in one fundamental matter: that the destination of this ship was not as important as the voyage itself. Having read history, and experienced Jungle and Inner City, Luis wondered if part of the Zero Generation's intent might have been to give at least a few thousand people a place where they could escape such horrors. A place where human existence could be controlled, as in a laboratory experiment. A controlled experiment in control.

Or a controlled experiment in freedom?

That was the biggest word Luis knew.

He mentally perceived words as having various sizes, densities, depths; words were dark stars, some small and dull and solid, some immense, complex, subtle, with a powerful gravity-field that attracted infinite meanings to them. *Freedom* was the biggest of the dark stars.

For what it meant to him personally he had a clear, precise image. His asthma attacks were infrequent, but vivid to his mind; and once when he was thirteen, in gymnastics, he had been under Big Ling at the wrong moment and Big Ling had come down right on him. Being about twice Luis's weight, Ling had squashed the air entirely out of Luis's lungs. After an endless time of gasping for air, the first breath, raw, dragging, searingly painful: that was freedom. Breath. What you breathed.

Without it you suffocated, went dark, and died.

People who had to live on the animal level might have been able to move around a lot, but never had enough air for their minds to breathe; they had no freedom. That was clear to him in the history readings and the historical v-worlds. Inner City 2000 was so shocking because it wasn't "wild nature" that made the people there crazy, sick, dangerous, and incredibly ugly, but their own lack of control over their own supposedly civilised "nature."

Human nature. A strange combination of words.

Luis thought about the man in Quad Three, last year, who had attacked a woman sexually, beaten her unconscious, and then killed himself by drinking liquid oxygen. He had been a Five, and the event, disturbing to everyone in the world, was particularly horrible and haunting to the people of his generation. They asked themselves *could I have done that? could that happen to me?* None of them seemed to know the answer. That man, 5-Wolfson Ad, had lost control over his "animal" or "natural" needs and so had ended up without any freedom at all, not making choices, not able even to stay alive. Maybe some people couldn't handle freedom.

The angels never talked about freedom. Follow orders, attain Bliss.

What would the angels do in the Year 201?

That was an interesting question, actually. What would any of them do, what would happen to the controlled experiment, when the laboratory ship reached the Destination? Shindychew was a planet — another huge mass of wild stuff, uncontrollable "nature," where they wouldn't even know what the rules were. On Dichew, at least their ancestors had been familiar with "nature," knew how to use it, how to get around in it, which animals were dangerous or poisonous, how to grow the wild plants, and so on. On the New Earth they wouldn't know anything.

The books talked about that, a little, not much. After all there was still half a century to go before they got there. But it would be interesting to find out what they did know about Shindychew.

When he asked his history teacher, 3-Tranh Eti, she said that the education program would provide Generation Six with a whole lot of education about the Destination and living there. Generation Five people would mostly be so old when they got there that it wasn't really their problem, she said, though of course they would be allowed to "land" if they wished to. The program was designed to keep the "middle generations" ("That's us," the old woman said drily) content with their world. A practical approach, she said, and well meant, but perhaps it had encouraged the mentality that was now so very prevalent among the proponents of Bliss.

She spoke frankly to Luis, her best student, and he told her as frankly that whether he got there or not, no matter how old he'd be if he got there, he wanted to find out now where he was going. He understood why; he didn't need to understand how; but he did want to understand where.

Tranh Eti gave him some help in accessing information, but it turned out that the education program for Generation Six was not accessible at present. It was being reviewed by the Educational Committee.

His other teachers advised him to finish his studies in high school and college and worry about the Destination later. If at all.

He went to the Head Librarian, old 3-Tan, his friend Bingdi's grandfather.

"To speculate about our destination," Tan said, "is to increase anxiety, impatience, and erroneous expectations." He smiled slightly. He spoke slowly, with pauses between sentences. "Our job is to travel. A different job from arrival." After a pause he went on, "But a generation that knows only how to travel — can they teach a generation how to arrive?"

THE GARAN

Luis continued to pursue his interest. He went back, on his own, to Jungle.

He had to follow the trail, of course. However through-composed a virtual-reality program was, you could do in it only what there was to do. It was like a dream, any dream, especially a nightmare: only certain choices are offered, if any.

There was the trail. You had to take the trail. The trail would lead to the ugly, degraded little savages, and they would scream and shoot poisoned darts, and then he would have to make one of the choices. Methodically, Luis made them, one after another.

Attempts to reason with the savages or run away from them ended quickly in blackout, which was, of course, v-death.

Once when they attacked him he fired the gun and killed one of the men. This was horrible beyond anything he had ever imagined and he escaped the program within moments of firing the weapon. That night he dreamed that he had a secret name that nobody knew, not even himself. A woman he had never seen before came to him and said, "Add your name to the wolf."

He went back into Jungle, though it was not easy. He found that if he showed no fear, threatened them with the gun if they attacked but did not fire it, the little men eventually, very suddenly, accepted his presence. After that another set of choice-forks opened out. He could keep his weapon in evidence and force the savages to lead him to the Lost City (which was supposed to be why you'd entered the jungle). He could make them obey him, but always he blacked out before he got far; the savages had murdered him. Or, if he behaved without fear, not threatening them and asking nothing of them, he could stay with them, living in a half-ruined hut. They accepted him as some kind of crazy man. The women gave him food and showed him how to do things, and he began to learn their language and customs. These were surprisingly intricate, formal, and fascinating. It was only v-learning; it only went so far, and seemed more than it was; when you came out you didn't come out with much. A program could hold only so much, even in implication. But what little he recalled of it had strangely enriched his thinking. He intended to go back some time, work his way to that final choice, and redo living with the savages.

But he had a different purpose, this time. This time when he entered Jungle, he moved as slowly as he could, and once he was well in he stopped and stood still on the path. He was no longer afraid of meeting the savages. Now that he knew them, had lived among them, it would have been sad to see them come at him, as they inevitably would, screaming and trying to kill him. He wanted not to meet them, this time. They were virtual human beings made by human beings. He had come to try to experience a place where nothing was human.

As he stood there, beginning to sweat at once, smelling the stinks, slapping at the creatures that buzzed and flickered around him and landed on his skin and bit, listening to the uncanny noises, he thought about Hsing. She would not admit VR as experience. She never went to V-Dichew unless it was required by a teacher. She never played v-games, wouldn't even try the really interesting one

Luis and Bingdi had worked out using "Borges's Garden" as a matrix. "I don't want to be in another person's world, I want to be in mine," she said.

"You read novels," he said.

"Sure. But *I* do reading. The writer puts the story there, and I do it. I make it be. The v-programmer uses me to do *his* story. Nobody uses my body and my mind but me. OK?" She always got fierce.

She had a point; but what struck Luis, standing alert and tense on the narrow incredibly intricate jungle pathway like a corridor gone crazy, watching something full of legs crawl away into the sinister darkness under a huge thing that he decided was a tree, but a tree lying down instead of standing up — what struck him was not only the choking, senseless complexity of this place, its quality of chaos, even though it was only a re-creation, the program of a sensation-field — but also how hostile it was. Dangerous, frightening. Was he experiencing the programmer's hostility?

There were plenty of sadistic programs; some people got hooked on them. How could he tell whether "nature" was in fact so terrible?

Certainly there were VR programs in which Dichew appeared simpler, more comprehensible — Countryside or Walking to the Mountains. And watching films, where the only sensations you had to cope with were sight and hearing, you could see that even though it was chaotic, "nature" could be pretty. Some people got hooked on those films, too, and were always watching sea turtles swimming in the sea and sky birds flying in the sky. But looking was one thing and feeling was another, even if it was only virtual feeling.

How could anybody actually live their whole life in a place like Jungle? The discomfort of the sensation-field was constant, the heat, the creatures, the changes of temperature, the rough, gritty, filthy surfaces of things, the endless unevenness — every step you took you had to look to see what your foot was going to land on. He remembered the natives' disgusting food. They killed animals and ate pieces of animal. The women chewed the root of some kind of plant, spat the chewed mass into a dish, let it rot a while, and then everybody ate it. If these stinging and biting poisonous animals were real not virtual, you'd come out of Jungle full of toxins. Indeed, what finally happened to you in the choice-fork where you lived with the savages was that you put your hand on a vine and it was a poisonous animal with no legs. It bit your hand, and within a few minutes you felt terrible pain and nausea, and then blackout. They had to end the program one way or another, of course; it was ten cycles subjective, ten actual hours, the maximum permitted length of a v-program. He had been not only virtually dead, but actually extremely stiff, hungry, thirsty, exhausted, and distressed when he came out of it.

Was the program honest? Did people on Dichew actually live in such misery? Not for ten cycles/hours, but for a lifetime? In constant fear of dangerous animals, fear of enemy savages, fear of each other, in constant pain from the thorns on plants, bites and stings, muscle strains from carrying heavy loads, feet bruised by the terrible uneven surfaces, and enduring still greater horrors, starvation, diseases, broken or deformed limbs, blindness? Not one of the savages, not even the baby and its young mother, was sound and clean. Their lesions and sores and scabs and calluses, bleared eyes, twisted limbs, filthy feet, filthy hair had only become more painful to look at as he began to know them as people. He had kept wanting to help them.

As he stood now on the v-path there was a noise near him in the darkness of the trees and long stringy plants, epiphytes like Yao's, only huge and knotted. Something among all these weird crowded-together lives that made the jungle had made a noise. He stood stiller than ever, remembering the garan.

He had gone with the men of the savage tribe, understanding that they were doing "hunting." They had glimpsed a flash of spotted golden light. One of the men had whispered a word, *garan*, which he remembered when he came back. He looked for it but it was not in the dictionary.

Now it came out of the chaos-darkness, the garan. It walked across the pathway from left to right a few meters in front of him. It was long, low, golden with black spots. It walked with indescribable softness and skill on four round feet, the head low, followed by a long graceful extension of itself, a tail, the tip just twitching as it vanished into the darkness again in utter silence. It never glanced at Luis.

He stood transfixed. It's VR, it's a program, he said to himself. Every time I came into Jungle, if I stood here just so long, the garan would walk across the path. If I was ready for it, if I wanted to, I could shoot at it with my v-gun. If the program includes "hunting," I would kill it. If the program doesn't include "hunting," my gun wouldn't fire. I could not make anything happen. The garan would walk on and vanish in silence, the tip of its tail just twitching as it disappears. This is not the wilderness. This is not nature. This is supreme control.

He turned around and walked out of the program.

He met Bingdi on his way to the gym to run laps. "I want to develop a technology for VU," he said.

"Sure," Bingdi said, after a moment, and grinned. "Let's do it."

WHERE ARE WE GOING?

Programs, photographs, descriptions — all representations of Dichew were suspect, since they were products of technology, of the human mind. They were interpretations. The planet of origin was inaccessible to direct understanding.

The planet of destination was less even than that. As he continued to explore the Library, Luis began to understand why the Zero Generation had been so eager for information about Shindychew. They had none.

The discovery of what they called a "Terran planet" within

"accessible range" had set off the whole *Discovery* project. The sub-Zeroes had studied it as exhaustively as their instruments permitted. But neither spectrum analysis nor any form of direct observation of a small non-self-luminous body at that distance could tell them all they needed to know. Life had been established as a universal emergent within certain parameters, and all the parameters they were able to establish were highly favorable. All the same, as he read in an ancient article called "Where Are They Going?" it was possible that a very small difference from "Earth" could make "New Earth" utterly uninhabitable for humans. Chemical incompatibility of the life forms with human chemistry, making everything there poisonous. A slightly different balance of the gases of the atmosphere, so that people could not breathe the air.

Air is freedom, Luis thought.

The Librarian was reading at a table nearby. Luis went over and sat down by him. He showed old Tan the article. "It says it's possible that we won't be able to breathe there."

The Librarian glanced over the article. "I certainly won't be able to," he observed. After the usual pause between sentences, he explained. "I'll be dead." He smiled a benign, semi-circular smile.

"What I'm trying to find," Luis said, "is something about what they expected us to do when we got there. Are there instructions somewhere — for the various possibilities — ?"

"At present," the old man said, "if there are such instructions, they are sealed."

Luis started to speak, then stopped, waiting for Tan's pause to end.

"Information has always been controlled."

"By whom?"

"Primarily, by the decisions of the Zero Generation. Secondarily, by the decisions of the Educational Council."

"Why would the Zeroes hide information about our destination? Is it that bad?"

"Perhaps they thought, since so little was known, the middle generations needn't worry about it. And the Sixth Generation would find out. And send them the information. This is a voyage of scientific discovery." He looked up at Luis, his face impassive. "If the air is not breathable, or there are other problems, people can go out in suits. Evamen. Live inside, study outside. Observe. Send information to the *Discovery* in orbit. And thence back to Ti Chiu." He pronounced the Chinese word in Chinese. "There are Unreplaceable Supplies for twelve generations, not six. In case we could not stay there. Or chose not to. Chose to go back to Ti Chiu."

It took Tan quite a while to say all this. Luis's mind filled the pauses with imaginings, as if he were illustrating a text: the vast trajectory slowing, slowing towards a certain star; the little shipworld hovering above the surface of the immense planetworld; tiny figures in evasuits swarming out into Jungle. . . . Vivid, improbable. Virtual Unreality.

" 'Back,' " he said. "What's 'back'? None of us came from Dichew. Back or forward, what's the difference?"

" 'How much difference between yes and no? What difference between good and bad?' " the old man said, looking at him approvingly, yet with that expression in his eyes that Luis could not interpret. Was it sorrow?

He knew the quotation. Hsing and her father Yao had both studied with 3-Tan, who as well as being the Librarian was a scholar of the Chinese classics, and all three were fans of Old Long-Ears. Growing up in Quad Two, Luis had heard the book quoted till he read a translation of it in self-defense. Recently he had re-read it, trying to figure out how much of it made sense to him. Liu Yao had copied the whole thing out in the ancient Chinese characters. It had taken over a year. "Just practicing calligraphy," he said. Watching the complex, mysterious figures flow from Yao's brush, Luis had been moved more strongly than he ever had been moved by the seemingly comprehensible translated words. As if not to understand was to understand.

CIRCULATION

Paper, made from rice straw, was rare stuff. Little writing was done by hand. Yao had got permission to use several meters of paper for his copying, but he could not keep it out of circulation for long. He gave pieces of the scroll to Chi-An friends. They would put them up on the wall for a while, then recycle them. No inessential artifact could survive more than a few years. Clothes, artworks, paper copies of texts, toys, all were given back to the cycle, sometimes with a ceremony of grief. A funeral for the beloved doll. The portrait of Grandfather might be copied into the electronic memory bank when the original was recycled. Arts were practical or ephemeral or immaterial — a wedding shirt, bodypaint, a song, a story in an all-net magazine. The cycle was inexorable. The people of *Discovery* were their own raw material. They had everything they needed, they had nothing they could keep. The only poverty such a world could suffer would follow from the loss or waste of energy/matter tied up in useless objects or ejected into space.

Or, in the very long run, from entropy.

Once upon a time a dermatologist doing eva to repair a slight encounter-graze on the underhull had tossed his alloy gun to his companion a few meters away, who missed the catch. The film-story of the Lost Gun was a dramatic moment in second-grade Ecology. Oh! the children cried in horror as the tool, gently revolving, drifted among the stars, farther and farther away. There — look — it's going to away! It's going to away forever!

The light of the stars moved the world. Hydrogen acceptors fed the tiny fusion reactors that powered the electrical and mechanical systems and the Fresno accelerators that sped *Discovery* on its way. The little world was affected from outside only by dust and photons. It accepted nothing from outside but atoms of hydrogen.

Within itself it was entirely self-sustaining, self-renewing. Every cell shed by human skin, every speck of dust worn from a fabric or a bearing, every molecule of vapor from leaf or lung, was drawn into the filters and the reconverters, saved, recombined, re-used, reconfigured, reborn. The system was in equilibrium. There were reserves for emergencies, never yet called upon, and the store of Unreplaceable Supplies Tan had mentioned, some of them raw materials, others hi-tech items which the ship lacked the means to duplicate: a surprisingly small amount, stored in two cargobays. The effect of the second law of thermodynamics operating in this almost-closed system had been reduced to almost-nil.

Everything had been thought about, seen to, provided for. All the necessities of life. *Why am I here? Why am I?* A purpose for living: a reason. That, too, the Zeroes had tried to provide.

For all the middle generations of the two-century voyage, their reason for being was to be alive and well, to keep the ship in good running order, and to furnish it with another generation, so that it could accomplish its mission, their mission, the purpose to which they were all essential. A purpose which had meant so much to the Zeroes, the earthborn. Discovery. Exploration of the universe. Scientific information. Knowledge.

An irrelevant knowledge, useless, meaningless to people living and dying in the closed, complete world of the ship.

What did they need to know that they didn't know?

They knew that life was inside: light, warmth, breath, companionship. They knew that outside was nothing. The void. Death. Death silent, immediate, absolute.

SYNDROMES

"Infectious diseases" were something you read about or saw hideous pictures of in history films. In every generation there were a few cancers, a few systemic disorders; kids broke their arms, athletes overdid it; hearts and other organs went wrong or wore out; cells followed their programs, aged, died; people aged, died. A major responsibility of doctors was seeing that death did not come too hard.

The angels spared them even that responsibility, being strong on "positive dying," which made of death a devout communal exercise, leading the dying person into trance induced by hypnosis, chanting, music, and other techniques; the death itself was greeted by ecstatic rejoicing.

Many doctors dealt almost entirely with gestation, birth, and death: "easy out, easy in." Diseases were words in textbooks.

But there were syndromes.

In the First and Second Generations many men in their thirties and forties had suffered rashes, lethargy, joint pains, nausea, weakness, inability to concentrate. The syndrome was tagged SD, somatic depression. The doctors judged it to be psychogenic.

It was in response to the SD syndrome that certain areas of professional work had been gender-restricted. A measure was put up for discussion and vote: men were to do all structural maintenance and dermatology. The last — repair and upkeep of the skin of the world where it interfaced with space — was the only job that required doing eva: going outside the world.

There were loud protests. The "division of labor," perhaps the oldest and deepest-founded of all the institutions of power-imbalance — was that irrational, fanciful set of prescriptions and proscriptions to be reinstituted here, where sanity and balance must, at the cost of life itself, be preserved?

Discussions in Council and quad meetings went on for a long time. The argument for gender-restriction was that men, unable to bear and nourish children, needed a compensatory responsibility to valorise their greater muscular strength as well as their hormone-related aggressivity and need for display.

A great many men and women found this argument insupportable in every sense of the word. A slightly larger number found it convincing. The citizens voted to restrict all evas to men.

After a generation had passed, the arrangement was seldom questioned. Its popular justification was that since men were biologically more expendable than women they should do the dangerous work. In fact no one had ever been killed doing eva, or even taken a dangerous dose of radiation; but the sense of danger glamorised the rule. Active, athletic boys volunteered for dermatology in numbers far larger than were needed, and so served on a reserve rota with regular training evas. Evamen had a distinctive way of dressing: brown canvas shorts, a carefully embroidered sleeve-patch of stars on black.

The outbreak of SD had leveled off eventually to a low endemic level, a drop that some said was connected to the eva restrictions and some said was not.

The Thirds had dealt with a high incidence of spontaneous abortions and stillbirths, never explained, and fortunately lasting only a few years. The episode had caused an increase in late pregnancies and two-child families until the optimum replacement ratio was recovered.

In the Fourth and Fifth generations a perhaps related, even more debilitating set of symptoms appeared, diagnosed but as yet unexplained, tagged TSS, tactile sensitivity syndrome. The symptoms were random pains and extreme neural sensitivity. TSS sufferers avoided crowds, could not eat in the refectories, complained that everything they touched hurt; they used dark glasses and earplugs and covered their hands and feet with things called sox. As no explanation or cure had been found, myths of prevention sprang up and folk remedies flourished. Quad Two had a low incidence of TSS, and so the Chi-An food style — rice, soy, ginger, garlic — was imitated. A reclusive life seemed to ease the symptoms, so some people with TSS tried to keep their children out of kidherd and school. But here the law intervened. No parental decision was permitted to impair the welfare of the child and of the community as determined by the Constitution and the judgment of the Council on Education. The children went to school and suffered no visible ill effects. Dark glasses, earplugs, and sox were a brief fad among high-schoolers, but the disorder affected few people under twenty. The angels asserted that no practitoner of Bliss suffered from TSS, and that to escape it, all you had to do was learn to rejoice.

ANCESTORS OF THE ANGELS

0-Kim Jan had been the youngest of the Zeroes, ten days old at Embarkation.

0-Kim Jan was a power in the Council for many years. Her genius was for organisation, order, a firm, impartial administration. The Chi-Ans called her Lady Confucius.

She had a late-born son, 1-Kim Terry. Her son led an obscure life, interrupted by bouts of somatic depression, as a programmer for the primary schools innet, until 0-Kim died in the year 79. She was the last of the Zeroes, the earthborn. Her death was felt as momentous.

Her funeral was attended by a very great crowd, far too many even for the Temenos to hold. The ceremony was broadcast on the allnet. Almost every person in the world watched it and so saw the inception of a new religion.

CHURCH AND STATE

The Constitution was explicit in decreeing the absolute separation of creed from polity. Article 4 specifically named the monotheisms that figured so large in history, including the religion that had controlled the dominant governments at the time the voyage of *Discovery* was planned. Any attempt "to influence an election or the deliberation of a legislative body by overt or covert invocation of the principles or tenets of Judaism, Christianity, Islam, Mormonism, or any other religious creed or institution," if confirmed by an ad hoc committee on Religious Manipulation, could be punished by public reprimand, loss of office, or permanent disqualification from any position of responsibility.

In the early decades there had been many challenges to Article 4. Though the planners had consciously tried to select *Discovery*'s crew for what they saw as scientific impartiality of mind, the monotheist tendency to limit understanding to a single mode was already deeply embedded in much of their science. They had expected that in a deliberately, widely heterogeneous population the practice of tolerance would be not so much a virtue as a necessity. Still, in the Zero Generation, after several years of space travel people who had never given religion much thought, or who had thought of it as inimical, often took to identifying themselves as Mormon, Muslim, Christian, Jew, Buddhist, Hindu. They had found that religious affiliations and practices gave them needed support and comfort in their sudden, utter, irrevocable exile from everyone on Earth and from the Earth itself.

Faithful atheists were incensed by this outbreak of piety. Actual memories of the horrors of the Fundamentalist Purification and historical evidence of endless genocides in the name of God cast their shadows across the mildest forms of public worship. Eclecticism waved its ineffectual hands. Accusations were hurled, challenges made. Ad hoc Committees on Religious Manipulation were convened and reconvened.

But the generations after the Zeroes had no experience of exile; they lived where they were born, where their parents had been born. And miscegenation made ancestral pieties irrelevant. It was difficult for a Jewish Presbyterian Parsee to choose which of his Puritanisms to obey. It was not difficult to forgo the incompatible righteousnesses of a Sunni-Mormon-Brahmin inheritance.

When 0-Kim died, Article 4 had not been invoked for years. There were religious practices, but no religious institutions. Practice was private or familial. People sat vipassana or zazen, prayed for guidance or in praise. A family celebrated the birth of Jesus or the kindness of Ganesh or the memory of the Passover on more or less appropriate days of the monthless year. Of all ceremonies, funerals, which were always public, were the most likely to bring the trappings as well as the essentials of religion into play. Beautiful old words in beautiful old languages were spoken, and rites of mourning and consolation were observed.

THE FUNERAL AND THE BIRTH OF BLISS

0-Kim had been a militant atheist. She had said, "People need God the way a three-year-old needs a chainsaw." Her funeral was scrupulously free of references to the supernatural or quotations from holy books. People spoke briefly — some not briefly enough — about her effect on their life and everyone's life, about her charisma, her incorruptibility, her powerful, parental, practical care for the future generations. And they spoke with emotion of this death of the "Last of the Earthborn." Children of children watching this ceremony, they said, would be alive when the Mission that the Founders sent forth came at last to its fulfilment — when the Destination was reached. Kim Jan's spirit would be with them then.

Finally, as was customary, the child of the deceased rose to say the last words.

1-Kim Terry came up on the podium in front of the people and the innet camcorders beside the bier where his mother's body lay draped in white. There was great intensity and purposefulness in his movements. To people who knew him, he looked changed — assured, calm. He was not tearful or shaky-voiced. He looked out over the crowd that filled the whole floor of the Temenos. "He shone," several people said later.

"The last of those whose body was born of Earth is gone," he said in a clear, strong voice, which reminded many of his mother, a fine speaker in Council. "She has gone to the glory of which her body was the bright shadow. We here, now, travel away from the body into the realm of the soul. We are free. We are utterly free of darkness, of sin, of Earth. Through the corridors of the future I bring the message to you. I am the messenger, the angel. And you, you are angels. You are the chosen. God has called you, called you by name. You are the blessed. You are divine beings, sacred souls, who have been called to live in bliss. All that remains to us to do is to know who we are, that we are the inhabitants of heaven. That we are the blessed, the heavenborn, chosen for the eternal voyage. That we are, each one of us, sacred, born to live in bliss and die to greater bliss." He raised his arms in a great, dignified gesture of blessing over the startled, silent multitude.

He spoke on for another twenty minutes.

"Unhinged with grief," some people said as they left the Temenos or turned off the set; cynics responded, "Maybe with relief?" But many people discussed the ideas and images Kim Terry had put into their minds, feeling that he had given them something they had craved without knowing it, or felt without being able to say it.

BECOMING ANGELS

The funeral had been epochal. Now that no living person in the world remembered the planet of origin, was there any reason to think anyone there remembered them? Of course they sent out radio messages concerning the progress of the *Discovery* regularly, as specified in the Constitution, but was anybody listening?

"Orphans of the Void," a mawkish song with a good tune, sung by the Fourth Quad group Nubetels, became a rage overnight. And people talked about 1-Kim Terry's speech.

They went by his homespace to talk to him, some concerned, some curious. They were received by a couple named 2-Patel Jimmy and 2-Lung Yuko, his next-door neighbors. Terry is resting, they said, but he'll talk this evening. Did you feel the wonderful feelings while he was speaking in the Temenos? they asked. Did you see how different, how changed he is? We've watched him change, they said, watched him become wise, radiant, eloquent. Come hear him. He'll speak this evening.

For a while it was a kind of fad to go hear Terry speak about Bliss. There were jokes about it. Atheists railed about cult hysteria and hypocritical egotrippers. Then some people forgot about it, and others kept going to the Kim homespace cycle after cycle, year after year, for the evening meetings with Terry, Jimmy, and Yuko. People held meetings in their own homespaces, with little feasts, songs, meditations, devotions. They called these meetings angelic rejoicings, and called themselves friends in bliss, or angels.

When these followers of Kim Terry began to preface their kinname with Angel as a kind of title, there was a good deal of disapproval and discussion in the councils. The angels agreed that such group identification was potentially divisive. Terry himself told his followers not to go against the will of the majority: "For, whether or not we know it, are we not all angels?"

Yuko, Jimmy, and Jimmy's little son Inbliss lived with Terry in the homespace he had shared with his mother. They led the nightly meetings. Kim Terry himself become increasingly reclusive. In the early years he now and then spoke to meetings held in the Quad One Circus or the Temenos, but as the years went by he appeared

PARADISES LOST | 297

less and less often in public, speaking to his followers only over the innet. To those who went to the meetings at his homespace he might appear briefly, blessing and encouraging them; but his followers believed that his bodily presence was unimportant compared to his angelic presence, which was continual. Bodily matters darkened bliss, obscuring the soul's needs. "The corridors I walk are not these corridors," Terry said.

His death in the year 123 brought on a deep hysteria of mourning combined with festivity, for his followers, embracing his doctrine of Actuality as explained by his energetic interpreter, 3-Patel Inbliss, celebrated his apparent death as a rebirth into the Real World, to which the shipworld was merely the means of access, the "vehicle of bliss."

Patel Inbliss lived on alone in the Kim homespace after Terry's and his parents' death, holding meetings there, speaking at home Rejoicings, talking on the innet, working on and circulating the collection of sayings and meditations called *The Angel to the Angels*. Patel Inbliss was a man of great intelligence, ambition, and devotion, with a genius for organisation. Under his guidance the Rejoicings had become less disorderly and ecstatic, indeed were now quite sedate. He discouraged the wearing of special clothing — undyed shorts and kurtas for men, white clothing and headscarves for women — which many angels had adopted. To dress differently was divisive, he said. Are we not all angels?

Under his leadership, indeed, more and more people declared themselves to be angels. The number of conversions in the first decades of the second century brought on a call for an Article 4 hearing on Religious Manipulation by a group who claimed that Patel Inbliss had formed and promulgated a religious cult which worshipped Terry as a god, thus threatening secular authority. The Central Council never actually called a committee to investigate the charge. The angels asserted that, though they venerated Kim Terry as a guide and teacher, they held him to be no more divine than the least of them. Are we not all angels? And Patel Inbliss argued cogently that the practice of Bliss in no way conflicted with polity and governance, but on the contrary supported it in every particular: for the laws and ways of the world were the laws and ways of Bliss. The Constitution of *Discovery* was holy writ. The life of the ship was bliss itself — the joyful mortal imitation of immortal reality. "Why would the followers of perfect law disobey it?" he asked. "Why would those who enjoy the angelic order seek disorder? Why would the inhabitants of heaven seek any other place or way to live?"

Angels were, in fact, extremely good citizens, active and cooperative in all civic duties, ready to fulfil communal obligations, diligent committee and Council members. In fact, more than half the Central Council at the time were angels. Not seraphim or archangels, as the very devout and those close to Patel Inbliss were nicknamed, but just everyday angels, enjoying the serenity and good fellowship of the Rejoicings, which were by now a familiar, accepted element of life for many people. The idea that the beliefs and practices of Bliss could in any way run counter to morality, that to be an angel was to be a rebel, was clearly ridiculous.

Patel Inbliss, now in his seventies, indomitably active, still occupied the Kim homespace.

INSIDE, OUTSIDE

"Could it be that there are two kinds of people ... " Luis said to Hsing. Then he paused for so long that she replied crisply, "Yes. Possibly even three. Daring thinkers have postulated as many as five."

"No. Only two. People who can roll their tongue sideways into a tube and people who can't."

She stuck out her tongue at him. They had known since they were six that he could make his tongue into a tube and whistle through it, that she couldn't, and that it was genetically determined.

"One kind," he said, "has a need, a lack, they have to have a certain vitamin. The other kind doesn't."

"Well?"

"Vitamin Belief."

She considered.

"Not genetic," he said. "Cultural. Metaorganic. But as individually real and definite as a metabolic deficiency. People either need to believe or they don't."

She still pondered.

"The ones that do don't believe that the others don't. They don't believe that there are people who don't believe."

"Hope?" she offered, tentative.

"Hope isn't belief. Hope's contingent upon reality, even when it's not very realistic. Belief dismisses reality."

" 'The name you can say isn't the right name,' " said Hsing.

"The corridor you can walk in isn't the right corridor," said Luis.

"What's the harm in believing?"

"It's dangerous to confuse reality with unreality," he said promptly. "To confuse desire with power, ego with cosmos. Extremely dangerous."

"Oooh." She made a face at his pomposity. After a while she said, "Is that what Terry's mother meant — 'People need God like a three-year-old needs a chensa.' What was a chensa, I wonder?"

"A weapon, maybe."

"I used to go to Rejoicings sometimes with Rosa before she went seraph. I liked a lot of it, actually. The songs. And when they praise things, you know, just ordinary things, and say how everything you do is sacred. I don't know, I liked it," she said, a little defensive. He nodded. "But then they'd get into reading all the weird stuff out of the book, about what the 'voyage' really is, and what 'discovery' actually means, and I'd get claustro. Basically they were saying that there is nothing at all outside. The whole universe is inside. It was weird."

"They're right."

"Oh?"

"For us — they're right. There is nothing at all outside. Vacuum. Dust."

"The stars — the galaxies!"

"Light-specks on a screen. We can't reach them, we can't get to them. Not us. Not in our lifetime. Our universe is this ship."

It was an idea so familiar as to be banal and so strange it unnerved her. She pondered.

"And life here is perfect," Luis said.

"It is?"

"Peace and plenty. Light and warmth. Safety and freedom."

Well, of course, Hsing thought, and her face showed it.

Luis pressed on — "You did History. All that suffering. Did anybody in the subzero generations ever live as well as we live? Half as well? Most of them were afraid all the time. In pain. They were ignorant. They fought each other over money and religions. They died from diseases and wars and food shortage. It was all like Inner City 2000 or Jungle. It was hell. And this is heaven. Angel Terry was right."

She was puzzled by his intensity. "So?"

"So did our ancestors arrange to send us from one hell to another hell, by way of heaven? Do you see potential danger in that arrangement?"

"Well," Hsing said. She considered his metaphor. "Well, for the Sixes, maybe it'll seem kind of unfair. It's not going to make much difference to us. We'll be too doddering to go eva at all, I suppose. Although I'd like to dodder out and see what it looks like. Even if it is hell."

"That's why you're not an angel. You accept the fact that our life, our voyage, has a purpose outside itself. That we have a destination."

"Do I? I don't think so. I just sort of hope we do. It would be interesting to be somewhere else."

"But the angels believe there is nowhere else."

"Then they're in for a surprise when we reach Shindychew," Hsing said. "But then, I expect we all are. . . . Listen, I have to do that chart for Canaval. I'll see you in class."

They were second-year college students, nineteen years old, when they had this conversation. They did not know that sophomores had always discussed belief and unbelief and the purpose of existence.

WORDS FROM EARTH

Messages had followed, or preceded, them, of course, ever since *Discovery* left the planet Dichew, Earth. During the First Generation many personal messages were received. *Descendants of Ross Betti: Everybody in Badgerwood is rooting for you!* Such transmissions had become rarer as the years went on, and finally vanished. Occasionally there had been major interruptions in reception, once lasting for nearly a year; and as the distance grew, and for some reason particularly during the last five years, distortions and delays and partial losses were the norm. Still, *Discovery* had not been forgotten. Words came. Images arrived. Somebody, or some program, on the Planet of Origin kept sending out a steady trickle of news, information, updates on technology, a poem or a fiction, occasionally whole periodicals or volumes of political commentary, literature, philosophy, criticism, art, documentaries; only all the definitions had changed and you couldn't be sure whether what you were watching or reading was invented or actual, because how could you possibly tell Earth reality from Earth fiction, and the science was just as bad, because they took discoveries for granted and forgot to define the terms they were using. Generations One and Two had spent a lot of time and passion and intelligence analysing and interpreting receptions from

Dichew. There had been whole schools of opinion in Quads One and Four about the reports concerning apparent conflict between what were apparently philosophical-religious schools of thought, or possibly national or ethnic divisions, called (in Arabic) The True Followers and The Authentic Followers. Thousands or millions — the transmissions spoke of billions but this was certainly a distortion or error — at any rate a great number of people on Dichew had killed one another, had been killed, because of this conflict of ideas or beliefs. On *Discovery*, there were violent arguments about what the ideas, the beliefs, the conflicts were. The arguments went on for decades, but nobody died because of them.

By the Third and Fourth Generations the general content of Earth transmissions had become so arcane that only devotees followed them closely; most people paid no attention to them at all. If something important had happened on Dichew somebody or other would notice, and in any case whatever was received went into the Archives. Or was supposed to be going into the Archives.

4-CANAVAL

When she came to College Center to enroll for her first-year courses, Hsing found that the professor of Navigation, 4-Canaval Hiroshi, had requested that she be skipped over the first year of his course and put into the second. "What if I wasn't intending to take Nav at all?" she demanded of the registrar, indignant at this high-handed order. But she was flattered; clearly Canaval had been watching the High School math and astro classes, and had his eye on her. She signed up for Nav 2.

Navigation was an honored profession but not a glamorous one, not like being an evaman or an innet entertainer. To many people the idea of navigation was a little threatening. They explained it by saying that in most jobs you could make a mistake and of course it would cause trouble (any event in a glass bowl is likely to affect everything in the glass bowl), but in jobs like atmosphere control and navigation, a mistake could hurt or even kill people — hurt or kill *everybody*.

All the systems were full of failsafes and backups and redundancies, but there was, notoriously, no way to failsafe navigation. The computers, of course, were infallible, but they had to be operated by humans; the course had to be continually adjusted; all the navigators could do was check and re-check their calculations and the computers' calculations and operations, check and re-check input and feedback, check and correct for error, and keep on doing it, over and over and over. If the calculations and operations all agreed with each other, if it all checked out, then nothing happened. You just did it all over again forever.

Navigation was about as thrilling as running the bacteria counts, also an unpopular job. And the mathematical talent and training required to do it was formidable. Not many students took Nav for more than the required first year, and very few went on to specialise in it. 4-Canaval was looking for candidates, or victims, as some of his students said.

If the unpopularity of the subject rose from some deeper discomfort, some dread of what it dealt with — the voyage through space, the very movement of the shipworld, its course, its goal — nobody talked about it. But Hsing thought about it sometimes.

Canaval Hiroshi was in his forties, a short, straight-backed man with coarse, bushy black hair and a blunt face, like the pictures of Zen Masters, Hsing thought. He was related to Luis; they were half-cousins; at moments Hsing saw a resemblance. In class he was brusque, impatient, intolerant of error. Students complained: one insignificant mistake in a computer simulation and he tossed the whole thing out, hours of work — "worthless." He was certainly both arrogant and obsessive, but Hsing defended him against charges of megalomania. "It's not his ego," she said. "I don't think he has an ego. All he has is his work. And it does have to be right. Without error. I mean, if we get too close to a gravity sink, does it matter whether it's by a parsec or by a kilometer?"

"All right, but a millimeter isn't going to do any harm," said Aki, who had just had a beautiful charting deleted as "worthless."

"A millimeter now, a parsec in ten years," Hsing said priggishly. She saw Aki roll his eyes. She didn't care. Nobody else seemed to understand the excitement of doing what Canaval did, the thrill of getting it right — not nearly right, but *exactly* right. Perfection. It was beautiful, the work. It was abstract, yet human, even humble, because what you wanted didn't matter. And you couldn't rush it; you had to get all the small things right, take care of all the details, in order to get to the great thing. There was a way to follow. It took constant, ceaseless, alert attention to that way to stay on it. It was not a matter of following your wish or your will, but of following what was. Being aware, all the time, being centered. Celestial Navigation: heaven-sailing. Out there was infinity. Through it there was one way.

And if knowing this went to your head, you always got reminded, immediately and inarguably, that you were completely dependent on the computers.

In third-year Nav, Canaval always gave a problem: *The computers are down for five seconds. Using the coordinates and settings given, plot course for the next five seconds without using the computers.* — Students either gave it up within hours, or worked days at it and then gave it up as a waste of time. Hsing did not hand the problem back in. At the end of term, Canaval asked her for it. "I thought I'd play around with it in vacation," she said.

"Why?"

"I like the computations. And I want to know how long it'll take me."

"How long so far?"

"Forty-four hours."

He nodded so slightly that perhaps he didn't nod, and turned away. He was incapable of showing approval.

He did, however, have a capacity for pleasure, and laughed when he found things funny, usually quite simple things, silly mistakes, foolish mishaps. His laughter was a loud, childish ha! ha! ha! After he laughed he always said, smiling broadly, "Stupid! Stupid!"

"He really is a Zen Master," she told Luis in the snackery. "I mean really. He sits zazen. He gets up at four to sit. Three hours. I wish I could do that. But I'd have to go to bed at twenty, I'd never get any studying done." Observing a lack of response in Luis, she said, "And how is your v-corpse?"

"Reduced to a virtual skeleton," Luis said, still looking a bit absent.

College students chose a professional course in third year. Hsing was in Nav, Luis in Med. They no longer had any classes together, but they met daily in the snackery, the gyms, or the library. They no longer visited each other's room.

SEX IN THE GLASS BOWL

Lovers do not run away (where is away?). Lovers' meetings are public matters. Your procreative capacity is a matter of intense and immediate social interest and concern. Contraception is guaranteed by an injection every twenty-five days, for girls from the onset of menstruation, for boys at a time determined by medical staff. Failure to come to the Clinic for your conshot at the due date and hour is followed by immediate public inquiry: Clinic staff people come to your class, your gym, your section, corridor, homespace, announcing your name and your delinquency loud and clear.

People are permitted to go without conshots on the following

conditions or undertakings: sterilization, or completion of meno-
pause; a pledge either of chastity or of strict homosexuality; or an
intention to conceive, formally declared by both the man and the
woman. A woman who violates her undertaking to be chaste or
conceives a child with anyone but the declared partner can get a
morning-after shot, but both she and her sexual partner must then
go back to conshots for two years. Unauthorised conceptions are
aborted. The inexorable social and genetic reasons for all this are
made clear during your education. But all the reasons in the world
wouldn't work if you could keep your sexual life private. You can't.

Your corridor knows, your family knows, your section, your
ancestry, your whole quadrant knows who you are and where you
are and what you do and who you do it with, and they all talk.
Shame and honor are powerful social engines. If enforced by total
publicity and attached to rational need, rather than to hierarchic
fantasies and the will to dominate, shame and honor can keep a
society running steadily for a long time.

A teenager may move out of the parent's homespace and find a
single on another corridor, in another section, even change quadrants; but everybody in that new corridor, section, quad will know
who goes in and out your door. They will be observant, and interested, and vigilant, and curious, and mostly well-disposed, and
always hoping for a scandal, and they will talk.

The Warn, or Warren, was the first place many young people
moved to when they left parentspace. It was a set of corridors in
Quad Four, close to the College; all the spaces were singles; due to
the shape of the housing of the main accelerator, walls in the Warn
weren't all at right angles, and some of the spaces were substandard
size. The students moved partitions around and created a maze of
cubicles and sharespaces. The Warn was noisy and disorganised and
smelled of dirty clothes. Sleep there was occasional, sex was casual.
But everybody turned up on time at Clinic for their conshot.

Luis lived near the Warn in a triple with two other medical students, Tan Bingdi and Ortiz Einstein. Hsing was still in the Quad Two homespace with Yao. She had a twenty-minute walk to and from college daily.

After the usual adolescent period of experimenting around, when she entered college Hsing had pledged chastity. She said she didn't want conshots controlling her body's cycles, and didn't want emotion controlling her mind; not till she was through college.

Luis continued to get his conshot every twenty-five days, did not pledge, but did not go to bed with any of his friends. He never had. His only sexual experiences had been the general promiscuities of teenparties.

They knew all this about each other because it was public knowledge. When they were together they didn't talk about these matters. Their silences were as deeply and comfortably mutual as their conversations.

Their friendship was of course equally public. Their friends speculated freely about why Hsing and Luis didn't have sex and whether and when they'd get around to it.

Beneath their friendship was something that was not public, and was not friendship: a pledge made without words, but with the body; a non-action with profound results. They were each other's privacy. They had found where away was. The key to it was silence.

Hsing broke the pledge, broke the silence.

"Reduced to a virtual skeleton," Luis said absently, evidently thinking of something other than the v-cadaver which had been teaching him Anatomy. The cadaver had been programmed by its ghoulish author to guide and chastise the apprentice dissector. "The medulla, idiot!" it would whisper cavernously from moveless lips and lungless rib-cavity, or "Surely you don't take *that* for the caecum?" Hsing liked to hear what the cadaver had been saying. If you made no mistakes it occasionally rewarded you with bursts of poetry. "Soul clap hands and sing, and louder sing!" it had cried, even as Luis removed the larynx. But he had no cadaver-tales for her today, and went on sitting at the snackery table, brooding.

She said, "Luis, Lena — "

Luis held up his hand so quickly, so silently, that she fell silent, having said nothing but the name.

"No," he said.

There was a very long pause.

"Listen. Luis. You're free."

His hand was up again, warding off speech, defending silence.

She insisted: "I want you to know that you are — "

"You can't free me," he said. His voice was deepened by anger or some other emotion. "Yes. I'm free. We both are."

"I only — "

"Don't, Hsing! Don't!" He looked straight into her eyes for an instant. He stood up. "Let it be," he said. "I have to go." He strode off among the tables. People said "Hi, Luis" and he did not answer. People saw a quarrel. Hsing and Luis had a fight in the snackery today. Hey, what's up with Hsing and Luis?

YIN YANG

A young woman may find it difficult to withstand the urgent sexual advances of an older man in a position of power or authority. Her resistance is further compromised if she finds him attractive. She is likely to deny both the difficulty and the attraction, wishing to maintain her freedom of choice and that of other women. If her desire for independence is strong and clear, she will resist the pressure of his desire, she will resist her own longing to match the strength of her yielding to the strength of his aggression, to take him into herself while crying "Take me!"

Or she may come to see her freedom precisely in that yielding. Yin is her principle, after all. Yin is called the negative principle, but it is Yin that says "Yes."

They met again in the snackery a while after commencement. Both were in intense training in their chosen specialties, Luis interning at the Central Hospital, Hsing as an apprentice in the Bridge Crew. Their work consumed them. They had not seen each other alone for two or three tendays.

She said, "Luis, I'm living with Canaval."

"Somebody said you were." He still spoke with that vagueness, absentness, a kind of soft cover over something hard and set.

"I just decided to last week. I wanted to tell you."

"If it's a good thing for you . . ."

"Yes. It is. He wants us to marry."

"That's good."

"Hiroshi is — he's like the fusion core. It's exciting to be with him." She spoke earnestly, trying to explain, wanting him to understand. It was important that he understand. He looked up suddenly, smiling. Her face turned dusky red. "Intellectually, emotionally," she said.

"Hey, flatface, if it's good it's good," he said. He leaned over and lightly kissed her nose.

"You and Lena — " she said, eager.

He smiled a different smile and replied quietly, mildly, absolutely, "No."

INTEGRITY

It wasn't that there were pieces missing from Hiroshi. He was complete. He was all one piece. Maybe that's what was missing — bits of the other Hiroshis who might have read novels, or played solitaire, or stayed in bed late mornings, or done anything but what he did, been anyone other than what he was.

Hiroshi did what he did and doing it was what he was.

Hsing had thought, as a young woman might think, that her being in his life would enlarge it, change it. She understood very soon after she came to live with him that the arrangement had changed her life greatly and his not at all. She had become part of what Hiroshi did. An essential part, certainly: because he did only what was essential. Only she had never truly understood what he did.

That understanding made a greater change in her thinking and her life's course than having sex and living with him did. Not that the pleasures, tensions, and discoveries of sex didn't engage and delight and often surprise her; but she found sex, like eating, a splendid physical satisfaction which did not take up a great deal of her mind or even her emotions. Those were occupied by her work.

And the discovery, the revelation Hiroshi brought her, had nothing to do, or seemed to have nothing to do, with their partnership. It concerned the work he did, they did. Their whole life. The life of everybody in the worldship.

"You got me to live with you so you could co-opt me," she said to him, half a year or so later.

He replied with his usual honesty — for though everything he did served to conceal and perpetuate a deception, he made scrupulous efforts never to lie to a friend — "No, no. I trusted you. But it simplified everything. Doesn't it?"

She laughed. "For you. Not for me! For me everything used to be simple. Now everything's double . . ."

He looked at her without speaking for a while; then he took her hand and gently put his lips against her palm. He was a formally courteous sexual partner, whose ultimate surrender to passion always moved her to tenderness, so that their lovemaking was a reliable and sometimes amazing joy. All the same she knew that to him she was ultimately only fuel to the fusion core — an element in his overriding, single purpose. She told herself that she did not feel used, or tricked, because she knew now that everything was fuel to Hiroshi, including himself.

ERRORS

They had been married for three days when he told her what the purpose of his work was — what he did.

"You asked me a year ago about discrepancies in the acceleration records," he said. They were eating alone together in their home-space. Honeymooning, it was called, a word that didn't have many reverberations in this world without honey or bees to make it, without months or a moon to make them. But a nice custom.

She nodded. "You showed me I'd left out some factor. I don't remember what it was."

"Falsehood," he said.

"No, that isn't what you said. The constant of — "

He interrupted her. "What I said was a falsehood," he said. "A deliberate deception. To lead you astray. Make you think you'd made an error. Your computations were perfectly correct, you omitted nothing. There are discrepancies. Much greater discrepancies than the one you found."

"In the acceleration records?" she said stupidly.

Hiroshi nodded once. He had stopped eating. She knew that when he spoke so quietly he was very tense.

She was hungry, and pushed in one good supply of noodles before she put her chopsticks down and said, through noodles, "All right, what are you telling me?"

His face was strained. His eyes lifted to hers for a moment with an expression of desperation? pleading? — so uncharacteristic that it shocked her, moved her as his vulnerability in lovemaking did. "What's wrong, Hiroshi?" she whispered.

"The ship has been decelerating for over four years," he said.

Her mind moved with terrific rapidity, running through implications, explanations, scenarios.

"What went wrong?" she asked at last, quite steadily.

"Nothing. The deceleration is controlled. Deliberate."

He was looking down at his bowl. When he glanced up at her and at once looked down again, she realised that he feared her judgment. That he feared her. Though, she thought, his fear would not influence his actions or his words to her.

"Deliberate?"

"A decision made four years ago," he said.

"By?"

"Four people on the Bridge. Later, two in Administration. Four people in Engineering and Maintenance also know about it now."

"Why?"

The question seemed to relieve him, perhaps because it was asked quietly, without protest or challenge. He answered in a tone more like his usual one, even with a touch of the lecturer's assurance and acerbity. "You asked what's wrong. Nothing is. Nothing went wrong. We have always been on course, with almost no deviance. But an error did occur. An extraordinary, massive error. Which allowed us to take advantage of it. Error is opportunity. Chierek and I spotted it. A fundamental, ongoing error in the trajectory approximations, dating from our passage through the CG440 sink, five years ago, in Year 154. What happened during that passage?"

"We lost speed," she answered automatically.

"We gained it," he said. He glanced up to meet her incredulity. "Our acceleration increase was so great and so abrupt that the computers assumed a factor-ten error and compensated for it." He paused to make sure that she was following him.

"Factor *ten?*"

"By the time Chierek came to me with the figures and I realised that it could only be explained as a computer compensation error, we'd accelerated to .82 and were forty years ahead of schedule."

She was indignant at his joking, trying to fool her, saying these enormities. "Point eight two is not possible," she said, cold, dismissive.

"Oh yes," Hiroshi said with a grin that was equally cold, "it's possible. It's actual. We did it. We traveled at .82 for ninety-one days. Everything you know about acceleration, Gegaard's calculations, the massgain limit — it was all wrong. That's where the errors were! In the basic assumptions! Error is opportunity. It's all clear enough, once you have the records and can do the computations. We can tell the physicists back on Dichew all about it when we get to Shindychew. Tell them where they went wrong. Tell them how to use a sink to whiplash an object up to eight tenths lightspeed. This is the voyage of the *Discovery*, all right. We could have made it in eighty years." His face was hard with triumph, the conqueror's face. "We're going to arrive at the target system five years from now," he said. "In the first half of Year 164."

She felt nothing but anger.

"If this is true," she said at last, slowly and without expression, "why are you telling me now? Why are you telling me at all? You've kept this from everybody else. Why?"

It was not only the enormous shock of what he was telling her, it was his victorious look, his triumphant tone, that brought up the surge of rage in her — the opposition he had feared at the beginning, the question *How dare you?* But her anger now didn't affect him; he was unshaken, borne up by his conviction of rightness.

"It's the only power we have," he said.

"'We?' Who?"

"We who aren't angels."

TO COUNT THE NUMBER OF ANGELS

When Luis was told that the Educational Agenda for the Sixth Generation was not accessible because it was being revised, he said, "But that's what I was told when I asked to see it eight years ago."

The woman on the Education Center info screen, a motherly sort, shook her head sympathetically. "Oh, it's always under revision or under consideration, angel," she said. "They have to keep updating it."

"I see," said Luis, "thank you," and switched out.

Old Tan had died two years ago, but his grandson was a promising replacement. "Listen, Bingdi," Luis said across their sharespace, "does the bodycount register angels?"

"How should I know?"

"Librarians are the masters of useful trivia."

"You mean, are angels listed as such? No. Why would they be? The old religious affiliations weren't ever listed. Listing would be divisive." Bingdi did not speak quite as slowly as his grandfather, but in a similar rhythm, each sentence followed by a small, thoughtful silence, a quarternote rest. "I suppose Bliss is a religious affiliation. I don't know how else it could be defined. Though I'm not sure how religion is defined."

"So there's no way to know accurately how many angels there are. Or put it another way: There's no way to know who is an angel and who isn't."

"You could ask."

"Certainly. I will."

"You'll go from corridor to corridor throughout the world," Bingdi said, "inquiring of each person you pass, Are you an angel?"

"'Are we not all angels?'" said Luis.

"Sometimes it seems that way."

"It does indeed."

"What are you getting at?"

"It's what I can't get at that worries me. The education program for the Sixes, for instance."

Bingdi looked mildly startled. "Are you planning on procreating a baby Six?"

"No. I want to find out something about Shindychew. The Sixes are going to land on Shindychew. It seems reasonable to assume they'll be educated to do so. Informed of what to expect. How to cope with living outside. Trained in doing long-term eva on a planet surface. That's going to be their job, after all. The Zeroes must have included information on it in the education program. Your grandfather said they did. Where is it? And who is going to train them?"

"Well, there aren't any Sixes even wearing clothes yet," Bingdi said. "A bit soon to terrify the poor little noodles with tales of an unknown world, isn't it?"

"Better too soon than never," said Luis. "Destination Date is forty-four years from now. *We* might want to go do eva on Shindychew. Dodder forth, as Hsing put it."

"May I think about it after a couple of decades?" Bingdi said. "Just now I need to finish this bit of useful trivia."

He turned to his screen, but in a minute he looked round again at Luis. "What's the connection of that with the number of angels?" he said, in the voice of one who glimpses the answer as he asks the question.

ENEMIES OF BLISS

She did not know 5-Chin Ramon well, though he was one of Hiroshi's circle. He had been on the Managerial Counsel for a couple of years now. She had not voted for him. He identified as Chinese Ancestry and lived in Pine Mountain Compound, which was mostly Chins and Lees. A lot of the Chins had become angels early on. Ramon had risen, as they said, high in Bliss. He seemed a colorless, conventional man; like many male angels he treated women in a defensive, distancing, facetious manner Hsing found despicable. She had been displeased as well as very surprised to find he was one of the ten — now eleven — people who knew that the ship was decelerating towards an early arrival at the Destination.

"So you made this tape without telling the people you were taping them?" she asked him, not trying to keep contempt and distrust out of her voice.

"Yes," Ramon said, without expression.

Ramon had had a crisis of conscience: so Hiroshi said. 5-Chatterji Uma explained it to Hsing. Hsing liked and admired Uma, a bright, elegant little woman, elected to chair the Managerial Counsel four years running; she had to listen to her. Ramon, Uma explained, had been admitted to Patel Inbliss's inner circle, the archangels; and what he heard and learned there had so disturbed him that he had broken his vow of secrecy, made notes of things said among the archangels, and given them to Uma. She had taken his report to Canaval and the others. They had requested Ramon to prove his allegations. So he had surreptitiously taped a session of the archangels.

"How can you trust a person who would do such a thing?" Hsing had demanded.

"It was the only way he could provide us evidence." Uma had looked with sympathy at Hsing. "Paranoid suspicions — rumors of plots to take over navigation, tamper with our genes, put untested drugs in the water supply — how many have we all heard! This was the only way Ramon could convince us that he wasn't paranoid, or simply malicious."

"Tapes are easy to fake."

"Fakes are easy to spot," said 4-Garcia Teo with a smile; he was a big, craggy, kindly engineer whom Hsing could not help trusting, hard as she was working to distrust everybody in this room. "It's real."

"Listen to it, Hsing," Canaval said, and she nodded, though with a sullen heart. She hated it, this secrecy, lying, hiding, plotting. She did not want to be part of it, did not want to be with these people, to be one of them, to share the power they had seized — seized because they had to, they kept saying; but nobody had to lie. Nobody had the right to do what they were doing, to control everybody's life without telling them.

The voices on the tape meant nothing to her. Men's voices, talking about some business she did not understand, none of her business in any case. Let the angels have their secrets, let Canaval and Uma have theirs, just leave me out of it, she thought.

But she was caught by the sound of Patel Inbliss's voice, a soft, old voice, iron-soft, familiar to her all her life. Through her resistance, her disgust at being forced to eavesdrop, her incredulity, she heard that voice say, "Canaval must be discredited before we can count on the Bridge. And Chatterji."

"And Tranh," said another voice, at which 5-Tranh Golo, also a member of the Counsel, nodded his head in a wry pantomime of thanks-very-much.

"What strategy have you formed?"

"Chatterji is easy," said the other, deeper voice, "she's indiscreet and arrogant. Whispers will cripple her influence. With Canaval it is going to have to be a matter of his health."

Hsing felt a curious chill. She glanced at Hiroshi. He sat as impassive as if in his morning meditation.

"Canaval is an enemy of bliss," said the old voice, Patel's.

"In a position of unique authority," said one of the others, to which the deep voice replied, "He must be replaced. On the Bridge, and in the College. We must have a good man in both those positions." The tone of the deep voice was mild, full of reasoned certainty.

The discussion went on; much of it was incomprehensible to Hsing, but she listened intently now, trying to understand. All at once the tape ended midword.

She started, looked around at the others: Uma, Teo, Golo, and Ramdas, whom she thought of as friends; Chin Ramon and two women, an engineer and a Counsel member, whom she knew as members of the secret circle but did not think of as friends. And Hiroshi, still sitting zazen. They were in Uma's homespace, furnished "nomad style," a recent fad, no biltins, only carpeting and pillows in bright paisleys.

"What was that about your health?" Hsing demanded. "And then they were talking about something about heart valves?"

"I have a congenital heart deformity," he said. "It's on my H-folder."

Everyone had an H-folder: genetic map, health record, school records, work history. You held the code on it; nobody could see your H-folder without your permission, until you died and the file went from Records to Archives. A considerable mystique of privacy surrounded these personal files. No one but a coparent or a doctor would ever ask to see your H-folder. That anyone could break or steal the code and look at it without your permission was unthinkable. Hsing had not seen Hiroshi's H-folder and had never asked to, since they weren't planning on a child. She did not understand why he had mentioned it.

"Records staff is about ninety percent angels," Ramon said, seeing her blank expression.

She resented his pushing her, forcing her to realise what Hiroshi had meant. She resented Ramon altogether, his too-soft voice, his tight, hard face. Whenever Ramon was around, Hiroshi got tense, too, tight-mouthed, obsessed with all this stuff about the angels taking over. Now Ramon had got control over her too, forcing her to collude, to listen to the tape he'd made betraying people who trusted him.

To her dismay she found that she felt like crying. She had not cried for years. What was there to cry about?

Chatterji Uma's sympathetic gaze was on her. "Hsing," she said quietly, as the others began talking, "when Ramon showed me his notes, I told him to get out. Then I threw up all night."

"But," Hsing said. "But. But *why* would they *do* all this?" Her voice came out unmodulated, loud. The others turned.

Both Ramon and Hiroshi answered: "Power," one said, the other said, "Control."

She did not look at either of them. She looked at the Counselwoman, the woman, for an answer that made sense.

"Because — if I understand it — " Uma said, "Patel Inbliss has taught the angels that our destination is not a stopping place — not a place at all."

Hsing stared. "You mean they think Shindychew doesn't exist?"

"Nothing exists outside the ship. Nothing exists but the Voyage."

SOUL, SAY WHAT DEATH IS

"Rejoice in the voyage of life, from life, to life,
  Life everlasting, bliss everlasting.
  We are flying, O my angels, we will fly!"

All the celebrants sang out the last line, sweet and exultant, and Rose turned to smile at Luis. They sat in a row, Luis, Rosa with her baby Jellika, her husband Ruiz Jen holding his two-year-old Joy on his lap. Angels were strong on what they called "whole families" and "true brotherhood," couples who had and brought up both their children together. *Mother sweet to cherish, Father strong to guide, little boy, little girl, growing side by side.* Luis's head was full of tags and rhymes and sayings. He had read almost nothing but angelic literature for the last four tendays. He had read *The Angel to the Angels* through twice, and Patel Inbliss's *New Commentaries* three times, and many other texts; he had talked to angel friends and acquaintances, and listened much more than he talked. He had asked Rosa if he could come to Rejoicings with her, and she had of course told him happily that nothing could make her happier.

"I'm not going to become an angel, Rosie," he said, "that's not why I want to come," but she laughed and took his hands — "Oh, you already are an angel, Luis. Don't worry about that. I would just love to bring you into bliss!"

After the singing there was the Session in Peace, during which the celebrants sat in silence until one of them was moved to speak. Luis had come to look forward to these sessions. What was said was usually quite brief — a joy shared, or a fear or sorrow, in trustful expectation of sympathy. The first time he had come with Rosa, she stood up to say, "I am so glad because my dear friend Luis is here!" and people had turned and smiled at her and him. There were cut-and-dried speeches about thankfulness and remembering to be joyful, but often people spoke from the heart. Last meeting, an old man whose wife had died said, "I know Ada is flying in bliss, but I am lonely walking in the corridors without her. If you know how, please help me learn not to grieve her joy."

Today people were shy of talking and said only conventional things, probably because an archangel was present. Archangels visited home or sectional Rejoicings to give brief talks or teachings. Some of them were singers who performed the songs called "devotionals," to which the celebrants listened rapt. Luis had found these songs musically and intellectually rich and complex, and readied himself to listen with interest when the singer, 5-Van Wing, was introduced.

"I will sing a new song," Wing said with angelic simplicity, paused, and began. His unaccompanied voice was a strong, sure tenor. He sang a devotional of a kind Luis had not heard before. The tune was a free, ecstatic outpouring, evidently largely ex tempore, built on a few linked patterns, but the words were at odds with the music; they were allusive, brief, obscure.

Eye, what do you see?
Blackness, the void.
Ear, what do you hear?
Silence, no voice.
Soul, say what death is?
Silent, black, outside.
Let life be purified!
Fly ever to rejoice,
O vehicle of bliss!

The last three lines rose in conventionally joyous cadences, but the song had lingered darkly on the words before them, repeating them many times, the singer imbuing them with a tremor of horror which Luis felt as strongly as the others.

It was a remarkable performance, and Van Wing was a real artist, he thought.

He recognised as he did so that he was defending himself against the song, trying to trivialise the effect those lines had had on him.

Soul, say what death is?
Silent, black, outside.

As he went back through the crowded corridors to his homespace in Four, the words kept singing their dark song in his head. When he woke next morning, he understood what they meant to him.

Sitting on his bed he began to write in a blank book Hsing had made for him as a birthday present when they were sixteen. Though he had always used it sparingly, over the years most of the pages had been covered top to bottom and edge to edge with his small clear handwriting. Only a few were left. The flyleaf was inscribed: "A Box to Hold Luis's Mind. Made with Love by Hsing," her name not in letters but in the ancient ideogram: 星. He read the inscription whenever he opened the book.

He wrote: "Life/ship/vehicle/passage: mortal means to immortality (true bliss). Destination metaphorical — for Destination read Destiny. All meaning is inside. Nothing is outside. Outside is nothing. Negation, nil, void: Death. Life is inside. To go outside is denial, is blasphemy." He stared at the last word a while, then leaned over and brought up the OED on his innetscreen. He studied the definition and derivation of "blasphemy" for some time. He then looked up "heresy, heretic, heretical," and then "orthodoxy," which he quit abruptly to begin writing again in the blank book: "Hu. sp. highly ADAPTABLE! Bliss a psych./metaorganic adaptation to existence in transit — near-perfect homeostasis. Follow rules, live inside, live forever. Maladaptation to *arrival*. Arrival equated with phys./spir. DEATH." He paused again, then wrote, "How to counteract, causing least possible argument, factionalism, distress?"

He stopped writing and sat for a long time thinking, brooding. The soft, steady, unvarying flow of air at 22° C from the atmosphere-intake of his sleepspace stirred the thin leaves of the book and laid them gently down to the right, revealing the flyleaf again. "A Box to Hold Luis's Mind." The word love. The ideogram that meant Hsing, that meant star. There really was nobody else to talk to.

She did not answer his first message, and when he got through to her she was busy, sorry, things are so busy just now, I just can't get away from work. . . . She could not possibly have become self-important. Canaval was self-important, not without justification. But Hsing pompous, Hsing evasive? No. Busy. Why so busy? What kind of work kept one from answering a friend? Probably she was still afraid of him. That grieved him, but it was not a new grief. And since it was herself she feared, not him, it really was her problem, not his. So he insisted. He refused to be put off. "I will come tomorrow at ten," and at ten he was at the door of her homespace. She was there; Canaval was not. She was brusque, awkward. They sat down facing each other on the biltin couch. "Is something wrong, Luis?"

"I need to tell you what I've learned about the angels."

It was a strange thing to say after half a year of silence between them, he knew that; still, he found her response even stranger. She looked amazed, dismayed. She covered her shock, began to speak, stopped, and finally, with what seemed suspicion, said, "Why me?"

"Who else?"

"What do you think I have to do with anything to do with them?"

Circuitous! Luis thought. He said only, "Nothing. And that's getting to be rare. This is important, and I need to talk it over with you. I want to know what you think about it. Your judgment. I've always thought best when I talked with you."

She did not loosen up at all. Tense, wary, she nodded grudgingly. She said, "Do you want tea?"

"No, thank you. I'll talk as fast as I can. Please interrupt if I'm not clear. Tell me if what I say is credible."

"I don't find much incredible lately," she said, dry, not looking at him. "Go ahead, then. I do have to be on the Bridge at ten-forty. I'm sorry."

"Half an hour will do."

In half that time he told her what he had to tell. He began with his realisation that the education committees and councils had been controlled for at least twenty years by a large, steady majority of angels. It was now impossible to find what curriculum the Zero Generation had originally planned for the Sixth. Those plans had evidently been deleted — possibly even from the Archives.

Every time he considered that possibility it still shocked Luis, and he did not try to minimise his concern. Hsing continued to conceal any reaction she felt. He began to wonder if she already knew everything he was telling her. If so, she wasn't admitting that either. He went on.

The elementary and high school curriculum had been scarcely altered since Hsing's and Luis's schooldays. The most striking change was a decrease in information and discussion concerning both Dichew and Shindychew. Children now in school spent very little time learning about the planets of origin and destination. Language concerning them was vague, with a curiously remote tone. In two recent texts Luis had found the phrase, "the planetary hypothesis."

"But in 43.5 years we will arrive at one of these hypotheses," Luis said. "What are we going to make of it?"

Hsing looked stricken again — frightened. He didn't know what to make of that, either. He went on.

"I've been trying to understand the elements in angelic theory or belief that lead them to deny the importance — the fact — of our origin on one planet and our destination on another. Bliss is a coherent system of thought that makes almost perfect sense in itself and as a belief-system for people living as we live. In fact, that's the problem. Bliss is a self-contained proposition, a closed system. It is a psychic adaptation to our life — ship life — an adaptation to a self-contained system, an unvarying artificial environment providing all necessities at all times. We of the middle generations have no goal except to stay alive and keep the ship running and on course, and to achieve it all we have to do is follow the rules — the Constitution. The Zeroes saw that as an important duty, a high obligation, because they saw it as an element of the whole voyage — the means glorified by the end. But for those who won't see the end, there's not much glory being the means. Self-preservation seems self-centered. The system's not only closed, but stifling. That was Kim Terry's vision — how to glorify the means, the voyage — how to make following the rules an end in itself. As he saw it, our true journey is not only to a material world outside in space, but also to a spiritual world of bliss — which we will attain, by living rightly *here*."

Hsing nodded.

"Over the last decades Patel Inbliss has gradually changed the emphasis of this vision. *Here* is all. There's nothing outside the ship — literally nothing, spiritually nothing. Origin and destination are now metaphors. They have no reality. Journey is the sole reality. The voyage is its own end."

She was still impassive, as if he was telling her nothing she didn't know; but she was alert.

"Patel isn't a theorist. He's an activist. Acting on his vision through his archangels and their disciples. I believe that in the last ten or fifteen years, angels have been making many of the decisions in Council, and most of the decisions about education."

Again she nodded, but warily.

"The schools teach almost nothing about the original purpose of the interstellar voyage — to study and perhaps settle a planet. The texts and programs still have information about the cosmos — star-charts, stellar types, planet formation, all that stuff we had in Tenth — but I've been talking to teachers and they tell me they skip most of it. The children 'aren't interested,' they 'find these old material-science theories confusing.' You realise that almost all school administrators and about 65 percent of the teachers — 90 percent in Quad One — are members of Bliss?"

"So many?"

"At least that many. My impression is that some angels conceal their beliefs, deliberately, to keep their dominance from becoming too plain."

Hsing looked uneasy, disgusted, but said nothing.

"Meanwhile in the archangelic teachings, 'outside' is equated with danger, physical and spiritual — sin, evil — and with death. Nothing else. There is nothing good outside the ship. Inside is positive, outside negative. Pure dualism. — Not many young angels are going into dermatology these days, but there are some older ones who do eva. As soon as they're through the airlocks, they undergo a ritual of purification. Did you know that?"

"No," she said.

"It's called decontamination. An old material-science-theory word with a new meaning. The soul is contaminated by the silent black outside. . . . Well, that aside. Angels are eager to follow the rules, because our life lived well leads us directly to eternal happiness. They are eager for us all to follow the rules. We live in the Vehicle of Bliss. We can't miss bliss. Unless we break the one new rule. The big one: The ship can't stop."

He stopped. Hsing looked angry, as she always did when she was worried, troubled, or scared.

His gradual discovery of the change in the angelic teachings and the extent of angelic control over various councils had alarmed but not frightened him. He had seen it as a problem, a serious problem, that must be addressed. The way to solve it was to bring it out into the open, forcing the angels to explain their policies and making the non-angels aware that Patel Inbliss was trying to change the rules, and exerting clandestine power to do so. When they saw that, they'd react against it. There need be no crisis.

"We've got 43.5 years," he said. "Plenty of time to talk it over. It's a matter of getting things back in proportion. The more radical angels will have to agree that we *do* have a destination, that people *are* going to do eva there, and that they'll need to be trained to do eva, not to look on it as a sin."

"It's worse than that," Hsing said. The tight, stricken look had come over her again. She jumped up and walked across the room — a neat, severe room, not like the messy nest she used to live in — and stood with her back to him.

"Well, yes," Luis said, unsure what she meant, but encouraged at her saying anything at all. "We all need training. We'll be in our sixties at Arrival. If the planet's habitable, we've got to get used to the idea of at least some of us living there — staying there. While maybe some of us turn around and head back to Dichew. . . . The angels never mention that, by the way. Inbliss seems to think only in a straight line extending to infinity. The flaw in his reasoning is that he assumes a material vehicle is capable of an eternal journey. Entropy does not seem to be part of Bliss."

"Yes," Hsing said.

"That's all," he said after a minute. He was puzzled and worried by her non-response. He waited a little and said, "I think this must be talked about. So I came to you. To talk about it. And you might want to talk about it to non-angelic people in Management and on the Bridge. They need to be concerned about this revision of our mission." He paused. "Maybe they already are."

"Yes," she said again. She had not turned around.

Luis had very little anger in his temperament and was not given to fits of pique, but he felt let down flat. As he looked at Hsing's back, her pink cheongsam, her short-legs-no-butt (so she had described her Chi-An figure), her black hair falling bright and straight and cut off sharp at the shoulder, he also felt pain. A hard, deep, sore pain at the heart.

"There was a flaw in my reasoning too," he said. He stood up.

She turned around. She still looked worried beyond anything he had expected. It had taken him a long time to realise how powerful angelic thinking had become, and he had dumped all his discoveries on her at once — yet none of it had seemed to surprise her. So why this reaction? And why wouldn't she talk about it?

"What flaw?" she asked, but still distrustful, holding back.

"Nothing. I miss talking with you."

"I know. The work in Nav, it seems like it never lets up."

She was looking at him but not looking at him. He couldn't stand it.

"So. That's it. Just sharing my worries, as we say in Peace Session. Thanks for the time."

He was in the doorway when she said, "Luis."

He stopped, but didn't turn.

"I want to talk more about all this maybe with you later."

"Sure. Don't let it worry you."

"I have to talk to Hiroshi about it."

"Sure," he said again, and went out into the corridor.

He wanted to go somewhere else, not corridor 4-4, not any corridor, not any room, not any place he knew. But there was no place he didn't know. No place in the world.

"I want to go out," he said to himself. "Outside."

Silent, black, outside.

ON THE BRIDGE

"Tell your friend not to panic," Hiroshi said. "The angels aren't in control. Not as long as we are."

He turned back to his work.

"Hiroshi."

He did not answer.

She stood a while near his seat at the navigators' station. Her gaze was on *Discovery*'s one "window": a meter-square screen on which data from the epidermal sensors was represented in visible light. Blackness. Bright dots, dim dots, haze: the local starfield and, in the left lower corner, a bit of the remote central galactic disk.

Children in the third year of school are brought to see the "window."

Or they used to be.

"Is that actually what's ahead of us?" she had asked Teo not long ago, and he had said, smiling, "No. Some of it's behind us. It's a movie I made. It's where we'd be if we were on schedule. In case somebody noticed."

She stared at it now and remembered Luis's phrase, VU. Virtual Unreality.

Without looking at Hiroshi she began to speak.

"Luis thinks the angels are taking control. You think you're in control. I think the angels are controlling you. You don't dare tell people that we're decades ahead of schedule, because you think that if the archangels knew, they'd take over and change course so as to miss the planet. But if you go on hiding the truth, you're guaranteeing that they'll take over when we reach the planet. What are you planning to say? *Here we are! Surprise!* All the angels will have to say is, *These people are crazy, they made a navigation error and then tried to cover it up. We aren't at Shindychew — it's forty years too soon — this is some other solar system.* So they take over the Bridge and we go on. And on. To nowhere."

A long time passed, so that she thought he had not listened, had not heard her at all.

"Patel's people are extremely numerous," he said. His voice was low. "As your friend has been discovering. . . . It was not an easy decision, Hsing. We have no strength except in the accomplished fact. Actuality against wishful thinking. We arrive, we come into orbit, and we can say: *There's the planet. It's real. Our job is to land people on it.* But if we tell people now . . . four years or forty, it doesn't matter. Patel's people will discredit us, replace us, change course, and . . . as you say . . . go on to nowhere. To 'bliss.'"

"How can you expect anybody to believe you, to support you, if you've lied to them right up to the last moment? Ordinary people. Not angels. What justifies you in not telling them the truth?"

He shook his head. "You underestimate Patel," he said. "We cannot throw away our one advantage."

"I think you underestimate the people who would support you. Underestimate them to the point of contempt."

"We must keep personalities out of this matter," he said with sudden harshness.

She stared at him. "Personalities?"

THE PLENARY COUNCIL

"Thank you, Chairwoman. My name is Nova Luis. I request the Council discuss formation of an ad hoc Committee on Religious Manipulation, to investigate the educational curriculum, the contents and availability of certain materials in the Records and Archives, and the composition of the fourteen committees and deliberative bodies listed on the screen."

4-Ferris Kim was on his feet at once: "A Committee on Religious Manipulation can be convened, according to the Constitution, only to investigate 'an election or the deliberation of a legislative body.' School curriculum, the materials kept in Records and Archives, and the committees and councils listed cannot be defined as legislative bodies and thus are exempt from examination."

"The Constitutional Committee will decide that point," said Uma, chairing the meeting. Ferris sat down looking satisfied.

Luis stood up again. "Since the religion in question is the creed of Bliss, may I suggest that the Chair consider the Constitutional Committee as possibly biased, since five of the six members profess the creed of Bliss."

Ferris was up again: "Creed? Religion? What kind of misunderstanding is this? There are no creeds or cults in our world. Such words merely echo ancient history, divisive errors which we have long since left behind on our way." His deep voice grew mellow, gentle. "Do you call the air a 'creed,' Doctor, because you breathe it? Do you call life a 'religion,' because you live it? Bliss is the ground and goal of our existence. Some of us rejoice in that knowledge; for others that joy lies in the future. But there are no religions here, no warring creeds. We are all united in the fellowship of *Discovery*."

"And the goal appointed in our Constitution for *Discovery* and those who travel in it is to travel through a portion of space to a certain planet, to study that planet, to colonise it if possible, and to send or bring back information about it to our world of origin, Dichew, Earth. We are all united in the resolve to accomplish that goal. Do you agree, Councillor Ferris?"

"Surely the Plenary Council is not the place to quibble over linguistic and intellectual theories?" Ferris said with mild deprecation, turning to the Chair.

"An allegation of religious manipulation is more than a quibble, Councillor," Uma said. "I will discuss this matter with my advisory council. It will be on the agenda of the next meeting."

THE SOUP THICKENS

"Well," Bingdi said, "we have certainly put the turd in the soup-bowl."

They were running the track. Bingdi had done twenty laps. Luis had done five. He was slowing down and breathing hard. "Soup of bliss," he panted.

Bingdi slowed down. Luis gasped and stopped. He stood awhile and wheezed. "Damn," he said.

They walked to the bench for their towels.

"What did Hsing say when you talked to her?"

"Nothing."

After a while Bingdi said, "You know, that bunch on the Bridge and Uma's advisory council, they're as tight as the archangels. They talk to each other and nobody else. They're a faction, as much as the archangels."

Luis nodded. "Well, so, we're the third faction," he said. "The turd faction. The soup thickens. Ancient history repeats itself."

THE GREAT REJOICING OF YEAR 161, DAY 88

Two days after the Plenary Council announced the formation of a Committee on Religious Manipulation to investigate ideological bias in educational curricula and the suppression and destruction of information in the Records and Archives, Patel Inbliss called for a Great Rejoicing.

The Temenos was packed. Everybody said, "It must have been like this when 0-Kim died."

The old man stood up at the lectern. His face, dark, unwrinkled, the bones showing through the fragile skin, loomed on every screen in every homespace. He raised his arms in blessing.

The great crowd sighed, a sound like wind in a forest, but they did not know that; they had never heard the sound of wind in a forest; they had never heard any sigh, any voice but their own and the voices of machines.

He talked for nearly an hour. At first he spoke of the importance of learning and following the laws of life laid down in the Constitution and taught in the schools. He asserted with passion that only scrupulous observance of these rules could assure justice, peace, and happiness to all. He talked about cleanliness, about recycling, about parenthood, about athletics, about teachers and teaching, about specialized studies, about the importance of unglamorous professions such as labwork, soilwork, infant care. Speaking of the happiness to be found in what he called "the modest life," he looked younger; his dark eyes shone. "Bliss is to be found everywhere," he said.

That became his theme: the ship called "discovery," the ship of life, that travels across the void of death: the vehicle of bliss.

Within the ship, rules and laws and ways are provided by which each mortal being may, by learning to live in mortal harmony and happiness, learn also the way to the True Destination.

"There is no death," the old man said, and again that sigh ran through the forest of lives crowded in the round hall. "Death is nothing. Death is null, death is void. Life is all. Mortal life voyages onward, ever onward, straight and true on its course to everlasting life, and light, and joy. Our origin was in darkness, in pain, in suffering. On that black ground of evil, in that terrible place, our ancestors in their wisdom saw where true life, true freedom was. And they sent us, their children, forth, free of darkness, earth, gravity, negativity, to travel forever into the light."

He blessed them again, and some thought his sermon was done, but as if given new energy by his words he was speaking on: "Do not mistake the goal of our discovery, the purpose of our lives! Do not mistake symbol and metaphor for reality! Our ancestors did not send us on this great voyage only to return to where it began. They did not free us from gravity only to sink again into gravity. They did not free us from Earth to doom us to another earth! That is literalism — scientific fundamentalism — a dreadful mental myopia. Our origin was on a planet, in darkness and misery, yes, but that is not our destination! How could it be?

"Our ancestors spoke of the Destination as a world, because they knew nothing else. They had lived only in darkness, in filth, in fear, dragged down by gravity. When they tried to imagine bliss, they could only imagine a better, brighter world, and so they called it a 'new earth.' But we can see the meaning of that obscure symbol, and translate it into truth: not a planet, a world, a place of darkness, fear, pain, and death — but the bright journey of mortal life into endless life, the unceasing, everlasting pilgrimage into unceasing, everlasting bliss. O my fellow angels! our voyage is sacred, and it is eternal!"

"Ahh," sighed the forest leaves.

"Ah!" said Luis, watching and listening in his homespace with Bingdi and several friends, known among themselves as the Turd Group.

"Hah!" said Hiroshi, watching and listening in his homespace with Hsing.

ON THE BRIDGE, YEAR 161, DAY 101

"Diamant asked me yesterday about an anomaly he noticed in the acceleration figures. He's been following up on it for a couple of tendays."

"Lead him astray," Hiroshi said, comparing two sets of figures.

"I will not."

After some minutes he said, "What will you do?"

"Nothing."

His hands were flickering over the workboard. "Leaving it to me."

"If you choose."

"I have no choice."

He worked on. Hsing worked on.

She stopped working and said, "When I was about ten I had a terrible dream. I dreamed I was in one of the cargo bays, wandering around, and I realised that there was a little hole in the wall, in the skin of the ship. A hole in the world. It was very small. Nothing was happening, but I knew what had to happen was that all the air would rush out the hole, because outside was vacuum. The nothing outside the ship. So I put my hand over the hole. My hand covered it. But if I took my hand away, I knew the air would begin to rush out. I called and called, but nobody was near. Nobody heard. And finally I thought I had to go get help, and tried to take my hand off the hole, but I couldn't. It was held there. By the nothing outside."

"A terrible dream," Hiroshi said. As she spoke he had turned from the workboard and sat facing her with his hands on his knees, straight-backed, expressionless. "Do you recall it because you feel yourself in a similar position now?"

"No. I see you in that position."

He considered this awhile. "And do you see a way out of that position?"

"Shout for help."

He shook his head very slightly.

"Hiroshi, one or another of the students or the engineers is going to find out what you've been doing and talk about it before you can mislead, or co-opt, or silence them. In fact, I think it's already happening. Diamant's been going after this as if he's trying to prove something. He's very bright and extremely anti-authoritarian — I was in classes with him. He will not be easy to mislead or co-opt."

He made no reply.

"As I was," she added, dryly but without rancor.

"What do you mean by 'shout for help'?"

"Tell him the truth."

"Only him?"

She shook her head. She said in a low voice, "Tell the truth."

"Hsing," he said, "I know you think our tactics are mistaken. I'm grateful to you for bringing up your disagreement so seldom, and only with me. I wish we could agree on what is right. But I cannot put the power to change our course into the hands of the cultists until it is literally too late for them to do so."

"It's not your decision to make."

"Will you take it out of my hands?"

"Someone will. And when they do, it will appear that you've been lying for years, you and your friends, in order to have sole power. How else can they see it? You will be dishonored." Her voice still sounded low and rough. After a moment, biting her lip, she added, "Your question to me just now was dishonorable."

"It was rhetorical," he said.

There was another long silence.

He said, "It was dishonorable. I beg your pardon, Hsing."

She nodded. She sat looking down at her hands.

"What action do you recommend?" he asked.

"Talk to Tan Bingdi, Nova Luis, Gupta Lena — the group that's behind the ad hoc committee. They're working to expose Patel's power-tactics. Tell them whatever you like about how it happened, but tell them that we're going to be at the Destination in three years — unless Patel prevents it."

"Or Diamant," he said.

She winced. She spoke more cautiously, more patiently: "The

danger isn't people like Diamant, Hiroshi. It's a fanatic gaining access to the Bridge for two minutes to damage, disable the course-computers — that's always been a possibility, but now there's a *reason* for somebody to do it. Now they *want* us never to arrive. At least that's out in the open, since Patel's speech. So now the fact that we *are* arriving has to come out in the open, because we need all the support we can get to make it happen. We must have support. You can't go on alone with your hand over the hole in the world!"

She had felt him withdraw when she said the name Nova Luis. She grew more urgent and eloquent as she spoke, losing ground; she ended up pleading. She waited and he made no response. Her arguments and urgency ebbed away slowly into a dry flatness of nonfeeling.

At last she said, drily and flatly, "Or perhaps you can. But I can't go on lying to colleagues and friends. I won't give you away, but I won't collude any more. I will say nothing at all to anyone."

"Not a very practical plan," he said, looking up at her with a stiff smile. "Be patient, Hsing. That's all I ask."

She stood up. "The evil of this is that we don't trust each other."

"I trust you."

"You don't. Me, or my silence, or my friends. The lie sucks trust out. Into nothing."

Again he did not speak; and presently she turned and left the Bridge. After she had walked a while she realised that she was at Quad Two, at Turning 2-3, heading for her old homespace, where her father lived alone. She wanted to see Yao, but felt it would be somehow disloyal to Hiroshi to go see him now. She turned around and started back to the Canaval-Liu homespace in Quad Four. The corridors seemed tight and narrow, crowded. She spoke to people who spoke to her. She remembered a part of her old nightmare dream that she had not thought to tell Hiroshi. The hole in the wall of the world had not been made by something from outside, a bit of dust or rock; when she saw it she knew, as one knows in a dream, that it had been there ever since the ship was made.

AN ANNOUNCEMENT OF EXTRAORDINARY IMPORTANCE,
YEAR 161, DAY 202

The Chair of the Plenary Council put a notice on the innet of an "announcement of extraordinary importance" to be made at twenty hours. The last such announcement had been made over fifteen years ago to explain the necessity of an alteration in profession quotas.

People gathered in the homespace or compound or meetingspace or workplace to hear. The Plenary Council held session.

Chatterji Uma came on the screen precisely at twenty and said, "Dear fellow passengers of the ship *Discovery*, we must prepare ourselves for a great change. From this night forward, our lives will be different — will be transformed." She smiled; her smile was charming. "Do not be apprehensive. This is a matter for rejoicing. The great goal of our voyage, the destination for which this ship and its crew were intended from the very beginning of our voyage, is closer than we dreamed. Not our children, but we ourselves, may be the ones to set foot upon a new world. Now Canaval Hiroshi, our Chief Navigator, will tell you the great discovery he and others on the Bridge have made, and what it means, and what we may expect."

Hiroshi replaced Uma on the screens. The thickness and blackness of his eyebrows gave him a sometimes threatening, sometimes questioning look. His voice however was reassuring, quiet, positive, and rather pedantic. He began by telling them what had happened five years ago as the ship passed through a gravity sink near a very large area of cosmic dust.

Hsing, watching him alone in their livingspace, could tell when he began to lie, not only because she knew the actual figures and dates but because when he began lying he became both more authoritative and more persuasive. The lies concerned the rates of acceleration and deceleration, the time of the discovery of the computer error, and the navigators' response.

Without being specific about dates, Hiroshi implied that the first suspicions of anomalies in the ship's rate of acceleration had arisen less than a year ago. The magnitude of the computer error and its implications had been only gradually revealed. He sketched a scenario of incredulous but intrepid humans wresting their secrets from computers whose programming forced them to resist any override of their response to the original misreading, of navigators forced to try to outwit their instruments, trick them into re-compensating for their immense overcompensation, slowing the ship down from the incredible speed it had achieved.

Until this moment, he said, that struggle had been so chancy, they had been so unsure of what had happened and was happening, that they had felt it unwise to make any announcement. "To avoid causing panic by a premature or incorrect disclosure was our chief concern. We know now that there is no cause for alarm. None. Our operations were entirely successful. Just as the acceleration exceeded all speculative limits, we have been able to decelerate very much more quickly than had been thought possible. We are on course and in control. The only change is that we are well ahead of schedule."

He looked up, as if looking out of the screen, his black eyes unreadable. He was speaking slowly, carefully, a little monotonously, letting each sentence stand by itself. "We are continuing to decelerate, and will do so for the next 3.2 years.

"Late in the year 164, we will enter orbit around the planet of destination, Hsin Ti Chiu or New Earth.

"That event, as we all know, was scheduled to occur in the year 201. Our voyage of discovery has been shortened by nearly forty years.

"Ours is a fortunate generation. We will see the end of our long voyage. We will reach its goal.

"We have much work to do in these two years. We must prepare our minds and bodies to leave our little world and walk upon a wide new earth. We must prepare our eyes and souls for the light of a new sun."

THE TRUE WAY

"It doesn't make sense, Luis," Rosa said. "It doesn't mean anything. The Zeroes just didn't understand. How could they? They thought we were too sinful to be able to live in heaven forever. They were earthen, they couldn't help it, so they thought we'd have to be earthen too. But we aren't — how could we be, born here, on the way? Why would we want to live any life other than this one? They made it perfect. They sent us to heaven. They made the world for us so we could learn the way to everlasting life in bliss by living in mortal bliss. How could we learn it on some kind of earthen black world? Outside, unprotected, unguided? How can we keep going on the True Way if we *leave* the True Way? How can we reach heaven by stopping on an earth?"

"Well, maybe we can't, but we do have a job to do," Luis said. "They sent us to learn about that earth. And to tell them what we learn. Learning was important to them. Discovery. They named our ship *Discovery.*"

"Exactly! The discovery of bliss! Learning the True Way! The archangels are sending back what we've learned all the time, you know, Luis. We're teaching them the way — just as they hoped we would. The goal is a spiritual goal. Don't you see, we've *attained* the Destination? Why do we have to stop our beautiful voyage at some evil, terrible, earthen place and do eva?"

AN ELECTION, YEAR 162, DAY 112

5-Nova Luis was elected Chair of the Plenary Council. The general trust he had earned as a conciliator, negotiator, and peacemaker during the troubles of the past half-year made his election inevitable, and popular even among the angels. His year in office was indeed one of reconciliation and healing.

A DEATH, YEAR 162, DAY 205

At the age of eighty-seven, 4-Patel Inbliss suffered a massive stroke and began to die, amid a continuous frenzy of tearful prayer, song, and rejoicing. For thirteen days the celebrants occupied all the corridors surrounding the Kim homespace in Quadrant One, where Inbliss was born and had lived all his life. As his dying went on and on, weariness and tension grew among the mourner-rejoicers. People feared an outbreak of hysteria and violence like that which had followed the announcement of Arrival. Many non-angel occupants of the quadrant went to stay with friends or relatives in other quads.

When at last an archangel announced that the Father had passed to Eternal Bliss, there was much weeping in the corridors, but no violence, except for a man in Quad Four named 5-Garr Joyful who beat his wife and her daughter to death "so that they could enter Eternal Bliss with the Father," he said; he omitted, however, to kill himself.

The Temenos was filled solid for the funeral of Patel Inbliss. There were many speeches, but their tone was subdued. He had no child to deliver the final speech. The archangel Van Wing sang the dark devotional, "Eye, what do you see?" to end the ceremony. The crowd dispersed in the silence of exhaustion. The corridors that night were empty.

A BIRTH, YEAR 162, DAY 223

5-Canaval Hiroshi's child was born to his wife 5-Liu Hsing, and was given the name 6-Canaval Alejo by his father.

Though Nova Luis was not practicing medicine during his term as council chair, Hsing had asked him to attend the birth, and he did so. It was an entirely uneventful delivery.

When he came the next day to see his patients, he sat for a while with them. Hiroshi was on the Bridge. Hsing's milk had not come in yet, but the baby was rooting diligently at her breast or anything else that offered itself. "What did you want me for?" Luis said. "You obviously know how to have a baby a lot better than I do."

"I guess I found out," she said. "*Learn by doing!* — remember Teacher Mimi in third grade?" She was sitting up in bed, still look-ing tired, triumphant, flushed, and soft. She looked down at the small head covered with very fine black hair. "It's so tiny, I can't believe it's the same species," she said. "What do you call this stuff I'm leaking?"

"Colostrum. It's the only thing his species eats."

"Amazing," she said, very softly touching the black fuzz with the back of a finger.

"Amazing," Luis agreed soberly.

"Oh Luis, it was so — To have you here. I did need you."

"It was my pleasure," he said, still soberly.

The baby went through some spasms, and was discovered to have had a miniature bowel movement. "Well done, well done. He'll be a member of the Turd Group yet," Luis said. "Give him here, I'll clean him up. Well, will you look at that? A bobwob! A veritable bobwob! A fine specimen, too."

"It's a gowbondo," Hsing whispered. He looked up at her and saw she was in tears.

He laid the baby, swallowed up by its clean diaper, in her arms; she went on crying. "I'm sorry," she said.

"New mothers cry, flatface."

She wept very bitterly for a moment, gasping, then got control.

"Luis, what is — have you noticed anything about Hiroshi — "

"As a doctor?"

"Yes."

"Yes."

"What's wrong with him?"

He said nothing for a while, then, "He won't go to a physician, so you're asking me for a spot diagnosis — is that it?"

"I guess so. I'm sorry."

"It's all right. Has he been particularly tired?"

She nodded. "He fainted twice last week," she said in a whisper.

"Well, my guess would be congestive heart failure. I know a good deal about it because as an asthmatic I'm liable to it myself, though I haven't managed to achieve it yet. You can live with it for a long time. There are medicines he can take, various treatments and regimes. Send him to Regis Chandra at the Hospital."

"I'll try," she whispered.

"Do it." Luis spoke sternly. "Tell him that he owes his son a father."

He stood up to leave. Hsing said, "Luis — "

"Take it easy, don't worry. It'll be all right. This fellow will see to it." He touched the baby's ear.

"Luis, when we land, will you go outside?"

"Of course I will, if we can. What do you think I'm insisting on all this education and training for? To watch a bunch of evajocks running around in space suits on a vidscreen?"

"It seems like so many people want to stay here."

"Well, we'll find out when we get there. It's going to be interesting. It already is interesting. We found out what a whole section in Storage D is. We thought it was very heavy protective clothing, but the pieces were too large. It's temporary livingspaces. You prop them up somehow and live inside them. And there are inflatable toruses which Bose thinks are meant to float on water. *Ships.* Imagine enough water to float a ship on! No. I wouldn't miss it for the world. . . . I'll look in tomorrow."

THE REGISTRY OF INTENT UPON ARRIVAL

In the first quarter of Year 163, all people over sixteen were required to declare Intent Upon Arrival in an open registry on the innet. They could change their declaration any time, and it would not be binding upon them until a moment of ultimate decision, to be announced after investigations of the habitability of the planet were complete and had been fully tested.

They were asked:

> If the planet proved habitable, would you be willing to be part of a team visiting the surface to gather information?

> Would you be willing to live on the planet while the ship remained in orbit?

> If the ship left, would you be willing to stay on the planet as colonists?

They were asked to state their opinion:

> How long should the ship stay in orbit as a support to the people on the planet?

And finally, if the planet was not accessible or not habitable, or if you chose to stay on the ship and not visit or
colonise the planet:

If and when the ship left, should it return to the planet of
origin, or continue on into space?

A return journey to Earth, according to Canaval and others,
might take as little as seventy-five years if the whiplash effect of the
gravity sink could be repeated. Some engineers were skeptical, but
the navigators were confident that *Discovery* could return to Earth
within a lifetime or two. This assertion met with little enthusiasm
except among the navigators.

The open registry of Intent Upon Arrival, accessible on the innet
at all times, went through interesting fluctuations. At first the number of people willing to visit the planet or live on it while the ship
stayed in orbit — Visitors, they were dubbed — was pretty large.
Very few, however, said they would be willing to stay there when the
ship left. These diehards got tagged Outsiders, and accepted the
name.

The largest figure by far was those who wished not to land on the
planet at all, and to continue the voyage out as soon as possible.
Over two thousand people registered immediately as Voyagers.

This angelic vote was so strong that there was no real question of
what the final decision would be. *Discovery* would not stay in orbit
around its Destination, would not turn back to its Origin, but
would go on to Eternity.

Urgent arguments about exhaustibility of supplies, about wear
and tear, about accident and entropy, swayed some Voyagers; but
the majority continued steadfast in their intention to live in bliss
and die to Bliss.

As this became clear, the number of people who registered as
willing to stay permanently on the planet began to grow, and kept
growing. It was clear that the angelic majority, eager to continue its

sacred journey, could not be kept tethered to the planet for very long. Few of the angels opted even to make an exploratory visit to the planet's surface. Many, following the teachings of the archangels, tried to persuade their friends that leaving the ship was unthinkably dangerous — not a bodily risk, but a sin, a temptation to seek unneeded knowledge at the cost of the immortal soul.

Gradually the choices narrowed, became absolute. Go out into the dark and be left there, or continue on the bright and endless voyage. The unknown, or the known. Risk, or safety. Exile, or home.

Throughout the year, the number of those who shifted their registry from Visitor to Outsider grew to over a thousand.

In the latter half of Year 163, the yellow star that was the primary of Shindychew's system appeared to the eye at magnitude -2. Schoolchildren were taken onto the Bridge to see it in the "window."

The education curriculum had been radically revised. Though teachers who were angels were unenthusiastic or hostile to the new material, they were required to allow "lay teachers" to present information about what the Destination might be like. The VRs of Old Earth — Jungle, Inner City, and so on — had allegedly deteriorated, and had been destroyed; but many educational films were salvaged, and others were found in Storage awaiting use by potential settlers.

Those who registered as Visitors or Outsiders formed learning groups, in which they studied and discussed these films and instructional books. Dictionaries were much called upon to settle misunderstandings and arguments over terms, though sometimes the arguments went on and on. Was a *ravine* a need for food, or a place where the floor went down into a hole? The dictionary offered gorge, gully, gulch, canyon, chasm, rift, abyss . . . . A low place in the floor, then. When you need food badly, that's *ravenous*. But why would you need food badly?

A PRAGMATIST

"No. I don't intend to leave the ship."

Luis stared at the Registry, where he had just discovered Tan Bingdi's name on the list of Voyagers. He looked around at his friend, and at the screen again.

"You don't?"

"I never did. Why?"

"You aren't an angel," Luis said at last, stupidly.

"Of course not. I'm a pragmatist."

"But you've worked so hard to keep the . . . the way out open . . ."

"Of course." After a minute he explained: "I don't like quarrels, divisions, enforced choices. They spoil the quality of life."

"You aren't curious?"

"No. If I want to know what living on a planet surface is like, I can watch the training videos and holos. And read all the books in the Library about Old Earth. But why do I want to know what living on a planet is like? I live here. And I like it. I like what I know and I know what I like."

Luis continued to look appalled.

"You have a sense of duty," Bingdi told him affectionately. "Ancestral duty — go find a new world . . . Scientific duty — go find new knowledge. . . . If a door opens, you feel it's your duty to go through it. If a door opens, I unquestioningly close it. If life is good, I don't seek to change it. Life is good, Luis." He spoke, as always, with little rests between the sentences. "I will miss you and a lot of other people. I'll get bored with the angels. You won't be bored, down on that dirtball. But I have no sense of duty and I rather enjoy being bored. I want to live my life in peace, doing no harm and receiving no harm. And, judging by the films and books, I think this may be the best place, in all the universe, to live such a life."

"It's a matter of control, finally, isn't it," Luis said.

Bingdi nodded. "We need to be in control. The angels and I. You don't."

"We aren't in control. None of us. Ever."

"I know. But we've got a good imitation of it, here. VR's enough for me."

A DEATH, YEAR 163, DAY 202

After recurrent episodes of illness, Navigator Canaval Hiroshi died of heart failure. His wife Liu Hsing with their infant son, and many friends, all the staff of Navigation, and most of the Plenary Council, attended the funeral service. His colleague 4-Patel Ramdas spoke of his brilliance in his profession, and wept as he finished speaking. 5-Chatterji Uma spoke of how he laughed at silly jokes, and told one he had laughed at; she said how happy he had been to have a son, though he had known him so briefly. One of his students spoke last, in the place of the child, calling him a hard master but a great man. Hsing then went with the technicians, accompanying his body to the Life Center for recycling. She had not spoken at the service. The technicians left her alone for a moment, and she laid her hand very gently on Hiroshi's cheek, feeling the death-cold. She whispered only, "Goodbye."

DESTINATION

In the year 164, Day 82, *Discovery* entered orbit around the planet Shindychew, Hsin Ti Chiu, or New Earth.

As the ship made its first forty orbits, probes sent down to the surface of the planet provided vast amounts of information, much of which was unintelligible or barely intelligible to those receiving it on the ship.

They were soon able to state with certainty, however, that people would be able to do eva on the surface without respirators or suits. There was a growing body of evidence that the planet might be accessible to long-range inhabitation. That people could live there.

In the year 164, Day 93, the first ship-to-ground vehicle made a successful landing in the area designated Subquadrant Eight of the planetary surface.

AFTER THIS THERE ARE NO MORE HEADINGS, FOR THE WORLD IS
CHANGED, NAMES CHANGE, TIME IS NOT MEASURED AS IT WAS,
AND THE WIND BLOWS EVERYTHING AWAY.

To leave the ship: to go through the airlock into the lander, that was a comprehensible thing — terrifying, fiercely exciting, absolute, an act of transgression, of defiance, of affirmation. The last act.

To leave the lander: to go down those five steps onto the surface of the planet, that was to leave comprehension behind, to lose understanding: to go mad. To be translated into a language where no word — ground, air — transgress, affirm — act, do — made sense. A world without words. Without meaning. A universe unde-fined.

Immediately perceiving the wall, the blessed needed only wall, the side of the lander, she backed up against it and at once turned to hide her face against it so that she could see it, the wall, curving metal, firm, limiting, see it and not see the other, the no walls, the vast.

She held her baby close against her, his face to her breast.

People were there with her, beside her, clinging to the wall, but she was only vaguely aware of them, even though they were all huddled close together they all seemed apart and distant. She heard people gasping, vomiting. She was dizzy and sick. She could not breathe. The ventilation was failing, the fans were far too strong. Turn down the fans! A spotlight shone down on her, she could feel the heat of it on her head and neck, see the glare of it in the skin of the wall when she opened her eyes.

The skin of the wall, the ship's epidermis. She was doing eva. That was all. She always wanted to be an evaman when she was little. She was doing eva. When it was done she could go back into the world. She tried to hold on to the skin of the world but it was smooth ceramic and would not let her hold it. Cold mother, hard mother, dead mother.

She opened her eyes again and looked down past Alejo's silky black head at her feet and saw her feet standing in dirt. She moved, then, to get out of the dirt, because you shouldn't walk in dirt. Father had told her when she was very young, no, it's not good to walk in the dirt gardens, the plants need all the room, and your feet might hurt the little plants. So she moved away from the wall to move out of the dirt garden. But there was only dirt garden, dirt, plants, everywhere, wherever she put her feet. Her feet hurt the plants and the dirt hurt the soles of her feet. She looked despairingly for a walkway, a corridor, a ceiling, walls, looked away from the wall and saw a great whirl of green and blue spin round a center of intolerable light. Blinded and unbalanced she fell to her knees and hid her face beside the baby's face. She wept in shame.

Wind, air moving fast, hard, endlessly blowing, making you cold, so you shivered, shuddered, like having a fever, the wind stopping and starting, restless, stupid, unpredictable, unreasonable, maddening, hateful, a torment. Turn it off, make it stop!

Wind, air moving softly, moving slender grasses in waves over the hills, carrying odors from a long way off, so you lifted your head and sniffed, breathed it in, the strange, sweet, bitter smell of the world.

The sound of wind in a forest.

Wind that moved colors in the air.

People who had never been of much account became prominent, respected, constantly in demand. 4-Nova Ed was good with the tenses. He was the first to figure out how to deploy them properly. Miraculously the shambles of plasticloth and cords rose and became walls, walls to shut out the wind — became rooms, rooms to enclose you in the marvelous familiarity of surfaces close by, a ceiling close overhead, a floor smooth underfoot, quiet air, an even, unblinding light. It made all the difference, it made life livable, to have a tense, to have a homespace, to know you could go in, be in, be inside.

"It's 'tent,'" Ed said, but people had heard the more familiar word and went on calling them tense, tenses.

A fifteen-year-old girl, Lee Meili, remembered from an ancient movie what foot coverings were called. People had tried syndrome-sox, those that had them, but they were thin and wore out at once. She hunted through the Stockpile, the immense and growing labyrinth of stores that the landers kept bringing down from the ship, till she found crates labelled SHOES. The shoes hurt the delicate-skinned feet of people who had gone barefoot on carpet all their lives, but they hurt less than the floor here did. The *ground.* The *stones.* The *rocks.*

But 4-Patel Ramdas, whose skills had put *Discovery* into orbit and guided the first lander from ship to surface, stood with a reading lamp in one hand, its cord and plug in the other, staring at the dark wrinkled wall-like surface of a huge plant, the *tree* under which he had set up his tense. He was looking for an electrical outlet. His gaze was vague and sad. Presently he straightened up; his expression became scornful. He walked back to the Stockpile with the lamp.

5-Lung Tirza's three-month-old baby lay in the starlight while Tirza worked on construction. When she came to feed him she shrieked, "He's blind!" The pupils of his eyes were tiny dots. He was red with fever. His face and scalp blistered. He had convulsions, went into coma. He died that night. They had to recycle him in the dirt. Tirza lay on the place in the dirt where the baby was lying inside it, underneath her. She moaned with her mouth against the dirt. Moaning aloud, she raised her face with brown wet dirt all over it, a terrible face made of dirt.

Not star: sun. Starlight we know: safe, kind, distant. Sun is a star too close. This one.

My name is Star, Hsing said in her mind. Star, not Sun.

She made herself look out of her tense in darkcycle to see the safe, kind, distant stars who had given her her name. Shining stars, bing hsing. Tiny bright dots. Many, many, many. Not one. But each . . . Her thoughts would not hold. She was so tired. The immensity of the sky, the uncountability of the stars. She crawled back into inside. Inside the tense, inside the bagbed beside Luis. He lay in the moveless sleep of exhaustion. She listened automatically to his breathing for a moment; soft, unlabored. She drew Alejo into her arms, against her breasts. She thought of Tirza's baby inside the dirt. Inside the dirtball.

She thought of Alejo running across the grass the way he had today, running in the sunlight, shouting for the joy of running. She had hurried to call him back into the shade. But he loved the warmth of sunlight.

Luis had left his asthma on the ship, he said, but his migraines were bad sometimes. Many people had headaches, sinus pain. Possibly it was caused by particles in the air, particles of dirt, plants' pollens, substances and secretions of the planet, its outbreath. He lay in his tense in the long heat of the day, in the long ebb of the pain, thinking about the secrets of the planet, imagining the planet breathing out and himself breathing in that outbreath, like a lover, like breathing in Hsing's breath. Taking it in, drinking it in. Becoming it.

Up here on the hillside, looking down on the *river* but not close to it, had seemed a good place for the *settlement*, a safe distance, so that children would not be falling into the huge, fiercely rushing, deep mass of water. Ramdas measured the distance and said it was 1.7 kilos. People who carried water discovered a different definition of distance: 1.7 kilos was a long distance to carry water. Water had to be carried. There were no pipes in the ground, no faucets in the rocks. And when there were no pipes and faucets you discovered that water was necessary, constantly, imperatively necessary. Was wonderful, worshipful, a blessing, a bliss the angels had never dreamed of. You discovered thirst. To drink when you were thirsty! And to wash — to be clean! To be as you'd always been, not grainy-skinned and gritty and sticky with smears of dirt, but clean!

Hsing walked back from the fields with her father. Yao walked a little stooped. His hands were blackened, cracked, ingrained with dirt. She remembered how when he worked in the dirt gardens of the ship that fine soft dirt had clung to his fingers, lined his knuckles and fingernails, just while he was working; then he washed his hands and they were clean.

To be able to wash when you were dirty, to have enough to drink all the time, what a wonderful thing. At Meeting they voted to move the tenses closer to the river, farther from the Stockpile. Water was more important than things. The children must learn to be careful.

Everybody must learn to be careful, everywhere, all the time.

Strain the water, boil the water. What a bother. But the doctors with their cultures were unyielding. Some of the native bacteria flourished in media made with human secretions. Infection was possible.

Dig latrines, dig cesspools, what hard work, what a bother. But the doctors with their manuals were unyielding. The manual on cesspools and septic tanks (printed in English in New Delhi two centuries ago) was hard to understand, full of words that had to be figured out by context: drainage, gravel, bedrock, seep.

A bother, being careful, taking care, taking trouble, following the rules. Never! Always! Remember! Don't! Don't forget! Or else!

Or else what?

You died anyway. This world hated you. It hated foreign bodies.

Three babies now, an adolescent, two adults. All under the dirt in that place, close to the little first death, Tirza's baby, their guide to the underground. To the inside.

There was plenty to eat. When you looked at the food section of the Stockpile, the huge walls and corridors of crates, it seemed it must be all the food a thousand people could eat forever, and the angels' generosity in letting them have it all seemed overwhelming. Then you saw the way the land went on and on, past the Stockpile, past the new sheds, and the sky went on and on over them; and when you looked back the pile of crates looked very small.

You listened to Liu Yao saying in meeting, "We must continue to test the native plants for edibility," and Chowdry Arvind saying, "We should be making gardens now, while the time of the revolu — of the year is the most advantageous time — the *growing season*."

You came to see that there was not plenty to eat. That there might not ever be plenty to eat. That (the beans did not flower, the rice did not come up out of the dirt, the genetic experiment did not succeed) there might not be enough to eat. In time. Time was not the same here.

Here, to every thing there was a season.

• • •

5-Nova Luis, a doctor, sat beside the body of 5-Chang Berto, a soil technician, who had died of blood poisoning from a blister on his heel. The doctor suddenly shouted at Berto's tense-mates, "He neglected it! You neglected him! You could see that it was infected! How could you let this happen? Do you think we're in a sterile environment? Don't you listen? Can't you understand that the dirt here is *dangerous*? Do you think I can work miracles?" Then he began to cry, and Berto's tense-mates all stood there with their dead companion and the weeping doctor, dumb with fear and shame and sorrow.

Creatures. There were creatures everywhere. This world was made of creatures. The only things not alive were the rocks. Everything else was alive with creatures.

Plants covered the dirt, filled the waters, endless variety and number of plants (4-Liu Yao working in the makeshift plant test lab felt sometimes through the mist of exhaustion an incredulous delight, a sense of endless wealth, a desire to shout aloud — *Look! Look at this! How extraordinary!*) — and of animals, endless variety and number of animals (4-Steinman Jael, one of the first to sign up as an Outsider, had to go back permanently to the ship, driven into fits of shuddering and screaming by the continual sight and touch of the innumerable tiny crawling and flying creatures on the ground and in the air, and her uncontrollable fear of seeing them and being touched by them).

People were inclined at first to call the creatures cows, dogs, lions, remembering words from Earth books and holos. Those who read the manuals insisted that all the Shindychew creatures were much smaller than cows, dogs, lions, and were far more like what they called insects, arachnids, and worms on Dichew. "Nobody here has invented the backbone," said young Garcia Anita, who was fascinated by the creatures, and studied the Earth Biology archives whenever her work as an electrical engineer left her time to do so.

"At least nobody in this part of the world. But they certainly have invented wonderful shells."

The creatures about a millimeter long with green wings that followed people about persistently and liked to walk on your skin, tickling slightly, got called dogs. They acted friendly, and dogs were supposed to be man's best friend. Anita said they liked the salt in human sweat, and weren't intelligent enough to be friendly, but people went on calling them dogs. Ach! what's that on my neck? Oh, it's just a dog.

The planet revolved around the star.

But at evening, the sun set. The same thing, but a different matter. With it as it set the sun took colors, colors of clouds moved through air by wind.

At daybreak the sun rose, bringing with it all the mutable, fierce, subtle colors of the world, restored, brought back to life, reborn.

Continuity here did not depend on human beings. Though they might depend on it. It was a different matter.

The ship had gone on. It was gone.

Outsiders who had changed their minds about living outside had mostly gone back up in the first few tendays. When the Plenary Council, now chaired by the Archangel 5-Ross Minh, announced that *Discovery* would leave orbit on Day 256, Year 164, a number of people in the Settlement asked to be taken back to the ship, unable to endure the finality of permanent exile, or the painful realities of life outside. About as many shipsiders asked to join the Settlement, unable to accept the futility of an endless pilgrimage, or the government of the archangels.

When the ship left, the nine hundred and four people on the planet had chosen to be there. To die there. Some of them had already died there.

They talked about it very little. There wasn't a lot to say, and when you were tired all the time all you wanted was to eat and get into your bedbag and sleep. It had seemed like a big event, the ship going on, but it wasn't. They couldn't see it from the ground anyway. For days and days before the leaving date the radios and the hooknet carried a lot of talk about the journey into bliss, and exhortations telling the people on the ground that they were still all angels and were welcome back to joy. Then there was a flurry of personal messages, pleadings, blessings, goodbyes, and then the ship was gone.

For a long time *Discovery* kept sending news and messages to the Settlement, births, deaths, sermons, prayers, and reports of the unanimous joyfulness of the voyage. Personal messages went back to the ship from the Settlement, along with the same informational and scientific reports that were sent to Earth. Attempts at dialogue, at response, rarely successful, were mostly abandoned after a few years.

Obeying the mandates of the Constitution, the Settlers collected and organised the information they gathered concerning Shindychew and sent it to the planet of origin as often as the work of survival allowed them time to do so. A committee worked on keeping and transmitting methodical annals of the Settlement. People also sent observations and thoughts, images, poems.

You couldn't help wondering if anyone would listen to them. But that was nothing new.

Transmissions intended for the ship continued to come in to the receivers in the Settlement, since the people on Dichew wouldn't hear about the early arrival for years to come, and then their response would take years to arrive. The transmissions continued to be as confusing as ever, almost entirely irrelevant, and increasingly difficult to understand, due to changes in thought and vocabulary. What was a withheld E.O. and why had there been riots about it in Milak? What was faring technology? Why were they saying that it was essential to know about the 4:10 ratio in pankogenes?

The vocabulary problem was nothing new, either. All your life inside the ship you had known words that had no meaning at all. Words that signified nothing in the world. Words such as *cloud, wind, rain, weather*. Poets' words, explained in notes at the foot of the page, or that found a brief visual equivalent in films, sometimes a brief sensory equivalent in VRs. Words whose reality was imaginary, or virtual.

But here, the word that had no meaning, the concept without content, was the word virtual. Here nothing was virtual.

Clouds came over from the west. West, another reality: direction: a crucially important reality in a world you could get lost in.

Rain fell out of a certain kind of cloud, and the rain wet you, you were wet, the wind blew and you were cold, and it went on and didn't stop because it wasn't a program, it was the weather. It went on being. But you didn't, unless you acquired the sense to come in out of the rain.

Probably people on Earth already knew that.

The big, thick, tall plants, the trees, consisted largely of the very rare and precious substance wood, the material of certain instruments and ornaments ontheship. (One word: ontheship.) Wood objects had seldom been recycled, because they were irreplaceable; plastic copies were quite different in quality. Here plastic was rare and precious, but wood stood around all over the *hills* and *valleys*. With peculiar, ancient tools provided in the Landing Stock, fallen trees could be cut into pieces. (The meaning of the word *chensa*, spelled *chainsaw* in the manuals, was rediscovered.) All the pieces of tree were solid wood: an excellent material for building with, which could also be shaped into all kinds of useful devices. And wood could be set fire to, to create warmth.

This discovery of enormous importance, would it be news on Earth?

Fire. The stuff at the end of a welding torch. The active point in a bunsenburner.

Most people had never seen a fire burning. They gathered to it. Don't touch! But the air was cold now, full of cloud and wind, full of weather. Fire-warmth felt good. Lung Jo, who had set up the Settlement's first generator, gathered bits of tree and piled them inside his tense and set fire to them and invited his buddies to come get warm. Presently everybody poured out of the tense coughing and choking, which was fortunate, because the fire liked the tense as well as it liked the wood, and ate with its red and yellow tongues till nothing was left but a black stinking mess in the rain. A disaster. (Another disaster.) All the same, it was funny when they all rushed out weeping and coughing in a cloud of smoke.

Cloud. Smoke. Words full, crammed, jammed with meaning, with meanings. Life-and-death meanings, signifying life, signifying death. The poets had not been talking virtually, after all.

> *I wandered lonely as a cloud . . .*

> *What is the weather in a beard?*
> *It's windy there and rather weird . . .*

The 0-2 strain of oats came up out of the dirt, sprang up *(spring)*, shot up, put out leaves and beautiful hanging grain-heads, was green, was yellow, was harvested. The seeds flowed between your fingers like polished beads, fell *(fall)* back into the heap of precious food.

Abruptly, the material received from the ship ceased to contain any personal messages or information, consisting of rebroadcasts of the three recorded talks given by Kim Terry, talks by Patel Inbliss, sermons by various archangels, and a recording of a male choir chanting, played over and over.

"Why am I Six Lo Meiling?"

When the child understood her mother's explanation, she said,

"But that was ontheship. We live here. Aren't we all Zeroes?"

5-Lo Ana told this story in Meeting, and it went through the whole community causing pleasure, like the flight of one of the creatures with fluttering transparent wings edged with threads of gold, at which everybody looked up and stopped work and said, "Look!" Mariposas, somebody called them, and the pretty name stuck.

There had been a good deal of talk, during the cold weather when work wasn't so continuous, about the names of things. About naming things. Such as the dogs. People agreed that naming should be done seriously. But it was no good looking in the records and finding that on Dichew there had been creatures that looked something like this brown creature here so we'll call it *beetle*. It wasn't beetle. It ought to have its own name. Tree-crawler, clickclicker, leaf-chewer. And what about us? Ana's kid is right, you know? 4's, 5's, 6's — what's that got to do with us now, here? The angels can go on to 100. . . . Lucky if they get to 10. . . . What about Zerin's baby? She isn't 6-Lahiri Padma. She's 1-Shindychew-Lahiri-Padma. . . . Maybe she's just Lahiri Padma. Why do we need to count the steps? We aren't going anywhere. She's here. She lives here. This is Padma's world.

She found Luis in the patty-gardens behind the west compound. It was his day off from the hospital. A beautiful day of early summer. His hair shone in the sunlight. She located him by that silver nimbus.

He was sitting on the ground, on the dirt. On his day off he did a shift at the irrigation system of little ditches, dikes, and watergates, which required constant but unlaborious supervision and maintenance. Patty grew well only when watered but not overwatered. The tubers, baked whole or milled, had become a staple since Liu Yao's success at breeding the edible strain. People who had trouble digesting native seeds and cereals thrived on patty.

Children of ten or eleven, old people, damaged people, mostly did irrigation shifts; it took no strength, just patience. Luis sat near the watergate that diverted the flow from West Creek into one or the other of the main channel systems. His legs, thin and brown, were stretched out and his crutch lay beside them. He leaned back on his arms, hands flat on the black dirt, face turned to the sun, eyes shut. He wore shorts and a loose, ragged shirt. He was both old and damaged.

Hsing came up beside him and said his name. He grunted but did not move or open his eyes. She squatted down by him. After a while his mouth looked so beautiful to her that she leaned over and kissed it.

He opened his eyes.

"You were asleep."

"I was praying."

"Praying!"

"Worshipping?"

"Worshipping what?"

"The sun?" he said, tentative.

"Don't ask me!"

He looked at her, exactly the Luis look, tenderly inquisitive, noncommittal, unreserved; ever since they were five years old he had been looking at her that way. Looking into her.

"Who else would I ask?" he asked her.

"If it's about praying and worshipping, not me."

She made herself more comfortable, settling her rump on the berm of an irrigation channel, facing Luis. The sun was warm on her shoulders. She wore a hat Luisita had inexpertly woven of grain-straw.

"A tainted vocabulary," he said.

"A suspect ideology," she said.

And the words suddenly gave her pleasure, the big words — *vocabulary! ideology!* — Talk was all short, small, heavy words: food, roof, tool, get, make, save, live. The big words they never used any more, the long, airy words carried her mind up for a moment like a mariposa, fluttering aloft on the wind.

"Well," he said, "I don't know." He pondered. She watched him ponder. "When I smashed my knee, and had to lie around," he said, "I decided there was no use living without delight."

After a silence she said, in a dry tone, "Bliss?"

"No. Bliss is a form of VU. No, I mean delight. I never knew it on the ship. Only here. Now and then. Moments of unconditional existence. Delight."

Hsing sighed.

"Hard earned," she said.

"Oh yes."

They sat in silence for some time. The south wind gusted, ceased, blew softly again. It smelled of wet earth and bean-flowers.

Luis said:

" 'When I am a grandmother, they say, I may walk under heaven,
   On another world.' "

"Oh," Hsing said.

Her breath caught in another, deeper sigh, a sob. Luis put his hand over hers.

"Alejo went fishing with the children, upstream," she said.

He nodded.

"I worry so much," she said. "I worry the delight away."

He nodded again. Presently he said, "But I was thinking . . . when I was worshipping, or whatever, what I was thinking, was about the dirt." He picked up a palmful of the crumbly, dark floodplain soil, and let it fall from his hand, watching it fall. "I was thinking that if I could, I'd get up and dance on it. . . . Dance for me," he said, "will you, Hsing?"

She sat a moment, then stood up — it was a hard push up off the low berm, her own knees were not so good these days — and stood still.

"I feel stupid," she said.

She raised her arms up and outward, like wings, and looked down at her feet on the dirt. She pushed off her sandals, pushed them aside, and was barefoot. She stepped to the left, to the right, forward, back. She danced up to him holding her hands forward, palms down. He took them, and she pulled him up. He laughed; she did not quite smile. Swaying, she lifted her bare feet from the dirt and set them down again while he stood still, holding her hands. They danced together that way.

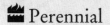 Perennial   EOS

Books by Ursula K. Le Guin:

THE BIRTHDAY OF THE WORLD *And Other Stories*
ISBN 0-06-050906-6 (paperback)

A superb collection of eight science fiction tales.

"[Le Guin's] work transcends the usual limitations of the genre, and this collection is no exception." —*The New Yorker*

THE WIND'S TWELVE QUARTERS
ISBN 0-06-105605-7 (mass market paperback)

Le Guin's first and perhaps most famous collection of short stories—17 in total—including the Hugo and Nebula Award-winning/nominated *Winter's King*, *Vaster Than Empires and More Slow*, *Nine Lives*, *The Ones Who Walk Away from Omelas*, and *The Day Before the Revolution*.

THE DISPOSSESSED
ISBN 0-06-105488-7 (mass market paperback)

Nebula and Hugo Award-winning Novel

The spellbinding story of a brilliant physicist who attempts to tear down the walls of hatred that have isolated his planet from the rest of the civilized universe.

THE LATHE OF HEAVEN
ISBN 0-380-79185-4 (paperback)

Nebula and Hugo Award-nominated Novel

The story of George Orr—a man who dreams things into being, for better or for worse. This fable of power uncontrolled and uncontrollable is a truly prescient and startling view of humanity, and the consequences of God-playing.

"A rare and powerful synthesis of poetry and science, reason and emotion."
                                                                —*New York Times*

Available wherever books are sold, or call 1-800-331-3761 to order.